Praise f

'Angela Slatter [is one] of the most daring and exquisitely
polished writers on today's speculative fiction scene'
Karen Miller, author of the Kingmaker, Kingbreaker series

'If you think you're going to be able to put *Corpselight* down
and go about your day, or read a chapter a night, you might want
to practise your fake-sick "reader flu" voice before you get started.
You might just need it'
HushHushBiz

'Angela Slatter once again shows that she is a writer to be reckoned
with, her characters and situations beautifully rendered
in a believable and realistic world'
Reader Dad

'One of the most important voices in fantasy'
SF Signal

'Simply put: Slatter can write! Beautifully, stylishly, accurately . . .
Read this writer. She'll drop the scales right out of your eyes!'
Jack Dann, award-winning author of *The Memory Cathedral*

'If you haven't read Slatter's work before,
you're in for an absolute treat'
Ree Kimberly, author of *Rat City*

'A brilliant new urban fantasy with elements of murder mystery
and magic – I'm already looking forward to the next
Verity Fassbinder adventure'
Alison Littlewood, author of *A Cold Season*

CORPSE LIGHT

Book 2 of the Verity Fassbinder Series

ANGELA SLATTER

Jo Fletcher
BOOKS

First published in Great Britain in 2017
This edition published in 2018 by

Jo Fletcher Books
an imprint of Quercus Editions Ltd
Carmelite House
50 Victoria Embankment
London EC4Y 0DZ

An Hachette UK company

A CIP catalogue record for this book is available
from the British Library

PB ISBN 978-1-78429-435-9
EB ISBN 978-1-78429-433-5

10 9 8 7 6 5 4 3 2 1

Typeset by CC Book Production
Printed and bound in Great Britain by Clays Ltd, St Ives plc

To my beloved uncle, Dr Rod Perry,
who has put more into the world than he has ever taken out.

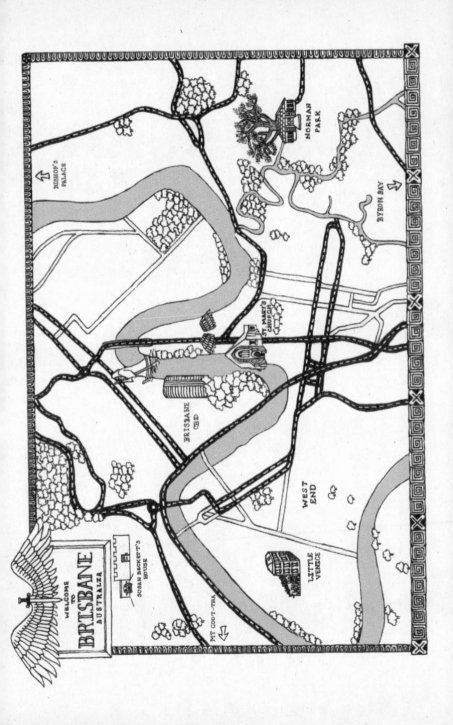

Mud

She took a while getting out of her car, smoothing the workday creases from her Donna Karan suit, collecting her handbag and the briefcase. She jingled the keys before inserting them in the lock of the house's front door, as if the noise might ward off evil spirits; as if it might let them know she was home and they should disappear now. The hallway looked fine, but the smell hit her before she'd taken a step inside. Had she caused it, *she wondered,* with her expectation? *She shook her head: magical thinking would get her nowhere. Steeling herself, she followed the stench.*

Mud.

Again.

It was all over the expensive silk and wool rug at the base of the new rocker-recliner that had replaced the last one: oblongs of insufficiently jellified gunk, almost like footprints but lacking definition. Up close, the odour was even worse. The whole chair wore a thick coat of the same crap — it wasn't just mud, but oozing filth. Foetid, contaminated liquefied death.

This was the third such occurrence in as many months: always on the same day. The mess was always there when she returned from work; the perpetrator had clearly waited until she'd left, then set about making its point, always in the same spots. None of her precautions had done a damned thing. She'd be having words with that bloody hippy chick at the St Lucia spook shop about her rubbish ingredients.

She couldn't imagine the insurance company would pay out, not again, even under the Unnatural Happenstance provision.

The first time this had happened she'd been unnerved, even afraid. The second time, she'd been annoyed. Tricks, *she'd thought*, shitty little tricks. Shitty, *spiteful* little tricks.

This time, the only thing on her mind was, Fuck you! *'It'll take a damned sight more than this,'* she shouted at the empty room, making sure her anger carried her words all through the house.

There was more, of course: the kitchen was awash with brown, slither-marks patterning the linoleum as if a nest of middling-sized snakes had run amok. The biggest puddle was in front of the fridge – well that was new. She picked her way across the floor, stepping on the clean patches, careful not to slip, not to get sludge on her expensive new Nicholas Kirkwood Carnaby Prism pumps.

The handle of the fridge door was pristine; she grasped it and pulled.

There was a moment, one of those frozen seconds when things stand still. In theory, in that moment, there was time to step away, to jump to safety. In reality, the shit-brown rectangle filling the matt-silver Fisher & Paykel quivered and slid out onto the neutral patent leather of her Kirkwoods with an obscene sucking sound, leaving her shin-deep in muck.

Then the doorbell rang.

Chapter One

'I've given this a lot of thought,' I said, 'and I've come to the conclusion that I can't go through with it.'

David put an arm around my shoulders – circumnavigating my waist had become more of a challenge than it used to be. 'Not to be negative or unhelpful, but I don't think that's an option any more, V.'

We were slumped on the couch, staring out over the sea of baby-related items we'd just schlepped home from what I prayed was our Last Ever Shopping Trip: a bouncer with an electronic 'vibrate' function that my friend Mel, from next door, swore I'd be grateful for; *two* colourful mobiles to go above the crib because we couldn't agree on which one to get (a roster system would be in place until the offspring could decide for herself). Bulk supplies of talc, nappies, wet wipes, rash cream and lavender-scented baby rub. Tiny hats, booties and singlets, so small they required four zeros to indicate sizing, all in nice neutral greens and yellows, because once we'd announced we were having a daughter, the pink gifts started arriving thick and fast. To combat princessification we'd bought Lego, Meccano, books from the Mighty Girl reading lists, science experiments and chemistry sets and Tonka trucks, as well as a good sturdy teddy bear. If we'd been stockpiling canned goods and weaponry in the same manner we'd have been called Doomsday preppers, but as it was, we looked like precisely what we were: very nervous expectant first-time parents.

David had even gone through the storage shed where we'd put all his stuff that couldn't fit into my house (once again avoiding having The Discussion about what would eventually happen to said stuff) and emerged triumphantly with the old microscope he'd been given as a boy. He'd polished it till it shone like new and now it sat on a shelf in the library, waiting patiently for our child to be seized by Science. Occasionally we wondered if we might be getting way ahead of ourselves – but we wanted to be *organised, ready*.

But that was the fun stuff, not what was making me want to back out of the whole baby-having deal.

It was all the *un*-fun stuff: bottles, sterilisers, a nappy bag big enough for a US Marine to pack her gear in, a pram that required an engineering degree to put together, let alone operate, a changing table with a simply *ridiculous* number of drawers, a plastic bath, a high chair and not even worst of all, an apparently irony-free potty shaped like Winnie the Pooh's head. But the thing that had me making for the hills as fast as I could waddle was the breast pump. It looked *nasty* – I couldn't imagine trying to attach it to my worst enemy, let alone *me*. I'm not thick: of course I understood that expressing milk would mean I didn't have to get up every time the bub needed a night feed – and it would also mean the *other* parent would have no good excuse not to do it – but still . . . Breast pumps make the iron maiden and the crocodile shears look appealing. The longer I stared at it, the less I liked it.

'Are you sure? I mean, there's got to be some kind of voodoo that can—'

'No voodoo, no hoodoo, no magic around the baby,' he said severely. 'Not until Maisie's older, anyway.'

'I think I would like a sandwich now.'

'You just had a sandwich. To be precise, you had two BLTs at that café, and then you ate half of mine.' But he got up anyway and stepped around the bench into the kitchen.

'Correction: *our daughter* had two and a half BLTs. While she's distracted by digestion, *I'd* like a sandwich.'

'I don't think it works like that. Cheese and vegemite?'

'Please.' I rubbed both hands over my five-storey belly. 'I can't wait to have soft cheese again. I miss Brie. And Gorgonzola.'

'I, for one, have not missed the stinky cheese.'

'You don't have to eat the stinky cheese.'

'No, but I do have to kiss you, who eats the stinky cheese.'

'That's true. It *is* in your contract.'

'There's a contract—?'

Any possible escalation was thankfully prevented by a knock on the front door. I levered myself upwards. 'I'll get it. It's critical that you finish that important task.'

'The fate of the world depends on it?'

'Sure, why not.'

The figure standing on the patio was recognisable only by the wisps of thin ginger hair that stuck up from beyond the pile of items in the bearer's arms. More pink things: soft toys, little fairy dresses, teeny-tiny ballet jiffies – and not a one was modestly hidden in shopping bags that might suggest actual purchases. I knew if I asked, the answer would be, 'I know a guy'.

'Ziggi Hassman, enough with the fudging pink,' I said, but stood aside to let him in, landing a kiss on his pale cheek as he passed. The eye in the back of his head gave me a wink. I'd removed almost all the wards from my house since the events of last winter, when Brisneyland in general and me in particular had been threatened by an archangel on a crusade, a golem made of garbage, an aggressive vintner and an especially ill-tempered mage, but I was starting to wonder if I should find one designed to ensure no Barbie doll could enter.

'I couldn't help it. Look at the shoes – how small are they?'

'So small. But you've got to stop: I'm only having one kid.' Not to mention that Mel had already pressed upon me all of her daughter Lizzie's baby cast-offs. We had enough gear to start our own line of black-market babywear.

'Also, *fudging*?'

'Trying to minimise the profanity so my daughter's first word doesn't rhyme with "fire truck".'

After I'd inhaled two sandwiches and Ziggi had dug through the mound of things we'd bought earlier, and after giving the breast pump an especially dubious glance, offering helpful comment on each and every one, he got to the point. 'So, V, fancy going for a ride?'

'That's phrased like a question, but I fear it is not.' From past experience my chances of bailing were not good, but I still tried, whining, 'Ziggi, it's *Sunday*.'

'It would be a *leisurely* drive.'

'Am I not on maternity leave?' I fidgeted with the ring David had given me for my birthday a few months ago: a vintage silver band set with a square-cut emerald; it was on a silver chain around my neck at the moment due to pregnancy-related sausage fingers. I'd noticed lately that whenever I didn't want to do something work-related, I touched the cool metal and stone as if it might somehow get me out of it. So far, it hadn't worked, but I wasn't quite prepared to give up yet.

'Technically, we don't have maternity leave, what with our jobs being secret, non-Union and all, but you're still getting paid for a lot of sitting around as far as I can tell.'

I knew he was right. Ziggi and I were employed by the Council of Five, the group which oversaw Brisbane's Weyrd population, keeping the community's existence as close to secret as possible, and its members – as well as the Normal populace at large – safe. A run-in with a nasty creature called a 'serker had seen me injured and in need of a chauffeur for a lot of months, and even after I'd swallowed my pride and let a Weyrd healer fix me up, we'd never got out of the habit of Ziggi driving me around. Besides, our boss, Zvezdomir – 'Bela' – Tepes (I'm positive his eyebrows were directly descended from Bela Lugosi) – wanted me to have back-up wherever I went. The memory of the pain inflicted by the 'serker's claws remained fresh enough to keep me from complaining about having a nanny.

'Will there be any sitting in cars? I warn you, my personal plumbing no longer reacts well to that sort of stress test.'

'There are many cafés where we're going.'

'Ooh, posh.' I looked at David, but the bastard just grinned and nodded. He'd been my last hope. David had adjusted astonishingly well to finding out about the Weyrd world that existed – *mostly* quietly – alongside the ordinary Normal world. Not that he'd had much choice: making a life with me meant getting used to some strange things, like folk who were the stuff of nightmares beneath their carefully cast glamours, the true sight of whom would send any respectable Normal running for torches and pitchforks. Also, like the fact that I was hybrid, a *strangeling*, with a Normal mother, a Weyrd father and a complicated history, not to mention ridiculous strength – but thankfully, neither tail nor horns nor any other sign of my heritage. And David had taken it all in his stride.

'Off you go,' he said. 'I have manly crib-assembling tasks to do.'

'You just don't want to make *your child* more sandwiches.' I grumbled a bit more then went to collect my leather jacket – because it was chilly outside – and the handbag I carried nowadays – because wearing the Dagger of Wilusa, the legendary weapon that had saved my backside more than once, on my ankle was no longer a comfy option. All I'd *planned* on carrying in there was the knife, a simple enough plan. So simple in fact that it hadn't taken into account what I was now calling Fassbinder's Law of Handbag Physics, which states that the number of items you want/need to put in a bag will always *just* exceed its actual capacity.

The house had once been a simple workers' cottage perched on the ridge of Enoggera Terrace that ran through Paddington. At some point it'd been renovated to within an inch of its life: the traditional white picket fence had been replaced by something looking remarkably like a rendered rampart in a fetching sandy hue, hiding everything except a covered carport that sheltered a silvery-grey BMW 3 Series sedan. I was surprised the vehicle wasn't stashed away in a highly secure garage, but maybe that upgrade was on the way: the Garage Mahal. The monotony of the wall was relieved only by a cedarwood door and a tastefully subtle intercom box.

We'd parked across the road in Ziggi's impossible-to-camouflage purple gypsy cab, which was neither tasteful nor subtle, and my driver sat quietly while I looked through photos of the house's interior and yard. It was built on a slope, like just about everything in this suburb; the lower section, originally stilts and palings, had at some point been enclosed and turned into four bedrooms and a family bathroom. The kitchen, lounge and dining rooms were upstairs, along with a small powder room. The polished floors were honey-coloured, and the VJ walls had been painted the colour of clotted cream. If those weren't the original leadlight windows, someone had made wonderful reproductions. Above each doorframe was a carved panel with a kangaroo and an emu giving each other the Federation eye.

The furniture was mostly in similar buttery tones, with the occasional item of contrasting burnt orange. The LED TV was supermodel thin and a sound system had been unobtrusively recessed into the walls so you barely noticed it. The kitchen had a lot of white marble, stainless steel and pale wood, with appliances that looked brand-new. The bedrooms were beautifully decorated, not a carefully plumped cushion or artfully draped throw out of place. A wooden deck off the kitchen had been accessorised with a cocoa-hued wicker and glass table and chairs for eight, but there was no sign of a barbeque – downright unAustralian, if you ask me – and looked out over the lap pool that took up the length of the back yard. A small tool shed sat in one corner, and drought-resistant plants ran around the fence line.

'Nice house,' I said, not at all envious.

Okay, maybe a little.

'Keep going.'

I flicked over to the second set of photos and whistled. The contrast was marked: what looked like mud was smeared throughout the place, on floors and walls; the claw-foot tub in the bathroom was filled with what appeared to be chocolate mousse. I examined the envelope the pictures had come in; the top left hand corner bore a logo and the name *Soteria Insurance*.

'And we're here because?'

'Because the owner, Susan Beckett, has recently made multiple claims on the Unnatural Happenstance part of her policy.'

'Oooooh.' Very few insurance companies had such clauses, and those who did generally had a particular kind of clientele and only consented to said clauses after a specific request and an impressive hike in premiums. After all, most people had no idea what 'Unnatural Happenstance' was and wouldn't think such cover necessary if they did, but there were clearly a few Normals, not to mention all of the Weyrd population, who knew better. The provision was specifically to cover losses and destruction occasioned by, amongst other things, poltergeists, demonic exertions, hauntings and other revenants — so was unlikely to appear in the paperwork next to anything as mundane as theft of your garden furniture or fusion of your washing machine.

'And when you say "multiple"?'

'Three times — the third was last week.'

'Who called us in?'

'The head honcho at Soteria is a friend of Bela's. He called Bela, Bela called me.'

'Why didn't Bela contact me?' I was less offended than curious.

'He's trying not to ring too late. He knows you're sleeping for two now. Also, you yelled at him on the last occasion. For quite a long time.'

That did sound like me. I was out like a light by eight-thirty most evenings, and spent half of my waking hours forgetting why I'd gone into a particular room. Pregnancy brain was doing me no favours.

'Okay, I'm grateful for that.'

'Plus he knows David doesn't like him.'

'It's not so much that he doesn't like him . . . well, yeah, he really doesn't like him.'

'*Anyway*, we are to surveil as subtly as we know how—'

'Not a lot of space to manoeuvre there.'

'—and not make any trouble.' He sighed. 'We just need to keep an eye out.'

'A bit difficult to do from here.' I shifted uncomfortably on the back seat. 'Do we ever get to interview her?'

'When we've surveilled enough.'

'Do you have a ball-park figure on how long that might be?' I peered at the house. 'It's just that, while I appreciate Bela putting me on low-stress tasks, I'm fairly bored.'

'Remain calm, sit quietly and see what we can see,' he said wisely. In the rear-view mirror I saw him tapping the side of his nose. With a grumble, I settled down to wait.

'There's a café not twenty metres away,' Ziggi objected. 'Can't you go there?'

'I love you, Ziggi, and I would do almost anything for you, except right now. I'm just going to ask the nice lady if she'll let me use her loo. Consider this multitasking.'

Opening the door, I manoeuvred my thirty-two weeks' worth of bulk out of the taxi with neither elegance nor dignity; it felt like an age since I'd been acquainted with either of those graces. I'd resisted giving up my favourite jeans for as long as I could, but separation was imminent. The belly-band that had kept me halfway decent during the last couple of months was either going to saw me in half, make me pee my pants or snap and ping off into the distance as if launched from a trebuchet. I wasn't sure which would be worse.

'But Bela said we should watch. *Just* watch. *Surveillance*, remember?'

I didn't reply, merely quickened my pace, gasping as circulation returned to my swollen ankles and my two-sizes-bigger-than-normal feet. The shirt I was wearing had a three-seater sofa's worth of fabric in it and ballooned behind me as I tried – and failed – not to walk like a duck. I looked as if I was setting sail. Like an idiot I'd left my jacket in the car with the enormous handbag and the winter air bit sharply; I moved faster.

Susan Beckett, Ziggi had told me while we *surveilled*, was a twenty-eight-year-old ex-pat lawyer from New South Wales, and had qualified three years ago to practice in Queensland. She worked for Walsh-Penhalligon, a medium-sized firm with nondescript offices on the edge of the CBD; no high-rise, high-cost Central Business District real estate for them. They dealt mostly with commercial litigation and insolvency in the building industry – Beckett was a bankruptcy specialist, indulging in asset-stripping by legal means, which couldn't have made her popular, so definitely an angle to investigate. The firm's name sounded familiar, but I couldn't quite recall why.

I reached the fortress wall and hit the buzzer, hoping with all my heart that Susan Beckett was actually at home – and that she was the type to respond promptly. My luck was in.

'Hello?' A cool voice trickled from the speaker and I suddenly realised there was a tiny camera lens embedded in the intercom panel.

I waved. 'I'm so sorry to bother you – I was out for a walk and I, err, seem to have . . .' I pointed at my belly.

'You're not going into labour are you?' The tone warmed with alarm.

'No, but I do need to . . . *go*. I'm so sorry to impose, but no one's home next door and . . .'

After a tiny pause, the gate clicked and I pushed through, thankful that Susan's relief that I wasn't going to give birth on her doorstep had combined with general human decency to allow me admittance. I stepped into a tiny, highly manicured front yard with a pocket-handkerchief lawn, all lush green stripes, surrounded by beds of architectural succulents, and moved briskly towards the open front door.

'I'm so sorry,' I said again to the chic blonde woman, clocking the cream woollen pants, blue linen-knit T-shirt accessorised with an Ola Gorie barn owl pendant on a long silver chain, and embroidered ballet flats from, if my eyes didn't deceive me, either Etro or Tabitha Simmons. No Ugg boots or trackie pants here.

She waved to a door at the end of a long hallway. 'Ensuite straight through there.'

Throwing any attempt at elegance out of the window, I waddled as fast as I could into a loo that was *Home Beautiful* perfect, with a sunflower-painted feature wall, a Carrara marble hand basin sitting perfectly in the centre of a golden pecan bench top, and bright yellow Sheridan hand towels hanging on polished brass hooks. Taps and spouts glowed in beams of light from the frosted-glass skylight and the stained-glass window that overlooked the back garden and across to Paddington and beyond, towards Bardon and Ashgrove.

Enthroned and considerably more comfortable, I could think more clearly. I must have appeared (a) convincing and (b) harmless for Susan Beckett to have let me in so easily. Or maybe she figured she could take care of herself. Or maybe she really didn't want to risk a puddle by her impeccably maintained front gate.

I was feeling a good deal more focused by the time I finished. I used the Creamy Honey Handwash from L'Occitane (which put my no-name whatever-was-on-special-offer soap to shame), and liberally spritzed Rose 4 Reines house perfume to make sure no trace of me remained. When I exited, it was to find my hostess hovering politely, uncertainly, in the hallway. I smiled as I covertly examined her more closely: wide blue eyes, pert nose, thin lips, sharp chin.

'Thank you very much. I'm so grateful.'

'No problem,' she said, with a distant smile, and swiftly returned to the front entrance. It appeared my visit was to be short – no girly chitchat, no 'when's the baby due; do you know what sex?' cooing – so I peered around, trying to take in as much as I could before I got ejected. There was a bare patch in the sitting room, a square of floorboards slightly lighter than the rest, a spot where maybe a rug was missing. Other than that, it was hard to pick anything off-key.

Except . . . *except* . . . under all the sweetness of the bathroom freshener, under the floral scents of all the lovely things I'd sprayed and washed with, there was a sour odour. I realised I'd smelled it on arrival, but I really had been too distracted to process it then. Now my pregnant-lady sense of smell went into overdrive and my stomach gave a little heave of protest.

It was bitter and brown, *rotten*, like ripe, nasty, wet shit, and it wasn't being helped by the warm air being pushed out by the ducted air conditioning.

But the perfectly groomed woman waiting in her stylish clothes, with her expertly straightened hair with the tiny upward flick at the ends, carefully applied make-up and subtle bouquet of Givenchy's Amarige, wasn't the source. I was willing to bet she'd done her best – or more likely, paid someone else to do their best – to get rid of the stink and whatever had caused it. Perhaps she couldn't smell it any more – perhaps she'd become accustomed to that after-note – or perhaps it only affected me, but those efforts at cleansing hadn't been entirely successful. It would fade only with time and frequent airing of the house as well as the regular squirting of expensive perfumes.

But I wasn't in a position to ask about it, not yet.

I followed as quickly as I could and let her hustle me out as I gave one last heartfelt thank-you. She was clearly glad to see the back of me, and that was okay. I'd been inside; I'd avoided a very embarrassing personal mishap and I'd learned something important.

Whatever kept hitting Susan Beckett's house liked to make its mark, and it *would* return, whether she wanted it to or not.

Chapter Two

'I saved your life.'

'Jeez, Fassbinder, I'm not disputing that.' Aspasia's long black locks shivered and kinked as if about to become snakelets, which they'd done on previous occasions, but she wasn't actually angry so the Medusa act was held in check. 'Seriously, though, how much cake can one pregnant woman eat?'

'How long is a piece of string, Aspasia?' I smiled.

With an eye-roll, she put two pieces of my latest craving into a container: hummingbird cake with vanilla frosting and coconut encasing concentric circles of marshmallow, lemon mascarpone and Lindt chocolate. Even Ziggi thought it was too sugary, which was saying something.

'Thank you,' I said sweetly.

'What, no coffee?' she asked, which earned her a full-on glare. It was a sore point. I hadn't had a coffee in months: I'd been banned. The first couple of weeks of cold turkey had not been pretty, and a few times I'd been so unpleasant that I'd put myself in the timeout corner.

'That was uncalled for.'

'I'm sorry.'

'No, you're not.'

'True.' She shrugged.

'And for Ziggi—'

'I know, I know. Mudcake and a latte.' She began the process of grinding beans and frothing milk. 'But really, don't you think about diabetes? All that sugar?'

'Well, I do now,' I whined. 'Are you trying to ruin this for me? I haven't seen my feet in months – let me take consolation where I may!'

'You're right, you're right.'

I'd convinced Ziggi that we deserved a treat after three hours of sitting in front of Susan Beckett's house, so now he was off in search of the ever-elusive West End parking spot while I settled precariously, thanks to my changed centre of gravity, on one of the high stools at the bar. Aspasia watched from the corner of her eye, a little with concern, a little with glee. We were never going to be besties, but we'd been getting on a whole lot better in recent months, which might have had something to do with me saving her and her sisters from a brush with an extremely bolshy angel. While the Misses Norn still bore the scars of that encounter – pinkly healed-over quadrate crosses on Aspasia's left shoulder, at the base of Theodosia's throat and high on Thaïs' right cheek – it had still taken several weeks of intensive arguing as to whether or not the angel's timely death had been merely a happy accident or the result of tremendous skill on my part before suitable reward had appeared. It might have been gratitude, or pity – because by then I was obviously pregnant – or maybe I just wore them down. I didn't care: it was free cake.

Improved relations might also have had something to do with the fact that while I was eating Little Venice out of cake and home, my presence was proving a deterrent for less savoury patrons. And after word got out that an actual *angel* had died upstairs in Thaïs' rooms, there'd been a stream of sightseers wanting to gawk at the scorch mark on the floor and the Sisters' scarred skin and to ask stupid questions. Even amongst the Weyrd there are death tourists. Who'd have thought I'd be the one to raise the tone of a place?

I ran my fingers over the grooves of the countertop, feeling the impression of ribs in the fossilised stone, and watched the reflections in the mirror behind the bar, a lovely thing that looked like lace made of snowflakes, indistinguishable from the one that had been shattered in an angelic fit of pique. The clientele of Little Venice was mostly Weyrd, with the occasional lost Normal who wandered in off West End's Boundary Road and found four big rooms filled with brightly coloured lanterns and incense. An enclosed courtyard out the back was paved with desanctified cathedral stones and covered by a tightly twined roof of leaves and vines that was sufficient to keep off the sun and rain, but didn't hide the baby snakes that lurked there. The emo-Weyrd waitresses had Lilliputian horns on their foreheads, just along the hairline, but there was enough body-modding in the Normal world that they didn't cause much comment; they didn't need glamours to cover them up.

The two floors above the bar formed the Sisters' private residence; Theo and Aspasia shared the second level and Thaïs had the entire third storey all to herself. Once upon a time, if anyone wanted to see Thaïs to have their fortune told, they had to go to her – never, ever the other way round – but her contact with the outside world had dwindled considerably since the incident with the angel. In addition to being purveyors of food, drink and fortunes, the Misses Norn collected information. News, rumour, and knowledge all flowed through Little Venice, with the Sisters choosing what they shared, what they kept to themselves and what they discarded. They liked to talk in riddles, but since the whole life-saving episode, they'd been more forthcoming with the useful snippets.

'So what's new?' I asked.

'What have you heard?'

'Nothing. I hear nothing, Aspasia. I stay at home and I eat. If I'm lucky I sit in cars and I eat, just for variety. Also, I pee a lot. My world has grown small as I've grown large with child.' I leaned forward and pleaded, 'Please, tell me something interesting!'

Aspasia snorted as she snapped the mudcake into a container and put it next to the others, then stuffed them all into a plastic bag. 'Sadly for you, not much is going on at the moment, Fassbinder. A couple of *kitsune* were in the other night, but they stuck to one drink each and didn't cause any trouble. Some foxfire reported at Toowong Cemetery.' She gave me a sly look and added, 'What I *do* hear, from several sources, is that the Boatman's still looking for you. Wants his knife back, I gather.'

'He'll get it. One day,' I said, not very convincingly, uncomfortably aware that said item was floating around in the bottom of my handbag.

'It's stealing, you know, if you don't return it.'

'No,' I said evenly, 'it's just borrowing something for a long time, like an overdue library book.'

'I'm sure he will appreciate the nuance.' She handed me the goodies.

'Look, that knife saved quite a few of us, so who would you rather have it? Me or the Boatman, who is less than spectacular at returning calls?'

'You. I would rather you have it, *but* this is just a PSA that he has been asking after it.'

'PSA?'

'Public Service Announcement. Have you not noticed, acronyms are the in thing these days?'

'Uh, no, not to so much. But okay, thanks.' I couldn't deny my relief that the return of the weapon known in some quarters as the *God-slayer* had been delayed for a while longer, and I probably shouldn't have been disappointed about the lack of arcane activities. I wasn't, really, but I *was* bored – for all I'd tried to weasel my way out of surveillance detail, that was more to do with avoiding sitting-in-a-car boredom, even though I wasn't best placed to do much more in my current state. All those times I'd wished for a quiet life? I should have known better. As an afterthought, I said, 'Do you know a woman called Susan Beckett? Normal.'

'Nope. Should I?'

'Probably not. She's made several claims under *Unnatural Happenstance*. I thought maybe—'

'You're doing *insurance* work? Shit, Fassbinder, no wonder you're bored.' There was genuine shock in her tone, which almost made my eyes water with self-pity. 'Sorry, haven't heard anything, but I'll keep an ear to the ground.' She picked up a cloth and began wiping down the bench. 'Haunting?'

'Maybe, maybe not. Inundation with a really nasty stinky kind of mud.' I paused in case she had something to add, but nothing was forthcoming. 'Ah, well. Whatever's bothering her is unlikely to go away.'

'My thoughts exactly.'

I rubbed at the ache in my lower back. 'How's Theo doing with the Council?'

'She complains a lot – and I mean *a lot* – but she hasn't stepped down or threatened anyone, so I guess it's okay. I hear the oldies are grumbling about upstarts and new bloods, but no one's tried to depose her, so again, it's okay.'

I grinned. The 'oldies' constituted calm, corpulent Sandor Verhoeven and the arcane hippy chick Titania Banks. The Council's numbers had been temporarily reduced to two last year by a combination of an attempted coup of sorts and some forcible early retirements. As a result, swift elevations were required to bolster the ranks.

Seats on the Council were generally inherited, but the rot exposed by my investigation meant that the ruling body had to be seen to be cleaning house, and although there were a *lot* of venerable Weyrd families who'd presented their credentials in hopes of a Council seat, most had been doomed to disappointment. There was much grumbling and dissent from the Odinsays, the DeCourceys, the Ballingruds and the like, but no one much listened. Bela had served the Five for a long time, so he was an obvious choice. Udo Forsythe – a gentleman with an impeccable Old Country bloodline – was an appeasement to the established order; he immediately nailed his colours to the mast by supporting Verhoeven and Banks in whatever they proposed. And then there was the wild card, Aspasia's youngest sister, Theodosia; the Norns held sway in the community and the perception that the only side they favoured was their own made them as close to neutral as could be hoped. The times they were a'changin' . . . if only a little bit.

'Say "hi" to Theo for me.' I didn't ask about Thaïs; she still made me nervous, although I couldn't put my finger on precisely why. I carefully wiggled off the stool.

'Oh, and hey, Fassbinder? They've finally hired a new Archivist – started last week.'

I'd never actually met the last Archivist, Ursa, but I *had* unwittingly spent some time with the mage who'd posed as her after he'd stolen her skin. Vadim Nadasy had gained unlimited access to the Council's records and removed almost every trace of himself and his wife, Magda – she of the fatal winemaking hobby – which had made my job even more difficult. I'd managed to dispose of them both, but only after a lot of effort on my part and a lot of death and destruction on theirs, leaving me with a not-entirely-irrational discomfort on the subject of archivists.

'Anyone we know?'

'Nope. An international.'

'You're a veritable wellspring of vagueness, Aspasia.'

She flipped me the bird as I turned away.

'What part of *surveil* did you have a problem understanding?' Bela's tone was strangely mild, kind of resigned, but his Lugosi-esque eyebrows spoke volumes. Ziggi and I had returned home to find my handsome Best Beloved and my exceedingly handsome ex-boyfriend sitting on the back deck, each with a Corona in hand, not saying much at all. The silence could at best be described as uncomfortable, cold war at worst. Feeling ashamed – but not enough to restrain myself – I'd hidden the cake in the fridge rather than share before Ziggi and I went out to join them.

The green canvas deckchairs were new, wider, sturdier, and much better for pregnant ladies to get into and out of. I sat next to David and reached across to hold his hand, while Ziggi flanked Bela, forming a semi-circle of social discomfort as we all stared at the enormous jacaranda tree holding centre stage on the lawn. The afternoon was closing in, the temperature dropping as the winter sun started beating a retreat, but we were all wearing coats. Sensible people would've gone inside and turned the heater on, but we shared a fondness for the back deck of the house.

'Relax,' I said. 'She didn't suspect a thing.'

Bela's expression was dubious. 'And what did you find out?'

'Not so much,' I admitted. 'But I could smell something.'

Eyebrows lifted, not so much in disbelief as in askance.

'Yes, it's my replacement superpower.' As the pregnancy progressed I'd gradually lost my Weyrd strength – I could barely open the Vegemite jar now – but if required, I could smell for Australia. 'There was a stink – I'm pretty sure the insurance assessors should have mentioned it, but it didn't appear in the report. It must have been awful, worse than all that flood mud a few years ago – and this wasn't just mud, there was a fair percentage of poop in there, too, if I'm not mistaken. Whatever is doing this is *very* unhappy.' I wriggled, trying to adjust the weight of the baby on my internals. 'So, is there anything else to this account, something not in the paperwork?'

'According to Alex Parrish, Soteria's CEO, Ms Beckett swears it only ever happens when she's not at home, and she's realised it's always the last Wednesday of the month. She claims not to know what brought it on, says she has had no contact with any arcane forces.'

'Then why does she have *Unnatural Happenstance* on her policy?' asked David. I gave him a surprised look; clearly he and Bela *had* been talking before we arrived. That showed either unexpected trust on Bela's side or unexpected tolerance on David's, or an unexpected combination of both; I wasn't sure which.

'She says she'd forgotten about the provision until the first incident, when she was reading said policy and came across it. Happy coincidence.'

'Why didn't she stay at home on those last two occasions? She knows there's a pattern, so she could lie in wait,' David said.

'Well, the first occurrence was a surprise, nothing you'd expect. No pattern was set. Second occurrence suggests there might be a pattern. The third time . . .' I said.

'Do you think she tried something else?' Ziggi asked. 'Attempted to deal with it herself?'

'Either that or she *knows* who it is. Maybe *both*. She doesn't need to lie in wait to find them *in flagrante de muddo*. In fact she probably doesn't want to be around them at all. I call shenanigans,' I muttered. 'It's not something that's just automatically added to a policy, or indeed accidentally. Besides, how many lawyers don't read the things they sign before putting pen to paper?'

'Definite case of pants on fire,' observed David, and the atmosphere lightened.

'If we can't get answers, straight or otherwise, from the woman herself, then we need to cast further afield. Ziggi, didn't you say she'd only been practicing in Queensland for the last three years?'

'Yup.'

'Then I'll do some digging. Or have someone else do said digging on my behalf.' I rubbed my stomach, which was starting to rumble.

'Are you going to bother McIntyre?' asked Bela.

'"Bother" is such an unpleasant word. I am going to draw on my mutually beneficial friendship with Detective Inspector McIntyre. *Friendship*.'

'Yeah, she'll be bothering Rhonda,' said David.

I ignored him and continued, 'So, think tank: any ideas on what might be making the mess?'

'Demon?'

'Angry cat.'

'Poltergeist?'

'Ghost?'

'Bad neighbour.'

'Some kind of spirit?'

'Anyone who's not helping has to stop talking.' I sighed. 'Aspasia said there were some *kitsune* at Little Venice.'

'Not really their style,' said Bela, adding, 'Bad drunks, though.'

'She said they were very well behaved. And you're right, they're generally not poo-flingers.' David gave me a look that said there would always be some things he wouldn't get used to me knowing. I gave an apologetic shrug.

Then, 'Bela, can I talk to your friend at Soteria? I'd like to ask him about, you know, stuff.'

For once he agreed without bitching, or telling me to be polite. Either my behaviour was improving or his spirit had been well and truly crushed.

'I'll let you know when,' he said after a moment.

After Ziggi and Bela had gone, David and I went back to the sofa to enjoy what remained of our weekend.

'You really dislike him, don't you?' I said after a few moments.

'It's more of a low-level hatred.'

'You know he's no threat to you, right?'

'It's not that, and it's also insulting to suggest that it is. It's just that working for him puts you in danger.'

'In all fairness, not so much lately. He has been better, David, he's genuinely trying to be more considerate. And he's been pretty lenient for a man with an employee who's been phoning it in for several months now.'

He sighed and pulled me in for a hug. 'But it's not just you any more, V. There's the baby. I don't want to lose either of you.' He held me even tighter for a moment, then said, '*But*, I also don't want you to feel like you've got to give up what you do, or think I want you to be different, because I don't. I'm just . . . worried. I can be worried sometimes, can't I?'

'I do understand, and I won't do anything to risk the baby, David. I promise.' I touched his face. 'This Beckett thing, I'm just doing research. I'll compile the information, then the guys can deal with it. I just need—'

'—to not be bored for a while.' He grinned. 'I know you.'

'There's only so much domestic harmony one can take,' I said, and leaned close to whisper, 'There's cake in the fridge.'

'Hummingbird?' he asked hopefully. Not too sugary for *him* then.

'And because I love you, I'm sharing.'

'You really *do* love me.'

Chapter Three

Ah, Monday. What could possibly make the day any better than a trip to my OB/GYN? The answer was pretty much anything. My gynie was running late, which wasn't unusual, and I didn't find the sickly pastel pink of the treatment room as relaxing as others might. I had visions of half a dozen women on the other sides of the thin walls around me, all dressed in the same backless gowns, all wondering when they'd see the elusive specialist, all wanting to strangle the cheery nurse who stuck her head in the door every ten minutes or so to flash a toothy grin and say *Doctor will be with you shortly*, all wanting to shout *Liar!*

Trying to use my downtime productively, I made a discreet phone call. 'Rhonda?'

'Is that you, Fatso?'

When the inspector had been dying of throat cancer, I'd bullied an angel into saving her, which on a scale of one to ten rated as a pretty freaking spectacular twenty. And when I say 'bullied' it was really more by way of calling in a favour. As a result, you might have thought she'd be a bit grateful, but apparently nothing short of a jackhammer was going to make a dent in Rhonda McIntyre's carapace. She'd been in the Police Service for too long, and having to be the liaison for the Weyrd community – or what she liked to call the 'Strange Shit Basket' – has done nothing to improve her attitude.

'It's baby weight, Rhonda,' I said through gritted teeth. 'Plus actual, you know, baby.'

'Sure it is.' There was laughter on the other end of the line and I resolved to start an exercise regime immediately. Well, soon. Soonish. At some point in the future.

'And how can I help you today, Ms Fassbinder?'

'I know you'll find this hard to believe, Inspector, but there appears to be something weird going on.'

She sighed, a great put-upon sound. 'Isn't there always?'

'Well, yes. But at the moment I'm just doing background checks – nothing's spilled over yet and there's been no complaint made. But—'

'But something will probably go wrong and you want me to abuse the privilege of my position and get information for you in order to head something off at the pass?'

'If you wouldn't mind.' I carried on quickly before she had a chance to tell me precisely how much she did mind, 'Name is Susan Beckett, address is 182 Enoggera Terrace, Paddington.'

'What has Ms Beckett done to draw your baleful eye, and should I feel sorry for her?'

'I was not aware you were programmed for sympathy, Rhonda.' I spoke over the grumbling noises. 'She's had some uninvited house guests and her insurance company is concerned.'

'I'm going to assume that you don't mean white ants or relatives overstaying their welcome – and you know what? I don't need to know anything else, it'll just worry me. What do you want?'

'Anything. Any criminal record. Disturbances reported at the property. A list of licensed vehicles. If there's anyone else registered as residing at the house. Who's the person to contact in case of emergency. Oh, and any information you can pry out of your New

South Wales colleagues as she's not from here originally . . . so, you know, everything.'

'What's she do for a living?'

'Lawyer,' I said quietly, in the vain hope she might either not hear me or mistake my mumbling for 'harmless individual'.

There was a somewhat fluid noise, as though coffee or tea might have been propelled across the room. Then there was some coughing and some exuberant swearing. 'Are you trying to kill me, Fassbinder?'

'I think we both know the answer to that. Look, she's a commercial lawyer. Surely that's not as bad a criminal lawyer?'

'Would you rather have a Taipan in your bed or an Eastern Brown?'

'Fair point.' I sat back, stretched, then said hopefully, 'So you'll get that information to me as soon as humanly possible?'

She was still laughing when she hung up. I stuffed my mobile into the voluminous handbag, and lay back, trying to ignore the fact that there was a sheet of paper rustling beneath me on the poufy pink bench bed. Closing my eyes, I patted my belly, breathed deeply and awaited the doctor.

Since we were very nearly at the pointy end of the pregnancy and I'd passed all the danger stages, everything was pretty routine, so I'd told David I was happy enough to do these gigs on my own – and Ziggi was driving me wherever I wanted as it seemed to fall under the umbrella of 'keep the scary pregnant lady contented', a programme I was pleased to see the three men in my life had all got on board with. David was spending time tidying things up at the digital design agency before he took paternity leave. After all, how long can you stay excited about staring at something that looks suspiciously like a jellybean in a cyclone? Well, jellybean, then lizard, then kewpie doll with a disturbingly large head. What I hadn't told him was my tiny, niggling fear that our joint venture – even with the Weyrd blood from my long-dead father Grigor heavily diluted – might show nascent wings, tail, horns or, worse still, claws.

I knew we'd all be relieved when Miss Maisie Fassbinder-Harris finally made her debut, preferably with no visible signs of her genetic make-up from my side of the family.

A brisk knock pulled me from the least relaxing meditation ever. I opened my eyes to see a pretty round face with smooth light brown skin and wide dark eyes appearing around the door as if entirely disembodied.

'Are you decent?' Dr Ambelin Aarden asked with a blindingly white grin.

'Hope not.'

She chuckled and stepped into the room, white coat open over a blue jersey wrap dress with an enviably small bump beneath it. That frock looked infinitely stretchy and I was suddenly covetous. 'How are you, Verity?'

'Fine under the circumstances. But you're the one with the scans – why don't you tell me how I am?'

'Perfectly normal, although a little grumpy – although that's perfectly normal too. Let's get this underway.' She pushed up the hem of my gown, shook the tube of gel with enthusiasm, then squirted a goodly amount onto my distended belly.

'Cold,' I protested. 'So *cold*.'

She rolled her eyes, applied the transducer and my daughter showed on the screen as a landscape of white, black and grey; the sounds of her heartbeat and the rush of blood filled my ears. I squinted anxiously: no sign of tail, wings or claws. The unwelcome voice inside my head piped up, '*But there are still four weeks to go.*'

'Looking good,' sang Dr Aarden. 'Star pupil.'

'I bet you say that to all the fat ladies.' I stared hard at the tiny life pulsating on the monitor.

She knew what I was angsting over. 'Nothing to worry about: there's nothing that's not meant to be there, Verity.'

Finally, I allowed myself a smile. 'How long do you have to go?'

'Four months,' she said, and rubbed her own belly in sympathy. 'Already sick of the indigestion.'

'Your first?'

'Third. And no, it never gets easy. Sorry.'

'You comfort a lot of people, do you?' I sighed.

She just grinned a little wickedly. 'Are you all set with the hospital? Sister Bridget will tear you a new one if the paperwork's not in order.'

'Even I am not dumb enough to piss off Sister Bridget.'

It was sometimes hard to believe Sister Bridget Hazelton, the éminence grise of St Agnes of the Mercy Hospital up on Wickham Terrace, was not officially in charge. The place was small and had no emergency department, but it was well-known for its women's health programmes and its excellent maternity ward. The nurses had all been nuns, back in the days when caring was related to religiosity and wards were places where healthcare professionals spoke in whispers so their patients got some rest. These days the caregivers were highly trained nurses without any obvious religious calling, apart from Sister Bridget and two other ageing nuns. The phrase 'rules with an iron fist' was often coupled with her name, and while I wasn't precisely terrified of her, I did make sure that I dotted every 'i' and crossed every 't' when I dealt with her.

St Agnes' accommodated Normals, but it had long been the spawning ground of choice for the full and half-blood Weyrd of Brisbane, with some very specialised birthing suites and equipment for specific needs. I'd chosen Dr Aarden because she did a lot of deliveries there and she and the staff had a thorough knowledge of what could happen when Weyrd blood was in play.

We ran through the routine Q&A, as we did every time, and she told me what to expect at this point in my timeline, as if I hadn't read every bit of maternity literature I could put my hands on. When she finished with, 'Any other questions?' I stuck my hand in the air.

'Where did you get that dress?'

Something I've noticed over the years is that no matter how small the cemetery or how big a group you're with, you still feel utterly alone. Death is a great separator, the journey you can't take with anyone else. So it might have seemed a strange place for me to hang out after my visit to Dr Aarden's Bardon-based practice, but that was what I'd been doing every week since the pregnancy kicked in.

Toowong Cemetery is forty-four hectares of very hilly land, a mix of rolling green, stone and marble monuments of varying vintage, rusting fences, foliage and war graves, with bitumen avenues winding through the landscape. The Legacy Way Tunnel had dulled the noise of the M5 a bit, but not entirely; the rush of traffic still flowed up the hill in waves, breaking over tombs and trees. People have been buried there for a hundred and forty years, so there's a wide span of funerary decorations, from impressive gothic sculptures to some very minimalist slabs and wall niches for urns. My grandparents' neat little plot is under a crows ash tree at the top of 12th Avenue. Their marker is a simple slab of black marble with a couple of cherubs perching on either end, holding a wreath of calla lilies between them. Their names, *Albert Claude Brennan* and *May Helena Brennan*, are engraved and gilded, and underneath is my mother's, *Olivia Angelica Fassbinder*, complete with the epitaph *Lost and sorely missed* beneath, but no dates.

As usual, Ziggi dropped me at the top of the hill, then drove down the slope to park near the junction with 8th Avenue, an easy stroll when I was done. I think perhaps I felt drawn to the bone orchard after the events of last winter, which had made me appreciate the people around me more. I'd been in real danger of losing David, Ziggi, Bela, Rhonda, the Norns, Mel and Lizzie – not to mention my city – and for all the bickering and grumbling, they were my family, and no less or more dysfunctional than any connected by blood.

My grandparents had raised me from the age of ten, after my father had been arrested; he'd been killed in prison not long after he'd started his incarceration. My mother had died when I was so small I had not even a recollection of her face hovering over my crib, and Grigor never spoke of her. But my grandparents always brought me here: Grandma told me to talk to my mum, but I never really knew what to say; I had no memories to draw on, nothing in common but our blood. So I'd tell her the names of my toys, about the books I was reading, what I'd done at school, that I liked Grandma and Grandy. When I ran out of things to say, Grandma would smile a little sadly at a loss I didn't understand then and say it was time to go home. I don't know where my father lies; I guess he must have been buried at government expense in some potter's field, or maybe the Weyrd Council took care of his body.

After my grandparents' deaths I'd come here to leave flowers and tidy their gravestone, but it was never a regular pilgrimage, because I always felt them more at home, in their house, which I'd inherited. As Maisie grew inside me, however, I was thinking more and more about where I'd come from, those whose blood I shared, and becoming painfully aware that my daughter was the only living relative I had in the world.

So after every gynie visit I'd be here, sitting under the spreading crows ash, rubbing my swollen ankles, searching my handbag for a muesli bar and staring down the hill at the crumbling older graves. I'd talk to my dead about irrelevancies, complaining about the indigestion, the way my favourite jeans wouldn't do up any more, how hard it was going to be for me to get up again, talking about David and Maisie and Bela and Ziggi, Mel and Lizzie, the Norns and Rhonda and Ellen – the family I'd made for myself – and most of all, telling them how much I missed them.

Today, when I'd finished, I heaved myself to my feet and was stretching when something caught my eye: a flashing light, brief and bright, somewhere on the neighbouring hill, like the sun catching a mirror or a broken bit of glass. I watched a little longer, but gave up when it didn't appear again. I rolled my head around on my neck, enjoying the stretch of the tight muscles, shouldered my handbag (the weight of which might possibly have had something to do with the tight muscles) and started down the incline towards the lurid purple taxi.

Seeing me coming, Ziggi lifted a hand in acknowledgement. I'd reached the end of the avenue and was about to step into the car park when some instinct made me look to the right. I had one foot already reaching out over the gutter, but I pulled it back in so quickly I almost overbalanced as something intensely orange sped past: a compact Datsun Stanza, which appeared to have time-travelled from the '80s purely for the purpose of scaring the bejesus out of me. Had I been a few seconds faster, had I not looked, it would have knocked me flying.

I stumbled backwards, shouting '*Fuuuck!*' ruining all my conscious effort these past months not to swear in front of the foetus. The flood of adrenalin was making me feel sick, so I found a large rock to perch on while I tried not to throw up.

I was vaguely aware of Ziggi yelling, and soon he was crouched beside me, pale face paler than usual, shooting questions at me. I didn't even try to answer; I was practising restraint and anything I said would have been even more profanity-laden than usual.

'Did you see the driver?' was all I could manage once the shaking had lessened and I found my voice.

'No. They didn't slow down either, not even to take those bends.' He paused, rubbed at my shoulders. 'Did you recognise the car?'

'Nope. Didn't get the licence plate, either – it was covered with dried mud. The driver . . . was wearing a large sunhat.'

'Can't trust drivers who wear hats,' he said with feeling.

'A Datsun Stanza, for crying out loud!'

'How is it even still running?'

'I mean . . . seriously. After the Apocalypse there'll just be cockroaches and Datsun Stanzas.'

'C'mon. I'm taking you home.'

I didn't argue, but begged him, 'Just don't tell David, okay?'

Chapter Four

The next day, with my nerves and poise reinstated, I went to visit Soteria Insurance. The company was located in a nondescript building on Astor Terrace in Spring Hill, but the moment I stepped out of the lift on the third floor and opened the ornate red cedar door that sat self-consciously in the middle of the glass-walled corridor, I felt like I'd entered another world: Art Deco furniture and sculptures ahoy, wood panelling and amazing light fixtures constructed in highly polished metal and bright colours. Four doors of some exotic dark wood, all closed, were arrayed along one wall, each with a blank brass plaque, as if their occupants hadn't yet been decided.

The carpet was a merlot shade and so plush I wanted to kick off my low-heeled Mary Janes and scrunch my toes in like a cat, but I resisted the urge, which was for the best since I'd gone to the trouble of not looking like a hobo. I was wearing a newly acquired black jersey wrap dress, retail therapy after the near miss in the cemetery, and a charcoal coat that had replaced the one ruined in the sewers by the golem.

Behind an enormous honey- and maple-coloured desk sat a receptionist so exceedingly bubbly that I almost expected to hear the occasional *pop* when she spoke. Her black bob had a streak of cobalt blue vibrant enough to have been done just a few minutes ago.

'Mr Parrish is expecting you. He'll be out in a moment,' she said with a smile. She started to ask if I wanted coffee – then she noticed my belly and her face took on a sympathetic cast. 'Oh, sorry.'

'Green tea, please,' I said, then dragged myself off to drop onto a gilded daybed covered in a blue and silver brocade. Alas, just as I got comfy, one of the doors opened and a tall man who could have been Bela's only marginally less good-looking brother or very close cousin came out, all smiles.

'Ms Fassbinder? I'm Alex Parrish.' He offered his hand, which I took. 'How can I assist?'

'Well, first, you could help me up,' I said, and he laughed, surprised, and gently pulled me to my feet. 'Thank you. Let us never speak of this again.'

He ushered me into his office, where the décor changed dramatically, from luxurious Art Deco to equally expensive Minimalist. There was a lot of grey and silver, with some black for contrast, and the equally thick carpet was white. *White!* A sign of either madness or phenomenal optimism, neither of which are usually associated with insurance companies. But I was happy to note that the leather visitors' chairs were wide and high: easy to get into and out of with dignity.

'You're here about Susan Beckett,' he stated.

I nodded. 'I've read the report and talked with B—' Professional setting, I reminded myself. 'Um, Zvezdomir about the incidents, but I'd like to get your take on things. She's a Normal – do you know how she found out about *Unusual Happenstance?*'

He settled back in his chair and said, 'Well, first of all, you should know that we're not exclusively a Weyrd firm, so we don't only offer insurance for the inexplicable things: we've plenty of clients who just want coverage for their car or house and contents or pets, et cetera, for ordinary everyday mishaps. Our Weyrd clients do tend to ask specifically for it, but there're also a number of Normals who've had experiences which have led them to conclude that UH isn't such a bad idea. Some have made certain big investments and want to cover all bases – commercial concerns can be a lot easier if you know that you're covered for the stranger aspects of life. I believe Susan Beckett learned of us through her work – that's Walsh-Penhalligon. We insure many of their clients, so it's not at all unusual.'

'You didn't ask her why she wanted UH at any point? Like asking about a pre-existing medical condition?'

'Well, it seemed rude to do so. She requested the cover, she paid for it, so all's fair.' Alex Parrish leaned forward, elbows on his desk. His eyes were an icy blue, but there was nothing cold in his demeanour. In fact, he was downright charming, which I imagined was an asset in his business. He picked up a Mont Blanc Meisterstück Red Gold Classique fountain pen – there was a mortgage payment right there – and fiddled with it.

'How long's she had the cover?'

'Almost three years, since she moved to Brisbane, Ms Fassbinder.'

'Verity, please.'

'Verity.' He smiled, and I felt warm all over. I wondered if it was a pregnant lady hormonal thing. Hot flushes. Great.

'Well, she was paying the right premiums, so no grounds for complaint on that score?' I observed, tapping my fingers against each other, and was silent for a few moments.

He said, 'You look like you're plotting something evil.'

'Just thinking, but admittedly it looks quite similar.' I puffed out a breath. 'So, when you said "the stranger aspects of life", you meant poltergeists?'

'And hauntings. Angry *genii loci* – local spirits of a place can be disturbed by building works, that sort of thing. Ectoplasmic home invasion. Demonic possession. Doppelganger activity. We also offer services to clean up both the physical effects of such incursions and the psychic ones.'

'Exorcism?'

'Exorcism, laying to rest ceremonies, setting up wards, contact ceremonies to see what the spirit in question is after.'

'And has Susan Beckett taken advantage of any of these services?'

'Only the cleaning. And obviously, claiming the cash.' He broke off as the girl from reception came in carrying a tray; the smell of the coffee completely overwhelmed any scent my green tea might have produced. As I gave an involuntary groan, Alex Parrish grinned at her and said to me, 'Verity, this is Alicia, my daughter.'

'Mum was the same when she was pregnant with Lucy,' she told me. 'I put something out to make up for it.'

And she had, bless her cotton socks: a small mountain of pretty, coloured macarons sat on a plate she placed carefully between her father and me. But nearer to me. I decided I liked Alicia Parrish rather a lot.

When she'd returned to man the reception desk, Alex continued, 'Ms Beckett's refusal to use our more specialised solutions is one of the reasons we're about to cut off her cover.'

'Because she won't take reasonable precautions to stop recurrence?'

'Precisely.'

'Why not cut her off before now?'

'Well, Soteria gives three bites at the cherry. After the first claim, the measures we put in place generally clear up whatever's been causing the problem.'

'And those measures include . . . ?'

'Wards, mostly, sometimes a sacrifice – nothing appalling, nothing human, I hasten to add; but some fine livestock, or a piece of good jewellery buried in the garden, sometimes it's enough to pour a bucket of animal blood around the boundary of the property.'

'But Beckett won't let you do this?'

'We've done the standard blood boundary, but she won't let us deploy a clairvoyant or an exorcist.' He dropped the pen and spread his hands in a gesture of helplessness. 'I've never seen someone so adamantly refuse assistance, but we can't keep haemorrhaging money like this – she's got an expensively furnished home. But it's too strange – and believe me, I *know* strange – which is why I called Zvezdomir. It strikes me as just *wrong*, unusually so.'

I really wanted to ask if he was Normal or Weyrd, but one doesn't do that when on one's best behaviour. 'Okay. Who took her call the first time it happened?'

'That would be me. I handle all UH claims personally.'

'That must suck up a lot of time.'

'Less than you might think, but it's necessary. We offer a specialised service and clients pay a premium for personalised attention.'

'How did she sound?'

'Rattled, afraid, but trying to hide it. I'd never heard her anything but cool, calm and collected before in business dealings—'

'So you've dealt with her on commercial matters too?'

'As I said, we've got common connections through Walsh-Penhalligon. She's always tough, yet that afternoon she sounded bad. It was after five and I was driving home, but I turned around and headed straight to her place to do the initial assessment.'

'And you found mud.'

He laughed wryly. 'In Paris in the seventeen hundreds there was what they called *la boue*; no matter what social stratum you were in, you had to walk through it at some point, and it was *foul*: a thoroughly unpleasant mix of mud and decay and excrement, both animal and human. That's the closest I can get to describing what I found in Ms Beckett's home. Needless to say, we put her up in a hotel while the place was cleaned.'

I was dying to ask if he'd actually seen the stuff in the seventeen hundreds or if he was merely a keen student of history, but I restrained myself. Bela would have been proud of me. As a reward, I helped myself to a pistachio macaron. 'And the smell lingers.'

'Doesn't seem to matter what kind of cleaning agent or deodoriser you use, it hangs around like, well, a bad smell.' He tapped his fingers on the handsome leather blotter in front of him. 'And the more it happens, the stronger the scent left behind is getting.'

'She's the only person living there?'

'To the best of my knowledge.'

'Do you know about any family she might have?'

'As long as I've known her, she's been single – of course, I can't speak to her dating habits – and I've never heard her mention relatives.'

'And she bought that house when she first moved to Brisbane?'

'I believe so.'

'And no trouble prior to this?'

'None whatsoever.' He scratched his head. 'Here's what I can't understand: these things usually go away with the application of magic. If they don't, then people generally move and the thing, whatever it is, stays behind because it's attached to the house or the land or the locality.'

'Unless it's a poltergeist, or someone's the subject of a curse,' I said.

'Curses,' he said, 'are tough. But we can deal with them. It often comes down, in the end, to a lot of negotiating with the curser on behalf of the cursee. It's all about the wording.'

'Do you think that's what this is? A curse?'

He shrugged. 'Could be, but with Ms Beckett's unwillingness to let anyone help . . . who knows?'

I sipped my green tea and thought about how much I hated it. Figuring I deserved another macaron, I went for what looked like a cookies'n'cream.

Alex Parrish asked, 'Where to from here?'

'Well, I go home and start researching.' Well, right after I did the groceries. 'I'll phone if I learn anything, or need something clarified.'

'Do you think she's in any danger? Susan Beckett?'

'I don't think so – at least not yet. My instinct is that whatever it is could have hurt her at any time – could have drowned her in that noxious mud – but it hasn't. It only acts up when she's not at home, which suggests to me it wants to torment her. It's got a schedule, although we don't know what that is, but I'd say it's going to want to draw things out before doing anything permanent.' I gave up on the green tea and set it down, then handed Alex Parrish a business card.

He gave me one in return and said heavily, 'I need to tell her that her policy is going to be cancelled. Give her fair warning, for her own safety.'

'Maybe . . . listen, don't cut Susan Beckett off just yet – only, that might be something that triggers either her or whatever's trying to get to her. Let's keep things stable for a while, hey?'

'Based on the past pattern, you've got about three weeks before the next attack.'

'Always on the last Wednesday of the month, yeah?'

'Always.'

'Thanks for your time, Alex. Either Zvezdomir or I will be in touch.'

In the lift I thought about Alex Parrish. He hadn't been evasive or unhelpful, and that was a rare thing in the people I usually dealt with. It made me inclined to like him. Plus, his daughter had brought me baked goods. I wondered again if he was Weyrd or Informed Normal. I should have asked Bela before, I guess. Ziggi was waiting downstairs, maybe he knew. But for now, I had to go shopping, then I'd hit the books, and if I couldn't find anything in my own personal library, I'd have to make the acquaintance of the Weyrd Council's new Archivist. It had to happen sooner or later anyway, although I couldn't guarantee I wouldn't be tugging at his skin to make sure it wasn't going to come off in a hurry.

Perhaps I'd get more help and less trouble out of the new guy.

Chapter Five

The trolley was filled with sickeningly healthy things: lots of fruit and vegetables, white meat, fish, no treats; David would be proud of me. Disbelieving but proud. This burst of virtue, however, didn't mean I wasn't going to be distracted by the deli counter, which was unusually deserted. It wasn't like I was going to eat any of the processed foodstuffs – I'd waved the server away twice and they'd gone to hide out back – but I could stare longingly at salamis and soft cheeses for a while.

'Look good, don't they?'

The speaker was a smiling young Asian woman with an astonishing hairdo that mixed brutal undercut with baby-doll ponytails. She wore black jeans that must have been mistreated by acid, razorblades, sledgehammers and possibly some kind of rabid animal. A studded belt was slung low on her hips and her throat was encircled by a spiked leather collar. WHITE NOISE was shouted in jagged lettering on the front of her fluoro-pink singlet top, and only a black cami underneath saved her from overexposure at the gaping armholes; her Docs were emblazoned with Sailor Moon characters. Her voice was devoid of any accent, and I wondered if that was the result of nature or nurture.

'Yeah,' I said at last.

'Not good for babies, though,' she continued and reached out to touch my belly, which had somehow become public property the moment it swelled. When I instinctively moved back, she sidled closer, nails sharp and painted, the left side red, the right black.

I was raising my hands to ward her off when the baby went *nuts*. By nuts I mean, totally hyperactive: kicking, twisting, whatever a foetus could manage to do *in utero*, Maisie was doing – and hurting the hell out of me into the bargain. I gasped and doubled over, trying not to collapse onto the grimy linoleum tiles. When I glanced sideways, I found an unfriendly smile on the girl's pretty face.

She moved nearer and Maisie delivered another internal judo chop. I looked back at the floor, certain I was going to vomit. I hunched over and started trying to crabwalk away when someone brushed past me, almost making me topple. Then I heard the girl's uninflected voice say 'You!' in an accusatory tone; next there was a gasp, and then a *thud*.

Almost immediately, Maisie calmed down and stopped trying to karate-kick her way out; it took some moments before I was able to straighten. Through tears I saw two things: one figure prone on the ground in front of me and another person, who was not prone, moving swiftly towards the checkouts and the exit. The Asian girl lay bleeding, black liquid seeping out from a stab wound high in her side. As I stared, her umber-coloured eyes faded then flashed bright yellow; she shuddered as if fitting, her outline shimmered and she grew smaller and smaller until she wasn't a girl any more.

A fox with dark red fur, a sharp snout and a fluffy brush of a tail lay still and sad on the dirty oyster-coloured floor. The whole incident hadn't created enough noise to attract the attention of any of the deli servers, and no other shoppers had happened past, which was plain dumb luck.

Abandoning my shopping trolley, I went after the other figure, less lope and more hobble, one hand supporting my belly. Needless to say, I was anything but fast and agile, unlike my quarry, so by the time I got to the registers there was no sign of anyone. I interrupted the closest checkout server and asked, 'Did you see anyone?' which earned me precisely the look I deserved from both her and the middle-aged woman whose groceries she was ringing up.

I tried again. 'Someone tall – male or female, with a calf-length black coat and jeans . . . and a hat, a kind of green army cap.'

They both just watched me rub my stomach, then the checkout girl said, 'Nuh.' I could see the older woman's mind working as she visibly relaxed: *Pregnant woman's fancies.* Resisting the urge to yell, 'I'm not crazy!', and mindful that I'd no hope of putting on a burst of speed even if I knew which direction to take, I gave up. The only thing I was likely to catch here was a cold, thanks to the air-conditioning on full-blast, circulating all the germs the unwashed masses brought to the shopping centre.

Slowly I made my way back to my trolley. The *kitsune* – one of the fox spirits who'd been at Little Venice? – was nothing more than a pile of red dust. At least I didn't have to explain away anything difficult.

The baby had settled, but I kept talking to her, whispering, 'It's okay, Maisie-moo, it's okay. All safe now.'

But I was rattled. My last seven-odd months had been pretty much danger-free. As soon as we'd found out I was pregnant Bela had adjusted my workload, cutting down on opportunities for me to get stabbed or punched, which made both David and me happy, especially when it became obvious my Weyrd strength had unexpectedly gone the way of Samson's after a short back and sides. This was the first time since then that I'd been faced with my inability to defend myself, or anyone else – the first time in my life, really, and I discovered I was not overly fond of the feeling.

There I was in Woolies, for the love of all that's holy, innocently staring at forbidden things, and something nasty had felt comfortable enough to threaten me and my baby — and Maisie knew it too, even cocooned deep inside me. I'd become complacent, assuming everything in the world would give me the same kind of consideration as my friends had; that the worst I had to fear was indigestion and the deleterious effects of soft cheese.

I thought uncomfortably about Aspasia's comments about the Boatman wanting his knife back — the very knife that was lurking somewhere in the bottom of my very large handbag.

When the being who accompanies souls on their final journey had given me the Dagger of Wilusa last year, he'd been pretty miserly with details, including what he wanted me to do with it. I'd had no idea he'd expected me to stop a posse of rebel angels from breaking the sky in their search for God and, coincidentally, letting in all the nasties that lived between dimensions. I'd had to figure just about everything out for myself, which might account for why I didn't feel in too much of a hurry to return the Swiss Army Knife of the Occult.

I pushed the trolley towards the checkouts and contemplated my next move.

It was after lunchtime by the time Ziggi dropped me home, so I made myself some sandwiches, then spent the afternoon ensconced in my library, sitting on the creaking leather chair at the wide old banker's desk with its green leather insert, my stomach bumping on the edge. There was an armchair in the corner that would've been more comfortable, but I didn't like the idea of balancing a laptop on my daughter's first home. I played around on the internet, doing an initial pass at 'surface research' before I hit the actual books.

What the net gave me confirmed one of my suspicions: that mud wasn't a particularly common weapon of choice amongst the ghostly or the poltergeistly or the demonly. However, there were a few recorded incidents.

In 1645 a great tempest had covered all of Paris in stinking, reeking mud, which had vastly augmented the already fairly enormous amount of *la boue* in the city's streets – but this lot had fallen from the sky. Eighty-seven people were reported drowned, mostly in the 'miracle courts', the slum areas where folk who spent their days posing as disabled beggars quite astonishingly regrew missing limbs and suddenly learned to walk again the moment they set foot in their own territory.

Then, in 1798, in the Warwickshire village of Burton Dassett, mud rained down from the ceiling of the library in the house of the area's richest landholders. The home was owned by the Temple family, local magistrates for decades, and the mud-storm continued inside for three days until the vicar was called in to banish the ill-spirit. A footnote suggested that the turning point might actually have been when the Temples opened their substantial grain stores to the starving villagers. No one was ever accused of causing the incident, which struck me as unusual.

In 1842 in the town of Randolph, Vermont, Mrs Julia Sadler found her two sons almost drowned in a bath of mud at their home. She rescued them and the family fled, never to return either to the house or the town. Rumour had it that she'd had an altercation with another woman on the subject of a stolen silver salver, sullied laundry or a wayward husband; the sources disagreed. No charges were ever laid, and the house was later destroyed in a mysterious fire.

The incidents were few and far between, but they existed; they'd been recorded, even if in sparse detail. Ideas of 'why' and 'how' were clearly thin on the ground; no one even speculated on whether the cause was specifically ghostly or demonic or witchly, or even poltergeist-related, and there were no in-depth accounts left by those who'd experienced the phenomenon. All this meant that, unless my books yielded something good, I'd need to attend at the Weyrd Archives, which in turn meant politely asking Bela to snip the Gordian knot of red tape that engulfed the centre of Weyrd power and set up an appointment for me.

Another trip to Little Venice wouldn't go astray either, so I could ask if Aspasia'd seen the *kitsune* again and check in with Thaïs to plumb the depths of her eldritch knowledge. Maybe she knew more about magical malignant mud attacks in history; maybe she'd caused a few herself. You could never tell with Thaïs.

Outside the window, night had fallen and I could no longer see the jacaranda tree in the back yard. I was shutting down the desktop and easing my way out of the chair just as the sound of keys in the lock reached me.

As David opened the front door I asked cheerily, 'How was your day?'

'Same old, same old. Build website based on client instructions, show website to client, re-do website based on client not liking exactly what they'd asked for.'

'Maybe do something they don't ask for in the first place?'

'That's so crazy it just might work.' He dropped his messenger bag onto the floor of our bedroom, then went through to the kitchen, me following along like a hunting hound. 'And how was your day? Anything interesting?'

'Met the boss of Soteria Insurance, talked about mud and stuff.'

'Mmmm, anything else?'

I probably should have recognised that tone, but I didn't. 'Nope.'

'So, nothing? Nothing happened? Not even a fox lady approaching you in Woolies?'

'You saw Ziggi, didn't you? I *told* him not to tell.' Actually, I reminded myself, I'd told him not to tell about the incident with the orange Datsun at the cemetery. He'd been even more upset about the fox-girl incident and it'd taken some time to calm him down.

'Correction: Ziggi *called* me.' He began pulling items from the fridge.

'I can cook if you like?'

'No one's prepared for that. Look, I'm not going to freak out, I don't want to wrap you in cotton wool, but if there's something going on that might put you in danger, I really would prefer to know about it in advance.'

'I'm sorry,' I mumbled into his neck. He smelled good. 'I didn't want you to worry. And in my defence, you just walked in the door and I might have been planning to tell you over dinner.'

'Were you?'

'Not as such, no.'

'I always worry where you're concerned, but it's fairly obvious that no matter what job you're in, trouble will find you. If I told you to quit, you'd probably hurt me. If by some miracle you did quit, then you'd get bored and resentful, and that wouldn't be much fun for either of us.' He rubbed his nose against mine. 'Just be careful and don't lie to me, okay?'

'Okay, promise.' I leaned out of the hug and said, 'Then I should probably tell you that I almost got hit by a car the other day at the cemetery because I wasn't watching where I was going.'

'I know that, too.'

Ziggi and I were going to have words very soon.

While David made dinner – my idea of teamwork was me doing the shopping, him doing the cooking – I talked him through my discussion with Alex Parrish.

'What I'd really like to do is go to Walsh-Penhalligon's offices and have a poke around, but I've got no good reason to do so and I'm sure Susan Beckett would recognise the pregnant lady who accosted her at her home. Also, I cannot imagine doing a break-and-enter, not in my current condition.'

'What do you need?' he asked slyly.

I shrugged. 'I don't know. Stuff. You know how I work: start with All of the Things, then whittle it down as I go. Maybe something that suggests what's happening to her is work-related — or eliminates that avenue. That'll help narrow things. Walsh-Penhalligon deals with Soteria Insurance, they take out *Unnatural Happenstance* cover for themselves and clients, so they're cheek-by-jowl with the Weyrd stuff. Maybe Beckett had a case or a development that upset someone with superpowers? I don't know. It could be nothing, it could be something.'

'Did I mention I'm working on the website for Walsh-Penhalligon?'

That sparked a memory. 'Why, yes — yes, you did. Which is why the name was familiar to me when I read the Beckett file . . .'

'I might be able to access something.'

'Are you talking about hacking? What do you know about hacking? You're so straight-laced.'

'After my parents died I went through a bad patch, did a few things I wasn't proud of. One of those things was playing around with cracking secure systems.' He shrugged. 'But strictly speaking, this isn't hacking as I've got access to their website and logins. It's more like "working from home" than "inappropriate access".'

'You'd break the law for me?'

'Well, bend it, maybe.'

'Right then. Show me what you've got, Mr Harris.'

He booted up his laptop and after an hour all we'd been able to find of interest were Susan Beckett's billing records. Even then, there was nothing specific I could put my finger on, except for a whole series of items that were listed as 'payment-in-kind', which seemed bizarre for a legal firm. I thought they were supposed to be all about the cash, the trust accounts, the billable hours and the getting paid on time, or they got all litigious.

'I think we should call it a night, my love,' I said, and sighed.

David logged off, echoing my sigh. He pushed a strand of hair away from my face and said, 'So, what are you going to do about staying safe?'

'The dagger? I need to make sure it's accessible.'

'The ankle sheath's not practical at the moment.'

'Are you saying I'm too fat to bend down?'

'I would never say that for I am not stupid. I am, however, suggesting that gravity might not currently be your friend.'

'That's beside the point.'

'It's not really,' he said. 'Maybe I can jury-rig the sheath inside the giant handbag so it's easier for you to find when required?'

'Is there anything you can't do?'

'Play the violin.'

Chapter Six

The next morning I slept in; David had been gone for ages by the time I rose and I spent most of the day being lazy and feeling unwell. I'd been lucky so far with no morning sickness, but Mel had warned me when I'd crowed about it that it might just be late-onset. I'd felt quite strongly that the indigestion, no matter what I ate, more than made up for that tender mercy, but it looked like she was right. I was feeling sluggish and exhausted, so I spent more than my fair share of hours on the couch, alternatively napping and watching programmes that made me yell at the TV.

It was late afternoon by the time I managed to maintain a state of uprightness and hit some actual books for a more in-depth search on ghosts and mud and hauntings. I pulled out volumes I'd not looked at in an age, and even some I didn't recall owning. As my girth had increased, my never-very-strong interest in housework had declined and now even the library shelves had gathered a coating of dust. That made me guilty enough to vow that as soon as I was unencumbered by a belly that entered every room five minutes ahead of me, I'd be wielding the feather duster with a vengeance.

Said books – possibly purely coincidentally, possibly in an act of retaliation – gave me virtually nothing back. There was the general and the random: mud monsters who lurked in ponds waiting for children to wander too close; the occasional recountings of folks in

North America waking to find muddy footprints on their floors and doors open that had been locked before bed; muddy handprints left on windows of cabins in the Ozarks, no bodies found but drag marks were evident. But mostly walls tended to bleed blood or seep water, not mud. There was nothing like what I was looking for, and nothing in Brisbane or its surrounds . . . in fact, nothing similar reported in all of Australia, as far as I could establish.

Still, I ploughed on with a bloody-minded determination, which wasn't to say that the business-like knock didn't bring an immense sense of relief. I took the time to use the peephole David had, with adorable optimism, installed in the hope I'd be more wary about opening doors to strangers. I made a mental note to let him know I'd used it: no point in virtue if no one else knows about it.

Caution proved unnecessary, however: it was my regular delivery guy. I liked Len. Lanky and loose-limbed, with neatly pressed khaki shorts and navy polo shirt with the lime-green Mercury Couriers' logo (a winged letter) on the left breast pocket, and his dreads tied back with a braided leather thong, he was friendly, efficient, polite – and knew when it was time to leave.

'Hey, Miz F.'

'Hey, Len. Busy?'

'Always. Can never deliver anything fast enough. People be crazy. Sign here.' He handed me the electric signature thingy and I used the stylus to try to produce something that looked like my scrawl. Len said, 'Seriously, you could draw a paw print and it would be fine.'

'Have a good day,' I said and took the padded envelope that looked like an overstuffed chicken.

Back in the library I returned to the armchair in the corner and the cushions I'd spent the last few hours crushing and gave the parcel an experimental squish. For a moment I worried it might be too squishy, then I squished it again. Upon realising there was no accompanying squelch, I decided it was safe and pulled the little red ripcord.

Inside were three dresses, none for a newborn but maybe for a one-year-old, each with a plain bodice in green, purple and yellow; one skirt had dinosaurs, one had a π symbol and the last a chemistry set. The labels read 'Princess Awesome' and they were indeed awesome. Someone either knew me well or had taken a really good guess. I looked for a card but came up empty, and there was no return address either. Maybe they were from Rhonda and her girlfriend Ellen; a note seemed like the kind of thing McIntyre would be too grumpy to include and Ellen too vague. I'd ask McIntyre when I called to nag her about the information on Susan Beckett.

I heard my phone ring from the kitchen where I'd left it charging on the bench and made it there before it rang out.

'Is that puffing I hear?'

'I was just thinking about you.'

'And lo, I appear.'

'Bad things often do. Is there a reason for this call or were you just bored? Run out of flies to pull the wings off?'

'Be nice, I have information for you.'

'Is it useful information?' My mood lifted.

'I didn't say that.'

'Aw.'

'Susan Rosaline Beckett, age 28, in the Byron Bay area. Parents Marian and Acton Beckett, 56 and 62 years of age respectively, still living close to Byron. Mum's a retired schoolteacher and Dad works as a mechanic, but he also owns property down that way, several rental houses. And there are two younger sisters, thirteen and fourteen, Unity and Hilda. Also, terrible names.'

'That's a sizeable age gap.'

'Indeed it is; must have been quite a shock to poor old Marian. Anyway, Susan did her law degree at the University of Sydney, got a position in a big firm there and looked set to be on the fast track until she sidestepped to Brisneyland, apparently voluntarily. Applied for a practice certificate in Queensland three years ago. Got the job with Walsh-Penhalligon and bought the house on Enoggera Terrace as soon as she moved up; owns no other property. She is the only person listed in the electoral rolls as living at that address. Her bank vaults appear to be filled with gold and she pays off her credit card – it's a black one, which I'm given to understand is impressive – every month without fail. One vehicle is registered to her, a Havana-Mojave metallic beamer.'

'Is that car-wank speak for silvery-grey?'

'Silvery-grey, yes. She owns no companies or other businesses.'

'That's a lot of information, Rhonda.'

'I have friends,' she said cagily.

'You do?'

'Well, I know a lot of people who owe me favours and are scared of me. Also, I have a new constable who needs breaking in. That's what they were invented for, constables, for doing legwork and boring searches.'

I grinned. 'Thanks, McIntyre. That was both helpful and pain-free.'

'Which should be enough to make you suspicious,' she said and laughed like a super-villain.

'Oh no.' I closed my eyes in defeat; before pregnancy brain I'd never have been this easily outplayed. 'You *were* unusually amenable.'

'It's not for me,' she said, then her voice dropped, as if embarrassed, 'it's for Ellie's birthday.'

'Okay?'

'Well, you know she likes tattoos.'

'I do indeed.' Artworks in miniature swarmed across Ellen Baxter's skin: her hairline was inked as though her face peeked from a broken eggshell and a collage of mouths and faces, tears and roses, pearls and breasts, beasts and bells bloomed over her shaved head.

'I want to get her an appointment with one of the artists, but I can't.'

'And you think I can?'

'It's one of your lot.'

'Grumpy pregnant women?'

'*Weyrd*, you idiot.' She pushed out a frustrated breath, which told me how important this was to her.

'And you think I might be able to . . .'

'Put in a good word. This woman doesn't work on Normals, Fassbinder. Believe me, I have already tried talking to her.'

'Oh shit, were you rude?'

She gave a sniff meant to indicate offence, then confessed, 'Maybe. A little.'

'So I have to smooth over your mess *and* get your girlfriend an appointment?'

'Yes. That would be the optimal outcome.' I could hear her tapping a pen on the desk at her end. 'Ellie's tatts . . . they're special. They tell a tale, and they've all got some meaning for her. This one, the one she wants, has protective powers apparently . . . she *believes* in it. Look, Fassbinder, it'll be our third anniversary and she wants it as a memorial, a binding to make us stronger, she says. I want to make it happen for her.'

'You old softy.'

'Shut up,' she growled. 'Will you do it?'

'I'll do my best. What's the name?'

'Kadie Cross. She works out of Mindy's Mehndi at West End.'

'Actually, she *owns* Mindy's Mehndi. Give me a couple of days.'

'You've got a whole two weeks.'

'Okay then. Thanks, McIntyre.'

She'd already hung up when I realised I'd not asked her about the baby clothes. It could wait.

I went outside for some fresh air, leaning my belly against the wooden railing of the back deck. The big old jacaranda tree spread dark against the sky; in a few months it would be heavy with brilliant purple blossoms, and the fat kookaburra that lived in its branches would be deeply displeased at having to share his home with a fleet of seasonal lorikeets, a mass of chittering and bright green, red, blue and yellow flashes of colour.

To my left was Mel's house, all quiet and lonely while Mel and Lizzie were on their month-long cruise around the South Pacific, funded from the Weyrd Council's coffers – as both mother and daughter had been having nightmares about the basement of a certain glamoured Ascot house, I'd made a – *slightly* forceful – suggestion that they should be compensated for the Nadasys' actions. Being trapped on a ship with a bunch of strangers was my idea of hell, but a floating theme park was Lizzie's idea of heaven, and Mel pointed out that if she didn't have to cook or clean for a month, she'd be a very happy camper too. I was missing them both – I wanted Mel there to answer all my stupid questions about pregnancy stuff, and I missed Lizzie coming to visit, hiding in the hollowed trunk of the jacaranda and reading a comic.

It's only a month, I told myself, *and a mere three weeks to go.* I'd have a baby by then, and Mel'd be starting her new job at a spa in a rare patch of rainforest in Indooroopilly, lots of trees and quiet, incense and calm people drifting in and out, with hours that let her drop

Lizzie to school and pick her up. Things would go back to the everyday status quo.

I turned away from the empty windows of the Wilkes house and stared at the base of my tree.

Something shiny was bobbing around one side of the trunk, dodging back and forth, hidden, then seen. In a moment it was joined by a second small ball of bright light. Each had a misty outline; sometimes they faded as they pulsed, like it was taking real effort to pull themselves into a cohesive shape and maintain it – almost as if it was something they had to *remember* to do.

Foxfire.

Will-o'-the-wisps.

Corpselights.

Aspasia had mentioned a sighting at Toowong Cemetery. It wasn't uncommon for such things to wander off and float through the 'burbs – very few graveyards are set up to contain them nowadays. As a rule they weren't really looking for anything, just kind of drifting along like the fluff blown off a dandelion head. My visitors didn't appear to be any exception: they zipped around for a bit, then headed towards the high back fence. They bumped into the vine-covered wood, then climbed until they were sailing over the top, which was where I lost sight of them. They'd probably be ping-ponging through the block of new townhouses behind my place.

I shivered. With the darkness, the cold intensified, designed to drive sensible folks indoors. David would be home soon; it was time for me to make myself presentable. I went back inside.

It was date night.

Chapter Seven

'What did we just watch?' I asked as we descended from the first floor of the Southbank Cinemas. We'd waited till the very end, watching the last of the credits roll, to let the masses depart before I negotiated my way out of the chair and down two flights of stairs.

'I think the first one was called *Shit Explodes*. The second one was definitely *More Shit Explodes*.'

'Why did we think a Superman double-bill was a good idea?'

'Did we? I can't recall. I'm sorry.'

'No apologies necessary. We both chose it, therefore we share the blame equally,' I said magnanimously. 'Is it wrong that I was cheering for General Zod in *Shit Explodes*?' I was silent for a moment. 'But Wonder Woman was cool in *More Shit Explodes*.'

'Wonder Woman is always cool as a matter of course,' he pointed out. 'Ice cream?'

'Don't faint, but I'm not hungry.'

David gave me the side-eye, then raised a hand to my forehead to check for fever. I swatted at him, then had to hang on to the rail for support. Below us the crowd for the next showing was milling, while outside, through the glass frontage, I could see cars flashing by, moving too quickly when there were so many people crossing the road with little regard for their own safety.

'Let's walk along Southbank – the night markets, not the river,'

I added hastily. The markets sat in the middle of the parklands, separated from the water by the stalls, a lot of bougainvillea and the artificial beach that would likely be deserted now.

David sensibly didn't say anything, but he knew why I was avoiding the Boatman's habitat.

We reached the bottom of the steps and I found someone standing in front of me: lanky in jeans and a skivvy, a denim jacket over one arm, dreadlocked and grinning. It took me a moment.

'Hey, Miz F.'

'Len! Didn't recognise you out of uniform.'

I did the introductions, and as they shook hands, David said, 'So: date night?'

'First date.' Len blushed, grinning, and pointed over to where a trail of people, mostly women, were disappearing down the corridor to the loos. One figure stood out: she wasn't tall, but her outfit drew the eye, even from the back: short black dress with a layered lacy skirt with red ribbons and bows and silver zippers and petticoats, high-heeled laced knee-high boots, artfully ripped fishnets and fingerless gloves that ended in long crimson-painted nails. A cross-body bag in the shape of a silver skull with rabbit ears rested on one hip. A tiny hat sat on hair that had been teased to within an inch of its life and lacquered into place: Alice in Goth Wonderland. I couldn't see her face, but I imagined a lot of eye makeup, lips as red as blood and maybe a heart-shaped stick-on beauty mark high on one cheek.

'That's great! Good luck!' I wasn't sure that was the appropriate response, but it wasn't like we were related; I didn't get to question him closely about the girl of his dreams and his intentions towards her. What was the correct etiquette for wishing your delivery dude a fun date?

'What are you seeing?' asked David, coming to my rescue.

'*Batman vs Superman.*'

Aha. In which case *good luck* was the appropriate response. 'Okay, well, enjoy.'

We waved and left Len waiting for his date to powder her nose. When we got outside, David said, 'Who was that?'

'The delivery guy.'

'Right.'

We scurried across Grey Street to take Ernest Street, then across Little Stanley and over the grassy area until finally we found the pavers of actual Stanley Street underfoot. Red lanterns hung in the trees and brilliantly hued bougainvillea looped over the giant metal and steel wire trellis that covered the walkway along South Bank Parklands. Ahead of us were the stalls, each neat canvas tent stuffed with all manner of goods: clothing, food, natural soaps and cosmetics, artwork, woodwork, jewellery, organic honey, fruits and vegetables, fudge and other sweets, toys, quilts, second-hand books, wine, biltong . . . you name it, it was there.

The crowd was manageable, with not too many people trying to shove their way along to the Plough Inn for a late-night tipple, but I spotted the Max Brenner Chocolate Bar and decided I wasn't entirely *un*hungry. I nudged David in the right direction, catching a smile as I did so.

Miraculously, when we went inside there was no queue. We placed our orders and found a table at the back.

'See?' I said. 'It's meant to be.'

'Well, obviously. What would the Norns say if they knew you were cheating on Little Venice?' asked David with a grin.

I shrugged. 'I'm allowed to see other cafés. Also, they're very bad at hot chocolate.'

'And what did you do today? You were dead to the world when I left.' David reached across the table and held my hand, stroking the pale skin of my inner wrist gently.

'I slept, lay on the couch, slept, watched TV, slept, ate, slept, and did some research on mud.'

'*Mud for Fun and Profit*? *Mud for Beginners?*'

'*The Idiot's Guide to Mud*, more like.' I relayed the little information I'd gleaned from the books, the large amount of information from McIntyre about Susan Beckett, and the sad tale of how I'd been lured into doing a favour for her. 'And to top it all off, there were a couple of corpselights in the back yard. Might have been the same ones Aspasia mentioned, of course.'

He tilted his head the way he did when he'd heard something new and was analysing it; his fingers on my wrist stopped moving. 'What's that, and should I be worried?'

'Not really – well, not unless you're crossing a moor or a bog, or other stretch of land where you should be concerned about sinkholes, cliffs or wells or general all-purpose quagmires.'

'Yeah, but what are they precisely?' A waiter brought out our suckaos and there was a pause while we began scooping the little chocolate buttons into the heated cups, then adding the milk and stirring enthusiastically with the weird metal spoon-straws. Do-it-yourself hot chocolate is not just for five-year-olds, you know.

'The overarching term is will-o'-the-wisps,' I continued after my first slurp, 'but they're also known as foxfire or corpselights or *ignis fatuus*, which means fool's fire. And there's also friar's lantern, hobby lantern or my personal favourite, hinkypunk.'

'*Hinkypunk?* Seriously?'

I ignored his amusement and continued my lecture. 'They're variously described as being the ghostly dead, fairy lanterns, spiteful fae or even the spirits of unbaptised babies. Some are supposed to show where fae treasure is buried. They're often seen over swamps or marshes, bobbing lights that maintain the same distance from you no matter how fast you run after them; their goal, for the most part, is to lead travellers astray. Those ones are quite definitely malicious.'

'Okay, so like Min Min lights?'

'Kind of – but I've never heard of corpselights proper being particularly spiteful; they're the ones I associate specifically with cemeteries. Sometimes they appear as balls of light or fire over a grave; just sometimes they wander. I think they're actual spirits, something left over from a person.'

'Doesn't your friend the Boatman take souls?'

'"Friend" is a very strong word,' I hedged. 'On the whole, yes, he starts them on their final journey – but not always. Most folk just gravitate his way after death, or so I'm given to understand, although sometimes they do slip away – it's not like he runs after them. Some spirits flee because they're scared, or they feel they've still got things to do, revenge to be taken, justice to be sought, or maybe they just want to watch their kids grow up . . . and sometimes they don't really know what they're doing, or what they're meant to do. Sometimes they're just lost and they maunder.'

David sucked up the last of the chocolate and smacked his lips. '*Maunder?* Good word. So what happens to the maunderers?'

'Sometimes they transform . . . they become ghosts, poltergeists, haunts or spectres, things more active than corpselights, with a more directed intent or purpose . . . and sometimes they just fade until they're nothing more than echoes.'

'I wonder . . .' he began, and then stopped, put his cup down and stared at it. 'I wonder if my mum and dad went with the Boatman.'

That question hovered in the air between us. I knew his parents were dead, had been for some years, but we'd never discussed the whys and the wherefores. It hadn't ever felt like the right time; that was the problem with fast-moving relationships, a lot of the basic information doesn't manifest upfront. My grandmother would have clicked her tongue, waggled her finger and said 'Marry in haste, repent at leisure.' *Well, fie on you, Grandma, we're not married at all*.

But now I asked quietly, 'What happened to them, David?'

The expression that shifted over his face made me think he might not answer; that I'd ruined our evening. Then he grinned ruefully and began scraping up the remnants of melted chocolate. 'There's never enough in these things.'

'Never enough for a long story?' I asked, but I was prepared to let my original question slide, to never ask it again, if only I could feel that we were on safe ground once more.

'I'd better make it the short version then.' David took a deep breath. 'My parents were murdered.'

I lost my appetite for the hot chocolate, or indeed, everything and anything. My mouth went dry and my heart hurt for him; my clumsy brain searched for the right words. *Sorry*. A normal – Normal – person would say *I'm so sorry*. Alas, I was neither of those things. I was the daughter of a murderer who'd dealt death to vulnerable children. I reached across the table and touched David's free hand.

'Why didn't you tell me before?' I asked gently. 'I told you about my father—'

'I'll show you my childhood trauma if you show me yours?' He tilted his head quizzically.

'Well, when you say it like that it just sounds competitive.' I lifted his hand, kissed his palm.

'Honestly, it never felt like there was a right time. I know that sounds stupid, but some days it feels like it's hard enough to find time to do the ironing, let alone do a recap of my life to-date.'

'You don't have to tell me any more if you don't want to.'

'There's nothing special about it. It's quite mundane, really. My father had an affair.' His lips pressed into a tight white line, suppressed anger no less fresh for the years of grief that had followed. 'He worked with a woman called Vida Russell. It was a distraction for him, and I suppose he thought it was for her too. Well, maybe that's how it started, but she decided she wanted more, so she wrote to my mother, Adelaide, told her what had been going on, thinking it would break my parents up, but Mum always was a patient, pragmatic person. She gave Dad an ultimatum: finish it, or lose us.' He breathed out heavily.

'Dad called it off at once, but Vida didn't take it so well.' He stared out through the glass wall of the café at the passers-by, the walkers and shoppers, not really seeing them.

After a bit, he resumed, 'One night Vida Russell turned up at our home with a shotgun and made short work of Mum. Then she told Dad there was nothing in their way any more. "Peter, we can be together now."'

'Jesus.' Then I said, less helpfully, 'Unusual for a woman, a shotgun.'

He looked at me strangely.

'I'm sorry. I mean, historically, women go for poison or pillows,' I explained, digging myself deeper into a hole. 'Guns are messy and loud. But that's not the right response,' I blathered, then swallowed. *Please don't leave me because I'm weird.*

'Women are changing, I guess, like everyone else.' He held my hand tighter. 'When she finally realised that Dad wasn't on board with her master plan, she shot him too.' He cleared his throat. 'I was thirteen. Vida . . . She was going to kill me too, but . . . she didn't. I'd seen my parents die in the kitchen, but I couldn't run. I was frozen. I supposed I thought, as much as I thought anything, if they were gone, nowhere was safe. Vida reloaded the shotgun and pointed it at me – then she stared at me for a *really* long time, and I stared back . . . but there was this moment when it was like she somehow just emptied out. I could see it in her face, as if all that want and need and greed drained away and she somehow saw herself; as if she suddenly thought, "All this just because of my *whim*?"'

'What happened?' I asked in a very small voice.

'She turned the gun on herself.'

I wrapped both of my hands around his and said quietly, 'Cry if you want to.'

'All cried out. Some days it feels like it happened to someone else. I lived with my Aunt Harry, Mum's sister. She was kind and it was *almost* like having Mum back. She died the year I started uni. But I'd made the choice long before to move on, to keep living my life – if you let it, the past will drag you back, drag you down, drown you. If you let it.'

I leaned as close as my belly would allow, ran my fingers through his hair and breathed in the scent of him, then hugged him to me.

'You know,' he said, a catch in his voice, 'sometimes . . . sometimes I can't remember what my own mother looked like. But I *never* forget Vida Russell's face.' He pointed to his own. 'So full of want, *selfish* want. If she couldn't have what she desired, no one else would.'

He bent in and our foreheads met. There was nothing I could say to soothe the hole inside him, so I just held him, and I thought about what it cost him every time I went off to face something dangerous while he stayed at home, and it dug a deeper hole in my own heart.

There was no point saying that I understood, because he knew it, and they would have been wasted words.

Instead I said, 'I love you', and I held onto him for dear life. After a time, I felt the heat of fresh tears on my neck. I knew they'd never be truly gone.

Chapter Eight

Later that night I woke from a dream where parents – sometimes David's, sometimes mine – were killed in front of me, over and over. David snored softly, untroubled by my thrashing, as if he'd passed his nightmares on to me with the story; his ability to sleep through anything was truly impressive. I wondered how that would work when Maisie arrived. Perhaps a small cattle-prod on the bedside table was the answer.

The clock by the bed said it was 2 a.m. If I tried to go back to sleep, I'd go straight back to the same film reel; I had to do something to break the connection. I let my legs dangle over the side of the bed until gravity took over and I was standing up. My Ugg boots had slid under the bed so I wandered out to the kitchen, swearing quietly as my bare feet touched the cold polished wooden floors. I tried to move quickly to minimise the amount of contact between skin and flooring, but the odds were against me: by the time I was curled on the couch with a crocheted rug around me, my toes were icy.

To distract myself I thought about Susan Beckett and her immaculate house and the stink of malignant magic she couldn't quite get rid of. I tapped my fingers on my belly where the pyjama top rode up, amused by the drum-like resonance, then stopped; the kid might not appreciate her upstairs neighbour tap-dancing. Was Beckett really

68

alone in that big house? How long would she insist that she had no idea why what was happening kept happening?

Why wasn't she hiring anyone to exorcise her home? Why refuse Soteria's eldritch cleaning services? You'd think that would be the first step for someone who knew enough to claim on *Unusual Happenstance*. Had she tried a private contractor, wanting to avoid Alex Parrish's solutions for whatever reason? Most freelance exorcists worked out of the city's spook shops, so I made a mental note to visit a few of them, ask some questions. The fact that it had happened three times suggested that if she had sought help there, she was getting ripped off – and Susan Beckett hadn't struck me as the kind of person to throw good money after bad. If she had made her displeasure known, I might not have to ask too many questions.

I could only conclude that Ms Beckett had secrets that an exorcism or other psychical cleansing might expose: secrets she was willing to put up with this crap – *literally* – to keep hidden. Something was definitely rotten in the suburb of Paddington.

I was still tugging at the threads of the problem when I finally drifted off to sleep an hour later.

Mindy's Mehndi was located on the bottom floor of a house in one of the side streets off the main drag of Boundary Road at West End. It wasn't your ordinary tattoo parlour – and it certainly wasn't what you'd expect if you were thinking of bikies or bands or hipsters or the sort of person who made bad decisions about body art late at night. There were no designs on the wall showing you how awesome a muscular Mickey Mouse might appear on your backside, or a mermaid with your mum's face on your bicep, or a bulldog in a tutu nestled between your boobs.

When you stepped through the sliding glass doors, it looked and smelled like the upmarket spa it was, with incense wafting gently on the breeze and a water feature trickling in one corner, featuring four exquisitely carved *apsaras*, lotus blossoms floating in the pond at their feet. The bright reception area was painted white and decorated with snowy wicker chairs, a glass-topped table covered with a mix of magazines designed to shave off a few IQ points and make you feel bad about your appearance. A hallway to the back of the building was punctuated by several doorways curtained with heavily embroidered silks in rich jewel colours; perhaps they might have gone more naturally against sandalwood and cedar, but they still looked pretty damned fine here in this light, airy place.

There was no sign out the front. Mindy's Mehndi wasn't easy to find unless you knew what you were looking for, and trying to keep Normal walk-ins to a minimum, they didn't advertise for business either. The owner, Kadrū 'Kadie' Cross, made a good living without having to ink skulls and crossbones and roses on the hairy, sweaty backs of bikers, although any Normals who did arrive looking for mehndi or massages got them. Mind you, they paid through the nose for the privilege.

It should be no surprise that the Weyrd enjoy massages and facials and mani-pedis as much as the next being, and are sometimes in greater need. And it's nice to relax, lose the glamour and let it all hang out – and that's best done in an environment where no one's going to scream if they notice you've got claws or a tail. The Weyrd clientele often came for something more than the treatments too: tattooed sigils and wards and spells to hide their nature, to repel curses, to keep them safe from a variety of dangers. Some brought their own designs, some asked Kadie for her expertise – rumour had it she could ink a glamour that would last for years, stopping the world seeing you for what you were. That was a particularly handy thing if you had wings or horns or any of the infinite number of alternative bits with which some of the Weyrd are blessed.

However, the tattoos weren't for everyone, and there were those who didn't want something they couldn't change. Some, the elder Weyrd in particular, frowned on the practice as too easy, too *undignified*. They felt one's magic should take *effort*; that they should have to be aware of it and in control of it. They'd actually prefer to wear the scars of their failures, rather than hide behind a drawing. My father, Grigor, had been of that mindset; I remembered his disgust when a drinking buddy had showed up one night – before our lives were torn apart – with a pattern freshly engraved on his chest. '*Graffiti*,' Grigor had sneered, '*a brand*.' Luckily for Kadie, not everyone felt that way.

I had no tattoos myself, but I had no need of them. My Weyrdness had manifested only in my ridiculous strength. I was eternally grateful there was nothing else I needed to cover up – Weyrd existence was hard enough without having to hide what you were from prying eyes. Besides, my grandmother had made it very clear that my life would be measured in seconds if I ever came home with a tattoo and the echoes of that warning had never disappeared. I really didn't want anything that couldn't be removed with water or spit . . .

Of course, I knew of Kadie Cross, though I'd never met her before. I hit the bell on the white marble counter; its clear ring echoed through the room. There was a moment of silence after the sound finally faded, then there was a gentle rustle and *shush* of someone approaching, someone who might be slithering or trailing a long tail behind them, or both.

The owner of Mindy's Mehndi was her own best advertisement: not only was she so lovely she could give the fountain *apsaras* a run for their money, but she'd used herself as a canvas that was both beautiful and practical. I'd put on my new green wrap dress, polished my Docs and brushed my overcoat but I felt frumpy. I could see why Ellen Baxter wanted this artist's work on her body. The smooth brown skin of her arms and legs (and probably other places not generally viewed by the public) were covered in flowers and vines, with snakes woven so cleverly amongst them I had difficulty distinguishing one from the other. They all ran together to create a glorious garden across her flesh that seemed to shift with her movements. It was sinuous and graceful and positively hypnotic, which wasn't surprising when you realised that beneath her own drawn-on glamours she was a *naga*, an Indian snake deity. Her abbreviated cream-coloured shorts were teamed with a matching vest that was waist-high in the front and so long in the back it trailed on the tiles. Her thick black ponytail hung past her backside and she was barefoot, her nails painted a deep shimmery red.

'Good morning. How can I help you?' Her voice was deep, musical, a slight Indian accent with an Australian twang – quite an acoustic achievement to get them to mix into something that didn't cause the listener to wince, but somehow she managed it. I smiled and offered a hand, which she took with only a small hesitation.

'Hi, I'm Verity Fassbinder,' I started.

'I know who you are.' She fidgeted, and I wondered why this regal woman was so nervous, especially when I was heavily pregnant and quite unable to undertake any kind of pursuit, until she asked, 'Are you here in your official capacity?'

That was it. Ever since I'd dealt summarily with the Nadasys, people had been extra nervous around me. It wasn't that I was particularly dangerous, and I'd only done what I'd needed to protect others, but I guess some had started to wonder about my ruthlessness. Perhaps I'd have to start carrying flashcards: *Hello, I'm not here to hurt you.*

I gave her my best non-threatening smile. 'Nope. Here to ask a favour, actually. For a friend.'

Her expression cleared and her own smile, limned by relief, was stunning. 'A friend?' she asked.

'Yes, really, a *genuine* friend, not just the friend people say they've got when they're too embarrassed to ask for themselves. My friend wants to buy her girlfriend a tattoo for her birthday.'

'And you're approaching me on behalf of a Normal? There are many parlours I can recommend.'

'Well, here's the problem: said girlfriend doesn't want just *any* tattoo, she wants one of yours – not a glamour, but a protective. And I promised I'd do my best to make that happen.'

'You owe a favour?' she asked slyly, and I sensed a trap opening.

I sighed, trying to work out how much I was willing to do for McIntyre. 'I guess so,' I admitted.

'I very seldom work on Normal folk, you know,' she said, sliding into one of the white cane chairs and gesturing that I should do the same. I judged the height and width of the seat, decided that I could probably manage both landing and take-off and half-sank, half-dropped into it. I was so nostalgic for the days when gravity didn't have quite such a grip on me.

'I know that, yes.'

'Which is why Inspector McIntyre sent you to ask,' she stated, not a little gleefully.

'Oh. You know Rhonda then?' I could only hope McIntyre hadn't made an impression like a meteor strike.

'She did call to ask for this service herself.'

'I hope she wasn't too rude.'

Kadie grinned widely, and I caught a glimpse of a forked tongue flitting against her pearly whites. 'She was mostly polite, although I suspect it took some restraint on her part.'

'You're very perceptive.' I shifted against the cushions, trying to find a more comfortable position. 'And if Rhonda was showing restraint, then you can imagine how much she wants this gift for Ellen.'

'It's nice to do favours for friends,' she said, dark eyes gleaming.

This time I sighed out loud and gave her a look that might have withered a lesser woman. Perhaps I'd lost my touch, just as I'd lost my strength? 'Ms Cross, you seem like a reasonable person, open to negotiation. What can I do for you?'

'I am so pleased we can communicate in this fashion.' She crossed her arms and relaxed into the chair now she was assured of getting her way. 'An object was stolen from me. I would like it back.'

'You're going to have to be a little more specific.'

'A large stone – a sort of crystal really, black and green and blue, almost like an opal. It's pretty, and has no real value to anyone but me.'

'Yet you want it back?' I thought I could feel the song of her lie vibrate against my ears, but I didn't think it wise to bring it up so bluntly. Maybe she didn't trust me – she didn't really know me, after all.

'It's important to my work.' She looked away for a moment, then turned back to me. 'And I even know who took it.'

What I thought was, *You'd rather get a pregnant lady to do your running around for you?* but what I said was, 'And you've not confronted them?' I didn't quite manage to keep the peeve out of my tone and her delicate little nostrils flared. Seeing Ellen's birthday present – not to mention any future dealings with Rhonda – hanging in the balance, I held up my hands in surrender. 'Sorry. Please give me the details.'

'Wilbur.'

I inclined my head: *And?*

'Wilbur Wilson. Small man, bald. Piggy eyes.'

'Anything else? Address? Job? Known associates?'

'Do I have to do your work for you?' She puffed up, offended.

Yep, definitely not telling me the whole truth, and getting defensive about it.

'The more information I have, the faster I can find your thief, so let's try again, shall we? Why was he here?'

'He was asking about tattoos — he wanted something more potent than the glamours he currently has.'

'What was he trying to cover up?' I said gently.

She shrugged, as if the matter couldn't have interested her less. 'He didn't tell me what he was underneath and it's not polite to ask. If I'd taken on the job, I'd have needed to know, of course . . . He wanted . . . a change. A total makeover: taller, fitter, handsome, more hair.'

'Could you have done that?'

'I'm good, but I'm no miracle maker. You've got to start with the base materials, enhance or diminish whatever's there as required. I can hide things, but even if he hadn't told me I'd've sensed that he already had some kind of magic at work on him. It was powerful, and quite frankly, if that level of enchantment couldn't make him look the way he wanted my tattoos weren't going to fix anything.'

I scratched my head. 'And how do you know he took the stone?'

'Because when he was here, it was here, and when he departed, it was gone.'

'You left him alone at some point?'

'I had a client in one of the rooms and the timer went off for her facial peel. It's not a good idea to leave those on too long, so I nipped in for a couple of minutes to clean her up. When I came back . . .' she lifted her empty hands in resignation. 'And he was not happy at my refusal. If I'd been alone here I'm not sure what would have happened.'

'Where'd you keep the stone?' I looked around the room.

She jerked her chin towards the fountain with its *apsaras*, and said in a disapproving tone, 'With my girls.'

I noticed then there was a kind of basin against the wall where something the size of an emu egg might once have nestled. The eyes of the stone nymphs moved, their lids dipping like wings, lashes batting; they looked ashamed. *Guardian goddess fail.* 'Do they walk around at night?'

She ignored the question, just glared, so I hurriedly continued, 'Was there anything else he said? About *why* he wanted to be changed?'

'He told me he was judged by his appearance in his personal life and at work, that he couldn't get any higher on the legal ladder unless he looked *better*.'

'A lawyer?'

'I didn't really get that sense. Maybe an assistant, or a paralegal? The guy in the mailroom with delusions of grandeur? He just didn't have the slickness I associate with lawyers. I could, of course, be wrong.'

'Did he say where he worked?' I asked hopefully.

She shook her head, and I wasn't really surprised. Disappointed, but not surprised.

'Okay. I'll look into this for you. I take it I can tell Rhonda to call you?'

'And you will find my stone.'

'I'll do my best.'

We rose and she took my hand. 'Ms Fassbinder, another thing. I'll be happy to do any protective work you might want at the family and friends discount.'

'Thank you,' I said, thinking it wasn't an offer I was likely to take up any time soon.

'You might be glad of it some day . . .' She shifted her grip to my elbow and guided me towards the door, a kind of gentle manhandling that it was hard to complain about without appearing churlish.

Ziggi was sitting was outside in the cab, his white-framed fly-eye sunnies perched at the end of his nose, a battered copy of Charlotte Brontë's *Villette* held between his callused fingers. Say what you will about his fashion sense, his taste in literature cannot be faulted. As I approached, I looked up and down the street, checking for anyone who might be lurking; since the *kitsune* had buttonholed me in the supermarket I'd been a little nervous.

It was Thursday, day of hitting the spook shops to see if Susan Beckett had been looking for quick fixes that Alex Parrish and Soteria didn't know about, but as I was about to open the taxi door, my mobile rang, displaying McIntyre's name on the screen. This led me to wonder if she'd developed some kind of psychic power as a result of her contact with the angels. Or maybe her ears had just been burning.

'Hey, Rhonda. Perfect timing. Give Kadie Cross a call. *Be nice.*'

'Fantastic,' she said, sounding distracted.

'And once more with feeling? I had to take on a job in order to get this for you; I want to hear actual full-on *gratitude*.'

'Sorry. I've got a situation here.'

If Rhonda was apologising – and being sincere about it – then something was up. '*Here* being?'

'Mt Coot-tha, at the lookout.'

'And the situation?'

'Is distinctly weird.'

'And Weyrd?'

'Probably.' She sighed. 'Just get here, Fassbinder. This is bad.'

Chapter Nine

The guy looked to all intents and purposes as if he'd just keeled over
– a heart attack, or an aneurysm perhaps. The lookout and accompanying café and restaurant were usually packed with local peeps
and tourists with a hankering for over-priced ice cream and food,
but McIntyre'd had it cleared. Ziggi parked on Sir Samuel Griffiths
Drive, but I'd still had to walk a fair way, pushing through the crowd
milling beyond the crime scene tape, all jostling for position, trying
to see why they'd been banished from the best view in the city. One
of the cops recognised me and let me past without comment.

The body was lying near one of the pay-per-view telescopes. He
wasn't looking happy or unhappy, just dead. He wore a pair of faded
jeans, a red-and-white chequered shirt and red rubber flip-flops. His
longish hair was dark, and he was sporting a three-day growth. I
reckoned he was in his mid-thirties. To his left was a little white paper
boat containing what smelled like melted rum'n'raisin ice cream.

In the glare of the midday sun I squinted at McIntyre, who was
standing next to him.

'Poke him,' she said.

That sounded pretty disrespectful. '*Pardon?*'

'Poke him in the chest. Doesn't have to be too hard. Just do it.'

Embarrassingly, she had to hold my hand to keep me from toppling
over as I sank onto my haunches. Underneath the dead man was a

kind of shiny shadow – closer inspection showed it was a puddle, drying slowly. I felt his clothes and they were damp too, and what I'd taken to be some kind of hair-slick was also water, not product. I did as instructed and jabbed at his chest, just over the heart where his shirt had been unbuttoned.

The skin and flesh beneath my fingers positively *rippled*. It was firm and whole, a real body, but somehow the poor man had taken on the consistency of a waterbed: push at one end and get an equal and opposite reaction at the other. Oh, and fluid spurted from his nose and mouth: it was like an *under*-enthusiastic fountain, but there was spurting nonetheless. I prodded him again for good measure, just to make certain I'd not imagined it, and sure enough, more rippling and wobbling and spurting followed.

I was grossed-out and fascinated at the same time.

'Wow,' I said, 'wow!'

Rhonda helped me up. 'Look at you with the articulateness.'

'I *swear*, I have *never* seen anything like that before. Perhaps you could offer something helpful? Maybe like background details?'

She rolled her eyes, then took an old-school Police notebook from her jacket pocket. 'Mr Toby Malone, aged thirty-two, late of Ashgrove, currently an unemployed fitter and turner, was here with his girlfriend, Anna Valentine, taking in the view and enjoying some of the creamy comestibles on offer.'

'Someone's been reading the thesaurus.' I stared down at Toby Malone, all mysteriously soggy and dead. 'Poor bugger. Any ideas?'

'That's why I called you,' Rhonda said rather curtly. 'Expert-type person.'

'I hate to admit it, but I am all out of ideas on this one. Did anyone see what happened?'

'His girlfriend.' Rhonda pointed her chin towards a woman seated under one of the sunsails in the company of an extremely young female uniformed officer who seemed to have an endless supply of tissues in the pockets of her navy combat pants. She wore an expression of resigned bewilderment as she mechanically patted the woman's heaving shoulders.

Rhonda saw it too. 'Lacy Oldman, my newbie.'

'I kind of figured. Way to throw her in at the deep end.' I put my hands into the small of my back and arched a little to relieve the pressure. 'What did Anna Valentine say?'

'One minute they were arguing, the next he's making weird noises and water starts pouring out of all visible orifices.'

'Should that be orifi? And no one was standing near them? No one saw anything suspicious?'

'Fassbinder, you know what this place is like – between the busloads of tourists and the Brisbanites who just want to view the city from another angle, you're either packed in like sardines in a can, or it's a post-apocalypse shopping mall – and then the other sardines come back in. It's tidal.'

'Mr Malone certainly found it so,' I said without thinking, then quickly, 'Ellen doing the autopsy?'

'Uh huh.'

'Okay, get her to test the water in him, see if there's anything weird about it – apart from the obvious. At least that way we might be able to work out where it's from.'

'We'd need something to compare it with first,' she said.

'Rhonda, try to be part of the solution, not the problem.' I rubbed my lower back again and sighed. 'I'll talk to the girlfriend. Also, McIntyre, my preference would be to *not* go to the morgue.' My aversion to the place, always quite pronounced, had grown in the last eight months as my sense of smell had become more acute.

'Fair enough. Keep in mind that it'll take some days to get the test results back.' She gave a whistle that sounded too loud in the still air and gestured for the waiting Scene of Crimes Officer to start doing his job before sending Toby Malone on his lonely way to a cold steel bed. 'Any ideas?'

'I . . . I can chat with some of the undines. They might have a clue about whether their element is being misused.' Of course there was no guarantee, especially if the liquid that had drowned Toby Malone was from different source, like bottled or transported from elsewhere. Not that I was entirely happy about going anywhere near the river – but surely I'd see the Boatman coming? Surely I could waddle away before he demanded his so-called 'stolen' property back? But if he was around, I knew he'd sense it, that close to the river.

But if I wanted to talk to the undines, I didn't have much choice; I could only hope. 'Call me when Ellen's done?' I said at last.

McIntyre gave me a thumbs-up.

The young policewoman eyed me suspiciously as I approached, but that could have been for any number of reasons. Perhaps she'd heard about me? Or that I wasn't afraid of her legendary boss? Maybe she resented the amount of research McIntyre had made her do on my behalf. Or even that this day was so filled with bizarre shit she just didn't know where to look – after all, there probably wasn't a class on this at the Police Academy. Idly I wondered what she'd done – right or wrong – to pull duty with Rhonda.

She didn't say anything as she vacated the seat next to the crying woman for me.

Anna Valentine was in her mid-twenties, with bouffant hair bleached a little too hard, a line of five gold studs in each ear, pale pink '60s lipstick and black eyeliner that had run down her cheeks.

She looked about as dazed as someone would on the worst day of their life.

'Hi, Anna. Can I talk to you about Toby?'

She nodded, but I could see she wasn't really focusing.

'I'm Verity Fassbinder. I work with the police.'

'How could this have happened? We were talking, just talking and then . . .' Her voice trailed off and she started crying again. The constable handed her another wodge of tissues.

'Take your time, Anna. Talk me through what happened, please.'

She took a deep breath and dashed away the tears. 'He started spluttering – at first I thought he was taking the piss, making burbling noises just to annoy me 'cause I'd been talking about a spa holiday in Bali, making it sound romantic, like it could be a honeymoon thing, y'know? And he said we couldn't afford it – we couldn't afford to get married until he got another job, so we'd have to put the wedding off for another year . . . and I just thought he was trying to get out of it. Again.' Sobs bubbled up around the words, made them come out all wet. 'So I started yelling at him and then . . . then I looked at him and all this water started coming out of his eyes and I thought he was crying 'cause I was angry at him, but he never fucking cries! Not even when the dog died . . . but it gushed out of his mouth and his ears, and . . . Then he was on the ground and he looked like a fountain . . .'

She began to shake again, weeping. Constable Oldman offered more tissues as I put an arm around Anna's shoulders and waited until she'd calmed a little before I went on, 'I know this is really hard, but what you're telling me is *really* important, Anna, okay? You didn't see anyone? There was no one close to Toby? No one spoke to him, started a fight, handed him anything?'

'No, nothing. One moment we were bickering, the next . . .'

More sobbing ensued. It was obvious I wasn't going to get anything useful from her, not at the moment.

'Okay, Anna, I'm going to leave you be now, but if it's okay with you, in a few days I'll come and see you, yes? See how you're doing? Maybe you'll have remembered something else . . .'

She hiccoughed a *yes* in between sobs as I offered her my condolences and a business card, just in case she did think of anything in the meantime. I thanked Constable Oldman for her time too, but she just gave me the hairy eyeball.

As I headed back towards the blue and white tape barrier I shook my head in Rhonda's direction: *Nope, nothing more. No point talking now.* I looked back over my shoulder at Anna Valentine and as I did, I noticed a flash of glass on the beam above her head: a security camera. I caught McIntyre's eye and pointed. She waved me off, impatient; *Yes, I know they're there; yes, they'll be examined – and no, not by me.* I suspected Constable Oldman had many boring hours ahead of her; I couldn't rustle up much sympathy given her lack of warmth.

I knew Ziggi had a dinner date with Louise Arnold, the Weyrd healer who'd fixed my leg last year, and he'd be getting anxious to go home and primp his thinning ginger hair, make sure all three of his eyes were sparkling and bright. And why not? He deserved a life outside of work as much as I did. Visiting the undines would wait until tomorrow, but I had someone else I wanted to talk to. I'd let Ziggi drop me off there before he disappeared; I could nab a lift home with David, or even catch a Normal cab for once.

Look at me, being so thoughtful.

'It's nice to see you again, Verity. How can I help?' said Alex Parrish, and he sounded genuine, which, let's face it, was something of a new experience for me. More often than not, I'd noticed people were *less* enthused about my presence on a second or third meeting – or if you're Constable Oldman, even the first. I wondered why that was, then remembered my mission.

'I have a few questions about insurance and clauses and maybe about firms who deal with Weyrd clients, or business that might involve Weyrd elements. Or just matters that might not be entirely mundane – or indeed, legal.'

'Like eldritch banking?'

'I have not even heard of that and now I am scared, although that could go some way to explaining the current global economy.'

He laughed and offered me green tea. I refused.

'That's very wise – Alicia's at lunch and I make the worst tea in the world. Much better with cocktails. So, what do you need to know?'

'Specifically, the phrase "goods in kind". As in a bill from a legal firm might have a notation against some sort of services as being paid for in that manner.'

'And how did you come across this term?' he asked evenly.

I grinned. 'I don't believe you need to know that, but rest assured it was in the pursuit of your interests.'

'Well, don't I feel like a puppy who's been swatted with a rolled-up newspaper,' he said, but laughed.

'Sorry, didn't mean that at all. But the less you know, the less you can disclose.'

'You are wise.'

'Once burned . . . Anyway, I was curious about what might constitute appropriate goods in kind when they're set against things that have a value of fifty thousand dollars and up.'

He steepled his fingers, an unconscious echo of my gesture the other day, then rested his chin on the tippy-top.

'That's a lot of "in kind",' he mused, and stared into a corner of his office for a few moments. 'Some firms, some larger commercial enterprises – *not* Soteria, might I add – do deals that don't require cash payments, but the monetary value needs to be recorded. The nature of the goods does not, which is handy because otherwise there might be some inconvenient questions asked by auditors, accountants, the Tax Office, the police. As I think I said before, it's all in the wording. You must be careful with phrasing.'

'I take it we're not just talking about a three-thousand-dollar bottle of 1961 Grange Hermitage in a brown paper bag?'

'Not generally. Might be a few cases of something rarer, maybe a vintage like the one you put the kibosh on last year?'

I was kind of surprised that Alex knew I'd put an end to the winemaker, who had been bottling the tears of children, because it wasn't the sort of thing Normal society was generally aware of – but maybe Alex Parrish wasn't Normal. Maybe Bela trusted him a lot. Or just maybe Soteria insured those who'd been affected by some of the property damage I'd had a hand in.

'Right. And?'

'And sometimes it might be arcane artefacts. An ancient treasure of some description. It might be turning someone, Normal or Weyrd, into a thrall or slave for a period of service. It might be the offering up of a soul. It might the sacrifice of a life, or several.'

'For a building project?'

'Bodies have been buried in foundations for thousands of years to protect structures, ensuring stability, longevity – the custom's aeons old in both Normal and Weyrd cultures. To make a multi-million dollar development go through, some investors might consider it worth the cost of a soul or twelve.' He sighed. 'It's essentially the same kind of thing the small-scale dark mages do, only for a bigger reward, you'll pay a bigger price.'

'And a legal firm might . . . ?'

He puffed out a breath. 'Might employ specialist contractors. Might employ legal experts whose forte is writing particularly watertight contracts. Or perhaps those who can source the kinds of offerings required.'

I tapped my fingers on the arm of the chair. Susan Beckett worked for a law firm that dealt with commercial dealings; Kadie Cross' thief, Wilbur Wilson, claimed to be in the legal profession. I let those things percolate in my brain, and said, 'Hmmmmm.'

'That sounds ominous.'

'It often is,' I admitted. 'Thanks, Alex, you've been a big help.'

'Anything else I can do?'

I rose slowly. 'That's it for the moment.'

He walked me to the door. 'Any progress on your enquiries into Ms Beckett?'

'Nothing big. Gathering crumbs. No one's really at risk as far as I can tell – well, except for her highly expensive furnishings, and possibly your company's bank balance.'

He snorted. 'I hope it's that simple. I really do.'

'And you're sure she's never mentioned family to you?'

He considered for a moment, trying to recall. 'No. As I said before, we don't have a social chitchat kind of relationship.'

'Well, I hope to have some answers for you before next mud-date.' We shook hands and I added, 'Thanks, Alex. I'll be in touch when I know more.'

The elevator delivered me to the foyer and I was just about to step from the building when I saw the girl.

Her face was identical to that of the *kitsune* who'd tried to make too-friendly in the supermarket, but she wasn't wearing the same kind of punk outfit. Instead, she sported a short black dress, layered lacy skirt and petticoats, with red ribbons and bows and silver zippers, high-heeled boots laced up to the knee and artfully ripped fishnets, fingerless gloves. A handbag shaped like a silver skull with rabbit ears hung over her shoulder and a tiny hat sat on a nest of high-teased hair. A heart-shaped beauty mark kissed her left cheek.

I narrowed my eyes as she walked casually, carefully, as a woman in six-inch heels invariably must, past the glass doors that let onto the street. I let her get a good head-start, then followed.

Alice in Goth Wonderland. A dead ringer for the first fox-girl – and Len the delivery guy's date, if the outfit was anything to go by.

Curiouser and curiouser.

Chapter Ten

The stroll down from St Paul's Terrace felt kind of slow, even for me, but I was still sweating under my coat. The girl kept stopping to browse the windows of the various chi-chi clothing boutiques, cheapie homeware stores and noodle joints. When she reached the Wickham Terrace end of the Valley Mall, she went right and continued on past the Asian eateries sitting side by side with so-called 'gentlemen's' clubs. At last she turned left into the Chinatown Mall.

I picked up my pace and rounded the corner just in time to see her disappear into one of the alleyways to the left of the herring-bone-paved plaza. Puffing like a steam train, I passed under the elaborate red-painted gateway and continued up the slight incline to the lane where I thought the girl had gone. When I peeked in, I could see it was a dead end – but there was no one to be seen.

Maybe I'd been wrong? Maybe it was further up?

I thought I'd better make sure she wasn't hiding behind one of the three dumpsters or the pile of pulpy cardboard boxes, so I took a few steps in . . . then a few more. There were several stackable supermarket trays; the rotting bread and single-portion containers of fermenting fruit salad gave off a terrible stench – even without my pregnant lady olfactory sense I'd've felt horribly nauseous. Not only that, the waste annoyed me. *Food banks*, people! Still I kept on, hand over nose, moving deeper into the shadows to make sure there were no hidden ratways or doors the girl might have taken.

Nothing.

Then I felt my stomach — and my daughter — begin to react to the stench: it was leave or throw up time. I turned, planning to head back out as fast as I could waddle . . . until two clouds appeared; buzzing, roiling masses of what at first looked like flies. They slowly coalesced, turning from black to grey, then to red and to white, finally becoming solid shapes, low to the ground. Their shape became clearer, vulpine, then the creatures reared up on hind legs and grew taller: Gothic Alice and another girl, this one looking like a librarian in a brown knit dress with sensible burgundy Mary-Janes. A tan satchel strap was slung across her chest; thick black-framed glasses settled on her pert little nose. She looked only marginally less threatening than her companion, whose smug grin was doing nothing to soothe my nerves. I wish I'd been at least a little surprised that their faces were identical to the *kitsune* who'd attacked me in the supermarket.

'What do we have here?' said Gothic Alice.

'A mouse,' replied the Librarian quietly, drawing from her satchel a short knife in a sheath. *A tantō*, I thought, *a good assassin's weapon*. Ninja Librarian, apparently.

'A wandering mouse who's gone where she shouldn't.'

'A mouse outside of her house.'

'You two really need to work on your double act,' I said, hoping I sounded more confident than I felt. It didn't help that Maisie had clearly been well aware of the threat, and long before I was. Now she was somersaulting good and proper. I put a hand to my belly, trying to calm her down, trying to stop the pain that was reverberating through me, begging, 'Not now, sweetie.'

Misunderstanding, the Librarian said, 'We're not interested in *that*. Or you. We just want to know where *it* is.'

'It?' I asked, backing away even though I had nowhere to go.

'The Apostate,' spat Gothic Alice, and began to pull something from her rabbit skull bag. She continued pulling for a long while until I could see the object: a naginata, a reaping sword; a thirty-centimetre-long blade attached to a wooden haft just over a metre long. Bewitched weapons were the order of the day. I wondered if reaching into my giant handbag would trigger an attack; even if it didn't, I couldn't guarantee finding the dagger in time, given how much crap I'd taken to lugging about.

'Still not helpful.'

The Librarian rolled her eyes. 'The traitor – the betrayer – the runaway. The one who is without faith.'

'We seem to have a failure to communicate,' I said, rubbing hard at my belly. As the *kitsune* took slow, sure steps towards me, Maisie began a kind of heavy metal thrashing, and it was *hurting*.

'The Guardian's *Hound*,' sneered Gothic Alice as if I were a particularly thick student.

That made me laugh, even though it hurt. 'Still not helpful!'

That made the Librarian pause, her certainty visibly wavering, but Gothic Alice snarled, 'She's lying. She knows.'

'I really, really don't – and I've got to tell you that if I had any clue who you're after I'd give them up right now just to get rid of you two.' I gritted my teeth.

'How does it feel to come from a family of liars?' asked the Librarian.

'Look, I don't think I am who you think I am . . .' Unless, of course, they knew Grigor. My father might be long gone, but he'd left plenty of landmines in my life.

'You're the woman who killed our sister.'

'Nope, not me — although I'll admit I was there. Ladies, I would love to discuss this further, but— *ARGH—!*' The pain in my belly was phenomenal — and I was also suddenly very, *very* wet below the waist . . . I felt as if I'd stepped in a puddle right up to my middle.

My waters had broken. Maisie Fassbinder-Harris was arriving whether I liked it or not — and the two assassins did *not* look like they had their first-aid badges. As I put a hand against the dumpster, trying to steady myself, I dropped my bag. The mobile fell out and skidded across the concrete — just my luck; why couldn't it have been the dagger landing precisely at my feet?

The noise I made at the first contraction sent the fox-girls skittering backwards a few feet, which would have been hilarious, had I not been being split in two.

'We haven't even touched you!' The Librarian looked more perplexed than I thought a stone-cold killer should.

I made a grab for the handbag, still hoping I might find my go-to weapon, but I was gripped by another vice-like squeeze and froze mid-lunge.

'It's the baby, stupid,' snapped Gothic Alice.

'She hasn't *told* us anything,' the Librarian complained. 'What do we do?'

'We help things along,' said Gothic Alice with relish and took a determined pace towards me.

I really didn't want my daughter to be born in a filthy, stinky back alley. I didn't want us both to die here, with me unable to defend us. I didn't want David to hear about our deaths, not this way — indeed, not any way.

I staggered backwards and caught the edge of the dumpster again so I could lever myself upright; no way in hell was I going without a fight – but my daughter had other ideas: shrieking pain lanced through me once more and I screamed.

'Shut her up before someone hears!' cried Gothic Alice sensibly, but she was too late: a figure had dropped in front of me, giving a cry of such rage it stopped us all in our tracks.

Whoever (or *what*ever) might have come from the sky or the roof, I neither knew nor cared; at this point I was going take *any* help I could get. The figure spun, a long black coat fanning gracefully, dark hair in a braid whipping from side to side. A leg kicked out, and then an arm, and there was that peculiar sound of air being cleaved, a voice of metal tempered by blood. There was a pause, a hesitation, as if the metal had hit something denser . . . and then it sang again as it came out the other side.

Gothic Alice's head, wearing a surprised expression and way too much mascara, flew off in one direction while her body toppled in another.

The woman who'd come to my rescue hesitated and looked at me, then at Victim #1. Then she set her sights on the Librarian – who was too busy staring at her sister's corpse to do much about defending herself. Luckily for her, that was when I screamed with all my might as Maisie tried to claw her way out; my unholy shrieking was enough to distract my rescuer and give the last fox-girl the moment's respite she needed. She bolted – but in the moment before she went, she gave the woman a look of such terrible hurt and betrayal and disbelief that in other circumstances I might have felt sorry for her. Well, as long as those other circumstances didn't include her trying to kill me and my soon-to-be-born child.

My knees gave way and I collapsed onto the ground, shuffling just enough to rest my aching back against the filthy dumpster. I realised I was bawling like a little kid; I wasn't sure how long that had been going on. I put both hands to my belly, as if that might stop any hasty exits, trying to control the uncontrollable, and did my best to remember everything Dr Aarden had told me about the breathing and the relaxing and the calm thoughts, but it was hard when all I could think about were the tales of women who'd given birth to offspring with talons and teeth and no compunction about using them against their mothers.

A hand touched my shoulder and I flinched. I was so focused on not exploding that it took me a moment to realise that my rescuer was crouched beside me. She'd retrieved my phone from the rapidly decaying mess of the *kitsune*; there was a long scratch on the screen, but I hoped it would be otherwise okay. The woman had an oval face framed by dark hair shot with silver. Her large hazel eyes looked sad. A thin scar started at the left corner of a full mouth and went almost up to her ear. Beneath her coat worn jeans were teamed with a black sweater; her Blundstones were plain, no-nonsense.

In a low, soothing voice she said, 'It's okay, Verity. It'll be all right. C'mon, steady inhalations.' She began to breathe in a calm, rhythmic way, making encouraging noises, trying to get me to imitate her. I reached for the mobile, but the contraction got worse instead of better and all I could do was stare at her and whimper, 'I want David.'

It didn't occur to me to ask how she knew my name.

Chapter Eleven

I slept and I woke, then I slept again – although 'waking' wasn't actual consciousness, because every time I managed to drag my lids open, Morpheus pulled them straight down again. Sometimes slumber was a comforting darkness with dreams I couldn't remember, sometimes it was a film on repeat: flickering images of the attack in the alleyway, my rescuer's devastating defence of me, Gothic Alice's head flying off in slow motion, me being bundled into the back of the ambulance and dragging the tall woman along with me, being wheeled down the corridors of St Agnes' Hospital, the ceiling lights flashing past as the trolley was pushed along . . . but there the memories ceased.

When at last I roused for more than a moment, I couldn't believe how *thirsty* I was, how my throat *ached* – had they intubated me? I dug through my foggy brain, but found no answer. The sheets felt rough against my skin, but I must've developed some sort of hyper-sensitivity, because they looked like a high thread count, not the usual stuff you'd get at a hospital. And the soft light coming from the bedside lamp felt too bright, making me blink. But there was no smell of antiseptic, no undercurrent of noise. As I looked around, I finally realised this was not the small, tidy, private cubicle I'd booked for Maisie's birth.

I was not in the maternity ward at St Agnes' Hospital.

I was pretty sure I'd started there, but I definitely wasn't in Kansas any more. For one thing, I was lying in a king-sized bed, and David was beside me, sleeping on top of the covers. The room was painted in a hue so snowy it had a tinge of blue to it, like a Scotsman's skin after winter, and the décor was French Provincial, the chest of drawers, bedside tables and dressing table all distressed white and gold. A sunburst mirror hung high on the opposite wall, and there were floor-to-ceiling shutters to my right, presumably covering windows. A chaise longue and a coffee table made up a comfy sitting area, and a small fridge hummed in a corner. A door sat ajar, showing a blizzard-white bathroom just beyond.

Definitely not St Agnes'.

And quite apart from the fact I wasn't where I was supposed to be, something didn't feel right – even given what I'd been through; it felt *extra* not right – and it took me long moments to realise what was missing.

I slid my hands to a soft, empty belly and felt suddenly, *terribly* alert. I tried to speak, but managed only a kind of caw. That was enough to wake David, who sat up and stretched before leaning over to rub his slightly stubbly cheek against mine. Clumsily, I put my arms around him.

'Hey.' He kissed me softly, which made the tears start.

'Did I lose her?' I croak-sobbed. 'Is she gone?'

'Oh! Oh, V— No! *No!* She was a little early, that's all, so her lungs aren't quite there, but they've got her in a humidicrib, she's all hooked up like a Dalek.' He smiled, crying and laughing at the same time, and I couldn't stop the sob that rose to my lips.

Then my stomach muscles contracted and I discovered that I had stitches somewhere *very* uncomfortable.

'Is she . . . ? Does she . . . ? Has she—?' *Got a tail? Wings? Claws?*

'She's perfect, V. Ten fingers, ten toes. A full head of ginger hair and she's very, very red, but she's *gorgeous*.' He squeezed my fingers. 'Beautiful.'

And we spent the next long while crying like big idiots.

A knock heralded the end of our private time as the door opened to admit Ziggi and Bela, the former windmilling his hand to hurry the latter. As soon as Bela's highly polished tan Ferragamo Oxfords got out of the way, Ziggi swiftly sealed the entrance.

'All clear?' he whispered

I gazed blankly at him, but David gave the thumbs-up and Ziggi gave a relieved grin. At my quizzical look he said by way of explanation, 'Sister Bridget.'

It didn't really explain anything.

Both of my friends held enormous bouquets. Ziggi with his burden of carnations, gerberas and lisianthus in reds, pinks, oranges and purples looked like a parade float as he moved towards the bed and enfolded me in a bear hug. I kept the wincing to myself as I was being shaken around for joy, so as not to hurt Ziggi's feelings.

Bela remained by the door, the large and eminently tasteful hand-tied arrangement of roses and baby's breath held in front of him as if he didn't quite know what to do with it and wasn't really sure how it had got there. I wondered if seeing me like this, with my life so utterly changed, being with someone other than him, was uncomfortable for him; with Bela it was always hard to tell. When I'd broken up with him, he'd never tried to convince me that it was the wrong decision, so maybe there was a good chance the situation didn't bother him at all. Maybe he'd stuck his thumb on a rose thorn.

David, with the great generosity of heart I loved so much, stood and went over to shake his hand. Bela said quietly, 'Congratulations!' and his face cleared as David drew him towards the bed.

My boss leaned over and gave me a hug a good deal more gentle than Ziggi's. 'I'm glad you're okay, V,' he said, waving the flowers around. David took them from him and carefully put them into a crystal vase sitting on the table. Bela looked infinitely lighter without the blooms.

'That makes two of us. But why do I appear to be at a ridiculously upmarket B&B and not at the hospital of choice?'

'It wasn't safe to have you in a public place and there was no way I could surround the hospital with a security team,' he said. The vision of Bela's ragtag collection of muscular, aggressive and frequently not-too-bright Weyrd – the equivalent of a Praetorian guard – hanging around the maternity wing of St Agnes' made me laugh, but I had to admit the idea didn't fill me with joy, even if they were there to protect me. 'So we brought you here. This is Ocean's Reach, it's a . . . well, a kind of sanatorium . . .'

'A nineteenth-century nuthouse?'

'. . . a retreat really,' Bela finished, ignoring my interjection. 'It's safe, run by a woman called Wanda Callander.'

The name didn't ring any bells. 'Who knows we're here?'

'Us, Sister Bridget, Dr Aarden. Wanda, obviously.'

'And Mike and Jerry,' added Ziggi.

'Monobrow Mike and Hairy Jerry?' I asked, my voice going up an octave. Mike Jones and Jerry Stormare had *one* job last year: to keep an eye on ex-Council member Mercado White. White had given them the slip in under an hour and departed for places unknown. As yet, no one had managed to track him down.

Bela raised his hands. 'They've been making up for their mistakes. They specifically asked for this detail. They feel like they've got something to prove.'

'Which they do,' I said.

'Don't worry, Galina is in charge of them,' said Ziggi.

'And who the hell is Galina?' Oops, there it went, up another couple of octaves.

'V, you're safe, Maisie's safe. We're just outside of Byron Bay.'

I looked at David, who continued, 'There was a helicopter ride. It was very exciting, although Sister Bridget wasn't best pleased.'

'Aaaannd why do we have Sister Bridget here?'

'Because Dr Aarden wouldn't release you without a medical professional on hand.'

'Okay then.' I scratched my head. 'We have a helicopter?'

Bela sighed. 'Alex Parrish organised a loan. *Focus*, V.'

'So Alex also knows where we are? People are going to be looking for me, you know – actual people who don't wish harm.'

'I called around, let McIntyre and the Norns know you were okay, that you'd be in touch.' Ziggi planted himself on the couch and put his feet on the coffee table.

'There are other things we need to talk about, V,' said Bela.

'How long have I been out?' I asked.

'It's only Friday. Maisie came along pretty quickly. You were in the hospital by half-five yesterday, she was out by half past six and we were in a helicopter by eleven,' David answered. 'Don't you remember *anything*?'

I didn't want to admit that part of me was doing its best to forget what little I did recall. I had an awful feeling I'd been babbling about *horns and tails and teeth, oh my!* in the ambulance, but the woman with me hadn't batted an eyelid; she'd just shushed me gently and reminded me again to breathe. Obviously the paramedics were used to dealing with hallucinating mothers too, because they'd just laughed.

I cannot claim this to have been my finest hour.

'Oh—! I just remembered there were two more *kitsune*, and I'm pretty sure one of them was on a date with the guy who delivers my parcels, which may or may not mean anything, but is still weird and warrants looking into. And there was this other woman—'

'The one who rang me on your mobile?' David asked.

And as he said it, I remembered that too: her calmly phoning David after she'd called the ambulance, telling him I was okay, that he should head to the hospital. She'd promised him she'd stay with me, keep me safe.

'She was gone by the time I arrived. The admissions staff had seen her but didn't get her name.' He grinned. 'But other people saw her, so you weren't imagining her, if that's what you're worried about.'

I wasn't going to admit it, but there might have been a tiny element of that.

'So let's discuss the woman,' Bela said, then looked around and gestured at Ziggi; together they dragged the *chaise* closer to the bed and settled in while I told my nearest and dearest how that same woman had just happened to be in the vicinity when two *kitsune* assassins decided I'd make a great sashimi platter. I told them how efficiently she'd wielded that *very* sharp sword of hers – and how it had disappeared by the time she knelt beside me, so it was probably just as enchanted as the fox-girls' weapons – I guessed it had probably shrunk right down to fit into her coat pocket. We discussed how interesting it was that she owned such a thing when she'd appeared to be completely Normal.

'But she couldn't have been entirely, could she?' I said, my restless fingers pleating the soft white sheets while David stroked my hair. 'Not the way she moved, not with her speed and precision. Maybe she's a mix like me, just gifted differently?'

'Then who is she?' asked David, and I could tell he was worried, about me, about the baby. About how the life I led might impact on us.

I touched his hand, squeezed it gently. 'She didn't do me any harm, love – in fact, she protected me at considerable personal risk, so I think it's fair to say she's on our side.'

'Or she wants you safe for the moment,' suggested Bela, earning himself glares all around. He shrugged. 'We're all thinking it. It's not like you to put your head in the sand, Verity Fassbinder.'

What he didn't say was, *Or maybe she wants the baby safe.*

'Any idea who she might be?' David directed the question towards Bela, an edge to his tone. It looked like the truce was on shaky ground.

'Until we know more, we need to be prepared. We don't know what she wants. You're all staying here until we're in possession of considerably more information than we currently have.'

Though I bridled at the idea of being told what to do, of being made to stay put, I knew Bela was right – and *here* was a luxury boutique hotel with zillion-thread-count linen. I was about to say so when David broke in with, 'Okay. That's a good idea.'

There were a few moments of heavy silence as I digested the fact that David had *immediately* sided with Bela, then I said evenly, 'I think I'd like to see my daughter now.'

A wide parquet-floored hallway lined with closed doors led from our room to a sitting room, brightly lit by winter sun pouring in through tall glass windows. I saw overflowing bookshelves, a broad coffee table stacked with magazines and the bulks of Monobrow Mike and Hairy Jerry filling two of the three over-stuffed couches. They each silently raised a hand when they saw me (*We're on duty*, they meant) and I replied in kind (*Don't fuck up*, I meant): cool people being cool. No sign of the mysterious Galina, though. Beyond that lay a kitchen with a comfortably battered pine table, a sideboard filled with crockery, an Aga in one corner with pots and pans hanging from a re-purposed ladder overhead, and a huge silver fridge.

But we didn't go that far. David led me to a door on the opposite side of the hallway and pushed it open, revealing a large room that had been turned into a nursery. A double bed had been pushed up against one wall to make space for the humidicrib in the centre. Sister Bridget was standing next to it, apparently checking something, but I barely saw her. I was focused on the jungle of extension cords keeping the high-tech whatsit working; it was making a *shushing* noise as it helped my little girl to breathe. She was so small, a little scrap of a human with a shock of red-gold hair that came from who-knows-where. The high, serious forehead and the teeny little ski-jump nose, currently filled with tubes, were all David. I couldn't see anything of me in her and, irrationally, that made me sad; I'd carried her around for so long you'd think I'd get a look in somewhere. I couldn't believe we'd made her, that the cause of so much heartburn and indigestion, so many uncomfortable nights, and so very much flatulence could be this adorable, could make my heart hurt so much just by looking at her.

David and I leaned against each other, shoulder to shoulder, Ziggi and Bela lined up on either side of us.

'Isn't she's beautiful, V?' breathed Ziggi, a beatific smile on his freckled face. He wiped tears away from all three of his eyes. I stole a sidelong glance at Bela and even he looked moved.

'Why's there a tube up her nose?' I asked, a bit trembly.

'It's a gastro-nasal feeding tube, V,' said David and rubbed my back. 'But Sister Bridget said you'll need to start expressing soon to ensure . . . errr, the flow starts and keeps going.'

Breast pump. *Oh God*. While I'd been sleeping, David had been learning everything we needed to know. Everything *I* should already know. 'How long does she need to be like this?'

'Her lungs need to develop further,' explained David. 'Maybe ten to fourteen days.'

'Can I hold her?' I asked.

'I'm sorry, Ms Fassbinder,' said Sister Bridget, reminding us she was there, thank you very much. Her blue uniform was neatly pressed and a spotless white wimple covered her iron-grey hair. Her olive skin was youthful, though, and her blue eyes alert and kind. 'She's got to stay where she is – but you *can* touch her without gloves, as long as you're very careful about disinfecting your hands. You can change her nappy, if you like, then give her a gentle massage while she's in the crib.'

'Awww,' said Ziggi. Anyone would think *he'd* given birth and was being denied access.

He pulled me into a hug and whispered, 'There's another option when Wanda gets back,' and I realised he didn't want Sister Bridget to hear in case she disapproved.

By the time night fell, I was shattered, even though all I'd done was sit beside the plastic box containing my daughter and touch her. Oh, and the expressing of the milk; the less said about that the better. I'd have stayed in Maisie's room, but that would have meant a turf war with Sister Bridget over the bed, and I realised I was too tired to fight anyone.

David had fallen asleep in no time. He was snoring softly and holding me close; it was a comfort to feel his warm weight beside me, his familiar scent so strong. But for all my exhaustion, when I closed my eyes and tried to drop off, all I could think of was the little girl separated from me by walls and plastic.

When I'd changed her nappy I'd never felt so happy to wipe up something so *nasty*; I didn't even mind the discomfort of the breast pump. I didn't think I'd ever get over the particular guilt of not being able to give Maisie her first feed (so she'd missed out on all that mumly goodness) – mind you, given that I'd walked us into danger, got her born prematurely and almost got us both killed, perhaps the missed feed wasn't the most stellar of my failings. And somehow I doubted it would be my last.

I couldn't help but think about the mystery woman too – if she hadn't been there in that dirty, dangerous alleyway . . . even in my mind I veered away from what might have happened. The more I thought about it, the more I became convinced she'd saved me in the supermarket too, then slipped away, although why she would've been following me was anyone's guess; or was it the fox-girl she'd been tailing? I'd got no sense of threat from her, but then again, sometimes I don't register a threat even when it's right under my nose: the former Councillor Eleanor Aviva and Vadim Nadasy as Not-Ursa were prime examples. That was the thing: people were like icebergs. You only glimpsed bits of them, and oftentimes it was only what they wanted you to see. Many folk, Weyrd in particular, were good at casual concealment . . . or maybe I was just dumb.

Frankly, it was a wonder I trusted anyone.

There was a difference now, though: Maisie and David. My pregnancy had made me vulnerable, and not just because of my strength going. I had so much more to lose now. I held David tighter, sent my last waking thought to our little girl and finally dropped off.

Chapter Twelve

Behind me a turf maze had been carved into the lush green grass of the back lawn, representing – depending on which book you were relying on – either a penitents' path in a cathedral, some strange Rosicrucian map to the lost treasure of the Templars, or even a means of trapping what Swedish fishermen called the *smågubbar*, the little people who allegedly brought bad luck to those looking to fill their nets. I sat down on a bench built into the stone garden wall, almost too close to the cliff edge for comfort, and stared out at the misty blue-green horizon, listening to the sound of the ocean breaking on the rocks thirty metres below.

My morning wander had revealed the beauty of this place. From the front, it looked like a farmhouse transplanted from the south of France. The main building, two storeys of buttery grey stone with newer single-storey extensions on either side (more rooms for when the place was used as an actual B&B and not a hideout), had French doors and sash windows in a chalky green hue, with shutters in the same pale green pinned back against the stonework. Climbing roses, heavy with white and purple blossoms, crawled across the façade. The gravel drive from the road to the front door surrounded a round lawn with a picture-book red-roofed wishing well sitting in the middle.

When I squinted, I could make out the wards neatly lettered over the doors and window lintels in silver paint; they couldn't be too strong or prescriptive or most of our little party wouldn't have been able to cross the threshold. I guessed Bela was betting on the remote location and the small number of people who did know where we were keeping us safe.

I took a deep breath of salty sea air, scented by flowers and herbs; the beds all around me looked untouched by the cooler winter temperatures. In fact, the whole place felt warmer than it should at this time of year – I'd grabbed my jacket, but I was quite comfortable in my long-sleeved T-shirt. I moved on from staring at the turf maze to examine the plants Wanda Callander used in her healing arts. Wanda's Weyrd blood showed up as what Ziggi described as 'positive sorcery': apparently, she was a good witch.

She still hadn't returned from her scavenging trip – Ziggi said she was in the hinterland somewhere looking for rare plants – and I was getting nervy waiting for her. Having to express milk every three hours wasn't doing much for my mood either, so I'd exiled myself to the garden before I said something anyone else might regret. And I didn't want to admit it, but I felt like bursting into tears every five minutes.

What the hell is wrong with me?

'V?'

Bela sounded tentative. He was carrying two cups of coffee, but stood politely waiting for permission to join me. I waved my hand in a non-committal fashion, which he took to mean *Sit right down*, and handed me one of the blue ceramic mugs. It was black and hot, without sugar – and the smell made me nauseous. My first coffee in seven months and that's what happened? *So unfair.* I set the cup on the wall.

'How are you feeling?' he asked and I had to resist the immediate urge to bite his head off.

'I'm okay. Tired. Confused. Guilt-ridden. Pissed off. Maybe a little bit irrational and murdery.'

'Will it help if I say that's normal?'

'Not really.'

'Right.' He lifted a hand and in not many seconds at all a stocky woman I'd never seen before strode over and stood stiffly at attention in front of us. I fought the urge to bark, 'At ease!' She was wearing a black short-sleeved T-shirt (presumably to show the weather who was boss) and black combat trousers tucked into serious steel-toed boots. Her eyes were blacker than black with no discernable pupils; her equally dark hair was cut into a sharp bob that kissed her square jaw. I'd have guessed she was somewhere in her mid-thirties, except that Weyrd didn't age the same way as Normals; she could have been a hundred years old and not showed an extra day. It made me wonder what glamours were at work on her; Ziggi didn't need much, for example, and some Weyrd, like Bela and the Norns, didn't need any at all. Some like the mysterious Wilbur Wilson apparently needed a whole lot.

'Verity, this is Galina Vasilieva. She comes to us from the St Petersburg chapter, very highly recommended. Galina specialises in personal security. Mike and Jerry will report to her. If you have any concerns about your safety, she's your first point of call.'

I resisted the urge to think up scenarios that involved Galina being unavailable and just said, 'Thank you, Bela. Thank you, Galina.'

She spoke with an accent that was vaguely Eastern European. 'Your family will come to no harm while I stand watch.'

Bela gave her a nod of dismissal and she headed back the way she came. I looked over my shoulder a moment later and she was nowhere to be seen. We weren't that close to the house. *Nice.*

'Can I trust her?'

'I trust her,' he said evenly.

'Not what I asked.'

'Yes.' Bela sighed. 'You can trust her. *I* trust her. I'd trust her with my life.'

'That's a big call.'

'I've known her a long time. I knew her family. Believe me when I say she will take her obligation seriously.'

I thought *obligation* was a strange word to choose, but I decided to be magnanimous and let it slide. 'More to the point, I suppose, is can I trust Mike and Jerry?'

'Look, they fucked up last year. They *know* they fucked up. They've spent a lot of time making up for it.' He sipped his coffee. 'But just in case, there's Galina.'

'Thank you,' I said, realising I really meant it.

'Ziggi and I need to go back to Brisbane tonight. The Councillors want an update, and Eleanor Aviva has been asking to see me.'

'I don't understand why she's still alive.'

'Yes you do: she was one of the Council of Five for a long, long time and she knows where the bodies are buried – even the ones she didn't put in the ground herself. Eleanor is smart. She's collected a lot of secrets over the years and now she's doling them out in return for certain . . . *privileges*.'

'Quite a nice reward, considering the shit she put Dusana Nadasy through' – Dusana, whom Bela had dated in one century or another – 'and considering she held back information that might have saved lives, and considering that she was more than happy to buy wine made from the tears of dead children by Magda Nadasy.'

'I know what she did, V,' he said quietly. 'I don't like it either, but I have to be a realist. This is the way the world works.'

'I *know* that. I don't have to be happy about it,' I grumped.

'If you need anything, V, call me. I'm not abandoning you. Galina will keep you safe, but if you need anything at all, call.' He tilted his head listening, and a moment later I heard the purring of an expensive engine. 'That'll be Wanda.'

Despite David's very specific ban on magic around the baby, he was pretty cool when I told him what Ziggi had suggested.

'It would be healing, just some non-traditional medicine – it would be fixing what I fucked up.'

'You didn't fuck anything—'

'Please, David – it's just, Wanda might be able to give things a kick along in the getting well department.' The tears I'd been fighting spilled over. '*This* is the one thing I can do for her . . .'

He hugged me and said, 'Just promise this won't give her super-powers.'

'I promise,' I said with relief, and didn't add, *I can't vouch for anything she's been born with*.

So now Wanda Callander, tall, red-haired, looking in her early fifties, was waiting for Sister Bridget to hand her my daughter. The nun wore a distinctly disapproving expression, but she still opened the crib and unhooked Maisie from the various machines. It didn't take long for things to begin beeping unhappily.

Ziggi had refused to leave before this was done; now he put one hand on my arm and one on David's. 'It'll be okay, Wanda's worked on even younger kids.' *How young did they have to be?* I wondered; Maisie was barely out of her wrapping. 'You'll need to be patient, V, okay? You might not see an immediate result, but within a day or two the improvement should be noticeable.'

David added, 'And we'll be able to take her home sooner.'

Apparently he'd forgotten the whole 'safe house' thing, that we were here for a reason.

As Sister Bridget lifted an unencumbered Maisie into Wanda's arms, the healer touched her hand and gave the sister such a warm smile that the nun returned it, looking surprised. The healer cradled Maisie in the crook of her left arm and where her slender right hand moved over the delicate arms and chest, throat and face, the sticky-out little tummy, chubby legs and teeny feet, the baby's skin took on a glow. She was pinker and healthier and just a little shiny, as if glitter cream had been rubbed over her.

It couldn't have taken more than five minutes but it felt like an eternity, although Maisie, displaying her father's ability to sleep for Australia, had not stirred. At last Wanda said, 'She shouldn't be touched for a while – the energies need to settle.' She returned the tiny scrap of human to the crib and I had to bite back a cry; I'd wanted so desperately to hold her myself.

Sister Bridget's face was far more serene than it had been, shining as if some of Wanda's work had rubbed off on her.

The healer came towards us and I held out a hand in thanks – which she ignored, instead folding me into a bear hug and not letting go. I almost started to struggle, then I felt a familiar *buzz*, like when Louise had worked on me. By nightfall my bruises would have faded, the aches and pains would be gone and the bits of me currently held together by stitches would be well be on their way to a full recovery.

When she let go, she said, 'You're always welcome,' even though I'd not yet managed to get the words *thank you* out.

'Thank you,' David said for both of us, and hugged her, then turned and enfolded me in his arms.

'I'll get dinner started,' said Wanda and disappeared.

'Thanks, Ziggi.' I grabbed his hand and squeezed. 'What would I do without you?'

He smiled. 'Pay for cabs, for a start.'

David stayed with Maisie and Sister Bridget while Ziggi and I joined Bela in the sitting room. He was talking to Jerry and Mike, Galina at his side like a stocky little shadow. She looked up as I came in, gave the merest incline of her head, then slipped out through the French windows that led into the back garden. *Patrolling*, I thought, then, *prowling*, which sounded even more appropriate. There was something dangerous about her, something predatory. I was glad she was on our side.

Bela rose. 'We've got to head home, V, but you'll be safe here.'

Mike and Jerry nodded sincerely; I didn't doubt their commitment.

I walked Bela and Ziggi to the front door, then hugged them both. 'Thank you,' I said and I meant it. 'For everything.'

'If you need anything, you call,' said Bela. He stroked my cheek and I managed to stop myself flinching, but he must have seen the surprise in my face. The gesture was intimate, unwelcome – Bela was so cool he made Antarctica look like a hot mess. He didn't usually let himself get close like that; it was a sign of how worried he was – and that was enough to worry me just that bit more.

'I will,' I said hastily. 'Let me know how it goes with the Council.'

Ziggi hugged me hard, squeezing the breath out of me until I had to tap on his back to get him to let go.

'Drive carefully,' I said. 'Keep me posted – you know *he* won't and I'll just go nuts down here.'

'Paradise is wasted on you, Verity Fassbinder.'

'Well, you know, pearls and swine.'

He disappeared around the hedge and soon I heard the sound of two very different engines come to life, then a '74 Porsche 911 Turbo and a purple gypsy cab roared past me and disappeared down the long driveway in a cloud of dust.

When I got back inside, Hairy Jerry and Monobrow Mike were sprawled across the two three-seater couches, the only chairs big enough to comfortably contain their bulk. I'd seen them only once without the glamours that made them look like nothing more ominous than overly zealous body-builders, but the sight had been seared in my memory: they both had leathery black wings, negligible noses and ears, glowing red eyes and a lot of spiky black fur all over them. But now the glamours were firmly, professionally, in place.

'Thanks for doing this guys,' I told them. What I *wanted* to say was, *Don't fuck up!* but I controlled myself.

'Fassbinder,' they said simultaneously, their large heads tilting at the same angle, then retracting identically.

'How's it going?'

'All quiet on the Western Front,' said Jerry, thick black hair curling from the neck of his green T-shirt.

'I don't think Sister Bridget likes us,' Mike confided, sounding a little hurt. His eyebrow looked so much like a caterpillar on steroids that I had to force myself to concentrate on his mouth, addressing it directly, hoping he didn't notice and say, *Hey, my eyes are up here*.

'I wouldn't take it personally,' I started. 'I'm not convinced she likes anyone much. Except maybe Wanda.' As I thought about that, a suspicion started taking hold. 'Old-school nun, guys: they specialise in all forms of misery and disapproval,' I added, but I kept my voice down; I didn't want her *extra* not liking me, even more than she *already* didn't like me. I wondered why she'd agreed to come here if she really didn't approve of the Weyrd — which also begged the question why she was working at St Agnes'. More questions with a distinct lack of answers, but getting those wasn't *quite* high enough priority right now. 'But I really appreciate you guys and Galina being here.'

Neither of them took the bait, so I asked outright, 'What's she like?'

Mike said, 'Solid.'

Jerry said, 'Scary.'

Both of those character traits were okay with me.

'Either of you worked with her before?'

'Nope.'

'Nah.'

'So your assessment of "solid" and "scary" is based on your interactions here?'

'Well,' said Mike, 'here and at the office.'

The "office" would be the Bishop's Palace where Bela kept all the muscle. 'She's been around for a while?'

'A few months,' said Jerry. 'You probably haven't met her before on account of being, y'know . . .'

'Under-employed due to pregnancy?'

Again with the simultaneous nods. Did they work on that in their downtime? Whatever, I wasn't going to get the dirt on Galina from this pair. 'Right. Well, okay. This *kitsune*, she's on her own now, but don't underestimate her.'

Jerry made a finger-gun at me and Mike did the clicking sound with his mouth.

'No, guys, I mean *really*. I would have been in trouble – I *was* in trouble. If that woman hadn't shown up . . .'

And I could see in their faces that they thought there were obvious reasons for that: pregnancy, diluted Weyrd blood, no magic, *being a girl*. At least neither of them was dumb enough to say that out loud – but *honestly* . . .

I remained calm: I'm now a *mother*, a grownup. 'Guys, I'm counting on you two. Don't let me down.'

Which turned out to be the right thing to say. Appealing to fragile masculinity was not my style, but hell, I had a family to protect, so I'd use every trick in the book.

Chapter Thirteen

Maisie's improvement was phenomenal, so good that Sister Bridget even let me feed her properly the next morning. She was still glary and curt, given to one-word answers, if she deigned to answer at all, so I decided there was no point in trying the let's-get-to-know-each-other-better dance. She couldn't have been more of a stereotypical nun if she'd tried. The only people she didn't give the serious side-eye to were David (known to charm just about anyone except Bela) and Wanda Callander (jury still out on that one).

After breakfast I left David cooing over our daughter and took my phone and myself off to the turf maze garden.

'Morning, McIntyre.'

'Happy baby day, Fassbinder,' said Rhonda. 'Well, belated.'

'Thanks.'

'Is she okay? Are you okay? David said it was kind of rough.'

'My beloved has a gift for understatement, but Mother and Baby are now doing fine, exiled as we are to a very nice safe house.'

'So I hear. Can I do anything?'

'Just keep an eye out for a Ninja Librarian and a tall woman with a sword.'

'I'll get right on that.'

I summarised my encounters with the fox-girls, then told McIntyre about Len's recently deceased date, gave her the name of the delivery company he worked for and asked her to be gentle when she questioned him. I didn't know much about him, but I didn't for a moment believe he'd had anything to do with the attack on me. It was far more likely Gothic Alice had somehow worked out his connection to me, and that suggested someone had been watching my house for some time. If the reason for watching me was connected with the Apostate, the Guardian's Hound – *the woman who'd rescued me?* – then they must've felt there was even more reason after their sister's death in the supermarket.

'Wasn't fun at all, McIntyre,' I finished, 'and there's still one of them out there, but I want to go home – I want to be safe *there*, not here.'

'Well, I hate to add to your burdens,' she said, 'but there's been another drowning.'

'Oh, fuck it all!'

'A woman in a shopping centre at Kedron. It was about half past eight in the evening, so not many witnesses. We managed to pass Malone off as a fit, but that's not so easy when someone's gurgling water everywhere. Faraday Hannigan, a lawyer, single, no kids, lived alone.'

'Shit. Shit, shit, *shit*. Where'd she work?'

'Able and Baines. Big firm in the city, one of those high rises by the river.'

'And no one saw anything, no one near her?'

'Nope.'

'I need to get back to Brisbane and talk with the undines. Probably the Norns too, but them I can phone. The undines, not so much. But I don't know when I'm going to be able to leave here.' Then I thought, *No one's stopping me – I just don't want to leave.* It was quiet here, it was safe, no one was making demands on me – other than the whole seventeen-times-a-day feeding schedule, of course. I had David and Maisie and we were in our own little shell, separated from worlds both Normal and Weyrd. I liked it this way.

'I don't want any more of these deaths, Fassbinder,' she said, and I imagined her running a square hand through her greying hair. That tugged at me, the idea I was choosing to hide away instead of solving problems that would save lives, but I didn't say anything and McIntyre continued, 'I've got no idea why these two died – is it targeted, or are they just random victims? If it's the latter, well, we're in even deeper shit, because there's no connection that might point us to a pattern.'

'You said Toby Malone had been made redundant – any chance at all that he'd had contact with Faraday Hannigan? Did she do workplace law? Or maybe he was having an affair with her?'

'All good things for Oldman to check on.'

'Speaking of whom, did Constable Oldman have any luck with that security tape from the Mt Coot-tha café?'

'Not as yet. Many hours of video watching and much deep sighing and rolling of eyes has been engaged in.' She paused. 'It probably doesn't help that she doesn't really know what she's looking for.'

'Well, that makes two of us.' I took a deep breath. 'If it's a spell, then someone is casting it. Someone with an axe to grind and I don't know how to find them. As you said, if there's no common connection we know about then we can't discern a pattern.'

She sighed. 'Constable Oldman can do some old-fashioned police work and talk to people, wear out some shoe leather.'

'That'll make her like me even more,' I muttered.

'It's not like you to worry about being liked, Fassbinder. Are you going soft?'

'No, just not used to being disliked *before* I've actually done anything.' I stared at the garden, blue sky, magnificent trees, shining sea — it was only then that I really noticed them. Ziggi was right: Paradise *was* wasted on me. 'Who is she anyway?'

'Daughter of a retired assistant commissioner; he doesn't think she's serious about the job so he got her assigned to me.'

'Is he a friend of yours?'

'Not hardly. This way he pisses off two birds with one stone. On the other hand, I get to torture his daughter.'

'The milk of your human kindness has curdled, hasn't it, McIntyre?'

'You try thirty years in this job and see how at-one-with-the-world you are.'

'Yeah, maybe you're right. Anything on the Malone autopsy?'

'He drowned, no surprises there. Ellen's still waiting on the results of the tests they did on the water. As soon as I know anything, you will.'

'Thanks. Oh hey, see if you can find anything on a guy called Wilbur Wilson. Police record, abode, driver's licence.' There was a silence as she waited for more information that might actually help. 'That's all I've got. Let's say middle-aged, *maybe* in the legal profession but I'm doubting it, on the short side.'

'I hate you.'

'No you don't. And thanks for the dresses.'

'What dresses?'

'For Maisie? The Princess Awesome dresses?'

'Not us. We've got her a giant teddy bear.'

'Just tell me it's not pink.'

'Of course it's not pink! We're gay, not gauche!'

'My very dear and patient friend—'

She hung up.

No dresses from McIntyre and Ellen, then, and another giant stuffed toy to take up space in the nursery. Oh well, at some point someone would say 'Hey, did you get . . . ?' and the mystery would be solved.

Talking to Rhonda about Wilson reminded me I'd not yet checked for Wilbur Wilson on the Queensland Law Society lists of solicitors, so I did the Google thing and searched online for folk licensed to practice in the State of Queensland. No Wilbur Wilson came up. I changed my spelling three times – it wasn't really a name that lent itself to alternatives, to be honest – and got the same result.

So.

I tried the Bar Association of Queensland for barristers, just in case Ms Cross hadn't paid enough attention to detail, and again came up empty. I'd check other such organisations around the country, but I was rapidly coming to the conclusion that Mr Wilson was a fake, claiming legal credentials – and probably a name – to which he had no right. None of which was going to make matters any easier. I sighed, not really surprised, but wishing that just *once*, something was *simple*.

Our hostess sat across from me at the long, battered pine kitchen table and said with confidence, 'Your little one's coming along nicely.'

I smiled and peeled a carrot with care, doing my best not to take any of my skin with it. I'd kicked my slippers off and was enjoying the luxury of stone flags with underfloor heating. 'We're so very grateful. And I'm especially grateful for what you did for me, I've got to tell you.'

I'd been moving a lot more easily since Wanda had applied her healing powers.

'Not a problem.' She smiled. Her red hair was slowly being taken over by white. She had bright blue eyes and skin to die for, for a woman her age; hell, at any age. I couldn't work out if it was great

genes, a really good moisturising regime, or the judicious application of Botox. Then again, there was a lot of mobility in her facial
features, so I crossed botulinum off the list.

'How long have you been here?' I asked, looking around at the
excess of copper pots hanging from the ladder, the tiny crystal chandelier and the enormous navy-coloured Aga stove which must have
cost a bomb.

'Fifteen years?' She tilted her head, did some mental calculation,
'Yes – just after our youngest left home we decided on a change,
sold our house in Sydney and came up here. This place was a wreck
so we were able to get it for a song . . . mind you, we spent a year
renovating and *that* cost a damned sight more than a song.'

'Absolutely worth it,' I stated. 'Is your husband away?'

'He died five years ago, so it's just me.'

'I'm so sorry—'

'Nothing to be sorry about, love. We had our time, and it was
grand. I have company when I need it; the kids occasionally come
home, and there's always someone wants teaching or needs sanctuary
or just a place to catch their breath.' She smiled to show she meant it;
there was no deep hurt underlying her words. 'And I've had plenty
of referrals from Zvezdomir and your Uncle Ziggi.'

I snorted with laughter. 'Uncle? Ziggi's not my uncle – a work
mate. A good friend. Avuncular. Uncle-ish. But not my uncle. '

'Oh. I thought with the red hair on your Maisie . . . Silly me!' She
looked nonplussed for a moment. 'How long have you been married?'

I played with the square-cut emerald ring on the chain around
my neck; hopefully it would be back on my finger soon, once the
pregnancy weight magically melted away. I said, 'We're not. We do
all the married things, but we've not, you know—'

Her smile turned impish. 'Good on you. Gabe and I had three

kids, forty years together and not a wedding band between us – but it was easier to go by Callander, keep the old biddies – and there are *always* old biddies! – from poking their noses in.' She leaned over to whisper, 'I don't know about you, but there's something nice about the sense you can escape anytime you want to. Few things heavier than a wedding ring.'

We peeled and chopped, slaughtering vegetables with gay abandon for a while, chatting about trivial things until there was a lull in the conversation and I felt I could casually ask the question that had been burning a hole in me as soon as I realised Ocean's Reach was near Byron Bay. 'Don't suppose you know a family called Beckett?'

Her lips tightened just a little, as though someone had turned a dial, and she gave me a sideways glance. 'I do indeed. We bought this land from them – Marian, that's the wife – her parents had owned it and when they died, the Becketts sold it off. They still live nearby, over on Morwood Road. I'm collecting their mail while they're away.'

That was the address McIntyre had given me.

'Where are they?' I asked, even more casually.

'Trip to Europe – they've been away about four months. Their oldest daughter sent them.'

'Wow, that's very generous!'

'She's a good girl, Susan.' Wanda carefully slivered the apple in her hand into thin slices, then dropped them into the big blue bowl she'd filled with strawberries, pears, raspberries, lemon juice and a sprinkling of sugar, then let slip, 'It might have been a bit of a guilt gift.'

'What makes you say that?'

Wanda gave me the eye. 'What makes you ask?'

'I – ah, I met Susan Beckett. She seemed . . . interesting?'

She stirred the fruit pieces around with a wooden spoon, made sure they were well-coated with the mix so they wouldn't turn brown or be too sour, silent while she did it. When she was finished, she put her elbows on the table, and leaned towards me. 'Well, they're an interesting family.'

I rolled my eyes and made a *c'mon* gesture with my fingers.

'You know, Ms Verity, you do seem to be fishing.'

'And you, Ms Callander, unless I'm very much mistaken, are attempting to wield quite a powerful beguilement charm on me,' I said. The blush that stained her cheeks gave me my answer. 'Which explains why you've got our surly Sister Bridget under your thumb.'

'There's no harm in it. Makes people happier and more biddable. Except spoilsports like you,' she said a little sulkily.

'I won't tell, just keep it in check. You're more than a healer, aren't you? You're a witch.'

Wanda pouted, then nodded. 'Susan hasn't been home since she moved up to Queensland. She's a smart girl, always was, and always had her eyes on bigger things. Gabe reckoned she'd marry rich, but I told him, "She'll do it all on her own, she'll make her own money so no one can take it away from her."'

'Did someone take it away before?'

'Well, not from her . . . I wish I could say I don't like to gossip, but I do! When we bought this place, word is all the funds went into Acton's account – not a joint one, just Acton's. Marian doesn't even have an account of her own.'

'You are *remarkably* well-informed,' I said admiringly.

'My bank manager does like to chat after a glass of red or three, and I like to pour wine.'

'A father who keeps a stranglehold on the finances would explain a girl's determination to make her own money.' I set down the paring knife when I finished with my last apple. 'Has she got any talent, Susan? Is there anything Weyrd in the bloodline?'

'Clean as whistle. Now, I do believe I hear your daughter crying for feed.'

She was right, but I couldn't help but note that it was also a handy end to our conversation.

It was after midnight and I couldn't sleep. I looked in on Maisie and gave Sister Bridget a bathroom break; while she was gone I drew wards on the humidicrib, and then more on the outside of the nursery door after she came back and kicked me out. I used spit – I didn't think Wanda would appreciate me scrawling over the lintel in my own blood. She would have told me her house was safe – that *we* were safe – and that no one knew where we were; that my body-guards were alert and raring to go, that I had no cause to worry. But it wouldn't have mattered. I didn't even know if the gesture would work, but it was all I could do, so I did it. I was given to understand that mummy spit had special powers, but when I told David about it later he laughed at me. *A lot.*

I made hot chocolate for myself and coffees for Jerry and Mike, and asked in vain where Galina was. They both said '*Around!*' in mysterious tones and I might have glared at them, but that gained me nothing new, so I wandered off to the library I'd found and called Bela.

He was awake, or he sounded it, anyway. He'd always been a night owl.

'Baby okay? David?'

'Both fine; both sleeping.'

'You're not.'

'Sleeping? Not so much. McIntyre had another drowning.'

'I heard. I spoke with Eleanor Aviva today. She asked to see you.'

'Seriously?' I frowned. Aviva ranked pretty high on my list of *People I Never Want to See Again* – not right at the top, sure, but a solid number eight, maybe even a six. When cornered, Aviva had traded information in exchange for protection, but before that she'd let quite a few people die to keep her own life intact. But maybe now Vadim and Magda Nadasy were dead, perhaps she was regretting her decision. Perhaps being locked up at the Bishop's Palace was getting old and she wanted to renegotiate – or most likely, she was bored and just wanted to mess with me.

I whined, 'Why?' then, 'Do I have to?' Huh. So having a baby apparently doesn't automatically make you a grown-up.

Bela laughed. 'You don't have to, no, but she says she has things to tell you. So maybe you should?'

'What things?'

'Well, if she'd told me, that would defeat the purpose of asking you to come, wouldn't it?' There was a pause. 'You're getting fractious – *more* fractious. Lack of sleep.'

'And you're only saying that because I can't hit you at the moment.' I rubbed my eyes; I hated it when he was right. 'She should have been punished, you know, not rewarded. I'm pretty sure Dusana Nadasy would agree with me.'

'I'm sure she does, but Eleanor's a repository for a *lot* of knowledge, a *lot* of secrets, and on balance, I can't let all of that be thrown away. If she trades information for the return of one of her beloved Fendi purses, what harm?'

Aviva had a handbag fetish and, I had to admit, excellent taste. 'If she wants to invite me to a Tupperware party I'm going to hurt you, you know that, right?'

'V, she said she had something of value to tell you. That's it.'

'The bad guys always say that,' I grumbled. 'Unless she's got something about the drownings or the *kitsune*, or even bloody Susan Beckett she's going to go to end of the queue.'

'Understood. I'll see if I can extract any more details. Was there a reason for this call?'

'Yes, actually, I was wondering about Sister Bridget. She doesn't appear to like anyone much here and I'm wondering if it's Weyrd-Normal thing? And if it is, then why is she working at a hospital frequented by Weyrd mummies and babes?'

There was a pause before he said, 'Sister Bridget spent a lot of time in the Vatican in the late Sixties.'

'Never a good way to start a sentence.'

'She was an exorcist.'

'I . . . *wow*. I didn't think the Papal types were too keen on women in that kind of role – or indeed, *any* kind of role. Too easy to seduce, what with us being the Devil's handmaidens and all. Prone to witchery, et cetera. You know, the usual bad press.'

'They weren't, and still aren't. *Mulieres Bonae* was . . . well, an experiment of Vatican II. It gave especially virtuous women the chance to take part in the activities of the adjuristine-exorcism squads. That's where Father Tony met her.'

Father Tony Caldero was, in no particular order, a friend of Bela's, a strange ally for Brisbane's Weyrd Council, and an ex-member of the Vatican's adjuristine-exorcism squads. 'Like secret weapons? The Devil wouldn't expect chicks to sneak up on him?'

'Something like that.'

'And I am assuming it was not a success.'

'Not as such, no. Not due to any fault of the women, but because priests didn't like being told what to do by females. Things went wrong . . . *Mulieres Bonae* was disbanded about '69.'

'A four-year run, huh?'

'By all accounts, when left to their own devices they were very effective.'

'And Sister Bridget is now a nurse in Brisneyland.'

'She was from Brisbane originally. Father Tony says she's a good person – sometimes a little rigid, but no harm in her. Not really given to precipitous actions.' Father Tony was a kind man, intelligent and generous, and after all the things he'd seen in his long life he certainly knew that there were more things in Heaven and Earth. If he had faith in Sister Bridget, then the least I could do was respect that.

'Okay. Well thanks, that's one question answered. Night.'

'Goodnight, V.'

I sat a little longer, contemplating my chances of getting Sister Bridget to talk about *Mulieres Bonae*. It never hurt to learn as much as I could about the Weyrd and all its infinite varieties as well as the Normals and their combative religious observances. She wasn't exactly the chatty type. Maybe if I pitched it as a teaching opportunity for her . . .

The mobile vibrated in my lap. I didn't recognise the number that showed up – it was quite long, fort a start – and I was tempted not to answer in case I ended up shouting at some guy swearing black and blue that my computer was infected by a virus and only by providing him with the details of my bank accounts could it be resolved.

I took a chance, feeling brave. 'Hello?'

'Verity!' Lizzie's voice was high and fast and over-excited. 'We're on a *ship*!'

I grinned, felt joy run through me. 'I know, baby. How are you enjoying it?'

'Oh, Verity, there's *everything*! Every. Thing. There's clubs and shows and pools and games and ball pits and slippery slides and swings and a roller disco and dance classes and movies you can watch over and over and over, and my new best friend Celia and I watched *Brave six* times already and it's the best! And . . .' She didn't so much pause for breath as run out of it, then handed the phone to her mother.

'Hey, V. How goes?'

I was so happy to hear Mel's familiar soothing tones that I found myself sobbing.

'Oh, honey – Hon, what's wrong?'

'Baby. Had baby—'

'Oh no, what—?'

'It's okay – I mean, *she's* okay, David's okay, we're all okay. There's just been a bit of drama. As usual.'

'But you're safe now?'

'Uh huh. At a nice B&B in Byron Bay,' I hedged. Mel knew about the Weyrd, but I didn't want to worry her. Let her put the wibbly weeping down to post-partum hormone storms.

'That's great! I bet David organised that.'

'Yeah . . .' I pulled myself together and managed, 'So, how's your part of the cruise going? Sounds like you'll have trouble prising Lizzie off the hull.'

'I have never not cooked for so long in my life. Even when I was a kid, I was making dinner from when I was eleven. I might not get off the ship either, V. Do you reckon the Weyrd would notice if the cruise operator just kept sending the bills?'

'You might get away with it for a while. Like, a week. Then a flying monkey would come after you.'

'Ah, worth a try. No housework, no cooking, margaritas on tap.' She sighed, and I thought of her imagining a life on the high seas. 'You should try it sometime.'

'If I got on a ship pirates would show up.'

'Weyrd pirates, too.'

'Yeah.'

We chatted for a few more minutes about ordinary things and it made me feel grounded for the first time in days.

'Okay, V, I'd better go. This call will be costing the Weyrd Council an arm and a leg. I just wanted to check on you. Congrats on baby Maisie. I'm glad you guys are okay.'

When I climbed back into bed beside David I went straight to sleep.

Chapter Fourteen

There was water *everywhere*. The linens beneath me were soaked, liquid was cascading down the walls like a moveable skin, the floor had become a pool afloat with furniture and flower arrangements. In his sleep, David snorted and turned, making fluid squelch from the bedding. Yet he didn't wake.

And I wasn't just damp. I wasn't just covered in moisture, I was filled to the brim. My lungs overflowed, wet poured from my nose and mouth, my eyes, my ears. I touched my stomach and it rippled like jelly. I tried to scream, but produced nothing but a gurgle. I was going to drown – I *was* drowning. I kicked the sheets away and tried to sit up, but when I looked down it was just in time to see the lower part of my body dissolve, then cataract over the edges of the mattress and splash into the pond below.

I woke alone, panting and fighting. Outside the large windows it was daylight, but the storm in progress had darkened the sky and rain was being thrown against the glass, thudding a staccato rhythm. Our room was stylish and dry, with nothing amiss, but the smell of fear was strong on my pillow. The only wetness was where I'd sweated; my forehead was sticky and the roots of my hair were soaked.

Just as my heartbeat was starting to normalise, the loo flushed in the bathroom and I couldn't stop myself from jumping.

David appeared, his dark blond hair tousled, the three-day growth getting serious. He was grinning – until he saw my expression.

'What's wrong, V?' He wrapped me in a hug and I pressed my face into the warmth of his neck and breathed in his scent.

'Bad dreams,' I said. 'Bad, *bad* dreams.'

'Anything I can do about it? Ask Wanda for medicinal pancakes and bacon?'

'David?'

'Hmmm?'

'We're in danger.'

'That explains the safe house: for the safety.'

'I'm serious. Sooner or later, I'm going to have to start asking some questions.' I stroked his face, as if I might be able to smooth away the worry lines which were deepening as I spoke. 'Which means I need to track down that last *kitsune*. I need to know who's after me – and I have to find that woman, too, and work out what she wants.'

'V—'

'I'm sorry, I really am. It doesn't matter that Bela has Jerry and Mike sitting out there, or Galina roaming the boundaries.' I put a finger to his lips as I tried to explain. 'No one else is going to hunt for answers because no one else is invested like I am. We can't hide here for ever, David – you know that. And I can't protect us unless I know what's coming after me – and why.'

He pushed my finger away and hugged me, hard. 'Coming after *us*, V. You're not alone in this. If someone's coming for you, they're coming for Maisie and me, too. We're in this together.'

My voice was rough as I spoke, barely able to hold back the tears that were lodged in my throat.

'But you can't protect us from the things that come out of *my* world, and I'm sorry for that, I'm so sorry – for all the things I've dragged you into.' I made him look at me. 'I'm going to have to leave you and Maisie here until I get answers. I *promise* I'll be careful. I'll have Ziggi with me as back-up at all times. I won't go off on my own. And my strength is returning – I almost pulled the handle off the bathroom door in the middle of the night.' I might have been exaggerating a little, but I was definitely back on track for crushing things, which was an enormous relief.

'*Really* promise?' he asked, as if he had a choice in this.

'You stay here, keep an eye on Maisie.' I grinned, a wicked thought popping into my head. 'Keep Sister Bridget company!' As he groaned, I added, 'Galina and the guys will be on duty, and I *know* I don't need to say this, but I'm going to anyway: keep your eyes out, be aware of everything going on and anything weird—'

'That's a very broad spectrum,' he observed, tightening his grip on me as if he wouldn't let me go when the time came. 'When are you going?'

I rubbed my cheek against his.

'Not yet.' *But soon.*

He touched my face. 'You'll have the dagger, and Ziggi will be with you at all times?'

'I swear.'

As I held him tightly, I felt some of the tension leave him. He might not be happy, but there was no denying the truth of what I'd said. Quite apart from the *kitsune* threat, there were two drowned (presumably) innocents out there who needed justice, and I couldn't forget Kadie Cross needed her talisman back – that might not be the most pressing matter, but it was something I might as well attend to in my travels. And I was good at shaking people until they gave me answers.

★

'Morning,' I said, and Sister Bridget gave me the same disapproving look my grandmother used to when I'd appear at breakfast without having brushed my hair. Well, I *hadn't* brushed my hair, which was a dark mop of knots and tangles, possibly with a bird nesting in there for good measure. And I was still in my flannelette pyjamas at eleven a.m., without slippers or a dressing gown, so I was a sure sign of the inevitable fall of civilisation.

'Morning,' she answered shortly, and set about opening Maisie's crib so I could deal with the mid-morning feed.

When I was settled in the comfy chair with my daughter happily attached – and me being thankful that she didn't have teeth yet – I watched as Sister Bridget moved around the room, finding an apparently infinite number of small tasks that needed doing: draping a towel modestly over my boobs, folding the terrycloth nappies she'd brought from St Agnes', piling towels and sheets into the washing basket, wiping down surfaces until the antiseptic smell filled the room and tickled my nose, making sure her Bible was perfectly aligned with the corner of the bedside table . . .

When she started straightening the paintings – beautiful fantasy landscapes in soft hues – I knew she was getting desperate.

'What's wrong, Sister Bridget?' I asked gently.

Her head whipped around, the short white veil transcribing a lovely arc behind her head. Her blue eyes flickered alarm for a moment, then the usual flinty gaze reasserted itself. I looked at her properly, *really* looked at her, trying to discern . . . anything. Her nose was crooked, the result of a break at some point in her past, and when you paid attention you realised she wasn't really a small woman at all. A little shorter than me, maybe five seven or eight, lean but not scrawny; she had none of the gristly nature of too-thin women who got old and couldn't put any fat back on their bones. Her hands, sticking out from the cuffs of her long-sleeved uniform, were strong-looking, square and practical, the nails neatly trimmed. Her posture was excellent, as military as Galina's, and I wondered who'd poked her in the back and shouted *Stand straight!* when she was young. She stared at me for a long moment.

'Whatever do you mean, Ms Fassbinder?' Her voice was soft, almost daring me to explain. Never a good idea.

'I mean what's wrong with *you*, Sister Bridget. We appreciate everything you've done for us and Maisie – we wouldn't be in this happy state without your help – but not to put too fine a point on it, you've had a stick up your butt since I woke up, and there's been no sign of it being withdrawn.' I adjusted my daughter and sank back against the chair a little more, then looked at the nun again. 'What's wrong?'

I didn't think she'd answer but she clasped her hands in front of her in a ladylike manner, straightened her shoulders and said, 'It's not fair. Not fair to your daughter.'

'What in particular?' I wasn't saying she was wrong, but there were so many things Maisie was going to encounter as my child that fell under the umbrella of "unfair" that I was going to need a little more information on this one.

'It's not fair to bring her into this life – to have her around those brutes out there. To expose her to danger.'

All my determination to conduct this conversation calmly, in an adult manner, was swept away in a tide of angry mummy guilt – or guilty mummy anger, or something, and what came out instead was, 'Well . . . well . . . well, fuck you, lady!'

I shouted so loudly and sat up so quickly that I dislodged Maisie, who made her displeasure known with a hearty wail. Hastily I resettled her, trying to gather my thoughts for a better follow-up to yelling a profanity at an elderly nun. All I managed was, 'Do you really think I have much say in all of this?'

She looked away.

'Sister, I don't know what you know about me, but I didn't have a choice about my bloodline. I'm half and half' – the last time Bela had called me that I'd objected on the grounds it made me sound like a pizza – 'and I have walked with one foot in either world for most of my life. I have learned to negotiate them both, and Maisie will too – and believe me, I will do *everything* I can to help her. And those men you're calling brutes? They are risking their lives to protect my daughter!' I paused for breath. 'And if you're suggesting she simply shouldn't have been brought into this world, well, I'm pretty sure your church has a few opinions on that!'

'I didn't mean—'

'At this point I don't really give a shit what you mean: what sort of person disapproves of another for things they can't control?' I glared at her; she managed to hold my eye for a good few seconds before looking away again, her face bright red. After a moment I said, 'I know you were with *Mulieres Bonae.*'

Her head snapped up.

'I know the sort of things you've seen because I've seen them too, and I imagine you've done the things you never thought you would or could just to keep people safe from the darkness.' I pushed out a breath. 'Don't think I haven't done those same things. Don't judge me.'

She was shaking all over as if overcome by a very localised earth-quake.

'I think you should take a break, Sister. Wanda will be looking for help in the kitchen.' I paused, then added quietly, 'You were me once.'

She went without a word.

★

The driveway running off Morwood Road was even longer and windier than the one to Ocean's Reach, with the added complication of being so overgrown that I wasn't always sure I was still on the track until a house finally appeared between the trees. I passed a green-painted mailbox and stopped to lift the lid and check inside: no mail, no snakes, but two desiccated frog corpses that'd long ago left earthy concerns behind them, or at least whatever concerns frogs might be heir to.

My conversation with Sister Bridget had left me so angry that I didn't trust myself to behave in a civilised manner around anyone, so I'd dressed and headed out to work off some energy. Sure, I'd recently promised not go anywhere alone, but technically that referred to when I was back in Brisbane. Besides, it was an excellent opportunity to do some snooping.

The Beckett family home was a single-storey wooden affair held a couple of feet above the ground on thick wooden stumps. A blue-painted verandah ran around the entire building. The dirty white walls clearly hadn't been washed in some time, but although it was unkempt and decidedly less glamorous than Susan Beckett's Paddo house, it wasn't untidy or suffering long-term neglect. The lawn needed mowing, but the window boxes and flowerpots on the deck were overflowing with white jonquils and hot pink camellias; an orange trumpet creeper hung like lace from the roof. It looked a little downmarket for someone who owned several pieces of real estate, but then again, being cheap was how some people made their fortunes. The single carport at the side was empty, but maybe the Becketts had splashed out on long-term parking at the airport when they'd gone off on their jaunt.

There was no movement from the house, so I climbed the five stairs to the verandah and pulled on the rope of the brass bell next to the front door. The sound was so dissonant that I quickly put my hand to the metal to still it. My fingers came away covered in dust. I peered through one of the windows into what might have been the lounge and saw nothing except a bare minimum of furnishings; it looked more like a holiday rental than a home for four. Maybe the Becketts *liked* minimalist décor? There were no lights on to lift the gloom, no noises of someone moving around inside, no sense of any inhabitants at all.

I put my ear against the door and listened, and still I heard nothing – but this close, I *smelled* something. Thankfully, it wasn't the odour of dead bodies, but there was definitely *something* familiar. I couldn't quite place it. I tapped my fingers against the wood as I straightened.

The Becketts were away on holiday and there didn't appear to be anything actually *wrong*, so there was no good reason to break in – not that I had any aversion to a little B&E when required, but it didn't appear to be required here. No one had been reported missing, no one was obviously in danger, and technically I was trespassing. I pushed away from the wall and headed down the steps to circle around to the back yard.

There was an ancient rotary washing line listing to port, its metal strands rusted, a lean-to shed with a ride-on mower, and the usual gardening implements, many with purposes unidentifiable to those not in the know. A deserted chicken coop had a lot of feathers and a few dried-up splotches in the dirt that might have been old blood or recent shit. Maybe a fox had got in. Wanda hadn't mentioned feeding chooks, just collecting the mail.

A movement behind the coop caught my eye and the first sign of life on the Becketts' property showed itself to be a cat: a small, stocky, chocolate-coloured animal with bright amber eyes

I crouched and held out my fingers. 'Hey, puss.'

Puss didn't reply, just stared at me for a good minute in a considering and not entirely friendly fashion, then turned, tail held high, and sashayed back into the undergrowth. Maybe it was feral, but it was a little too dignified. I wondered in passing if the cat had got to the chooks, then turned away to check the back of the house. It was more of the same, but with fewer plants. A broken rocking chair sat waiting for someone to either fix it or put it out of its misery. Lengths of red and white twine had been strung up under the verandah roof, I guessed for rainy-day clothes drying. An old boiler covered in cobwebs sat in a corner. I hoped to all that was holy that Marian Beckett didn't have to do her washing in that.

'You shouldn't be here.'

'Fuck!' The voice was too close and too soft and I still did what could best be described as an aerial half-twist. I was a great loss to Olympic gymnastics.

Galina was about a metre away, a smug little smile on her face.

'*Fuck!*'

'You said that already.'

'And I will fucking say it again. Fuck!' My heart was hammering in my chest. 'What are you doing here?'

'I might ask you the same question.'

'Trespassing. Evidently.' I took a deep breath. 'Are you following me?'

'It's my job,' she said, as if there could be no argument.

'Well, what about the house? What about my daughter and David?'

'Mike and Jerry will keep them quite safe. After all, *they're* not the targets.'

I opened my mouth, closed it again. She was right, but how the hell had I even *become* a target? And was *I* really the main game? I didn't think so; the fox-girls weren't really looking for me, only using me as a way to find the Apostate. Which begged the question: what interest did the Apostate have in *me*?

'Why here, Ms Fassbinder? Why this place?'

'Has Bela told you about Susan Beckett?'

'The mud? Yes.'

'Her parents live here: parents and two little sisters. They're on holiday.'

'Are they?' It wasn't really a question, more of a musing. 'Time to go home, Ms Fassbinder.'

'It's not home,' I muttered, but I fell in step beside Galina and together we headed back to Ocean's Reach.

Chapter Fifteen

I think I roused in the dark hours of the early morning because of the silence. Even when everyone was asleep at Ocean's Reach there was still some sort of noise: the gentle murmur of Mike and Jerry talking softly out in the lounge, Wanda or Sister Bridget chatting, the soft pad of Galina's steps as she moved in and out of the house . . . But I was woken by an absence that penetrated the deep sleep of the totally relaxed. David was in a dead slumber, not even snoring — after checking to make sure he was still breathing I sat up, and realising that I was utterly alert and I'd never get back to sleep like this, I pulled on a dressing gown and slipped out of our room. Hot chocolate and watching Maisie for a while was what was called for.

My bare feet made no sound on the floor, which was dry and warm — until about three steps away from my door, when I stepped in a small puddle. I was grateful not to have slipped, and felt irritation rise. It *had* to be Jerry or Mike, because I really couldn't picture Wanda, Sister Bridget or Galina spilling something, or wandering out of the shower room, sopping wet. I peered into the lounge, where I had a clear view of whoever was sitting there.

But no one was.

There was no sign of either Jerry or Mike.

Not a hint of Galina.

I blinked and clenched my hands into fists and leaned against the wall. *Where the fuck were they?* There were no noises from the kitchen or from the bathroom back up the hallway. *No sound at all.*

I was about to scurry off to check on Maisie, but I froze, squinting at the door to the nursery.

Against the white glossy paint was . . . *something.*

Human-shaped, but definitely not human – *it was see-through.* I suspected only the night-time lighting and the rippling of its substance had made it visible. Inside the uncertain outline there were neither organs nor arteries, veins nor bones, just the constant shifting of fluid held together by – by *what?*

It was swaying back and forth on uncertain feet, all frustration and confusion as it pressed itself against the slick surface of the door. Rivulets trickled down the wood like rain, and when the creature pounded at the panels, sprays of liquid flew off in all directions, spattering the floor and walls opposite.

For a few moments I panicked, feeling my throat close over as the terror of my drowning dream warred with my fear for my daughter. Then I realised: *it couldn't get in.*

It couldn't get past the wards I'd scrawled over the lintel of the door.

Mummy spit for the win!

But how the fuck did it get into the house? Sure, the wards were low-level, but where were our guards? What was this thing? And most importantly, what the hell was I going to do? My baby was safe for the moment, but that thing was between me and her. I was willing to bet this was what had ended poor old Toby Malone and Faraday Hannigan and I had no desire to become the latest soaking corpse.

But that thing wasn't going away.

It didn't matter that my strength was back – I doubted it would care if I kicked or thumped or poked or scratched it. It wasn't like I could get hold of it and throw it against a wall or snap it in half. The dagger was in our room, still in the bottom of my damned bag, but even if I had it here, I seriously doubted it would do much against this *thing*. The garbage golem had had a human core, but this was transparent *nothingness*.

While I was hesitating, I heard the glass door in the sitting room slide open, and in seconds Jerry appeared from outside. I felt a momentary rush of relief and sent up an apology – he'd been doing his job, patrolling, not slacking – then almost immediately felt sick as what passed for the creature's head turned. It had no ears, but perhaps the thud of Hairy Jerry's great big boots had sent vibrations through the air, telegraphing his presence.

Whatever it was, it was enough: it turned and launched itself at the hulking Weyrd, moving like a horizontal waterfall, a torrent travelling on the air, its human shape gone as it flowed into a streak of transparency.

Jerry didn't see it – most people wouldn't – but I knew what I was looking for now, and just as a warning was clawing out of my throat, I watched it hit him like a wave in the face. It didn't splash off like ordinary water would, but forced itself between Jerry's lips, opened in surprise, down his throat, into his eyes, his ears, up his nose. The big guy was drowning, and there wasn't a thing he – or I – could do about it.

I watched veins of water rise up beneath his skin and trembling, spread along like snakes, almost as if they had lives of their own. He was on the ground in moment, and utterly still not long after that.

And the *thing* that had killed him was gone, completely absorbed into Jerry, leaving only a few small puddles on the floor beneath him. I tiptoed over, keeping an eye out for any more of its kind, but there was nothing, at least not where I could see. I knelt beside Jerry, touched his chest with one finger, and watched as the ripple effect travelled under his white T-shirt.

'I'm so sorry,' I muttered, and ran to the nursery. I flung open the door, my view obscured by my tears, and I had to blink rapidly before I could make out Maisie in her little plastic box, her chest rising and falling regularly, snuffling in her sleep. Her eyes blinked open for a moment, caught me, then closed again. Her hands clenched and unclenched, tiny pink flowers with teeny pearly nails, and her little feet kicked as if she were riding a bike until she fell into a deeper sleep. I felt the tightness in my chest loosen, relief rushing warm and strong through me, and only then did I notice Sister Bridget, in the bed beside Maisie, slumbering as deeply as David. I wondered if someone had cast a spell, used a hand of glory or some such thing to make everyone fall so impossibly asleep that they might die in their beds and never wake while it was being done.

Behind me there was a noise and I swung around, terrified I'd see a watery twin waiting in the hall. There was no one to be seen, but I recognised the noise of the sliding doors opening again and with even more than my usual caution, I left the nursery, pulled the door shut, and moved into the lounge. Every step away from Maisie felt as if a rope were tugging on my heart, but I kept going.

The glass door was wide open, the cold night breeze pouring in, and when I leaned through, I saw in the spilled light, the bottom half of someone wearing cream-coloured chinos with highly polished oxblood shoes; his hands hung at his sides, the cuffs of a blue business shirt just visible. There was no distinctive jewellery on the fingers, no watch on the wrist, but the hand itself was strangely large and square, the fingers short, the final joints like little hammers, nails dark against olive-hued skin. Whoever it was saw me silhouetted against the light in the lounge and bolted.

Finally, I shouted, yelling 'Hey!' and threw myself out into the darkness, pursuing the solid-sounding footsteps . . . and barrelled like a battering ram into someone else.

Panting, I ricocheted away into a flowerbed where I fell onto a mattress of lavender – but I could smell other less pleasant aromas: fertiliser and the dead things that had gone into it. A muscle in my right thigh felt as though it had ripped, my left palm was badly grazed and I was incredibly glad that my birthing wounds had already been fixed. I lay for long seconds feeling sorry for myself until I heard someone else moan, and then swear.

I found my feet, spotted my victim and hobbled over to offer a hand to haul Galina upwards. She wasn't best pleased. Her dark hair was dishevelled and a scrape on her cheek oozed red. The sound of running footsteps was long gone. We'd never find anyone in this darkness.

David was packing our bags and Maisie was warm in my arms, happily sucking away, oblivious to everything. Dawn had cracked the sky half an hour ago, but our day was already well underway. The helicopter had been and gone, taking Jerry's body with it. As long as I lived I'd never stop seeing Mike cradling his partner's head in his lap, silently weeping, that terrible keening when the heart is so broken it cannot produce a sound. And I'd realised for the first time that 'partner' had meant 'husband' – I hadn't known; I hadn't asked. I'd been so focused on their previous fuck-up that I hadn't any room to be charitable. They'd had risked their lives for me and mine and I'd held a grudge like a child.

I'd apologised to Mike before he'd left, although I wasn't sure how much he'd taken in. He'd hugged me, though, hard enough to hurt, but I didn't complain, because that pain could never compare to his loss. He'd raised his hand in farewell as the helicopter lifted off and watched me as the distance between us grew. When they were no more than a speck in the sky I'd phoned Bela again and told him – quite unnecessarily – to make sure Mike was looked after.

Galina was somewhere outside, patrolling – not that it had done much good last night, because we'd been focused on a different threat entirely. Wanda was in the garden, gathering what blossoms and herbs she needed to cleanse the house after such a dreadful death. I'd said a stiff goodbye to Sister Bridget, who'd taken the hospital equipment and gone with Mike. Ziggi was already on the road and would be here soon enough – I wasn't prepared to ride in a helicopter when I was conscious; those things freaked me out.

The lovely, restful safe house was no longer safe. We were going home.

There'd been an argument, of course, about leaving Ocean's Reach, but as I'd pointed out to Bela, (a) something knew where we were and (b) that something could get into a warded house and (c) it was something that might or might not be connected with the remaining *kitsune* – but was definitely connected with the Brisneyland drownings. So there was no point hiding out here. Our cover was blown.

Apart from anything else, I needed to be back on familiar soil, to have my family in our own house. I needed a home court advantage, to be in the place where I could ask questions politely and knock heads together somewhat less politely.

'What did Mike tell you?' I asked David as he zipped up the toiletries bag. When Galina and I had limped in after our abortive pursuit attempt, we'd found David kneeling beside Jerry's body, next to Mike.

'Jerry had told him to go and sleep, that nothing was happening, so he should get some zzzs.' They'd been taking turns napping during the day, even though that wasn't allowing much rest, but we'd all reckoned the night was the most likely time for a strike. We were right about that at least. 'He was blaming himself.'

'Honestly, Mike being there wouldn't have made one iota of difference. That thing . . . whatever it was, it would have taken one of them. But . . .' I paused. 'It wasn't after them. It was at the nursery door, but it couldn't get in.'

'The wards? The *spit* wards?' he asked incredulously.

'For which you mocked me, I'd remind you. You're welcome.'

'I stand corrected, and grateful to be so. Here, let me take her. You can go and shower.' I surrendered Maisie without a fight, not even bothering with the usual 'are-you-saying-I-smell?' banter.

'What was it, then?' he asked. 'The water thing?'

I swallowed, and once again found myself having to blink back tears of rage. 'I don't know. I just don't fucking know. But it was going for our daughter, I'm bloody sure of that.'

David leaned against me; I could feel him shaking. 'You don't have to be calm and reasonable all the time, you know,' I said quietly. 'You're allowed to yell and lose your temper. You're quite within your rights.'

'Would it help? Would it make you feel any better if I had a rant?' Green eyes held mine.

'Nope, it wouldn't help me, but it might help you. Keeping all that in can't be good for you.' I touched his face. 'Actually it might help me too, because I know you're holding so much back, and frankly, I'm waiting for the dam to burst, for terrible things to come out.'

'When have I *ever* said terrible things to you?' he asked, genuinely hurt.

'You haven't and that's what makes me nervous. What if you . . . I don't know . . . detonate?'

'I . . . I don't know how to respond to that.' He sighed, looked away, then looked me in the eyes. 'Verity Fassbinder, I have *chosen* to be with you, and I'm very much aware that entails a series of unexpected occurrences of an unspecified nature. I knew that when I signed on. I knew that when we got pregnant. Our parenting experience – our entire relationship – was always going to be challenging because we will always face more world bosses than most people. Think of it as XP.'

'Is that gamer-speak for our life is a quest?'

'Yes.'

I opened my mouth and nothing came out, so I rested my head on his shoulder and stroked Maisie's red-gold hair until the beeping of a car horn interrupted our fragile idyll.

Chapter Sixteen

We'd not been gone long, but our house had already developed that dusty, deserted air. It needed people moving through it to keep living. I settled Maisie in her new crib, then grabbed the spare keys to Mel's place and led Galina next door.

As I gave her the quick tour, I said, 'Keep it clean. Mel will be back in a couple of weeks and I don't want to have to come in and sanitise the place from top to bottom because people have no respect. You're in charge.'

She raised an eyebrow, stuck her hand out and I dropped the keys into her palm.

'I'll do an online shopping order – anything special you'd like?'

'Basics are fine.'

'Okay.' I headed to the front door, then turned back. 'Set some wards, and be careful.'

'You too.'

A couple more Weyrd would be arriving soon for her to whip into shape; I made a mental note to buy Mel a *really* big box of chocolates for when she got home and I had to explain why I'd used her place as a boarding house for the brute squad.

I'd mix oil and ink and added some of my own blood to paint new wards across the door lintels and windows of our home. That would keep out the *kitsune* at least, but I was wary of making them so strong that not even Bela or Ziggi or Galina's security detail could get in to help us. And I had not the foggiest idea what to do against beings like that which had killed Jerry: it had defied the wards at Ocean's Reach; low-level though they were, they still should have had some effect, but I'd seen no signs of any weakening. It kept its form, it found the nursery, it killed with efficiency. Yet my mummy-spit spells had worked – maybe it was the very personal nature of those that had kept it at bay? Or what if . . . ? What if someone had disabled Wanda's wards? You'd have to know about them, of course, but still, getting through them with no effect suggested Weyrd, or at the very least, well-informed Normal. Did the chino-wearing runner who'd disappeared into the night know the house?

I considered the conversation we'd had on the way home, Ziggi driving, Galina in the front, David and me in the back and Bela on speaker-phone.

'So, this monster,' David had asked, 'is it . . . sentient, do you think?'

'You mean *was*: it was done when it entered Jerry.'

'Not sentient, then,' he said with conviction, then asked, 'So what kind of creature would die just to kill another?'

I rubbed my face. 'I have the feeling it went for Jerry because he was there, he attracted its attention. He went outside, maybe to patrol – or did he hear a noise, did someone draw him away? – and left the damned door open . . . or maybe it was opened by someone else, to let the thing in?'

'Not sure we'll ever know that,' said Ziggi, and Galina grunted in agreement, which was pretty much her only comment the whole four-hour drive home.

'It couldn't get into the nursery,' I said, 'but that's what it was trying to do.'

'Are you sure, V?' Bela's voice was a little tinny through the speaker. 'What if its location was coincidental?'

'That's possible, but . . . Jesus, Bela, it was pressing itself against the door as if would pass through the wood if it could. It was determined.' I bit my lower lip a little too hard and felt blood well. 'Shit. What if . . . What if it's following an order, an urge, an imperative, but that imperative wasn't . . . *specific*. What if Jerry was just in its path and it hadn't been able to fulfil its imperative, so it attacked him?'

'You mean it's like a gun and needs to be pointed? Aimed?' asked David, holding Maisie tight.

'And Jerry wasn't part of the plan. If that thing's got no real volition of its own, no thought process, no ability to discern one target from another . . .' Ziggi stopped.

'. . . then whoever creates it needs to be close by? As if the radio signal can only go so far? So the thing might lose shape and purpose if not close to the controller? So it's just water held together by a spell and moved by the tiny bit of another's will that washes through it? It's a pretty sloppy plan,' Bela said, but he still sounded a little disbelieving.

'No independent thought – it's not like Nadasy's garbage golem last year. Needing to be around to keep things together – and to watch your handiwork – would explain the fleeing bastard.' I took a deep breath. 'Which makes me certain said fleeing bastard was the creator.'

'And you're sure it wasn't an undine?' David asked.

There was a chorus of negative noises. I explained, 'Definitely not. They're non-violent scroungers. Now, rusalkas are a different story; they're murdered maidens, or ones who've been unlucky in love and killed themselves, and they don't care who they take down. Their methods are quite specific: enchanting with song, then drowning anyone silly enough to wander within range. Besides, rusalkas can always be seen; undines are either visible or invisible but not anything in between. And they both look properly human, with features and hair and solid female form. That thing was just water in non-specific person-shape.'

'So, to summarise?' Bela said.

'Someone's creating – and I think it's definitely that more than summoning – and controlling a . . . well, let's call it an eidolon, shall we?' At David's look, I added, 'Because that's a cool word.' I frowned, trying to marshal my thoughts. 'So: an eidolon of water for the sole purpose of drowning people. Jerry makes number three. It's something that needs its maker to be close by to make sure it does its job, to hold it together. But there were no witnesses to the previous deaths, or at least, no one who's noticed anyone acting suspiciously at the time.'

'Someone drowning on dry land in front of you is probably going to take all the attention,' observed David. 'No one's going to be noticing what's going on at the periphery.'

'That's probably what they're banking on. And what if that person is someone you wouldn't notice anyway? Someone who can slink through a crowd like a black cat on a dark night, excite no attention and then – BAM!'

'That suggests a powerful glamour,' said my completely Normal boyfriend.

'You've been doing your homework.' I kissed him. 'Glamour, or a forgetting spell.'

'Forgetting?'

'Some things you can use an erasure for – letters, records, documentation – but that spell needs to be fairly specific about what you're targeting, and it's hard to remember every trace you leave behind.

It won't work on big stuff like people or houses, things that have *weight*; that's what a Glamour is for, hiding what's there or making it appear different, cheating the eye.' I was remembering the house at Ascot which had been largely burned to the ground as a result of my efforts; it had had such a supreme glamour around it that it hung around even after the woman who'd cast it was dead, and was so powerful that no one noticed when flames started devouring the Winemaker's house. No one called the fire brigade, because no one had noticed it was there.

'Now, a forgetting spell works on the memory, hides recollections of things you've seen, people you've met, rather like a glamour hides things.'

'Or maybe that person was close by, but not easily seen. Hiding in a dark corner?' suggested Ziggi.

'Possible. Bela, I'm going to need to talk to the Archivist about this. I need someone with a better library to rifle through.'

'I'm sure he'll be delighted to hear you want to rifle through his carefully curated collection of records,' said Bela drily. 'I'll let you know when.' He hung up.

'After all this time you still need to go through Bela to make an appointment?' asked David, and I could tell from his tone of voice that he was a little offended on my behalf.

I too would have thought that after saving their collective butts the Weyrd Council might have been a little more welcoming, but apparently arm's length would remain a unit of measure for me. I was still a half-blood, a strangeling, and I would always be the daughter of Grigor Fassbinder, the *Kinderfresser* extraordinaire who'd almost exposed Brisbane's Weyrd to the eyes of the Normal world.

'The Russian Royal Court was reputed to have referred to their own Weyrd community as a right bunch of stiffs, and the phrase 'you've got a stick up your arse" is from a transcript of the meeting between King Louis XIV and the Weyrd ambassador of Byzantium.'

'I think you made that up.'

'Maybe a bit. Let's just say they're a formal bunch.'

Now, back in my own home, I locked the front door, peeked into the nursery where David and Ziggi were gurgling over Maisie, then set myself up in the library. I pulled a few books from the shelves – *Mother Sykes' Annotated Compendium of Protections*, *St Ignatia's Guide to Darkness and Light*, and *Murcianus' Magical Wards* – to research wards of varying degrees, particularly specific ones that might repel something made of water. I'd just booted up the laptop when there was a knock at the door, tentative.

'I'll get it,' said David.

'Use the peephole,' I reminded him, which was answered by a mocking laugh.

There was the murmur of voices, polite, and the sound of someone coming in, then David calling, 'V? It's for you.' I was thinking he'd let someone in awfully easy as I made my way to the door of the library. The nursery was directly across from me and Ziggi was waiting in the doorway, a finger to his lips: *Be quiet, I'll jump in if needed.*

I walked out into the front room, which we mostly used as a place to store my asparagus-coloured velvet reproduction *chaise longue*, another desk and a bookshelf for the more innocuous books.

A woman about my height was standing beside David, in front of the still-open front door. She was slender, wearing a calf-length black coat over indigo jeans and a red skivvy, and Blundstones. Her straight dark hair was pulled back in a tidy ponytail. She smiled, as if unsure of her welcome.

'You!' I said louder than I should and crossed quickly to grasp her hand, tightening my grip in case she tried to run. She gasped as I inadvertently crushed her fingers; I guess my full strength had returned. I let go quickly, saying, 'Sorry. *Sorry!* Where have you been?' I demanded, and she laughed out loud.

Instead of answering she said, 'How are you doing? Everything go okay?'

I felt a goofy smile on my face in spite of myself, and said, 'A little girl, Maisie.'

Her answering smile was shaky; there were tears behind it.

'David, this is . . . um . . . the person whose name I don't know, who saved my life. Ziggi, come here—!'

As he stepped out of the nursery, I turned to introduce him, but he looked as though he'd been slapped. I glanced back at my visitor, wondering *what's going on?* Her expression was resigned, but lightened in amusement to see his shock.

'Hello, Ziggi,' she said evenly.

He moved his lips a few times without producing any sound. *Old girlfriend?* I thought.

Then Ziggi whispered, '*Olivia?*'

I didn't make any connection with the name, but I got distracted by a noise outside, the particular tread of a man who's never really put much weight on the earth, and Bela appeared in the doorway. As I watched, Mr Inscrutable's face changed, much as Ziggi's had.

He didn't say anything until he was right next to me, then he asked calmly, 'Verity, what is your mother doing here?'

I didn't pass out, although I wanted to.

I did say, 'Don't be so fucking stupid.'

I didn't ask what the hell was wrong with them.

'Isn't your mother dead, V?' asked David helpfully.

'Yes.' Bewilderment was fast turning to anger: they *knew* my mother was gone, so what kind of a sick joke was this? Why would two of the people closest to me pull this kind of crap?

Unless . . .

Unless . . .

Unless there was a perfectly reasonable explanation for *everything*. I stared at the woman who'd saved me, waiting for her to furnish that reasonable explanation. There would be a reason, a *good* reason – *a very good fucking reason* – and I would accept it. I would remain calm, even though all I wanted to do was yell at someone – almost *anyone* – a lot, *very loudly*. Of course, if she'd shown any sign of trying to leave, I'd have thrown a chair at her.

I cleared my throat and said, 'You're not Olivia Fassbinder.'

She stared at me. 'I am your mother, Verity.'

'Less expired than I've been led to believe, then.'

'Somewhat.'

I tried to find a memory of my mother's face from my childhood, before she disappeared, but I'd been too small, I didn't remember her at all, and the only photos my grandparents had of her were when she was little, when she was Olivia Brennan, before my father came between them. There was nothing to show that that girl might have grown into the woman in front of me – nothing except the looks on Ziggi and Bela's faces . . . nothing but the fact that I could see in her what my own face might look like, some way down the track.

Bela pushed himself away from the wall he'd been leaning against. My ex had never been pro leaning, considered it sloppy, so it was a fair sign of how much this woman's presence had shaken him. 'This is your mother, V, I'd stake my life on it. I've seen photos of her and Grigor in the Archives.'

Ziggi's hands were shaking. 'This is Olivia Fassbinder, V, although

I swear, I don't know how. Sandor Verhoeven identified her body after she'd been pulled from the river—'

That was something I hadn't known, but I'd long suspected Verhoeven had been one of those who'd held my father down while iron spikes were hammered into him to stop him from shifting before he was sent to prison. Now it turned out he'd been near my mother's purported death too?

'Did you die?' I asked quietly.

'It's complicated,' she said, then licked her lips as if they were suddenly dry.

'I'm pretty smart. I can probably follow if you use short words,' I said, but she didn't answer me. 'Do you, or have you ever answered to the title the Guardian's Hound? The Apostate, perhaps?'

When I said that she paled. She'd obviously not heard that part of the fox-girls' conversation in the alley, and she didn't know how much or how little I knew.

'Verity, you're angry and you've got every right. And we need to talk, about everything. But I'd rather—'

'You'll understand if I don't give a shit about what you want, okay, *Olivia*?' I was trying so hard to remain *not angry*. Turned out I wasn't very good at that.

She looked away and I suddenly wondered if she wanted to tell me not to swear, pull some mummy bullshit like that? Instead, I asked, 'How did you find me? How did you know where I live?'

'I have my sources. I've been away but there are still people who owe me favours.' She smiled. 'And I grew up in this house, remember?'

'Very cloak and dagger.' I pursed my lips.

'Verity, I didn't want it to be like this. I—'

'Would you have told me who you were if Ziggi and Bela hadn't recognised you?' She didn't answer. I wanted to sit down because my legs had gone a bit wobbly and my knees weren't feeling too supportive, but that would have caused people to rush over and try to offer comfort. There'd be plenty of time for emotional collapse after I'd set some ground rules. 'Olivia, you were dead. Grigor told me so.' She squirmed at the mention of her husband. 'Your parents grieved for you. They buried you. There's a headstone in Toowong Cemetery with your fucking name on it!' *Oops, losing the* not angry . . .

'Verity—'

I held my hands up to stop her, but to my disgust, they were shaking. I yelled, '*Why aren't you dead?*'

The echoes fell into silence and I finally separated myself from the delayed outrage of the three-year-old she'd left when she died. *If* she'd died. I knew myself well enough: if I kept talking when I was exhausted, shocked, fearful and angry, I would say things that couldn't be forgiven . . . and despite everything, I didn't want to burn this bridge. Then my daughter began crying and I hated myself all over again.

'Are you going to run away?' I asked quietly.

'It's time I stopped.'

I let out a tremulous breath and passed a hand over my face. 'I can't do this right now.'

Bela moved closer to Olivia, and I finally noticed two large shapes out on the porch: he'd brought Septimus and Velma to replace Jerry and Mike. My boss clasped his hands in front of his waist like Solomon about to consider how best to divide an infant and said, 'I think, Olivia, there are quite a few questions to be answered. I'd like you to come to the Bishop's Palace—'

'No fucking way!' I yelled again, not least because I'd seen Olivia's hand moving towards the pocket of her coat. In her room Maisie cried out more and David threw me a look, then went to get her.

I did not want my home turned into a gladiatorial arena, especially when I was pretty certain my mother would win, and at great cost to my friends and furniture. 'You're not taking her there, Bela. You're not taking her to prison. She's done nothing wrong' – *that we know of* – 'and anything you want to ask her, you can ask right here.'

Had Bela really thought I'd let him take her without a fight? But he hadn't seen her move like I had, or the stain, which was all that remained of the *kitsune* on the pavers in that filthy alley. And no matter *why* she'd deserted me or what she'd done in the time since, I wasn't going to let her disappear into the depths of the Bishop's Palace – and she sure as fuck wasn't going to get the chance to give them the slip on the way there which, having seen her disappear before, was another perfectly reasonable possibility.

Most importantly, she'd been gone so very long from my life I wasn't going to let her go now.

Bela began, 'I don't know if that's a good—'

'I don't care,' I snarled. I looked at Olivia Fassbinder and said, 'I have things to do, but do you promise faithfully you'll still be here when I get back? If the answer is no, then prepare to be hunted.'

There was a flare of amusement in her eyes, but she didn't know me, what I'd done and what I was capable of, so let her think it was funny.

'I'll be here. I promise.'

At least that meant I didn't need to worry about amping up the wards, not with my very own Universal Soldier Mum on guard. I looked at Bela again, pointed a finger at him and said, 'Do you swear she'll be safe and there won't be any ill-conceived attempts to relocate her?'

Bela glared, but said, 'So sworn.'

'Right, okay, I'm going out. I'm taking Ziggi with me, *like I promised.*' I didn't want to go when I had so many questions. Mind you, I wasn't at all sure I was prepared to hear the answers.

'Bela, fill Olivia in on . . . all of the stuff. Olivia, I'm trusting you with those I love. *Don't make me regret it.*'

There might have been some crying in the back seat of the taxi, but Ziggi very sweetly ignored it, and waited until I'd subsided to the snot-snuffling and hunting-for-tissues stage before he asked, 'Where to?'

I was profoundly grateful he'd driven away immediately, so no one had been able to watch me break down. I made a real effort to pull myself together. 'Um . . . the undines, I think. Given last night, talking to individuals connected to water has become a priority.' My hands were shaking.

'And then?' he asked patiently.

'Little Venice, for a chat with the Norns about the same matter, plus, Aspasia said the fox-girls had been in, so maybe the last one's been back.'

'And then?'

'And *then* maybe we'll talk about my *feelings*.'

'Okay then. Can't wait for that.'

Chapter Seventeen

Undines make themselves at home wherever they happen to wash up, but they aren't necessarily easy to find. Those in the know will tell you the bend of the river which accommodates Newstead House is a favoured spot.

Built in 1846 by one of the new city's new land barons, the simple two-storey sandstone and wood dwelling was Brisbane's oldest surviving residence. It had been home to graziers, state separatists and governor-generals in the making. Over the years it had been extended and renovated to within an inch of its life, until it resembled a mansion of sorts. It had served as an unofficial Government House, army barracks during the Second World War and home to the Queensland Women's Historical Society; its latest incarnation was as a museum decorated in late Victorian style. It sat on the crest of a gentle hill amid expansive parklands that rolled down to the river. There were lots of trees and shrubs, colourful flowers, benches scattered hither and yon, an impressive fountain, and a giant chessboard on the enormous green spread that comprised the 'front lawn'.

The undines gravitated there not just for the views and the conveniently located rocky outcrops where they could easily slip into and out of the water, but also because it attracted a lot of picnickers and wedding parties. Undines were cunning thieves, with a preference for stolen food: the Yogi Bears of the Weyrd world.

Like most of our kind they'd come here as migrants, or refugees from troubles in a variety of Old Countries. Generally they were harmless – they didn't steal babies or lure Normals to drowning, and I'd yet to hear of one eating humans – but difference is difference. Folks driving out flesh-eating sirens or soul-entangling rusalki didn't care too much if they sent innocent water nymphs on their way as well. But the undines were forgiving by nature (although that might be more to do with being intensely lazy) and weren't too resentful, and they liked the river-city. Occasionally there were reports in November of them becoming visible and wearing jacaranda blossom crowns on their hair while sunning themselves; when that happened, Normals took them for bikini babes hired for promotional purposes and didn't give them a second glance.

It started periodically raining soon after we left home; the on-and-off showers were, thankfully, off when Ziggi and I wandered down to the path towards the white gazebo. It was often reserved for weddings, but there weren't many people around today, just an older couple strolling along the covered verandah of the house who'd given the purple cab disapproving glances, making Ziggi bridle. The gazebo and environs were blessedly people-free, although that didn't mean there wasn't someone there who might be coaxed into view.

I wandered down to where the river lapped the banks, leaned against a rocky outcropping and dug about in the giant handbag. The paper bag with *Doughnuts to Die For* emblazoned in pink and green had been a bit crushed between the breast pump and the spare bottles, the lettering smudged by its own sticky contents.

The chocolate-glazed doughnut was slightly crushed on one side, but no less appetising for that, and my stomach rumbled with envy as I contemplated the thick channel of raspberry jam and mock cream inside. Not so long ago saliva would have flooded my mouth, now there was nothing. I tossed the pastry in the air, a little to the left of me.

It vanished.

If I hadn't been paying attention, I'd have missed the elegant, slightly scaled hand that appeared and disappeared as if through a curtain. I heard delighted noshing, then an impressively loud burp.

'There's more where that came from, you know,' I said.

A voice from somewhere beside me asked suspiciously, 'What's the cost?'

'Answers. Just a few.'

'You'd better have a lot more doughnuts, and *he* better leave.'

'Ziggi? He's my friend—'

'Well, send him away.' Petulant.

I looked at Ziggi, who frowned, not wanting to abandon me there any more than I wanted to be abandoned.

'Well, there's a problem with that,' I said. 'You see, there's at least one person wishing me harm, and so Ziggi's kind of non-negotiable.'

Silence.

'What's your problem with him? Let's talk—'

'Don't like his kind.'

'What kind is that?'

'*Jäger*,' she spat.

Hunter.

Ziggi shook his head, but I said, 'Ziggi, how about you go for a walk?'

He stared at me for a moment, then gave a put-upon sigh and said, 'Watch out for the Boatman,' which was a low blow.

I scanned the river nervously as Ziggi made his way back from the water and positioned himself near the war memorial to the Americans who'd been stationed at Newstead House during the Second World

War – from behind, the bald eagle perched atop the column looked like Batman. *Coincidence?* I wondered, then dragged myself back to reality.

'Okay, you can come out now.'

An instant later the space that had been empty was filled by a girl with skin the luminescent greeny shimmer of oil on water. Hair of gold and silver flowed down to what was now a tail, now a pair of long legs with webbed toes and delicate fins on the calves, now a tail again. She had full pouty lips, but her teeth were mean little triangles, small and sharp. Her nose appeared to have been broken once, but it gave her face character, cutting through the bland prettiness. The eyes that slanted at me were an unreliable blue-green that kept changing colour.

'I'm Verity,' I started. *Look at me being Ms Politeness.* 'Thanks for talking to me.'

She placed one hand against her chest and said something – a name, I assumed – so wet and full of sibilants and glottal stops we both knew I had no hope of pronouncing it.

'I'm going to call you Sam, if that's okay.'

She shrugged but didn't say *Don't*. She pointed at the bag in my hand and I handed her another doughnut.

'Good, huh?'

'I *really* don't like fish. You try living in a river. There's no drive-through.'

I'd not thought of it that way before. 'Can you tell me if you've noticed anything wrong with the river recently?'

'As in pollution? Hell, yes: there's a factory up at Murarrie pouring industrial waste into the water at night.'

'Not what I meant, but I'll mention it to some journalists of my acquaintance,' I promised.

She gave me a business name, looking satisfied, but she was now doubly indebted to me. I ran a hand across my stomach, feeling a strange aching at the absence of baby bump, and suddenly the distance between Maisie and me was almost too much to bear. But now was not the time for mummy tears, rational or otherwise. I pushed it away.

'What I'm specifically after is information regarding someone using the river to murder people.' I had no idea if the river had anything to do with the eidolon's kills, but I had to start somewhere, eliminating possibilities. 'Or any source of water, I guess.'

'Any more details?'

'A man died on Mt Coot-tha a few days ago – at the lookout. He just started spurting water and drowned. When I examined the body he was completely saturated with fluid, right down to his flesh, all his tissues. Same deal with a lawyer in shopping centre, and a Weyrd down at Byron – I saw it drown him right in front of me. Liquid in the shape of a person, but no face, no organs, no brain . . .'

'Not part of the river,' she said with certainty.

'Why not?'

'If it were connected with the river, I'd know. *We'd* know. Or the lakes and streams and ponds. We'd feel it being drawn away – that kind of act causes a link, a *lien*, between the source and the final effect. This liquid is being brought from elsewhere, or even *made*. This is something held together with magic.' She frowned, silvery brows knitting in concentration. 'We don't do that. We don't hurt people.'

'I'm not for a moment suggesting it's undines – I know your only natural prey is picnic baskets.' I noticed she'd scoffed the second doughnut and handed her a third. 'But maybe you've sensed something in the river apart from pollution? A change, an abuse, anything dark . . .'

The rain began to spit again, pattering on her skin, causing shifting oily reflections where it hit. 'It doesn't sound like . . . What it *does* sound like is something *separate*. Some magic that's not elemental as such, even though it uses water . . . Am I making sense? The liquid is just a tool.'

I sighed. Why was nothing ever easy?

She added, 'You might try the Boatman, of course. He's not of the river, he just uses it. He might know if something's amiss on dry land?'

Um . . . My ankle tingled where the Dagger of Wilusa, back in its sheath now that I was considerably thinner, pressed against my skin. The Boatman escorted souls to the next place, but he just *caught* the dead, he didn't create them.

I sighed. I was about to hand her the bag, then I paused and said carefully, 'You called Ziggi a "*Jäger*" and you obviously don't like him – but I've known him a long time and I'd trust him with my life. And not just mine, but my daughter's life, my partner's life.'

She slitted her eyes and stared at me, then the doughnut bag. After a moment, the tension went out of her body. 'Well, maybe *he's* okay. But not his kind—'

'How can you tell his kind?'

'The colouring, the pale skin, the ginger hair – there's an eye in the back of his head, isn't there?' I didn't bother trying to deny it and she went on, 'In the old days they used to hunt us for sport. The *Jäger* would net us and gut us, fillet us, drain our blood into the waters where we'd been born – where we *lived* – which contaminated the entire system. They'd feed us to their hounds, use our flesh as bait, take our skins to make their wet-weather coats; they'd sew a dozen together to make a shelter to keep the rain off when they slept in the open.'

'Why? Why undines?'

'Why do *Jäger* do anything? Because they could – because they were stronger than us, they were protected as the kings' hunters, whatever land they lived in. They could do what they wanted, with complete impunity.'

I looked at her and said firmly, 'I give you my word Ziggi is *not* one of that kind.'

Her silvery brows joined in a frown. 'You don't know that for sure. You don't know what he did before he came here. You don't know what life he had, how old he is, how many centuries he's lived. Trust me, the water's memory is long, and its daughters remember *his* kind.'

Well, she was right about at least one thing: Weyrd live for *ages* – unless they're murdered by each other or Normals. None of them had ever told me how old they were, and I couldn't even begin to guess how old my father Grigor was when he died. Ziggi himself had once told me that I was a blink of the eye to the Weyrd, and to Bela in particular.

'Well, thanks anyway.' I handed her the paper bag; she looked inside and chortled.

Back in the taxi, I told Ziggi most of what the undine had told me. I thought long and hard about what she'd said about *Jägers*. I wanted to know more, but equally, I didn't want to offend Ziggi by digging into his past; he'd always been pretty cagey and I'd respected that: I trusted him. But now I had a risen-from-the-dead mother, I'd been attacked twice in the space of a few days and watched someone die horribly, almost impossibly. Now I felt like I really needed to *know*.

'Little Venice?'

'Little Venice.'

Then 'Ziggi? What's a *Jäger*?'

Chapter Eighteen

Miraculously, we got to park in a West End side street, so Ziggi came with me to Little Venice. The way he looked around made me wonder when he'd last been there; when I thought about it, I'd always brought refreshments back to him in the taxi. The surprised look on Theodosia's lovely face was probably as much for him as me.

'Hey! What are you doing back?' She came from behind the counter and gave me a hard hug, then yelled, 'Aspasia!'

'No rest for the wicked, or even the morally grey,' I said and sank into the closest chair. I leaned my elbows on the table. I asked 'Is Thaïs around?' which was a stupid question because the oldest of the Sisters Norn didn't go out. People came to her. All three Sisters collected and pooled the whispers, gossip and truth that ran through the café, but Thaïs was the mistress of information, collating the snatches of conversation and rumours, anything that might be useful, stirring them into her cauldron to see which hint might gel with which suspicion and create a solid piece of knowledge.

'She's in, but she's not *in*,' said Theo.

That meant Thaïs was off on one of her astral travels and there was no waking her; sometimes she could be gone for days. 'Crap.'

'Can I help? Aspasia!' Theo yelled again, giving a head-tilt that set her mess of auburn corkscrew curls dancing. 'How's the little one?'

I opened my mouth but instead of, *She's fine*, all I got out was a howl – and tears, followed by more howls and more tears and some heavy snot action. It felt like I'd been crying for ever, but when I finally calmed down I found Aspasia, having at last answered her sister's summons, staring at me in horror. I wanted to tell her I was no less appalled, but instead I rummaged through the handbag for tissues, having to remove the breast pump – to collective intakes of breath – before I found them. I dried my eyes and blew my nose while Ziggi patted my shoulder ineffectually but comfortingly.

'Well. That was unexpected. Sorry, didn't know that was lurking. Maisie is fine. David is fine. The safe house was fine while it lasted. Apparently I'm messy and emotional.'

'What do you need?' asked Aspasia, less sharply than she might once have.

'Answers, as always.' I rubbed a hand across my face. 'Theo, Bela told you about the *kitsune*?'

'At Council, yes. Broad daylight attack's pretty risky.'

'Not the first time, either. One of them tried to hurt me when I was doing groceries last week.'

'Obviously didn't succeed,' noted Aspasia.

'Can you recall anything about the two fox-girls who were in here the other week? One dressed like a punk, or maybe a librarian or a Gothic Alice in Wonderland?'

'That's right – the last two.' She bit her lip. 'They didn't talk to anyone. They had one drink each and watched the crowd.'

Well, that did at least confirm the supermarket fox-girl was connected with the alleyway attackers.

Theo frowned. 'Bela said a woman helped you out in the alleyway?'

'Yes,' I said, but offered no more information. At least Bela hadn't seen fit to broadcast Olivia's existence yet. Theo would find out soon enough, but no one *needed* to know that rumours of my mother's death had been greatly exaggerated; that would give rise to more questions than I was unable to answer. I didn't look at Ziggi; that would have given the game away.

'And you're absolutely sure the fox-girls didn't ask after anyone?' Both Sisters were shaking their heads, even as I added, 'Didn't mention either "The Guardian's Hound" or "The Apostate"?'

'Nope,' they said together.

'Ever heard those terms before?'

Again, 'Nope!' in stereo.

'Shit. Here's the thing: there's still one around. The one that looks like a librarian, brown satchel, sensible shoes, black-framed glasses.'

'That's not really a fair description of librarians,' objected Theo. 'I dated a *very* sexy librarian. She was gorgeous—'

'By *dated*, she means slept with once,' Aspasia interrupted.

'If I offer a general apology for using a broad generalisation, can we move on? Good.' I rubbed my temples. 'Keep an eye out for her. She'll be looking for something – people, information, resources. I'm pretty sure she's not done yet, not when she's lost two sisters.'

Nods all around.

'Here's the thing,' I went on, '*kitsune* seldom work on their own, they like packs – which makes me wonder about the solo effort in the supermarket. What was she doing?'

'Trying to impress someone? Make a point? Show up the others?' Aspasia suggested. 'But if they thought threatening you would get a result, it's serious. Something bigger's afoot.'

I sighed. 'Isn't there always?'

Theo said, 'And it does sound like something Thaïs might have heard about.'

'How long's she been under?'

'Three days. It's just impossible to wake her.'

'I know.' *Bugger, bugger, bugger.* 'Call me as soon as she's up and about, okay?'

'Is that all?' asked Aspasia, making a move towards the bar as if to get back to work.

'I wish!' I filled them in about the unfortunate Toby Malone and Faraday Hannigan, and finally about Jerry – clearly Bela hadn't reported Jerry's death to the Council yet, because the colour drained from Aspasia's face and she sat shakily beside me. Theo reached over and held her sister's hand.

'They went out, a long time ago.' She frowned. 'I should know this. Why don't I know about this?'

'You've been ignoring your phone,' Aspasia breathed.

I said, 'I'm so sorry, Aspasia.'

She said, 'It was a *really* long time ago . . . but it's a shock, you know?'

I gently described what I'd seen, how the eidolon had looked, what it had done to Jerry, but I didn't sugarcoat it. Half-truths would serve no useful purpose. 'Any of this sound familiar?'

Theo rubbed at her chin. 'Sometimes . . . sometimes, in the old days, if a great witch thought a member of her coven was betraying the group, or likely to betray them, she might arrange for what's called a Grand Drowning.'

'The spell's a nasty thing to work, a nasty way to die, witches drowning witches,' said Aspasia. She passed a hand over her eyes. 'The new Archivist might be more help.'

But I was supposed to be waiting for Bela to make an appointment for me. I was supposed to be obedient and polite. I was supposed to work within power structures so strict it made Victorian mourning customs look off-hand.

'Yes,' I said thoughtfully. 'Yes, he might.'

★

The argument with Ziggi took much less time than I expected: he capitulated to my demand in under sixty seconds, which must've been some kind of a record. Maybe he figured it wasn't worth doing anything that might draw my attention back to the subject of *Jägers*. Maybe he figured I wouldn't get past the foyer. Or just maybe he agreed with me that we'd wasted enough time waiting for permission to pay a visit, but still wanted to be able to claim he'd tried to talk me out of it. Either way, he dropped me at King George Square, then drove off to do laps of the CBD until I texted.

The Weyrd's Archives are kept in Brisbane's City Hall, just not in *quite* the same place. In the auditorium there's a sweet spot where you can speak the right words and a door will open in the air for you, but you need to step through quickly before it vanishes again. The security guys on the front desk didn't even attempt to search me this time, just waved me through. I raised a hand in greeting as they watched me walk confidently down the corridor that led off from the central star of the lobby.

I stopped in front of an entrance I recognised. The last time I'd been here one of the guards had escorted Bela and me and undone the four locks that secured the entrance. I'd forgotten about that; so that's why the arseholes had let me walk through so easily. They'd been taking the piss, figuring I'd have to return to them, tail between my legs, begging to be let in.

Well, fuck that.

Fuckers.

I put my handbag on the floor and examined the locks before placing both hands on the doorhandle and beginning to pull. I exerted a gentle pressure at first, but it was solid, insistent, and I revelled in the strength I'd not exercised in months. Initially the deadlocked steel-banded barrier resisted, but soon enough there was a creaking sound as the wood began to give and a crack appeared between the frame and the edge of the door. I slipped my fingers into the gap and got better leverage. The process was slow and steady, nowhere near as spectacular as kicking it in, but nonetheless extremely effective.

When the sudden tearing sound of metal and wood giving up the ghost screamed clearly back along the corridor, I grinned. Nothing like a bit of physical exertion to make me feel better. When the douches on the desk appeared at the end of the hallway, faces slack with surprise, I swung my handbag onto my shoulder in a jaunty fashion, gave them a cheery smile and flipped the bird before heading down the stone stairs to meet Brisneyland's newest Archivist.

Of course, when I say 'newest', I mean 'of two'. After all, Ursa had been on duty for a couple of hundred years before she was murdered. I don't count Vadim Nadasy, for all he wore Ursa's skin for a while; he certainly wasn't what *she'd* have called a proper Archivist. Now there was the new guy. Ursa had always been a stickler for manners and protocol; she'd have taken a very dim view of me breaking her door instead of waiting for an invitation. I wondered what the new man would make of my unconventional entrance, and made sure to stomp my Doctor Martens so no one could claim I'd snuck up on them.

I stepped into a large cavern at the bottom of the stairs. Those walls not lined with bookshelves housed floor-to-ceiling compactus units. At the far end was a variety of tables and desks of varying sizes and heights, some flat, some sloped like those of mediaeval monks. Three figures – *clerks? That was a new feature* – were staring at me, inkpots and quills forgotten, while a server sat in one corner, whirring quietly to itself. The Weyrd always did like to mix things up; if there was ever any great e-collapse, all these records would be safe and sound, handwritten copies filed in three different locations.

As if I was innocent of any recent vandalism, I strolled towards the clerks.

'Ms Fassbinder?' The owner of the voice appeared from between the stacks and I guessed he'd been waiting there, getting the first look in and assessing me before I did him.

I turned.

The previous Archivist had been tiny and wizened, with thin silver hair, pink eyes and ears that were basically holes in the side of her head. She was several hundred years old and wore overalls and orthopaedic shoes. She didn't bother with glamours.

The man before me, on the other hand, looked like he'd stepped from the pages of *GQ*. He took my breath away just a little – which was saying something, because I'd dated Bela Tepes. Thick blond hair, big blue eyes, square jaw, pouty lips, perfect brows and impossibly high cheekbones. His navy blue serge Savile Row suit fit his gym-sculpted body like a glove – there was a large chunk out of someone's mortgage – while the light reflected from his highly polished shoes would have blinded any enemies his dazzling smile hadn't already taken out. The hand he offered was large, the nails beautifully man-icured.

This guy made Bela and Alex Parrish look like slobs. He was almost as beautiful as the rebel angels, but he certainly was no angel: his glamour was good, but there was something a little unstable about it. I suspected the quality of the lighting down there wasn't kind.

'Ms Fassbinder, I'm Jost Marolf.' Clipped accent, perfect English: which meant he was neither Australian nor English, and certainly not American. His handshake was firm, polite, not crushing.

'Hello. How did you know it was me?'

'You fit the description.'

He grinned, not unkindly, and I was suddenly very aware of

my battered jeans, T-shirt, leather jacket and Docs . . . and equally suddenly a little paranoid that there might have been some trace of baby-related substances down my top or under my fingernails.

'I understand congratulations are in order?'

'Thank you.' I pushed my hands into my pockets and rocked back on my heels. 'I have some questions.'

His expression sobered to 'business-time' face. 'Zvezdomir Tepes said that you would from time to time.'

'People are drowning on dry land,' I said, then corrected myself. '*Being* drowned.'

'Weyrd or Normal?'

'Does it matter?' I asked with an edge.

He raised his hands and in the second before he reconsidered the gesture and folded them away, I saw traces of tiny hairs on the palms. I'd not noticed any kind of stubble when we'd shaken, so he was doing something other than shaving; maybe electrolysis.

'It might to the kind of creature you're looking for. Prey may differ.'

I unprickled. 'Sorry, sore point. Both Weyrd *and* Normal, as a matter of fact. I saw it: it was made of liquid, and it was gone once it had finished killing.' I described in more detail what it had done to poor Jerry.

'So not a rusalka or a lorelei or an undine then.' He frowned, put a finger to his lips. 'An ashray, perhaps?'

That wasn't a term I'd heard before. 'I'm listening.'

'"Water lovers", they're also called. They're from Scottish mythology. They are translucent, sometimes known as "sea ghosts". They're entirely nocturnal—'

'Ah, then nope. Sorry to shoot that one down, but two of the deaths occurred in broad daylight.'

'Fossegrim?' he said, a little desperately.

'Again, no. Those I know of: closely related to water sprites, with a tendency to play the fiddle.' I scratched my head. 'How about I tell you what I think and we see if that narrows things down? Someone's suggested it might be the result of a Grand Drowning spell. When it – I'm calling it an eidolon for now – had done its job, it was gone. It didn't reappear, or leave the body. It's got no will of its own, it's been made for a purpose – and no, it's not a golem.'

He pondered that. 'If it is part of a spell, someone needs to have cast it.'

'Yeah – there was someone there, someone who ran away afterwards. I gave chase—'

'—and didn't catch him, obviously,' he said, snippily.

'It was dark. There were circumstances,' I admitted, lacking the energy to get irritated. 'I ran into someone else and we lost him.'

He waited for me to go on.

'Anyway, here's my theory: the person casting this spell has to be relatively close by to keep the thing together.'

He nodded slowly. 'All spells lose efficacy the further they are from their originator, but water is the worst because it has no inherent shape memory. If I recall correctly, a Grand Drowning is usually cast by an entire coven. That gives it greater power, greater reach. If it's just one person doing this, they would need to stay close because they wouldn't have the same ability alone, the same puissance.'

'Does any particular kind of Weyrd tend to use such a spell? It seems very particular. And do they need any specific tools or conditions or skills?'

He made a face. 'I'm ashamed to say I can't tell you that right away.' He gestured to the three clerks, now tapping away at keyboards.

'We're trying to modernise, but my predecessor hadn't got very far, I believe she was quite resistant to—'

'Well, she *was* dead for the last few months of her employment,' I broke in, although I had no idea why I felt so protective of the old lady I'd never actually met. Maybe because it wasn't fair that she was criticised while her flesh was being worn as a human suit.

'Ms Fassbinder, I meant no disrespect,' Jost Marolf said quickly. 'I am doing my best to become as familiar with the holdings as she was, but it's going to take some time. I would like us to get along. I believe I can be useful to you in your endeavours – I realise some parts of this community view what you do as interference, a disloyalty to our kind, but trust me when I say that I believe you to be entirely necessary. What you do is keep us safe. I understand you've had trouble prising information out of the old guard on occasion; I do not wish to continue that way.'

'*Oh!*' Such openness was quite a shock, and left me floundering for a moment, until I managed a gracious response. 'Well, thank you, Jost. That's very much appreciated. And in return, I will do my best to keep the pissy attitude, defensiveness and destructiveness to a minimum.'

'That would also be most appreciated,' Jost said and smiled.

I smiled back and we shook hands.

'Also, I'm really sorry about your door.'

'My door—?'

'So, any ETA on that information?' I asked quickly.

'I'll search through what we've already got digitised – maybe we'll get a lucky break?'

'Maybe,' I said, with not much hope. Experience had kicked most of it out of me.

'As soon as I find anything, I'll be in contact,' he promised, proffering a business card with, wonder of wonders, an actual mobile phone number and email address on it. Another turn-up for the books: the private contact details of one of the Weyrd inner circle. It was nothing short of a miracle, so who knew what else might happen?

I turned away, then a thought struck me. 'Oh! Can I ask you something else?'

Chapter Nineteen

'How'd it go?' Ziggi asked as I slid into the back seat of the cab. As usual, he took off at breakneck speed, with no regard for other cars; I'd almost got used to the sound of horns honking in our wake. 'How was *he*?'

'Very handsome, and very helpful,' I said. Ziggi's only reply was a grunt, so I asked, 'Do you know anything about our Mr Marolf?'

'According to Bela, he was in the Great Archives of Prague for six years, before that, in the Great Edinburgh Necropolis Archives. Supposedly, he was apprenticed in the Great Library of Alexandria, but I'm not sure how you reference-check that. Oh, and Marolf means "border wolf".'

I laughed. That explained the hairs on the palms. 'So, all the places with "Great" in the title, and now Brisneyland! What did he do wrong?'

Ziggi laughed. 'Had to be something – or maybe he just likes heat, sun and footy.'

We both grinned at that.

'I'm willing to bet there was an indiscretion of some moment.'

'That's a bet I'm not going to take,' Ziggi said firmly as he took the exit onto the Riverside Expressway. The relief at heading home washed through me as he added, 'So, do we know anymore than we did earlier? Apart from the handsomeness quotient of the new Archivist?'

'Miaow! Pull your claws back in! Well, it's not a fossegrim, nor a rusalka, nor a lorelei, nor an undine and it's certainly not an ashray.'

'So, not much more?'

'Not as such, no.'

'And we're going home now, right? I mean, I just assumed—'

'And you did so correctly. I need to feed Maisie. I need a shower. I need some food. I need to hug David.' I sighed. 'I need to talk to Olivia.'

He didn't say anything except, 'What about tomorrow's schedule?'

'I want to talk to Anna Valentine – Toby Malone's girlfriend. She's had a few days to process things so maybe she'll remember something new,' I said, and texted McIntyre for the address. I tapped a finger against the window. 'You know what? Let's make a quick detour and drop in to see Kadie Cross now. I've found no sign of her Wilbur Wilson, but maybe some gentle questioning might extract a few more hints.'

'Ms Fassbinder, how nice to see you again.' But Kadie Cross didn't look especially pleased as she swooshed out from one of the back rooms in answer to my ring – almost as if she knew I had nothing worthwhile to tell her. 'Be so kind as to keep your voice down. I have a client experiencing a . . . relaxing seaweed wrap.'

Which was code for, *Someone has utterly done away with their glamours and you do not want to peer behind* that *veil.*

'I'll do my best.' I sat in one of the reception chairs and she mirrored my action.

'You look different,' she observed.

'Considerably lighter – I can even get myself out of a seat without the use of a crane.'

'Wonderful.' Her brisk tone said otherwise. 'How can I help?'

'Well, I hoped to have better news for you by now. However, I've searched for your Wilbur Wilson in both the Bar Association of Queensland and the Queensland Law Society, to no avail. Then I did the same searches around the country' – which was not entirely true; David had done that – 'and I'm afraid I came up empty yet again.'

'Well, that doesn't bode well for your friend's birthday present,' she said smoothly.

I rolled my eyes. 'Don't threaten me, Ms Cross. I'm not saying all is lost, I'm saying it's more difficult than expected, which is why I'm here to ask if perhaps you've remembered anything else about him? Anything distinguishing about his appearance?'

She sighed, and I suspected the words, *Why am I doing your job for you?* were on the tip of her pretty forked tongue. 'I suppose I could show you the security tapes.'

I blinked, then I blinked again, not sure I'd heard correctly.

'*You've got a camera?*' My voice was rising, and she started flapping her hands in a shushing gesture, making a hissing noise that might have been meant to be soothing.

'Be quiet! Someone will hear you!'

Nope, not soothed. 'You fucking well bet they will! You had footage and you couldn't be bothered to tell me about it? You've been wasting my time, lady, and few things piss me off more!'

'Shut up, shut up!' She half-rose, reaching out to either beg or strangle me, and whispered, 'Listen, I didn't tell you because if my clients thought I was taping them without their glamours, I'd never work again – you *know* that. A lot of Weyrd don't want *anyone* to know they've got tattoos doing the heavy lifting – you know that's frowned upon in some circles.'

'Oh, frowns will be the least of your worries if I don't get some straight answers right now! What else aren't you telling me? You don't happen to have his name and address in a little black book somewhere?'

'*Nothing!* I know nothing more – just, *shut up*.' She grabbed my arm and pulled me into a small office secreted behind the reception desk, its door barely discernable from the wall, so cunning was the joinery. From there it was simply a matter of her finding a date-marked file on her computer and double-clicking on it, all so easy I was almost foaming at the mouth with rage.

'I want to hurt you *so much* right now,' I said.

'Just keep this quiet and I'll tattoo whoever you want, whenever you want, however you want, free of charge.' She wiped the sweat from her forehead, and watched the screen as she fast-forwarded until she hissed, 'That's him!' and hit *pause*.

There he was indeed, standing in front of the reception desk: a short man, bald of head, olive of skin, plain of face, flabby of belly. He wore a blue shirt and had his hands pushed deep into the trouser pockets of his dark grey pinstriped suit, as if it might make him look casual and cool. The tie was so ugly it could only have been very expensive. I squinted: his shoes were either unusually scruffy or very dirty. I could also see, off to his left, the fountain with the carved maidens, and the large stone that meant so much to Kadie Cross.

Mr Wilson was *very* ordinary-looking, nothing to excite interest or comment, which made him hard to remember. The video was grainy, but I could see that he'd tracked in a lot of dirt. I wondered what he was beneath his glamours, and how he thought Kadie Cross could improve him. Whether people wanted to believe it or not, magic did have its limits.

I thought over what she'd said on my first visit — that he felt a significant change in appearance would improve his work prospects — but I smelled a rat. Such desperation for change — and it *was* desperation — struck me as unlikely to be related to an office promotion. No, I'd bet good money that he wanted a transformation for another reason entirely, connected with gaining the attention of an unwilling, unaware or unwary object of affection.

I didn't need to watch for long. I had his face and wouldn't forget it, no matter how plain he was. But I made Cross email me a screen-grab.

'Why are you taping these people?' I asked.

'Because you know what this community is like! One I day I might need protection and that lies in having blackmail material,' she said flatly. I wondered what had happened in her life for her to believe this.

'Right. But now I can blackmail you?'

'Yes, yes, but you're honourable, so you probably won't.' *Oh, lady, are you for real?* 'Will you just get on with finding my stone?' she asked, sounding exasperated.

'You do not understand shifts in the balance of power, do you?' I held her stare until she looked away. 'Will you just trust me? Sooner or later I *will* find this man and I *will* find your rock.'

She puffed and pouting with ill-grace muttered, 'All right. Now, may I return to my client?'

'Just one more thing: I need a favour — yes, and it's the least you can do.' Her eyebrows went up and I lifted a finger to warn off any negativity. 'Just listen.'

*

By the time we finally got home I'd managed to avoid talking about my mother and her failure to be deceased. It was a conscious choice on my part, and Ziggi followed my lead; he knew me well. If I wasn't bringing up a subject, then he'd better be well and truly prepared for a fight if he tried to discuss it. It's nice to know that your friends have been taking notice of your less-than-charming habits and respect them.

Bela met me at the front door, and Septimus and Velma left the house to go to Mel's; maybe with me in residence they wouldn't be needed quite so much? While that appealed to my ego, there was a much higher chance that it was because Bela had given up questioning my mother as a bad joke and now everyone just wanted to go home. All I wanted to do was get inside and feed my daughter, but I practised patience instead.

'Hopefully you didn't notice when you drove in, but I've got people at both ends of your street.'

'I didn't notice, but I wasn't looking.' I sighed and sank down on the steps, exhausted, even though I'd spent a large part of the day sitting in the cab. Ziggi was parked on the street, sunk low in the front seat, his novel propped against the steering wheel. It was a front: he wasn't reading on duty. I'd tried to send him home, but all he'd said was, 'Later.' I made a mental note to bring him out a blanket and something to eat.

Bela sat beside me, his Clive Christian cologne a little overwhelming to my still super-sensitive nose.

'So, is my mother still here? What have you, my dearest Zvezdomir Tepes, prised from Olivia Fassbinder's cupid's bow lips?'

'Not much,' he admitted, then added a tad resentfully, 'It wasn't as if I could apply any kind of persuasion here.'

'Too gutless to use thumbscrews on my mummy? Well, I do think it's probably bad form to torture someone's mother.' He gave me a look and I punched him lightly on the arm. 'Bela, I'm joking. Or I think I'm joking. Actually I have no idea what to think or feel, and in fact I've made a point of not thinking about this whole situation for the last while. Ask Ziggi: he'll tell you that under the dictionary definition of "in denial" is a big picture of me.'

'I have no doubt, V.' He touched one of my wrists gently. 'She said she's been travelling, taking on work as and when she could with both Normal and Weyrd communities.'

'That's all you got?' I asked.

'There's more, but V, what you need to hear she needs to tell you herself. She promised me she would.'

I shook my head in disbelief and he waved his hands about, as if that might distract me. 'There is a lot she hasn't told me and I know that. I'm rather hoping she'll tell you. But at this point . . . we need to be patient with her.'

'What the hell is she *doing* here, Bela?' I whined.

'I don't know . . . but, V, maybe give her a break? She's been through some stuff . . .'

'Right.' I ran a hand through my hair, wondered how many more greys I'd have before this misadventure was over. 'But she *was* dead, right? I'm sure Sandor Verhoeven can recognise a dead person. Only she's not dead now.'

'Very much not dead,' he agreed and we sat in silence for a few minutes. 'What did you find in your travels?'

'One: no sign of the *kitsune*, which makes me happy on one hand and nervous on the other. Two: consensus that the eidolon is most probably the result of a Grand Drowning spell. Three: a distinct lack of Wilbur Wilson to be found.'

'Who?'

'This guy.' I pulled out my phone and showed him Kadie Cross' friendly neighbourhood rock thief. Bela's dark eyes slid over the image without recognition.

'And why are you involved in this?'

'He stole something from Mindy's Mehndi and I'm trying to get it back in order to pay off a favour to McIntyre. But you didn't need to know that.'

'No, I did not. However, just to be clear, I've never seen him before, if that helps.'

'Not really, but seeing as we're on the subject . . .' I told him what Wilbur Wilson had asked for, then said, 'Kadie reckons he's already got mucho-strong glamours operating. So what kind of raw material do you think they were working with?'

He hesitated as he got his thoughts in order. 'Trolls, ogres, demons – they're all pretty base metal. Glamours can only do so much, unless you're prepared to spill a lot of blood. Most individuals, supplicants and practitioners, baulk at that. Well, a lot of them. Not all of them.'

'Hmmmm.'

He examined his nails as if there might be something less than perfect about them. 'A Grand Drowning, you say?'

'I spoke to the Norns – alas, Thaïs is "on tour" at the moment – and the new Archivist – oh, don't bother about chasing up that appointment, by the way.'

He gave me some serious side-eye; my bit of redecorating at City Hall had probably been reported already, but all he said was, 'And how did you find Jost?'

'Pretty. Very pretty.' I grinned. 'And helpful. And non-judgemental about my commemorative Powderfinger Internationalist Tour T-shirt.'

His eyes went skyward as if begging for strength. 'A Grand

Drowning is serious. In the old days, witches drowning witches was a terrible punishment, some might even say a heresy, to treat your own like that, whether it's a Weyrd or Normal coven. But there's no sign the victims were witches of either Weyrd or Normal stripe?'

'None. I wanted to re-interview the first victim's girlfriend, but McIntyre tells me she's gone on holiday to help recover. Back in seven days, apparently.' I sighed and examined the tips of my Docs, noted how the embroidered red roses had darkened with age and the general muck associated with being walked on and in. I'd be in the market for new ones soon, which would cause grief; the Finda range had sold out long ago. I drew my attention back to Bela. 'But, and this where my broad ambit tendencies come in handy, Kadie Cross did this.' I held up my hand, revealing the wrist he'd not touched and showed him my new henna tattoo. 'This is the best chance of avoiding drowning. Tell your friends. Get whoever's watching over this house to head to Mindy's Mehndi and get this done. You and Ziggi both.'

He looked dubious and I said, 'I'm *serious*, Bela,' which elicited a reluctant, 'Fine.'

I couldn't imagine him happily getting a tattoo, even a temporary one.

'And nothing on the *kitsune*?' he asked.

'Nothing. No one's seen anything, as far as I can tell. If she'd been sighted, it would have got back to the Norns and they'd have told one of us.' I sat back, stretched.

'How about Susan Beckett? Anything new there?'

'Seriously? When have I had time?' Then I remembered I'd wandered around her parents' property the day before Jerry had died, so I moderated my tone and told Bela what I'd seen there – and shared the fact that Wanda was acquainted with Ms Beckett. 'And if things stay on schedule, it's just over two weeks until the next occurrence.'

We went back over what I'd learned about payment in kind from Alex Parrish before the *kitsune* attack, then Bela pursed his lips and frowned. 'Do you think it might be about a contract gone wrong?'

'Could be – could be business-related. But honestly, mud and shit and *filth* . . . ? That's pretty personal, pretty contemptuous.'

'It's childish, basic, primal.'

'Like flinging poo.'

'Indeed.'

'Whereas the drownings . . . it's somehow *disinterested*. The victims are random; I don't feel like there's genuine *ill-will* there.'

'Apart from the horrible deaths?'

'Precisely.

'Susan Beckett doesn't want help, so at this point I think our only option is to stake out her place on the next due date. Ziggi and I can wait until she goes to work, then sneak in. If it does happen again, maybe we'll catch someone brown-handed. If we scare he, she or it off, then we've saved Beckett some grief.'

Bela never approved of my plans when they involved bare-faced boldness and not much else, but some days there was no other choice; some days secrets were too well-buried. 'Well, Verity Fassbinder, what next?'

'Feeding my daughter. Cuddles with David. Then I'll talk to my mother.'

He smiled wryly. 'Good luck with that.'

Chapter Twenty

The scent of garlic bread wafted through the house, which immediately made me feel like I was *home*. I'd checked the nursery first thing, but it was back to being a spare bedroom. The cradle was no longer there, nor the change table, nor the rocking chair; a single duffle bag was at the foot of the bed, along with fluffy blue guest towels that I didn't even know we owned (they might have been from the stash of linen I'd inherited from my grandmother, or David had brought some unexpected dowry items). It looked like my mother had been well and truly installed.

I headed to our bedroom and found all the missing furniture had been crowded in there. David was lying on the bed, Maisie beside him on a crocheted rug, and they were both gurgling away happily. Only one was dribbling, which was a relief. Both of them smiled when they saw me, which was also a relief.

'Hey, you.' David sat up, and I leaned over and kissed him, then crawled onto the bed beside him and scooped up our daughter. 'Might as well have this one in here for a while. I thought your mum might want some privacy.' He rolled his eyes and added, 'It was the least I could do after she'd spent several hours being *very* politely interrogated by Bela.'

'Yup.' I arranged feeding matters to my child's satisfaction, then leaned back against the pillows and closed my eyes. I badly wanted to sleep for a very long time. I opened my eyes again and asked, 'Did you hear any of it?'

'Yeah. There was a lot of, "I fail to see how that's relevant, Zvezdomir".'

I couldn't help but grin. I bet Bela had been thinking, *Fucking apple doesn't fall far from the fucking tree!* Well, probably without the profanity.

'She's cooking dinner.'

'How very domestic. Bit late to play Mummy, though,' I said bitterly, then, 'Oh, shit, I forgot to order groceries.'

'I did that. Also, ixnay on the swearing in front of the babyay.'

'Worst pig Latin ever. But point taken.'

'So, honey, how was your day?'

Opening one eye, I gave him a long look, then surrendered any hope of napping and instead gave David the executive summary of the day's events, carefully leaving out precisely how handsome Jost Marolf was.

'So, partially productive then?'

'Partially. And there's one more thing.'

'What?'

His suspicious tone was entirely unjustified. I held up my right arm, showed him what Kadie Cross had put there.

'Oh.'

'It's just henna. It won't last, but it will offer some protection.' I hadn't said anything about how terrified I was when I'd told Kadie Cross about the drownings, but she must have sensed it, because she'd ordered me to sit, then without another word, she'd produced a small earthenware bowl, a bottle of henna, a brush and a scalpel, mixed the henna with a tiny bit of my blood, and painted a series of lines and curves on the inside of my wrist, rapping my arm when I fidgeted, tickled by the brush bristles. The tattoo looked kind of like a ladybird holding a sickle.

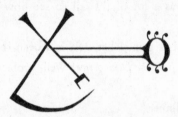

'This is *Vatnahlífir*. It's a protection rune against drowning,' I told David. I didn't repeat the rest of what Kadie Cross had told me: *It should keep you safe from the worst of it, but remember, it's only henna. You'll get about ten days, two weeks out of it, but it will eventually fade, so you might consider doing something more permanent later.*

One battle at a time.

'This is easy for you to copy,' she'd added. 'You'll want to mark your loved ones, keep them safe too. Give me your left hand.'

I did and she cut me again with the scalpel, a short, deeper slash on the fat pad of my palm, then held the injured limb over the bowl and let my thick dark blood dribble into the henna.

'Ouch!' I whined, but she just handed me a tissue and pointed to a little pile of Band-Aids and antiseptic cream on the desk. While I dealt with the first aid, she mixed the blood with the henna, which she decanted into a small bottle and handed to me, along with a new brush. 'This will bind your loved ones' safety to you, make it a stronger protection. Should be enough for three people, plus a touch up.'

That was David and Maisie, for sure. Ziggi and Bela both had the traditionalist's hatred of tattoos, the idea that it was an *easy* way of working magic. I loved them both, but I knew there was no way I'd be able to force them to sit down and be drawn upon. They were grown-ups; they would have to work out for themselves whether they were prepared to go to Kadie Cross for henna or the real thing. So: there remained only my mother.

There was some minor humming and hawing but, after Maisie, happy and full, fell asleep, I painted the rune on David's right wrist and our daughter's right heel. It felt like the easiest place to hide it, as neither of us particularly wanted some concerned citizen calling Child Safety Services down on us. As he waved his hand about to speed along the drying, David said, 'You know you're going to have to talk *to* her, V, and not least because she's living in our house.'

'I know,' I moaned, but I didn't yet know what to think about Olivia Fassbinder. She'd been dead pretty much my whole life and I had no memories of her. My grandparents hadn't talked about her; even when we went to visit her grave, it'd just been generalities. I was old enough to know that resenting her for dying was stupid and there wasn't much anyone could do about that – but now . . . ? Now she was decidedly alive – and worse, she must have been alive all along, which meant she'd *actively* chosen to leave me. Of course it was childish to think *abandoned* but I couldn't help but feel that sharp ache worming its way inside me. I'd spent so much of my life managing my emotions, trying not to lose my temper, trying not to give anyone the ability to hurt me, but now . . . now a big old ball of WTF had rolled into view. David and Maisie were *my* choices: I wanted them. I loved them. And Bela and Ziggi were there because I'd chosen them, made them my family . . . but Olivia Fassbinder? I had no happy childhood memories to hang onto, so she was just a mother-shaped absence in my life, and she had returned uninvited into it.

David was wise, and very much aware when to leave well enough alone; he'd made his point and now he'd let it percolate. I leaned my head on his shoulder and he kissed my hair, and we stayed like that until Maisie started snoring and my arms began to ache.

I got up and put her in the cradle. then I looked at David and poked out my tongue. 'Right then,' I said. 'Bullet being bitten.'

With dragging steps, and David following to make sure I didn't run away, I went out to the kitchen, where a not-dead woman was busy chopping tomatoes and crushing garlic.

'Olivia?'

She looked up.

'Got a moment? David will take care of things. Trust me, he's a far better cook than I am.'

'It's not that hard,' he said and I put a hand behind my back and flipped him the bird.

Olivia followed me out to the deck and as we sat, I took the bottle of henna from my pocket and shook it. 'Give me your wrist,' I said.

She didn't, just jerked her head at the bottle. 'What's it for?'

'Didn't Bela tell you? People are drowning on dry land,' I said.

'Yes, but what is this? No one marks me without my permission. Not any more.'

I lifted my sleeve and showed her the neat design drawn there. 'It's *Vatnahlífir*, a rune to—'

'—protect against drowning.'

'I have just enough henna for those I care about.'

Olivia blinked suddenly, fast. It took me a moment to realise she was fighting back tears.

'Don't be too overwhelmed,' I said meanly. 'You're under my roof and I've seen you in action. I want you alive and keeping my daughter safe when I'm not around.'

She snorted, all sign of tears gone, and held out her arm.

I'd drawn the first circle and was busy carefully adding the little legs on the side that turned it into a ladybird when I found myself asking, out of the blue, 'Did you cry? When you had me?'

'What?'

'When you had me. Did you find you were bawling for no reason?'

She laughed. 'All the time. I thought I was going mad. So did your father.'

That last part hung in the air like a stain. I cleared my throat. 'Why did you leave?'

I thought she wouldn't answer, and felt the anger growing inside me, but just as it was about to spray out, a great wash of profanity propelled by my inner spoiled brat, she began to speak.

'You . . . I . . . We . . .' She swallowed, took a deep breath and started again. 'When you were born, I was alone – I mean, I had your father, but my parents didn't want anything to do with me because they disapproved of him so much. We got married without much thought – I was pregnant, and that was just what you did then. I didn't even invite my parents to the wedding because I didn't want to give them any chance to snub me or make me miserable on that *special* day . . . and that was just the last straw, I think.' She licked her lips, and sighed. 'They'd gone on and on about Grigor – that he was no good, that he'd lead me to a bad end – and they were right, but who can see that when you're young and in love? I'd had a strict, sheltered upbringing, which made me easy prey for the first person who said he loved me. When you're so drunk on that first love, you don't notice what's in front of you, not even when all you've got to do is look.' Her voice dropped as she added, 'And you let them make a fool of you . . .'

She took the band off her ponytail and ran a hand through her hair, and now I could see the thick veins of white and silver running through. 'You make a fool of yourself because you think this man, who doesn't really care about *you*, who treats you like a convenience, or worse, a possession, is what love's all about, and you're terrified that at any moment that love will be taken away from you, and once it's gone, you'll never get it back.' She laughed, but it wasn't entirely bitter. 'You think that love is all there is in the world, and even if it's just a tiny scrap, it's the only amount allotted to you, and if you don't do everything possible to hang on to it – accept every insult, put up with every indignity – then you'll never be loved again.'

She looked at me, smiled. 'It's not true, you know.'

I swallowed and bent over her arm, trying to make sure the tremor I was feeling in my heart didn't make its way to my hand.

Olivia continued, 'When I had you I *really* had no one to turn to. There wasn't a soul I could ask all those dumb baby questions, no one who would care that was I crying at the drop of a hat. I didn't know anyone who could tell me that all that hormonal soup was perfectly natural. I had no family, no friends at all – I'd cut my Normal friends, girls from school, out of my life because of Grigor, but the Weyrd didn't like me at all, so no one on that side wanted to be my friend either. You should know that your father had been considered quite a catch, and I was really unpopular for landing him.'

Ah, there was the bitterness . . .

'I tried . . .' Her voice caught, trailed off and once again she had to gather herself. 'I tried, Verity – I tried really hard, for three *very* long years. And then . . . and then I found out what your father truly was.'

My heart went cold as I imagined Olivia, younger than I was now, left all alone, trying to cope with no support and then discovering that her husband, the father of her child, her '*catch*', was a *Kinderfresser* – not just a murderer, a killer of children, but the Butcher to the Weyrd, a child-*eater*, back when that sort of thing was still considered normal. I couldn't imagine how she must have felt, finding out that the man she loved, slept with, the man who held their baby and rocked her to sleep at night, was more monster than she could *ever* have imagined. Even knowing what she did about the Weyrd, that must have been a *huge* shock – and Grigor would have known it, because he'd deliberately kept that secret.

'That discovery came on top of untreated post-natal depression,' she added. 'It's no excuse, Verity. I shouldn't have run – or rather, I shouldn't have run without you. But it's a reason. Verity—' She stopped abruptly, then said, 'You've got corpselights.'

'Oh, are they back?' I felt as if I'd been pulled from a dream as I sat up and peered into the yard. The two little globes of foxfire were there again, peeking around the bole of the tree as if playing hide and seek, bright balls of light in the night.

'Been here a lot?' she asked.

'Only once – they're no harm. They're just wandering. They do that sometimes.'

Still my mother didn't relax. 'I think they're trying to get your attention.' She got up and moved to the verandah railing to watch the movement of the fool's fire. Then she started down the steps, and I followed.

The corpselights danced around and around the base of the big jacaranda tree until we reached the trunk, then they scootched back. We followed the odd little things, tracing the same path, until we came to the place in the trunk where there was a hollow, the spot where Lizzie kept a blanket, along with some of her dolls and comic books.

As we got closer I heard flies buzzing in spite of the cool winter weather, so I pulled out my mobile and hit the torch app. As I did so, I glanced over my shoulder.

'They're gone,' Olivia said, and she was right; they were nowhere to be seen, as if they'd done what they'd intended. We both sank into a crouch and I angled the beam of light into the maw of the tree.

The hollow was deep and shadowy, but the torch highlighted something that resolved into a single foot, still wearing a sneaker and sock, both of which were stained with old blood. The beam followed the foot which became a leg sticking out of the space; inside, was the body.

Chapter Twenty-One

'I'm sorry.' I sat on the grass in the darkness, the light from my mobile angled on Len the delivery guy's dead face, showing the sharp chin with its three-day growth, the dreadlocks with their colourful beads, the dried-up red-brown cataract at his throat where someone had run a knife across it. Galina and Ziggi had been down and examined the body, then returned to their respective posts, but I forced myself to keep looking at him, burning what had been done to him into my memory. It was the least I owed him: an enduring recollection, and the promise to punish whoever had done this.

No, not *who*ever.

I knew *who*.

Olivia had crawled in beside Len – no respect for crime scene preservation; I'd have to have a word about that – and examined the wound. Her voice echoed as she said, 'Cut's very clean. An extremely sharp knife, for up close and personal.'

'Like a tantō, perhaps?'

She looked over her shoulder at me, considering. We both saw the weapon the Librarian had drawn from her satchel.

'Odds are good.' Olivia backed out, a duck-waddle crouch, and turned without straightening, no wobbling, perfectly balanced. I couldn't have done that on my best day and she had twenty-odd years on me. My mother held out her hand. 'And then there's this.'

A tuft of reddish fur lay on her palm. Not that I'd had any doubt the fox-girl had been involved.

'Did she leave that behind, do you think? As a calling card? Or did he put up a fight?'

'No defensive wounds as far as I can see, but an autopsy in a better light might find differently. I think he followed willingly as she led him here – he's a man; he'd have followed, poor dumb bastard, especially if she asked for help and looked all sweet and innocent.' She spat. 'It's the sort of thing she'd do: she's less confrontational than the others, but sneakier.'

'So you know her? Them?'

'We've moved in the same circles,' my mother said evasively.

'Right.' I knew a half-truth when I heard it. 'That's all you've got to say?'

'For now.' She looked at me. 'That's all I've got that's useful, Verity.'

So that was it: our cosy conversation from earlier was done and I still knew nothing about her death, or lack thereof, her relationship with the *kitsune* – or whether she was anything to do with why they were targeting me. We'd be revisiting those subjects, but I reckoned I'd get more out of her if I waited until she was feeling vulnerable again. And for the moment I had enough on my proverbial plate.

'Might he have been involved with them?' she asked.

'As far as I could tell, he was a nice ordinary guy. He had a date with her sister, Gothic Alice, a couple of days before the incident in the Valley. Let's assume that was to ask about me: who was in the house, did anyone else get mail there, had my mother come visiting – stuff like that, basic intelligence-gathering. All the Librarian would have had to do was show her pretty face, say her sister wanted to meet him here. Or watch my house while we were away, approach him, make up some story, then a blitz attack . . .' I stared at the fur, strangely luminous in the torchlight. 'Poor bastard. But why him?'

'To send a message: kill an innocent, make you feel guilty.'

'What about you?'

She didn't answer. Time to call in the troops.

McIntyre wasn't delighted to hear from me when I told her she didn't need to question Len anymore and where to find him. We spoke briefly; the majority of the call was her cursing.

'She didn't sound happy. Will she come?' asked my mother, who clearly didn't deal with people like Rhonda McIntyre very often.

'She'll be along presently, complaining loudly. It's just part of her charm. Or something.' I rose, scratched my head and sighed. 'Olivia, do you know how to bake lavender bread and mix ward paint?'

She looked a little offended. 'Of course I do! I was doing that when you were still in nappies.'

'Will you tell David about Len – and ask him to show you where everything is. I'm going to wait down here until McIntyre turns up.' As she headed towards the steps, I called, 'Olivia?' and when she paused, 'It's a message for both of us, isn't it. You're the one she's after, aren't you?'

My mother didn't quite answer. 'Do you want me to leave?'

'Fuck no. I want you here where I can set wards – she only got in because there was nothing stronger than low-grade mozzie repellent; you might recall I was a little preoccupied with the whole giving-birth-in-a-filthy-alley-and-getting-airlifted-to-Byron-Bay thing. I want you and your sword and your special skills-set where I can see you, where I know you're safe, and where you can protect my daughter and my lover when I'm not around.' I stopped, catching my breath.

I want you here when you finally decide to tell me everything.

'So don't fucking leave, okay?'

Because if I have to hunt you down I'll be royally pissed.

'Okay,' she turned away, threw over her shoulder, 'And don't fucking swear.'

She stomped up the stairs, muttering about *potty-mouth* and it was all I could do not to laugh . . . right until I remembered poor old Len.

'I'm sorry,' I said yet again, but what else could I say? Len had the most tenuous possible connection to me, but that brief acquaintance had got him killed. He'd done nothing to deserve this, just been in the wrong place at the wrong time.

But something else was bothering me. I was missing something, but I couldn't quite put my finger on it.

A movement caught my attention: a small brown cat was padding along the fence. It froze when it realised it had been seen, but it was a calm reaction, more cool defiance than any kind of fear . . . then in the blink of an eye, everything changed. It raised its head and arched its back, its fur turning into something resembling porcupine hackles. Its legs stiffened, and in less than a second it was gone, trailing an astonishing *hiss!* behind it.

In another second, I realised why.

There was a bright flash to my right, then other: the corpselights had returned. They hovered about two metres in front of me, almost tentatively, as if they were uncertain of their welcome. I didn't want to spook them, so I spoke gently. 'Hi there.'

They didn't reply – not much given to chitchat, corpselights – but bobbed up and down, as if in response to my words. I remembered the Boatman had told me that the dead on their last journey have no voice and no power to object to their fate – but these corpselights weren't on their final voyage with the Boatman, which begged the question: had they escaped before that had come to pass, or had they got away from wherever he'd deposited them? Both options were equally disturbing, but either way, if they had no voice they couldn't tell me why they were here or what they wanted. Or why they'd chosen me. I'd always been crap at interpretive dance . . .

'I'm sorry, little ones, I can't do much if you can't tell me what you need . . .'

With that, they began to vibrate, slowly at first, then with increasing speed, as if some great invisible godly hand had hold of them and was shaking them like they were snow globes. They began to break into shards, each piece still whirring madly as it lengthened, until each shard had settled into a new place in a new shape.

Each column of light had legs and arms, hands and feet, and a head with facial features.

Two delicate girls stood before me, all washed-out hues. The elder was maybe fourteen, the other a little younger, but it was difficult to be sure because it was hard to look for too long into their shining faces. The smaller one clutched a battered teddy-bear. The older girl had her arm around her; on her wrist was a bracelet of coral pieces. I didn't need to see the colour to know it would be a lurid orangey-pink. I'd had the same kind of cheap trinket myself as a kid. They stared at me expectantly.

'I'm so sorry,' I said, 'but I don't know what to do. You have to tell me what to do, okay?'

But no information was forthcoming, and when the silence of the evening was shattered by McIntyre yelling at me from the driveway that ran down the side of the house, my visitors burst into points of light, coalesced into spheres once more and disappeared.

Skittish little things, corpselights.

I grabbed up my phone, scrambled to my feet – and glanced

back at Len. 'They'll take care of you now,' I said. I tried not to think of what that meant: lying on a slab in the morgue, with Ellen's tender mercies being visited upon him. His family would have to be notified, but that wouldn't be my job; somewhere, his mother and father would grieve for him, siblings, uncles, aunts – or maybe there was no one; perhaps there would just be me to remember.

I wondered if Len would quietly take his last ride with the Boatman, or just hang about my tree, looking for vengeance or justice? As far as I knew, most folk went willingly enough – which was just as well, otherwise we'd be overrun by spirits of all sorts. But there were some, particularly those with an axe to grind or gone too soon or unfairly, who made a point of sticking around in some form or other: a voice on a breeze, a crying in the night, or perhaps ghosts or corpselights, depending on the circumstances of their demise and their personal inclinations. They might become rusalkas or revenants, even vampires or zombies (not the Hollywood Romero kind but the traditional sort with no will of their own, who go back to being dead if you feed them salt).

Len didn't strike me as the type to hang around; he'd always seemed too laid back – but then, what did I really know about him? He'd always been polite to me, and appeared to be efficient at his job, but I didn't know the depths of his heart, or the weight of his sins.

McIntyre's two SOCOs began setting up portable spotlights so they could find anything that might have been dropped and I thought I'd better confess up front that (a) I'd been sitting on that spot of depressed grass, and (b) my mother had removed a tuft of fur from the victim's hand. I handed it over, and McIntyre didn't shout at me at all – but only because I'd asked her not to wake the baby. To placate her, I told her what I'd learned about Grand Drownings and that further information was on its way, but probably not at an acceptable speed for either of us. I told her about Jerry's death, then I advised her to take Ellen to Kadie Cross for their non-birthday-related tattoos. *Both* of them. Just in case.

When she finished swearing at the idea of getting a tattoo, I said soothingly, 'Rhonda, most of your officers have a bit of body art under their shirts nowadays. Why should you be an exception?'

'Someone has to be.'

'It'll make you cool.'

'Fuck off.' She pointed at Len. 'So, what's this guy's story?'

'My delivery guy. Story's simple: wrong place, wrong time.'

'Poor bastard. You're dangerous to know.'

I didn't feel like pursuing that line of conversation, so I asked after the hapless Constable Oldman.

'Young Lacy has declared the whole security footage viewing a dead-end. She's quite bitter – and she's not actually finished the task.'

'Kids these days: no staying power! Tell her to keep going. Remember, *she* doesn't get to call time, *you* get that privilege on account of being the boss with *years* of experience.' For once, I stopped there.

I turned to look at the back deck of the house, where David and Olivia stood silhouetted against the inside lights. 'Look, there's something else you need to know.'

Normally Rhonda McIntyre greets my pronouncements with a grumble and a grunted comment dripping vinegar about why couldn't I keep the Weyrd under better control (as if it were something I had a say in), and a pithy insult or three. Filling in the meagre details about my Lazarus mother for once knocked both pith and vinegar out of her.

Her eyes went wide and her eyebrows were raised, furrowing in her forehead; she blinked several times and her mouth moved for a while before words came out.

'I . . . I never thought of you as actually having a mother,' she managed at last.

'What? That I was *hatched*? Brought forth from the thigh of Zeus?' I sighed. 'That's her up on the deck. No, don't stare – what did you not get about *don't stare?*'

'Well, I . . . I – well.' She clearly didn't know what to do with her hands; perhaps they were destined to wave in ineffectual circles for the rest of the evening.

'There's not really any small talk to be made on the subject of Olivia Fassbinder, née Brennan,' I conceded. 'But, Rhonda, she was *dead*. More than one person has sworn to that fact. And yet she's been disturbingly silent on the matter of her resurrection.'

'And you can't beat it out of her?'

I tilted my head to one side. 'Don't think I haven't considered it – but even I have limits. Besides, she's freaky fast and freaky strong. She'd kick my arse in a matter of seconds.'

'I'd almost pay to see that,' the inspector said wistfully.

'Hey! You're on my side, remember? Look, my friend, I need your help. Shit-a-brick, I don't even know her birth date. She's in her early to mid-fifties, if that's any use.' I scratched my head and she gave me a flat stare. 'Oh, for fuck's sake, just be helpful for a change.'

And I told her what I wanted.

Although Wanda's precautions at Ocean's Reach hadn't stopped the water eidolon, I could at least keep the fox-girl at bay. After all, she hadn't got into the house, just the back yard, although I couldn't know if she'd actually tried the house or not. I'd "accidentally" not handed over all of the red fox-fur to McIntyre but given some to

Olivia to bake into the bread – foxes hate the smell of lavender, and adding the Librarian's own pelt personalised the wards.

Once the lavender loaves had cooled enough, Olivia and David buried one at each corner of the yard. With Maisie on one hip, I went around the house and painted extra wards over every door and window.

I called Bela to let him know about Len, so he could make sure his fellow Councillors understood that the fox-girl remained a threat; that she hadn't been cowed by the deaths of her sisters, then I took Ziggi out a hot chocolate and another blanket to try and make him a bit more comfortable in his cab. He was stubbornly refusing to come inside and sleep on the couch – he said he wanted to be out there where he could see any threat coming. I refrained from pointing out that threats didn't generally present themselves politely, proffering calling cards that said 'Threat' or 'Villain' like visiting Victorian gentlemen. If I concentrated, I could just about make out the shivering outlines of large Weyrd perched in trees up and down the street; there were more hidden in the yards surrounding my place.

I said in the back with my own cocoa and started, 'So, you ready to talk yet?'

He gave a big sigh, which I thought would precede a refusal to discuss the question of *Jägers*, but to my surprise, it didn't.

'My family . . . *my family*.' He half-turned in his seat, but didn't look at me, just stared out at the front fence. '*Jäger* means hunter, and my family was noted for producing very fine *Jägers* – not only that, but it's what we were particularly known for. The *Jägers* served the kings and queens of Europe, both Normal and Weyrd, those above and below the earth. The best stables held at least one of Hassman lineage – we were valued not only for our abilities, but for our viciousness too: we Hassmans gloried in the hunt, the chase, the kill. You know the legends of Herne the Hunter? He was one of ours – a distant cousin, but shared blood nonetheless.'

He took a sip, then went on, 'We were prized, it's true, but we were servants – no, not even servants, we were really no more than *pets*: kept in silken kennels and rewarded with toys of gold and rubies – but all the treasure in the world meant nothing, because we weren't free to leave our masters.' He rubbed his face and I noticed his fingers were trembling.

'The best of the *Jägers* were born with an eye in the back of the head so they could see what was coming behind them.' He lifted a hand and passed it over the place where his ginger hair was thinnest, where his own extra eye sat. 'By the time I was born, the world had changed. The Normal kings were being cast down and the Weyrd kings had gone further into darkness, trying to hide, to protect what was left. Their subject populations were scattering far and wide as Europe was shattered from within and without. But there were still places where the Weyrd held sway, and one of those was Thuringia. It's heavily forested and there are many places to hide, to live as what we are.' He looked at me then as if begging my understanding.

I wasn't sure yet what I needed to understand. 'Go on,' I said gently.

'When I reached the age of blooding, when I should have taken over from my mother as *Jäger* to the Dark Queen of Thuringia, I fled. I refused to do what was expected of me.'

'What happened?'

He didn't answer, and there was an impatient edge to my tone when I said, 'Ziggi?'

'My brother saved us. I'd have been hunted down and my family put to death because of my actions – but my brother . . . he bound himself to one of the Queen's sons, and that son interceded.' We sat in silence for a while. 'There's a good reason why the undines and their like have no fondness for my kind,' he added.

' But that's not you — *you* didn't hunt. You risked yourself and your family not to.'

'It doesn't matter; they only know that I wear the shape of a *Jäger*. My history's not written on my skin: there's no sign of my refusal to serve, my sacrifices. All they see is how I look, and they're afraid.'

I leaned forward and pressed my cheek against his. 'I'm sorry, my friend. I shouldn't have asked.'

'You had to know sometime, V.'

Back inside, I showered and climbed into bed. David ignored the vast empty acreage of our huge mattress and instead curled around my back, his breath tickling my ear, moving my hair gently. I welcomed the contact; I *needed* him there. We'd talked about Len, but I hadn't mentioned the corpselights, or their brief transformation. He had enough on his mind.

The more I thought about it, the more the *kitsune*'s act smacked of bravado. She'd seen what my mother could do — she'd lost two sisters to Olivia's wicked blade — and it looked like she wasn't going to make the mistake of getting too close. Maybe she'd try to pick off the people around us, death by a thousand cuts. Was she trying to force me into giving up my mother? Maybe she figured it would only take a few bodies, a few lost friends, and I'd turn on Olivia: one life in exchange for many.

Of course, the fox-girl didn't know me at all; she couldn't know that manipulation like that just pissed me off. It made me even more stubborn and determined. I would locate her boltholes, I'd make any allies regret the day they'd met her. I would find her in the end, and then I would be *very* unpleasant to deal with.

There was no way I'd give my mother up.

However, Olivia Fassbinder would be answering some questions for me, whether she wanted to or not . . . just as soon as McIntyre got back to me with the ammunition I needed.

Chapter Twenty-Two

The thing about spook shops is that after the second or third one they all start to blend together; sometimes you wonder if you've walked back into the one you just left. I had a photo of Susan Beckett from her driver's licence, which McIntyre might possibly have slipped my way when no one was looking, and was waving it about as I asked for the umpteenth time whether she'd been into whichever shop this was looking for information or supplies for cleansing rituals. In the spirit of 'two birds with one stone', I was also enquiring about a lone *kitsune*. Although the response was always *no*, I followed up with warnings about not offering her aid, as well as exhortations to call me *immediately*, should she happen to appear.

Thus far I was zip for zip on both counts and Ziggi was dropping increasingly unsubtle hints that it was well past time for lunch. I don't know where he puts all the food he consumes: yes, he's a tall, broad guy but he never gains a kilo. *Bastard*.

Asking the same questions, getting the same answers, smelling the same incense, needing to find somewhere to express milk every few hours, were all taking toll; by the time we were on our tenth or eleventh shop my temper was distinctly frayed. Third Eye Books was misleading; even though there were tomes on New Age Spirituality, Old Wicca, New Wicca, spells, magical cooking, magical thinking, magical dressing, brewing potions, how to get the best out

207

of a smudge ceremony and books by a bewildering array of gurus who swore by various methods of yoga, meditation, eating systems, mindfulness, body and attitude realignments, they didn't even fill a whole wall; it wasn't a book store per se. The shop was hidden away in the leafy suburban streets of St Lucia, not far from the University of Queensland campus, and it catered to the area's unique combination of bored moneyed housewives and impoverished and, in some cases not so impoverished, uni students.

When we walked in, the proprietor bustled out from the iridescent purple and green curtains that hid the backroom, her lip curling as she saw me.

Merrily Vaughan did a roaring trade telling fortunes – her readings generally managed to be broad enough to allow a range of interpretations – and selling charms to students not entirely confident about their exam results. She was mixed-blood, like me, but unlike me, she had no power. Some strangelings were okay with that. Some were okay with it, but only because they didn't know what they might be missing out on, so they didn't spend time bemoaning the loss of the greatness that might have been theirs had their DNA only combined a little differently.

Merrily Vaughan wasn't one of those: she heartily resented not having anything of the fantastical about her, so she'd spent her life trying to force magic to cling to her in some way, shape or form. She'd learned all the rituals and spells that would allow her to *occasionally* perform some tiny miracles – of course, you didn't need Weyrd blood for that, just intent, the right tools and a willingness to pay the price (in short: the more red stuff you spill, the greater effect you might have) – although it's true that having a touch of the Weyrd in your veins can make the spells stronger, more powerful; *more dangerous*.

She was mostly harmless, but the problem with Merrily was that even though she could *sometimes* do something spectacular, her spells tended to go wrong. In the way of deluded individuals the world over, she pretended she was better at it than she was; that she'd found a way to overcome the dud hand dealt her by the Universe.

That was generally where the problems started.

The day we met, a few years ago, she'd been employed by a gentleman best described as a fool looking to be rapidly parted with his money, who'd wanted her to bring his companion 'demon' through. A voice had been talking to him in his sleep, promising to make his life better if only he'd open the door for it, which showed a basic lack of understanding about demons. Merrily Vaughan took a sizeable chunk of his cash, conducted an ill-considered ritual – and succeeded in bringing *something* across. The *something* wrecked her shop and almost killed her and the client. They'd managed to hole up in the storeroom out back and she'd called Bela, who'd called me. To her credit, the *something* was trapped because she'd done a good job on the wards (although she did later admit she'd done that so the *client* couldn't leave the shop without paying extra). Luckily for me, my mixed heritage meant her spells didn't hinder me, so I was able to waltz in and clean up the mess. I still have a long scar on my left shoulder from razor-sharp claws, and Vaughan still owes me for a ruined leather jacket.

Some people aren't grateful even when you save their sorry arses from their own stupidity.

'Morning, Merrily,' I said, oozing cheer while Ziggi wandered around the store, taking in the stock: mass-produced tarot cards, overpriced candlesticks with equally expensive candles to go therein, incense, spiritual soap, wind-chimes, dream-catchers, massage oil, crystals, sarongs, fishermen's pants, scarves, shawls, tapes for meditation, yoga DVDs, magic make-up, perfumes heavy on patchouli, even some stuff I didn't recognise. Three bijou – for which read *very small* – tables were set up for tea and tarot.

'What do you want?' Merrily looked as if she was giving serious consideration to the 'flee' option, but unless the layout had changed, there was nowhere to go. This was a time when she could really have used an emergency exit, but there was none, which I was pretty sure was illegal.

'Is that any way to greet the woman who saved you from an angry *aka manah* demon?' I asked, and saw her hands stroke her backside, where I knew there was a series of scars made by the same talons that had scored my shoulder. She wouldn't soon forget them, although I had no doubt she'd like to, very much.

'How can I help you, Ms Fassbinder?' Her tone changed, suddenly so polite it made me wonder what she was up to.

I showed her the photo of Susan Beckett. 'Have you had any dealings with this woman recently?'

'Has she complained?' Her voice rose a couple of notches, and a red blush went from her neck up to the hairline where I could still see a little tidemark from her last dye job. Was it possible she disliked someone even more than she disliked me? *Bravo*.

'What would Susan Beckett have to complain about, Merrily?'

She harrumphed. 'I sold her a perfectly good protective ritual for home and hearth, all the trimmings, the primo stuff. If she didn't do it right that's not my look out. They seldom do, Normals; they don't have the attention to detail . . . And if she lied to me about the nature of the problem . . .' Merrily let her outrage hang for a moment. 'Well, that's her lookout. I don't give refunds.'

I opened my eyes wide; that wasn't entirely true. Her erstwhile demon-seeker had had his money back, and then some, to shut him up. 'What did she say it was for?'

Merrily clearly didn't want to tell me, but she just as clearly wanted me gone. I followed her gaze as she looked past me and through the store window. Across the road a group of five or six women were piling out of a silver 4x4, a Mercedes GLS 350. One of them was talking animatedly and pointing towards Third Eye Books. Ah: bored – *wealthy* – matrons; no doubt Merrily thought I'd be bad for business. Can't think why.

'Talk fast, Merrily and we'll be out of your hair before those plump pigeons get to the front door.'

'Right: so her house is flooding with mud once a month – well, puddles of it, really, and it stinks like a bastard. She claimed it was an unfriendly spirit.' Merrily pursed her lips, then said confidentially, 'But what she described didn't sound like a spirit to me, more like a curse. Well, that's what I thought, but calling a client a liar isn't a good business move.'

'On this rare occasion I'm inclined to agree with you.' I gave Ziggi the *Let's go* chin jut. 'Okay, Merrily, keep us both happy and stay out of trouble.'

Ziggi was outside already and I was almost at the door, although the women across the road were still fussing with hair and make-up and what I'd probably incorrectly assumed were fake Louis Vuitton totes, when Merrily said, 'Oi!'

I looked askance at her.

'What about me, Ms Big Shot?'

'What about you?'

'I've been the victim of a crime!'

'There's real police for that.'

'Not for this, not for what was taken,' she said, and smiled slyly.

I sighed. 'What was taken?'

'Powdered *Egeria densa*, a bag of labradorite crystals and seven toads' bladders.'

'Waterweed,' I said, frowning. 'Rocks and offal.'

'Well, yes.'

'Any idea who the perpetrator was?' I asked, more out of habit than hope.

'Some short-arsed bastard asking about love charms,' she said crossly. 'He must have gone out the back while I was dealing with another customer – it's not stuff I keep on display, you know. I'm not that irresponsible,' she said defensively.

'Okay.' I rubbed my head. Kadie Cross' rock had been taken in similar circumstances. 'What are those things used for?'

She shrugged. 'Together? I don't really know. I use the waterweed in a moisturiser, the labradorite in jewellery, and the bladders are for . . . well, I mix them with dried cranberries and—'

'Does this guy look familiar?' I selected the image of Wilbur Wilson and held up my phone.

Merrily's expression twisted with vicious joy, as if she'd found a way to screw with two people: me, and Wilbur Wilson. 'That's him! Ugly little shit! Love charms my arse, no one in their right mind—'

'Clients,' I said under my breath as the bell over the door clanged and the gaggle of women in search of their fortunes clattered in on sky-high heels. They'd have done better to go to Little Venice, although they might not have liked what they heard there. In Merrily's favour, she always tried to give happy fortunes, even if it had a lot to do with knowing on which side her bread was buttered.

'That's helpful, Merrily,' I said, to the surprise of us both. 'I'll get back to you if I find him.'

'Just get my stuff. I'm not made of money, Fassbinder.'

'Nor apparently of sugar and spice and all things nice.' I clicked my fingers. 'Oh, and any *kitsune* been around?'

'Wouldn't serve 'em if they did.'

'Not like you to be fussy.'

'Hey – they're *assassins*, Fassbinder. I do have standards, you know!'

Once back in the cab, I asked, 'So what spell needs those ingredients?'

'No idea,' Ziggi said. 'Remember, those might not be the only ingredients.' He jerked his head in the direction of Third Eye Books. 'Do you think that's all she knows?'

I shrugged. 'She's pretty much kept her nose clean since that last big mess. She doesn't like me, but she's also kind of afraid of me, so I don't think she'd dare mess me about, at least not much, and not on the big stuff.'

'Okay then,' he said. 'Where to now?'

'Let's go to Soteria. I'll have a chat with Alex Parrish and let him know we've found at least one place Susan Beckett went to for help outside of the insurance company.'

As he took off at speed, he said, 'Maybe let Bela know too. He might recognise those ingredients, or at least what they're used in.'

As soon as Bela picked up, I asked, 'Do you know what powdered *Egeria densa*, labradorite crystals and toads' bladders are used for?'

'If I do, is there a prize?'

'We've been to Third Eye Books, and not only did Susan Beckett buy a protective ritual from there, but the mysterious Wilbur Wilson – who you might remember from such thefts as Kadie Cross' favourite rock – stole those things from Merrily Vaughan, and Merrily is *not* happy.'

'With you in her store I'm not surprised.'

'Can you be helpful?'

'Waterweed, crystals and bladders.' There was a pause, then, 'I haven't heard of that combination, but maybe it would make more sense if we knew the other ingredients . . . there are so many spells, so many personal grimoires, every witch in the history of the world has mixed and matched their own spells . . .'

'MasterWitch. My Witchen Rules.'

He ignored me. 'And it might also be one of the great spells, the hidden spells, something powerful and personal and barely used nowadays. Have you heard from Jost yet?'

'Nope. That was my next request: can you give him a poke? See if he can't move a little faster on the whole researching and the finding of the answers things.'

'I'll ask nicely,' he said.

'Sure, that might work.'

'And, V? I wanted to let you know that Mike will be joining the team at your place.'

'Really? Shouldn't he be' – grieving? weeping? contemplating the wreck of his life? – 'resting?'

'I think he needs something to occupy his mind. You can understand that, surely?'

I nodded, realised he couldn't see me, then said, 'Yeah, you're right . . . but I think I have a better idea.'

When we got to the Soteria offices the wooden door was open, the lights were on inside, but the reception area was deserted. A cup sat on the top of the desk, steam rising from it, so it hadn't been there long. That's when I noticed dark patches of damp on the red carpet and a squelching beneath my boots. I yelled at Ziggi, '*It's here!*'

Only one of the office doors was closed, and it was locked. I kicked it, and the thing flew off its hinges. Even I was impressed.

With Ziggi close behind me, we staggered into a conference room mostly filled with a long oval table and comfy leather chairs. At the far end I could see a purple pagoda-style umbrella held up like a defensive weapon. Alicia Parrish was backed into a corner, and behind her was a slumped shape which might have been her father. On the table were splashes of water that were moving sluggishly back towards the row of windows, where they reassembled into an eidolon like the one I'd seen at Ocean's Reach. I wondered how long she'd held it at bay, and how long she could continue to do so.

The eidolon drew itself up, tensing for another attack, and Alicia screamed.

I sprinted towards her and with equal measures of idiocy and speed, put myself between Alicia and the eidolon just before it launched itself. Then it was on me and I was drowning and cursing the misplaced faith I'd put in Kadie Cross' *Vatnahlífir* rune.

Chapter Twenty-Three

'*What the actual fucking fuck—?!*'

I couldn't recall any time in our history when Ziggi had been quite so angry with me, or at least quite so sweary – not even when I'd wandered into a sewer tunnel on my own and got attacked by a garbage golem. Or when I wandered off on my own into a deserted house and got attacked by a 'serker. Mind you, my brain was feeling pretty scrambled, so I might have been forgetting something.

'What. Were. You. *Thinking?*' continued Ziggi, his voice getting even louder.

When I finally answered with all the dignity I could muster, what I managed to say was, 'Insofar as I was thinking at all, I figured my options were limited and it was as good a time as any to test out the rune.'

And it had kept me safe, despite my initial panic: the eidolon splashed up against me, going straight for my nose, mouth and ears, but it was expelled quick-smart. I was soaked through, my clothes and hair and skin dripping wet, but the creature had effectively been repelled and it dissipated, just as the one at Ocean's Reach had after its work was done. At least this one had achieved no job satisfaction at all.

While he was shouting at me, Ziggi propped me up in a chair at the head of the table. Alicia was dividing her attention between me and her father; Alex's forehead bore a vicious-looking cut. Ziggi started pacing back and forth, arms windmilling. 'Of all the irresponsible things! Leaving me to explain to David and Bela and your mother how you died—? You've got a *daughter*, V—'

'A fact of which I am well aware, so don't try to make me feel worse that I already do!' I yelled. It was taking all my self-control not to start crying, so the anger was good; the anger was my friend: it burned the tears away. 'Look, it was the only way I could think of to avoid more deaths – and we learned something about it.'

'Dumb-arse way to learn *anything*,' he muttered, his voice less shouty.

'Have you had your rune done yet?' I asked, knowing full well he hadn't. The lack of answer told me *no*, and I continued, 'Then you couldn't have fucking done anything, could you? It had to be me or we would have been mopping up one or both of these fine people.'

He huffed and puffed, sat and gave me some serious side-eye, but at least he'd calmed down.

'So how about you get a tattoo? How about you get it today? It doesn't even have to be permanent – it can be henna, just like mine. It can be hidden, so no one suspects you're taking the easy way out. How about you do it so I have one fewer person to worry about?' We glared at each other for long moments. If watching the eidolon go for me hadn't been enough to overcome his pride, then I didn't know what would be.

He muttered, 'I'll tell David what you did.'

'I'll tell Aspasia you said the angel's blessing cake is too rich.'

'You wouldn't!'

'Try me.' I looked at the bedraggled Parrishes. 'You guys should go and see Kadie Cross too – tell her I sent you.'

'While I'm enormously grateful for this timely visit, *what the hell was that thing?*' Alex sounded stunned.

'I'm calling it a water eidolon. It's already killed three people, and for some reason one of you was to be its next victim.'

'Why?' Alicia's eyes widened; she looked as if she was fighting to hold back the tears. 'What have we done?'

'Have you pissed anyone off? Cancelled anyone's cover? Or refused to pay out?'

Alex shook his head, then as he grimaced and put a hand to the seeping cut, Alicia said, 'He fell and hit his head on the corner of the front desk. It was the only thing that saved him – the eidolon missed him and hit the wall. That's the only reason we had time to get in here. We locked the door, but . . .'

'It went under, didn't it?'

'Yes.' She bit her bottom lip.

'The brolly was quick thinking.'

She looked pleased, in spite of her fear and worry.

'Get a doctor or a healer to look at your head, Alex, and after that, straight over to Mindy's Mehndi, okay?'

'Do you know anything else about this . . . monster?' asked Alex.

'It might be the result of a curse-spell, what's called a Grand Drowning – heard of it?' A blank look was my answer. I thought for a moment, then added, 'Actually, from what I just saw, I'm beginning to wonder if it's only got a limited time to do its thing . . . at least, I think that's it . . . it seemed kind of . . . well, more *anxious* than the last one, yet more sluggish.'

'There're *others* out there?' Alicia's voice was a lot steadier than I'd expected.

'Not as a naturally occurring phenomenon, if that helps. Someone's *sending* it, deliberately. There have been three dry-land drownings so far. I've been trying to establish links between the victims, but not with much luck, before you ask.' I sighed, staring at them. 'Do either of you know a Toby Malone, or a Faraday Hannigan?' I didn't mention Jerry; he hadn't been the intended victim, just in the wrong place at the wrong time.

Neither father nor daughter recognised either name. Back to Square One.

I pulled my damp shirt out of my jeans and wrung the tails, dribbling water onto the table, although it didn't make much difference to the dampness quotient; I was going to freeze the moment I stepped outside. 'Actually, the reason we came was to tell you that Susan Beckett went to a spook shop – Third Eye Books, by the St Lucia campus, if you know it – and purchased spiritual cleansing supplies. She told the owner she was dealing with a haunting.' I paused. 'Do you . . . do you think Susan Beckett might have done this to you?'

'I don't see why,' Alex said. He looked perplexed. 'She rang this morning to cancel her cover herself – I didn't even have to mention that we'd been intending to do just that. It was all very civil.'

'She cancelled *before* you cut her off? That doesn't mean she wouldn't want some payback . . .'

'No, I don't think she'd get anything out of something like that. Susan's always struck me as someone who only does something if she'll benefit from it. She's very calculating.'

I tapped my nails on the table, making little splashes in the puddles, then played with a tenuous thought running around in my head. 'Alicia, did you have any visitors this morning? New clients, old clients?'

'Just an odd little man, asking about policies – he wanted to talk to Dad, but he was on a conference call and I knew he'd be tied up for a while, so I asked him to come back later.'

'Was he okay with that?'

'He seemed fine.'

'Did he give you a name?'

'Nope.'

I gave my mobile a shake and prayed to whoever might be listening that it would still work after the inundation. The screen lit up and I breathed a sigh of relief, silently promising libations . . . well, at least the intent was there. I handed the phone to Alicia, who stared at Wilbur Wilson with horrified fascination.

'Did *he* do this to us? *Why?*'

'I don't know. You don't know him, apart from today?'

'Not at all. He was so polite!'

'What about you, Alex? Ever encountered Mr Wilbur Wilson? He claims to be in the legal profession . . .'

He took the phone and squinted in concentration. 'I don't recognise him at all, Verity, but . . . there's something . . .' He held the screen closer. 'Maybe it's the phone? Because of the water, perhaps? Or I'm just imagining it, but his outline looks—'

'—shaky,' I guessed. I couldn't see it, but it confirmed that Alex Parrish was more than he appeared: there was definitely Weyrd in his veins, if he could see the vibrations such spells made. 'Wilbur's got a lot of glamours over him – I'm not sure what he's trying to cover, but it's really battling with whatever he is underneath.'

I pushed my chair back and stood. 'Alex, my very strong recommendation is that you shut up shop for a while until you hear from either Bela or me. Don't answer the door to anyone who looks like a short, unhappy man – better yet, can you go away for a while? I don't know how Wilbur Wilson fits into this mess, but he does, and I'll find out – or die trying.'

'Don't even joke about that,' said Ziggi, and I patted his shoulder.

'What about Susan Beckett?' asked Alex Parrish. 'We don't cover her any more so she's no longer our problem – so there's no need to investigate any more—'

'Oh, she's still a problem, just not yours.' I zipped up my jacket, in the vain hope of not instantly icing up the moment we stepped outside. 'But in the event you do hear from her, let me know – and if she wants anything, refuse. Refer her to me.'

'Do you think she'll ask for help?' he asked sceptically.

'No, I don't, not willingly. But if we cut off other avenues, it might just funnel her towards me.' I rubbed my face. 'She wants to keep her secrets, but somehow, I don't think they're affecting only her.'

'Could . . . could she have sent Wilson?' asked Alicia, uncertainly.

That gave me pause; was the attack on the Parishes less random than the others? More targeted? Personal?

'I really don't know,' I admitted at last. 'Now, go. Healer, tattoos, henna, ink, whatever, then home. Lock your doors.'

When we got home, Ziggi refused to leave the cab again – part sulking, part determined to stay on guard. I promised I'd bring him dinner later – and I also promised I wouldn't have cooked it; I didn't have the heart to pile injury on top of insult. The moment I started up the path I heard the sounds of a heated argument from the front verandah, and spotted two figures gesticulating wildly. One was Galina, looking all fit and dangerous in her usual black outfit; the other was Constable Lacy Oldman, looking very policey in her light blue uniform shirt, blue leather jacket, navy combat trousers and big boots. Me, I was still damp and shivering and my breasts ached like nobody's business.

'Hey, hey!' I hissed as I approached. 'If you wake a sleeping baby and my mother doesn't get to you first, David will be really, *really* politely angry.'

They stared at me in surprise.

'Oh, c'mon. Everyone knows I'm phoning in the parenting.' The honesty was painful. I waved at Galina. 'It's okay, I know her. Well, kind of.'

My head of security said nothing, but she gave me *a look* as she moved away so quickly it was close to a disappearing act. I felt as though part of my brain had been blanked, even though I'd watched her go. Apparently Constable Oldman felt the same way. She blinked hard, as if she was doubting her own eyes. I wondered how long it would be before a small brown cat would appear and start slinking around, listening to private conversations. But Bela trusted her . . .

'Hi,' I said, noting an old manila folder in her hands. It was stained – looked like a mix of coffee, water and spilled ink – and, though it wasn't especially thick, it was tied with a length of frayed pink legal ribbon. There was some official-looking notation on the front, including a table for signing files in and out, with dues dates and signatures scribbled next to them. It looked as though it had come out of the ark. 'Is that for me?'

She held it out to me, and as soon as I took it, she turned to leave.

'Wait,' I said, and she did, keeping her expression carefully neutral. I smiled. 'You don't like me, do you?'

She didn't answer.

'See, I don't have to be especially sensitive to pick up on that, and you are perfectly within your rights to not like me. *However*, I would welcome a reason for the dislike, because painful experience has taught me that people who don't like me for some reason might well end up trying to stab me when my back's turned. So, *Constable*, what is your fucking problem?'

She stepped in close and hissed, '*You're* my problem. You wander into crime scenes, give orders, then wander off again – you've got no police training, no badge, no authority – and yet McIntyre lets you swan around while I'm stuck watching shitty security footage and digging around in dusty box-files.'

Jealousy? All this fucking attitude was about *jealousy*? Because she thought I was getting all the cool jobs, that I was the favoured child?

As I'd spent a large part of last year risking my life in various highly unpleasant and invariably painful ways, and this year added the chance of drowning, all in pursuit of safety for my city and its citizens, Normal and Weyrd alike, this version of sibling rivalry came as something of a surprise.

'Well, I don't think I've ever been accused of swanning before,' I said pleasantly, before grabbing her by the front of her shirt and giving her a hearty shake, which appeared to surprise her; it certainly made the blood drain from her face as she lost her feet from under her.

I had to steady her until she found them again.

'Now, do you know what happened to me today? I was almost drowned on dry land. Do you know what happened to me last week? I was attacked by assassins while I was not quite nine months' pregnant. And last year? I got beaten up by an angel, sucker-punched by an old witch who tried to roast me and almost eaten by a golem made of garbage. The year before that, I got nearly eaten by a berserker. So maybe you might want to do your research before you start accusing me of – well, whatever it is you think I'm guilty of – and you might like to consider if you really do want this job!'

We stared at each other for a moment, then I pulled out my phone. 'What's your mobile number?'

She was shocked enough to reel off the digits without thought; a couple of seconds later, her hip pocket buzzed.

'There's a photo there. You need to go back over the security footage from Mt Coot-tha – whether you want to or not – and then check if there's anything from the shopping centre where Faraday Hannigan died. See if you can find Mr Wilbur Wilson there. You'll need to look carefully as he might be hard to spot, but I'm betting he'll be there. Show me your police training's worth something. And Oldman?'

'Yeah?'

'I am not above tattling on you to McIntyre, so pull your bloody head in.'

She gave a short surprised snort of laughter as she walked away.

When I finally got inside I smelled beef curry and oh my gods, *naan bread*. I slipped into the bedroom and hid the manila folder under the mattress, then ventured to the kitchen to find David putting the finishing touches on dinner while plates were warming in the oven.

'Ziggi will love you,' I said, and kissed him. From Olivia's room I could hear singing and gurgling, which I put down to my mother and baby respectively. 'How was today?'

'About as exciting as it gets being housebound. It's a good thing I've got all this parental leave,' he said, with only the smallest trace of sarcasm, but he kissed me back. I let it go; he was entitled to the occasional whinge. 'How about you?'

'Hung out in flaky spook shops, asked a lot of stupid questions, saved Alex Parrish and his macaron-supplying daughter from drowning, did not drown myself,' I said lightly. That counted as a confession, just in case Ziggi decided to renege and squeal on my foolhardy – albeit highly successful – test of Kadie's rune.

'A positive outcome then. By the way, we're out of Maisie milk.'

'I got it,' I said, and went to feed my poor, neglected daughter, stock the fridge with expressed milk and make small talk with my mother.

★

After a shower and dinner, after I'd collected Ziggi's astonishingly clean plate, after settling Maisie into her cot in our room and waiting until she was breathing evenly and cuddled up to the plush green dragon the Norns had sent, I retrieved the file from beneath the mattress and climbed into bed. I propped pillows against the headboard and settled down to read, until David put his head in my lap, obstructing my efforts.

'What's that, then?'

'An old police file.'

'Which you shouldn't have?'

'Well, a police person gave it to me.'

'Of course.'

'It's Olivia's autopsy report.'

'Ah. That's a bit grim. Anything else you want to talk about? You know, pretend we're normal for a while?'

I dropped the file onto the floor and scootched down to lie beside him. I touched his face and he ran his fingers through my hair.

'I did *not* get drowned today, no matter what Ziggi might say in a fit of pique.' I thought about telling him about Ziggi and *Jäger*, but decided to leave that for the moment. There was enough on his plate without him starting to second-guess the people we trusted. 'See me, paying attention to you like I'm normal? See?'

'You're almost good at it,' he said and grinned.

'Shut up.'

Later still, when he'd fallen asleep curled around me, skin warm against my skin and holding on tight, I reached down and retrieved the file. I twisted onto my back and put my arm around David's neck and he settled into my shoulder without waking. I opened the file and read, page by page, the official tale of my mother's death.

Chapter Twenty-Four

Jost Marolf had clearly slept in his clothes. They were every bit as stylish and beautifully cut as his first outfit, but the grey herringbone suit was distinctly wrinkled, as was the pale blue double-cuffed shirt; the top button was undone and his understated silk tie hung loose around his neck. He smelled of manly perspiration and too much coffee. His hair, looked like it'd been electrified; he must have run his big hands through it several dozen times to make it look that spiky.

In spite of all that, he still looked pretty damned good.

Bela's enquiring poke had clearly done its job: he'd sent a very early morning text, and I had a strong suspicion that he'd fallen asleep as soon as he'd pressed *send*. But seeing our new Archivist slumped over his sloping desk, snoring softly and twitching a little, made me feel slightly guilty. The door to the Archives had already been replaced, and when I'd arrived one of the guys on the reception desk had greeted me politely and quickly run ahead of me to open it. It's rewarding to see the lessons you've taught be taken on board.

'Jost?' I called, taking in the piles of books surrounding him, stacked on the floor and the flat desks; some were still teetering, others had fallen in the night and lay scattered across the flagstones. Whatever noise they'd made can't have been enough to wake the Border Wolf, who struck me as the type who'd have instantly tidied them up if they had.

I thrust away the guilt and raised my voice. 'Jost? Rise and shine!'

'I . . . yes . . . I . . . Do I smell coffee?' He sat up with a start and pushed himself up from the desktop. His eyes were bloodshot, red-rimmed, with dark circles underneath; there was some reddish-gold stubble action on the chin, adding to the generally unkempt air.

'I didn't know how you took it.' I handed over a large long black and a small carton of light milk, then pulled sachets from my pockets, white and brown sugars and some kind of chemical sweetener I suspected was used to abrade rust from bridges. His eyes widened and I felt nostalgic for the joy of the first hit.

'Oh and this. Chocolate muffin.'

'Don't take this the wrong way, but I think I love you.'

'Never fear, the feeling will pass.'

He peeled the plastic lid from the coffee cup and splashed in milk and four packets of brown sugar: a sweet tooth to rival Ziggi's. I said, 'So, you've got something for me?'

He bit into the muffin, chewed then swallowed before saying, 'Two somethings, in fact.' Another sip of coffee, another swallow. 'I'm sorry it's taken so long. None of this was on the computers, so I've been going through the books one by one, and Honourable Ursa's filing system is . . . idiosyncratic.'

'I appreciate your efforts, Jost, I really do.' *Now get on with it!*

'So, first of all, the Grand Drowning. You know all magic costs?'

'Of course.' I resisted giving the hurry-up wave.

'Well, this conjuration is different: usually you make a personal sacrifice *before* getting what you want. In this case – as with a lot of the bigger, nastier workings – you just spill a little of your own blood to activate the magical forces, *then*' – he lifted an instructional finger – 'the rest of the price is paid by the fulfilment of the casting's goal: the death of the object of the spell.'

'So the victim pays your price, or most of it. Like you're over-charging someone,' I said, settling onto one of the tall stools by his desk.

He scoffed the last of his muffin. 'Yes, and they *must* die.'

'Ah. So Bela told you about the incident at Soteria?'

'Alex Parrish is a good man, I'm glad you were able to save him and his daughter.'

'And there was no death.' My palms had started to sweat, so I rubbed them against my jeans. 'I took the brunt of the eidolon's attack, but *I didn't die*.' I held up my wrist and showed him the henna rune, which was looking a little fainter than it had. 'Also, by the way, you should get one of these.'

'No death,' he breathed.

'No blood-price paid.'

'There's an outstanding debt in the air.' Jost whistled and sat back.

'So what happens to it?'

'Well, the cost will rebound on the caster, one way or another.'

'Will it be enough to kill said caster?'

'Eventually, but I can't say when.' He paused. 'You're thinking the mysterious Mr Wilson? I don't know what form the . . . *recompense* will take, Verity, but rest assured, he *will* be called to account, if this is his doing.'

'He's fast becoming my prime suspect.' I agreed. 'And the spell, what does it require? Apart from a death?'

'Powdered *Egeria densa*—'

'—labradorite crystals, toads' bladders—'

His eyes widened but he kept talking, '—crushed bloodstone, dried heather and cotton—'

'—which I'm sure he's got from elsewhere—'

'—and a stone that channels water energy, a big one, not just the little crystal pieces, which act as reflectors to intensify the power—'

'—and a partridge in a pear tree,' I sang, and as he snorted, 'Sorry, couldn't help myself. This big stone – something about the size of an emu's egg?'

'Labradorite is traditionally associated with water energy.'

'Of course it is. Wilbur Wilson stole a large crystal from Kadie Cross. She described it as "black and green and blue, almost like an opal". Sound like labradorite to you, Jost?'

'Unfortunately, yes. Yes, it does.'

We didn't talk for a few moments, until I had a sudden thought. 'Of course, we're forgetting the water in all of this. He's got to be getting water from somewhere,' I said, 'and the undines swear it's not anywhere they're connected with.'

'Any water will do but if it's water from a place the caster identifies strongly with or has a connection to, the control of the spell will be stronger.'

'Well, Jost, thank you. Really. That clears up a few things . . . Of course, it also poses a few more questions, but I'll take what I can get.'

'And that other matter you asked about? I found this.' He turned back to his desk and rummaged beneath some papers. He handed me a small blue book, the cover dotted with age spots, the gold foil peeling from the title and illustration. It was so old the pages showed signs of having been cut by the original owner. I made out the word *Jäger* in a jagged and aggressive-looking Germanic script. 'It's in English, a very rare translation, so please take care of it. It's a list of the family trees and histories of all the *Jäger* for the past five centuries.'

I'd asked Jost for anything about the *Jäger* when I was fairly sure Ziggi wasn't going to tell me anything, but instead, he'd opened up. I reached for it, almost had my fingers wrapped around the thing, but something stopped me. For a long while I stared at it, unable to quite rid myself of the feeling that accepting the book was . . . *wrong*. Ziggi had never given me the slightest reason to doubt him, or his loyalty. He'd saved my life on more than one occasion and I trusted him to do the same for David and Maisie, should the need arise. Maybe he hadn't told me everything, but everyone was entitled to some secrets. Besides, I could wait. I dropped my hand without touching the little blue book.

Jost looked at me in surprise.

'You know what, maybe some other time.'

The Archivist looked perplexed, but didn't ask anything more.

The mansion known as 'The Bishop's Palace' was perched on the high ground at Hamilton, overlooking not only the Brisbane River but also Newstead House. It was a few lots along from Toorak House, an equally impressive nineteenth-century sandstone building, but the Palace, glorious architectural piece of construction that it was, had one important difference: it was surrounded by a glamour that made the eye slide away. Even if you know what you're looking for, even if you've got the address and you've been invited there for a very specific purpose, even then you need to really concentrate or your gaze will slip right off it.

The Palace had a few voluntary full-time residents, including Sandor Verhoeven and his staff, and one unwilling full-time resident, Eleanor Aviva, in the specially constructed and warded cells in the basement. There's no great permanent population of criminals incarcerated there because if you're really, really bad, Weyrd justice tends to be more execute-y than rehabilitate-y. So Aviva, fallen Councillor, wicked witch extraordinaire (with something of the arachnid in her make-up), collector of phenomenally expensive handbags, had kept her life because she had secrets to trade, but there was no one to keep her company. However, I wasn't here to see her.

It always struck me that Sandor Verhoeven was waiting for something to happen so he could pounce on it; that's how it looked to me. As the physical resemblance to Orson Welles in his later years was remarkable, actual physical pouncing probably wasn't at the top of his list of recommended activities, but he'd been head of the Council for more than a hundred years so I reckoned he must be considerably more robust than he looked. Word had it he'd arrived in Brisbane in the 1800s with the first non-convict settlers sent north from Sydney. He was urbane, smart, calculating, and he did have a degree of compassion, although he was careful to ensure it didn't get trotted out often enough to make him look weak, which was probably why he'd survived so long. Well, that, and the cohort of very large bodyguards who saw to his continued health and wellbeing.

As we pulled up to the great black metal gate, Ziggi said, 'Let me do the talking!' I didn't argue, as yet again I'd insisted we show up somewhere without an invitation. I was happy to take the path of least resistance if it meant I got my own way.

Ziggi got out of the cab and approached the small dark red brick gatehouse, hands held up to show he posed no threat. The big blonde woman who stepped out peremptorily waved away the younger guards before they had the chance to pat down my chauffeur. She and Ziggi had a brief exchange, then he headed back to the cab and the gate was opened. I'd never been into the Palace before; occasionally I'd driven past, squinting really hard to make it out in defiance of the glamour. If I'd known it was going to be that simple to get in I'd have demanded a tour long before this.

'That was easy,' I said, suspiciously.

'Some days it just is, V.' He parked, and I was pleased when he

got out to accompany me: he still had no *Vatnahlífir* rune, and my
paranoia about leaving people on their own was gaining momentum,
even here.

Inside, the Palace was not as I'd expected.

It wasn't simply run-down, it was the next best thing to a ruin.
I half expected to see an archaeological team set up in the foyer,
grid-mapping the place and digging up ancient artefacts. I paused and
listened carefully just in case I could hear the sounds of excavation
elsewhere in the mansion, but there was nothing.

We'd been let in by a young man so fastidiously groomed he
might have given Jost Marolf a run for his money in the style department. He'd introduced himself as Guillaume before leading us up
the curved staircase to Sandor Verhoeven's living quarters – if you
could call that astonishing state of decay 'living'. We passed one
room with newspapers piled to the ceiling, even filling the doorway.
I didn't say anything, but my eyes felt as though they'd stretched to
the size of teacups, and the butler/major-domo/personal secretary
noticed.

'The Master does not like . . . change,' he said delicately.

It wasn't as if things were dirty, or not entirely; it was mostly
dust – but everything was ancient, like falling-apart ancient. There
were sideboards and hatstands, loveseats and round tables inlaid with
mother-of-pearl. The panelled walls were hung with paintings of
grim-looking men and women in clothing from a variety of historical
periods, all with the imposing jowls I always pictured when I thought
of Sandor Verhoeven. Flat surfaces were covered with candelabras,
vases of crystal, porcelain, brass and enamel, bronze busts, suits of
armour, unopened letters, gilded Ormolu clocks, stray books with
leather and gold-embossed covers: an antiques shop gone mad.

I'd noticed the hoarding habit in a number of Weyrd I knew.

The Norns did it, and Aviva's house, when we'd searched it, was chock-full too. While some embraced a more minimalist modern aesthetic – Bela's Highgate Hill apartment was all clean surfaces, smooth lines and expensive chairs that were uncomfortable to sit on – others obviously needed to feel familiar things around them. *Lots* of familiar things.

When we reached the landing, I took a closer look at the ceiling, which was painted with a fresco of some mythical scene with naked winged babies, women in diaphanous robes and warriors in imposing armour borne on clouds. Or perhaps it wasn't so mythical, as it was in the home of an ancient Weyrd leader. I squinted at the warriors, trying to see if one of them had the features of a younger – thinner – Verhoeven, and failed. Maybe one of the cherubs? As I stared, a fleck of gold paint broke away and floated down like a leaf to land on the marble floor far below. I wondered if Verhoeven's dislike of change extended to shoring up the structure of the house and shivered. I was really glad I'd not walked under the chandelier that illuminated the foyer.

'Miss Fassbinder. Mr Hassman.' The rich voice wafted over us as Guillaume opened the dark oak door, stepped aside and bowed us through, a lovely motion, smooth and glide-y with no hesitation. 'Do come in.'

Last year, when the Council members had been in hiding while I hunted for the garbage golem, Verhoeven had impressed me as the most reasonable, least unpleasant of the lot – but he was still Old School, and believed in having a layer of management between himself and the help, so I was a little surprised we'd been allowed in so easily. I was less dazzled that he'd chosen to greet us wearing a pilled grey sweatsuit and a pair of black Uggs with holes in the sides; his nails poked through like shards of glass. He was ensconced in a padded leather wingback chair in a small library filled to the brim with books. My fingers started itching; what I wouldn't have given to *borrow* a few tomes. On a small circular table beside him sat a Batman mug and a plate piled with chocolate chip cookies. His feet were elevated on an ornate Victorian mahogany footrest. An enormous desk loomed behind him, covered in more volumes, and a fire blazed merrily in the grate, overheating the entire room. I wasn't especially comfortable with so much paper so very close to an open hearth.

'Councillor,' I said.

'Sandor,' Ziggi said, to my surprise. First name basis? Bold.

'How can I help you this fine day? Bela tells me we have a series of Grand Drownings.'

'Amongst other things. But I'm not here to talk about that . . . unless you know something?'

'Alas, no. Do you wish to see Eleanor? She's been asking for you.'

'And she can keep asking. I wanted to talk to you about my mother.'

'Ah.' He set aside his newspaper; the headline looked like Dutch to my untrained eye. He gestured to a low recamier covered in worn golden fabric I wasn't at all certain would hold our combined weight. 'Have a seat.'

Ziggi obviously felt the same as he said, 'I'll stand.' He stayed near the door while I bravely stepped over piles of books and tentatively lowered myself onto the very uncomfortable but surprisingly sturdy couch.

'What do you want to know?' asked Verhoeven, staring at me intently. His eyes were a bright yellow; I couldn't sense any glamour around him, but that could have been because he was too damned good to let his metaphysical petticoat show.

'Ziggi said you found my mother's body.'

He nodded, but said nothing.

'And she was very definitely dead? Because that's what the autopsy report says.'

'Ah. You've seen that? Then why question me?'

'Because she is very obviously *not* dead, and equally, she is very obviously not *un*-dead, nor reanimated, neither zombie or revenant, ghost, ghoul or vampire, nor any of the other things I know about. According to the autopsy report, she was very dead indeed – very *drowned* . . . but the report also says her body disappeared from the old city morgue.' I concentrated on keeping my voice level. 'The cops looked for it – for *her* – but could find no trace. So: what happened?'

He sighed. 'This was before your father—'

'I know what happened to my father – but why was is *you* rather than Grigor who was called to identify her?'

'Before Zvezdomir came to work for us, our police liaison of the time would call me whenever someone connected to the Weyrd community had a brush with the law. When Olivia was discovered, the detective in question knew she was Grigor's wife. He contacted me and I went to the riverbank and identified her. I told him she was not of our kind, that she could be dealt with by the Normal authorities. There were no signs of violence on her; I thought it obvious she'd committed suicide.'

I clasped my hands to stop them from shaking; his casual tone punched all my buttons.

'Grigor was informed, as were her parents. When the body went missing . . . well, neither party wanted the matter pursued. Your maternal grandparents raised a memorial for her and that was the end of the matter.'

'There was no ride with the Boatman?'

He shrugged. 'There was no ceremony of *ours*, at least, but no one knows if her soul made its way to our enigmatic friend or not, or whether she escaped his clutches afterwards.' He raised his hands in a helpless gesture. 'What could we do, Ms Fassbinder? There were no signs, no clues. We truly believed she had taken her own life. And your father was the one who could have pressed for further investigation, but for reasons of his own, he had no interest in pursuing that.'

'Did he murder her? Did you ever think that?' I'd not even considered it myself until the words came out of my mouth. I felt sick to my stomach at the idea.

'I did wonder. But he was . . . There was no evidence . . .'

'And he was your friendly neighbourhood butcher; you didn't want to be without your *Kinderfresser*; that might interfere with the supply of Sunday roasts.'

He had enough sense not to meet my eye.

'So where did she go? What happened? Why is she back now?'

'Someone might have recalled her soul, or someone might have stolen it. She might have revived on her own, Miss Fassbinder. This world is not without miracles.' He hesitated. 'In truth, I do not know. You will need to ask your mother.' He pursed his lips with the smallest amount of smugness. 'If you'd let Zvezdomir bring her here for questioning, you might have more answers than you currently do.'

'And you might have had your arse kicked.'

I stood and started negotiating my way towards the door.

'Miss Fassbinder?' I stopped, but didn't turn. 'We failed your mother, I freely admit that. But we watched over you. When your father was gone, we watched over you. It was Zvezdomir's first task to do so when he came here, and we have had other guardians over the years, though your grandparents did not want you to have anything to do with your heritage. We did not abandon you, no matter what you might think.'

I kept on walking, Ziggi on my heels.

Chapter Twenty-Five

'Where to now?' Ziggi asked at last. He had wisely said nothing as we drove away from the Palace and I wept in the back seat. Would I have been this weepy if I hadn't just had a baby? Would the idea that my mother's death had been treated with such casual dismissal have made me ache so? Or the idea that my grandparents had also decided her loss could be ignored, at least until they inherited me? Was that why they were so accepting of me? So loving? Was it just guilt at failing their daughter? Perhaps I was their second chance, and they were determined to do it right at last, when they truly didn't know where the body of their only child lay . . .

Or . . .

Or . . .

Or did they?

Had Albert and May Brennan *known* Olivia wasn't actually dead? Was the headstone a red herring? If they had helped her escape from my father, then why hadn't they rescued me at the same time – why did they wait for years, until his arrest? Perhaps they believed him no danger to me . . .

The thoughts were whirling around in my head and I wanted to tell Ziggi to put his foot down and get me home fast, so I could shake my mother until I got all the fucking answers I wanted. But I didn't; I couldn't trust myself to keep my temper, to stop myself saying terrible things that once uttered, could never be taken back.

Plus, it would mean a lot of swearing around the baby.

I took a deep breath. 'How long before Beckett's next inundation?'

'A week?' said Ziggi, calculating in his head, then corrected, 'Week and a bit.'

'Then let's go there.'

'She could be at work—'

'Does it matter?' If she wasn't there I might jump over the fence and break some windows, just for the hell of it. I probably wouldn't.

Probably.

'Come on, Ziggi, let's channel this aggression into something constructive.'

He didn't answer, but took the turn off for Paddington. When we pulled up across the road from 182 Enoggera Terrace, right behind a red Jeep, he said, 'V, what Verhoeven said about your mother . . .'

'Mmmmm?'

'I . . . nothing. I got nothing. I'm just sorry. There was no excuse for anyone to behave like that, to show her such disrespect. She'd married in and she deserved better. She was a good person and she should have been looked after.'

If I hadn't had my mind on other things, if I'd been focused on what he said, I'd have noticed the problem with that sentence, but I was thinking about my mother and how she'd been less than forthcoming, keeping things to herself, and my anger at Olivia was mixing with my anger at Susan Beckett and *her* lack of honesty, making my feelings even more intense. Both women were refusing to reveal what they knew, and the secrets they were keeping were looking more and more likely to hurt other people – if they hadn't already. If I hadn't been dwelling on that . . .

But I wasn't paying proper attention and instead I just said, 'Thanks.'

After only a brief battle Ziggi conceded that my henna rune was likely to protect against eidolon attack and agreed to wait outside with Mike, who was staking her out in the bright red Jeep – apparently the Weyrd had never heard of using nondescript cars for surveillance work. Having noticeable eyes on Susan Beckett's place couldn't hurt, and although I wasn't really sure leaving Mike to sit on his own was the best thing for him, I figured he'd be super-alert, and which would be put to good use here.

Mike got out of his vehicle to talk to us. I noticed on his wrist the newly inked *Vatnahlífir*. I looked at Ziggi meaningfully; he chose to ignore me.

'Any activity, Mike?' I asked. The Jeep was pretty new, but the floor and seats were already scattered with takeaway bags and containers. Mike looked tired but intense, and I wondered how much sleep he was getting. Bela had agreed that perhaps grief-inflicted insomnia was best dealt with by some kind of watch like this, but now I wasn't sure how focused he really was with all those fast food additives coursing through him; we should have brought a salad sandwich, maybe sushi.

'Nothing so far, no one in or out, apart from the woman. She left this morning about eight, back a few hours later with groceries. Hasn't gone to work for two days.'

'Interesting.' I put a hand on his shoulder. 'How are you doing?'

'I'm okay. I can't sleep, or rather when I do it's for really short periods . . . but this is good, being here. In the house I was . . . sleepwalking, hearing voices. It's better in the car.'

'No dreams here?' I asked.

He hesitated as if he wasn't sure himself. 'No, not dreams. No dreams.'

I flicked a glance at Ziggi – *Keep an eye on him* – and was acknowledged by a slow blink. 'Well, I'll scream if I need you.'

The silvery-grey BMW was in the carport, and I noticed a series of long thin scratches on the right-hand side running from bonnet to boot. It had been keyed . . . or maybe clawed. I crouched to look more closely: it wasn't just scratches but a series of circular lines drawn inside a larger circle, like a puzzle, or a maze. I narrowed my eyes.

Susan Beckett answered when I hit the intercom button. 'Yes?'

'It's Verity Fassbinder.'

'Who?'

'You let me use your bathroom last week.'

'Oh. I'm sorry, I'm not feeling well.'

'It won't take long, Ms Beckett, just a few questions.'

'I'm afraid this really isn't convenient at all, Ms Fassbinder. Perhaps you could—?'

'Or perhaps you could open the fucking gate before I kick it in. I can do that, you know, and I'm just in the mood.'

There was a pause, then a buzz and a click.

She was waiting at the front door, pale hair pulled into a tight bun, wearing black leggings, a long-line black sweater and ballet shoes. Her right hand was bandaged. The wrapping was pristine, but the tips of the fingers were bright red and blistered. She wore no makeup and her skin was terribly pale, except for the dark bags under her eyes. Her lips looked dry and bloodless.

'What happened?' I asked, and she glanced down as if surprised by the concern and saw the injured digits as if she'd forgotten them.

'Oh, yes. Just clumsy. I wasn't paying attention at work when I poured hot water into a cup.' She gave me a weak smile. 'A few days off and it will be fine.'

'A tincture of marshmallow herb will help. It's got anti-inflammatory properties. You can get it at most spook shops. Third Eye Books has it in stock, but you probably already know that.'

If possible she went a little paler, but otherwise she ignored the dig. 'What do you want?'

'Let's talk inside, shall we?' I said as I pushed her aside, possibly harder than I'd intended – *yup, definitely got my strength back* – as she stumbled and did that running step-step-step thing to save herself. She recovered and I was glad she hadn't fallen, but I didn't help her. No point in wasting a perfectly good rush of fear.

She backed down the hallway until she reached the lounge room and placed the rocker-recliner between us. 'I'll call the police.'

'Oh, please do. They respond so quickly to calls from lawyers.' I sat on one of the couches, displacing one of the tasteful orange cushions as I did so, and gestured for her to sit, which she did after a moment's hesitation. 'How long do you think you've got?'

'Until what?'

'Before whatever's crapping mud all over your lovely house decides it's had enough of just tormenting you. I'm calling them "inundations", but maybe you've got another name for them? Maybe I should call it what it is: *a curse.*'

'I don't know—'

'Oh, for fuck's sake!' I yelled, as she cringed, 'do I *really* need to spell it out so you can stop pretending ignorance? Once a month for the last three months your house has been filled with nasty *shitty* mud. I can smell it even now, Ms Beckett, no matter how many expensive cleaning services you use or how many perfume diffusers you deploy. *I can still smell it.*' We stared at each. 'I cannot imagine you *want* this to happen; I cannot imagine you *chose* it. Which leads me to believe something's gone wrong.'

'It's none of your business.' She was shaking all over and her voice was trembling. '*How can you know?*'

'You've claimed on *Unusual Happenstance* once too often.'

'Soteria? I will sue Alex Parrish for all he's worth for breaking confidentiality! That bastard! I'll—'

'You'll do no such thing. Mr Parrish is entitled to investigate your claims. He's entitled to hire an investigator. I would have thought you'd be familiar with that part of the policy.' She glared at me until I said, 'Look: this is your last chance. You've not got long before it all happens again. Just tell me what's going on and I can help you. You're in danger—'

And she laughed so hard that she snorted; the sound was unhinged, unhappy. 'I'm in absolutely no fucking danger! There's no point if I get hurt!'

I took a deep breath and tried to unsettle her. 'Did you send Wilbur Wilson to kill Alex Parrish?'

She jerked as if struck. 'Wilbur Wilson?'

'Because as far as I can tell, that's what he was trying to do yesterday. And in the past week and a bit he's murdered three other people with no apparent connection to him or each other. But maybe you're the point of contact.' I pursed my lips. 'Alex is okay, by the way, thanks for asking.'

'I . . . I don't know any Wilbur Wilson.'

I fished out my phone, held up the photo of the little man. Her pupils contracted in shock, but she insisted, 'No. I don't know him.'

'You see, the thing is,' I said very calmly as I put away the phone, 'it appears Mister Wilson is conducting Grand Drownings, which would be my problem anyway, but it's made extra personal by the fact that he tried to kill my newborn daughter and he succeeded in killing someone else close to me, another innocent person. To say that makes me *unhappy* would be a very major understatement. So you can understand how I feel when you continue to lie to me.'

'I'm sorry about your daughter,' she said, her voice tremulous, 'but I don't know who that man is and I certainly didn't send him to hurt anyone. I can't help you. Please leave.'

'I've been to your parents' home,' I said, playing my last card. 'There was a smell at Morwood Road, just like the one here.'

She froze as if a chill wind had passed over her.

I continued, 'Did it start there, then move to your place? Or the other way around? Where's your family? Are they really on holiday?'

And for one tiny moment I thought she was going to break. I thought I'd got through. Then the moment died and she shook her head and gave me a cold stare. Even though Susan Beckett was clearly terrified beneath her ice maiden façade, she didn't crack.

Knowing I was beaten, I rose. At the front door, I made one last plea, 'Won't you at least help yourself? One of these days you're going to find you're drowning in mud or water or both.'

She said nothing, just shut the door quietly behind me.

'She knows *something*, Ziggi, I am absolutely bloody positive,' I said between gritted teeth. 'She knows something about Wilbur Wilson and she knows something about what's happened to her family and she most certainly knows what's happening with all that damned mud.' We sat in the taxi, watching Susan's Beckett's house as if it might do tricks or reveal truths if stared at long enough. 'Fuck, fuck and double fuck!'

'And you failed to charm this information out of her?'

'*Really?* Is this really the time to be obnoxious?' Things might have got worse from that point on except my phone rang and stopped me getting a good run up on my grump. 'Inspector McIntyre: got those tattoos yet?'

'Yes, and it itches like all buggery, thank you very much. I don't know how Ellen stands them all over her.'

'Did you call just to complain? Or do you, by some miracle, have good news?'

'Someone's been taking their bitch pills. We got the results back on the water from the drowning victims, but I'm not sure it's much help.'

'Well, don't keep me in suspense.'

'All samples contained diatoms – that's a form of algae to thee and me – of a kind not commonly found in Queensland.'

'And?'

'Common to New South Wales, though, specifically the Byron Bay region. If I remember correctly, Susan Beckett hails from that-a-way.' Rhonda sounded pleased with herself.

'Well done, you! Bloody well done!' She had just handed me a new means of leverage – maybe not with Susan Beckett, but with someone else for sure.

'Well, it's tentative,' McIntyre said quickly; 'it could be anywhere in Byron. But the mix is unusual: salt water diatoms and fresh. Strange, right? What are you going to do?'

'Ask more questions. Thanks, Rhonda.' I hung up and relayed the informed to Ziggi. He sighed when I gave him our destination and I said, 'Hey, at least it's not the Gold Coast.'

When his complaining lowered in volume and frequency, I called David.

'Hey, you. What's happening in the world of the Weyrd?'

'Oh, you know, stuff. I'm going to be home late tonight. Everything okay?'

'Uh huh. Maisie's sleeping again and I'm trying to read, but I keep nodding off, which turns out not to be the fault of the book at all.'

'I'm sorry,' I said. 'You shouldn't be doing this all on your own.'

'V, it's *okay*. Olivia's helping a lot. I think it's just adjusting to a new regime. Give me a couple of weeks and I'll be fine.' I could hear a smile in his voice as he added, 'I didn't say that to make you feel guilty, you know.'

'No, but it was a happy coincidence. Is Maisie good for milk?'

'Yup, your multiple express-o machine routines have produced plenty for today.'

'Oh, shit, now I really do feel like a cow. There's more to come.' I closed my eyes, loving the sound of him laughing. 'Is there anything else I should know?'

'Your mother's talking about learning to knit – should I be worried?'

'Only if she actually follows through, and even then only if it looks like a garrotte rather than a sweater.' I told him about my conversation with Sandor Verhoeven, then about diatoms, salty and fresh, and finally about Susan Beckett's refusal to be helpful. 'We're going to go to Byron, check on the Morwood Road house and see if we can't find a source of water that matches those diatoms. There's bound to be a dam or a spring somewhere close by.'

There was a pause, then he said, 'Don't forget there's a wishing well at Ocean's Reach, too. In Wanda's front garden.'

'You're right – and it's closer to the sea than Morwood Road. Evaporation, rain, ground water . . . which could lead to that specific mix.' I paused. 'You're a genius.'

'I know.'

'Modest, too.' I looked out the window, watched the landscape change as we went speeding further away from my lover and my baby; the ball of tension in my stomach grew bigger. 'Are you okay? *Really?* I mean, are you plotting to put a pillow over my face when I come home?'

'I'm more of a short-sheet-the-bed man: less lethal, more annoying.' He paused. 'I'll be glad when this is over, when you're back and we're a family, however strange that might turn out to be, what with your dead mother who's not dead, Uncles Bela and Ziggi and the rest of the clan. Do we know any Normal people any more?'

''course we do! There's Rhonda and Ellen. Mel and Lizzie. And . . .' I thought a bit. 'Okay, so that's pretty much it, but they are super-Normal. Also, we didn't have this conversation; if anyone asks you haven't heard from me and don't know where I am.'

'Got it: don't tell Bela. Okay, then. Just stay safe, hey? I love you.'

'Love you, too. I'll be late, but definitely home tonight.'

'Wake me when you get in.'

And I promised I would even though I knew he'd be sleeping like the dead when I tried.

Chapter Twenty-Six

'You know there are faster ways to do this,' griped Ziggi. 'Like a telephone call.'

'Yes, but it's harder to control someone over the phone, or to assess truth and deceit. Besides, I didn't want anyone else to know what we were doing.'

'Because——?'

I sighed. 'Because the more people who know, the less chance we have of maintaining the element of surprise.'

'And because Bela won't be happy to know you're going to accuse Wanda Callander of something?'

'"Accuse" is such an ugly word.' I watched the bushes along the side of the Ocean's Reach driveway flash past. We'd been pretty lucky with the traffic and there'd been no cops around to witness Ziggi's lead-foot antics – well, at least not that we'd noticed. It was just past half-three and the winter sun was on its way down. We'd stopped only for petrol, terrible sandwiches, and an express-o break, so I was feeling a lot more comfortable. 'Is she dangerous, do you think?'

'Wanda? She's a healer, V. Her place has been a trusted sanctuary for years.'

'I know, but something's not right. Wilbur Wilson is connected to a lot of dead bodies and the water in said dead bodies either came from the Becketts' property or Ocean's Reach. Wanda knows the family, she knows Susan – and somehow Wilbur Wilson knew we were at Ocean's Reach. I could be wrong – and if you ever tell anyone I said this, you're dead! – but I have *very* occasionally not been entirely right, however there's a link here somewhere. And I hope Wanda Callander can be convinced to tell me what it is.'

We pulled up in front of the charming stone-built house and the front door opened as if we were expected. Wanda had a broad smile on her lovely face, a tea towel draped over one shoulder, and jeans and shirt beneath an old-fashioned pinafore style apron. The wind tugged at her loose red hair.

'Verity! Lovely to see you again.' She opened her arms and I felt that *tug*, that *pull* of fondness that I'd recognised as a charm, even though it didn't work on me. Well, mostly not. I guess she thought of me as a challenge. I gave her a hug anyway, but said, 'Stop it, Wanda.'

She pouted, but I felt the drawing power dissipate, leaving nothing more than the ordinary fondness for someone who'd obeyed me. 'That's better.'

'It's such a little thing,' she complained, 'makes people feel at home, you spoilsport. Hello, Ziggi Hassman.'

'Wanda,' he said neutrally, and I wondered how much of her enchantment might have worked on him if I'd not been there to turn off the tap. 'We've some questions.'

'Of course.' She led the way, fidgeting with the tea towel, wiping her hands over and over as if she couldn't get them dry. 'How's Maisie? And your lovely David?'

'Very well, thank you.'

'And poor Mike?'

'As well as can be expected,' I said.

She led us to the kitchen and we sat while she bustled around making tea, putting homemade biscuits on a plate.

'We need to talk about Susan Beckett,' I said before biting into a jam drop. In other circumstances I might have felt bad eating her food when I was about to intimidate her, but we'd missed lunch.

'Susan?' she asked, but there was no real surprise in her tone. 'Ever since you asked about her last time . . . I wondered. Then I felt certain you'd come again. Just not so soon.'

'Did you teach her?'

'The craft? Yes. Small things. She's Normal and there's no talent there, but you probably know it's not really necessary, just knowledge and ritual and a willingness to pay the price. When I arrived here, Susan was fifteen, sixteen, terribly smart and terribly unhappy. She would visit to escape what was going on at home. At first her father objected, but I told him I'd employ her. She helped around when we were first setting up here, tidying rooms, doing laundry, helping with the guests. '

'And what did go on at home?' asked Ziggi, helping himself to another biscuit.

The kettle boiled and Wanda got up to fill the teapot. Ziggi got the mugs and found the sugar; I retrieved milk from the fridge.

'Acton hit her – not Susan, but her mother, Marian. Still does, I imagine. The local constabulary have been called out there more times than I care to recall, but Marian never files a complaint. She says nothing's wrong, even when she's got a bruise on her face or a broken arm's put her in hospital. She won't do anything about it. I tried to talk to her once – I thought I might be able to get her to leave. I told her I could help her get away and start again, and I could have, but she was terrified . . . that bastard had got her so afraid that she was convinced that no matter where she went he'd find her.'

'She was afraid he'd kill her?'

'She was afraid he *wouldn't* – that he'd drag her back and make her life even worse.' Her voice was a mix of sorrow and outrage; as she reached for her cup her hand shook. 'I tried to make her feel guilty. I asked, "What about your daughters?" and she sort of sneered, "He doesn't hit *them*."' Wanda looked away. 'It was . . . well, mean and childish, not like a grown woman protecting her children.'

'What about Susan?'

'Sometimes she'd bring the little ones – Unity and Hildy; dreadful names – and they'd sleep or play while she helped out, while she studied. She'd do her work quickly so she could come and learn something new. She's got a tremendous determination, does Susan. Normal witches need a lot of concentration, a lot of stubbornness, intense attention to detail and a greater command of the tools of ritual in order to make things happen, because they can't fall back on whatever enchantments blood might give them. Susan had that focus, but still and all, it was only little things that she mastered, for the most part.'

'For the most part?' I asked. 'What about the lesser part?'

'I'm sure it was an accident more than anything.' She licked her lips, sipped tea. 'I'd let her borrow some of my books – not the worst of them, mind you, and certainly not my own grimoire – that's come down from mother to daughter for almost a thousand years. I didn't even show it to her . . . but somehow she found out about it. She stole it.' Wanda bowed her head. 'There was no harm meant, I'm sure; it was just the curiosity, Verity, I promise you.'

'What did she do, Wanda?' I set my half-eaten biscuit aside, suddenly no longer hungry.

'You've seen the turf maze out the back? You know what they're for?'

'A lot of things.'

'I use the pilgrim's path for healing, but it can also be used to mark locations – and for summoning rituals. Well, Susan used it to summon one of the little folk, the mischievous ones.'

'*Smågubbar?*' I asked, and when Wanda nodded, Ziggi whistled.

'I found her one evening: she'd walked the path, chanted the spell, cut her wrist and given more blood than she could spare . . . it was too late for me to do anything but bandage the wound.' She rubbed her eyes with thumb and forefinger.

'That kind of a spell has a bigger cost than just a bit of blood,' I said, dreading what Wanda might say. 'How did she pay the deficit? No point making the *smågubbar* wear that cost when getting him was the whole point of the exercise . . .'

'We had an old German Shepherd—'

I held up a hand. *No more.*

'If you capture one of those little bastards, they're bound to you, you see?' she said. 'They have to do your bidding, and from the moment she had him, her life changed.'

'How do you mean?' said Ziggi.

'Suddenly there was money for university – she didn't have to rely on her parents, and more particularly, her father. Whatever she wanted, the little thing would provide. Gods, he was so small and so bloody ugly, and he followed her around like a pup. It didn't change, even as he grew. He was still ugly, and still utterly devoted to her. She wouldn't send him back, either, though I begged her, told her enough times that he didn't belong up here, not in this world, not for a long period. Creatures from the other side seldom thrive here.' She sighed. 'But she wasn't letting him go: he was her ticket out, away from her parents, and even from those poor little sisters of hers.'

'Wanda, did you see the Becketts before they took this holiday Susan sent them on?'

She said quietly, 'No. Susan phoned me and told me they'd gone, and she asked if I'd collect the mail' – she pointed to a pile of unopened letters, mostly junk, from what I could see, on one end of the kitchen bench – 'and feed the chickens. But I couldn't find the chooks when I went around there. A fox must have got into the coop. I could smell something when I went to the verandah – not death, but something not right.' She hung her head and said quietly, 'And I decided I was a coward and didn't want to know.'

'Do you think the Becketts are coming home, Wanda?'

She started to cry, shaking her head and searching for tissues in her pockets. I handed some over from my bag. 'Did you cast any glamours on him to make him look . . . acceptable?'

'Susan begged me to – I refused for ages, but when I realised she really wouldn't send him back, I did it, because . . . I felt sorry for her. And him, if truth be told. But it only ever made him *ordinary*, there was nothing I could do to make him beautiful. He's the most *ordinary* little bastard you've ever seen.'

'And she gave him a name?'

'No, she kept calling him *you*, and it felt wrong, so *I* named him – he reminded me of two of my uncles, tremendously ugly they were, both of them. Wilbur and Wilson.'

'Where's your grimoire now, Wanda?'

'I hid it so she couldn't get her hands on it again. I buried it out in the garden for safekeeping. But when I went to look for it a few months ago . . .' Her voice was trembling as badly as her hands. 'I don't know how long it's been missing.'

'Do you think Susan took it again?'

'Or she sent Wilbur. Or he came of his own accord. I was . . . I was too afraid to ask her . . . just like I was too afraid to ask about her family.' She wiped her eyes and visibly tried to pull herself together.

She said matter-of-factly, 'If she did whatever she did to her own family, what would she do to me?'

'That grimoire: might there have been a Grand Drowning spell in there?' I asked, and I watched her head droop with shame.

'A decent witch wouldn't *ever* consider drowning another, nor burning her. We shouldn't use the punishments of the Normal world against our own.'

'That's not a no.'

Her face looked pinched, her voice pitched low, as at last she answered, 'Yes. Yes, there are instructions for a Grand Drowning. These spells – they were written a long time ago, in a different age, by women who needed different means of protecting themselves. An ancestor of mine, she was the head of a coven and one of her followers tried to betray them. She took the only action she believed possible . . .'

'Is that where the mud-curse came from too? Something that inundates a house with shitty, noxious sludge?' The more I thought about it, the more I realised that enough mud would be a very effective way of killing someone . . . or four someones.

She frowned. 'No, there's nothing like that in there. It sounds like something pretty basic, though. Dirt, water, blood and your own shit for the primal material, then a suitable enchantment for transportation and expansion – the whole point would be to show utter contempt, to make life very unpleasant. What's that got to do with Susan?'

And I realised I hadn't actually told her about Susan's troubles. No one had. And as I did so now I watched the horror creep across Wanda's face. I took the opportunity to hit her with another of my suspicions. 'Did you tell her we were here? After I asked if you knew her?'

She blinked, but apparently realised lying wasn't a good idea, not at this point. 'Yes,' she said. 'I didn't know why you were asking about her. I thought she should know.'

'But she didn't tell you about the mud, or that she'd been in danger and was afraid?'

'No,' Wanda said quietly. 'I'm sorry. I didn't think it would—' She took a deep breath. 'I never dreamed she'd send . . .'

I didn't think she had either, but I wasn't in the mood to ease her conscience so easily. Wanda had warned Susan; Susan had passed the information on to Wilbur, whether through intent or accident, and Wilbur had come after me and mine because he thought I was a threat to Susan.

But he'd done something else for Susan. I was pretty sure of that.

I left Wanda with instructions to call if she thought of anything else that might be useful, but before Ziggi and I headed for home, we visited Morwood Road. Nothing had changed, except it was starting to look pretty neglected, the yard even more overgrown, the vines running riot everywhere.

This time I had no scruples about busting the lock on the front door. I knew no one was coming home. It was dark inside, and when I hit the light the glare was blinding; the electricity was still on, maintaining the illusion that someone would return.

The house contained only a few pieces of furniture, nothing expensive and certainly nothing as stylish as in Susan Beckett's Paddington abode. In the kitchen there was a refrigerator containing condiments that wouldn't go off, or at least, not so anyone would notice, like anchovies and mustard. A washer and dryer took up the tiny laundry out back, and there were three small bedrooms, one with a double bed, one with a single bed and the last with its door closed. As I pushed it open, the door banged back against the wall, the smell I'd detected in Susan Beckett's home overwhelmed us. There were two small single beds, each with a set of fairy wings on the end of the bed frame; a low chest of drawers sat between them, and on its top was what looked like a kind of altar, with bits and pieces of possessions heaped in front. A well-loved, threadbare teddy bear and a pinky-orange bracelet of coral pieces caught my eye and I swallowed, hard.

The stench was getting even worse. At first I thought the walls were painted a cappuccino colour in contrast to the stark white through the rest of the house, then I realised it was actually a thin veneer of mud, which also crunched beneath our boots when we walked across the floor. The fairy wings were encrusted with it, the teddy bear's fur was matted and the bracelet had brown sediment caught in its grooves and crevices. I picked them up, though I *really* didn't really want to.

'Wilson uses water,' I said.

'Doesn't mean he can't or won't change,' answered Ziggi.

'True. But where'd he get the mud-curse?'

'It's a mystery.'

Whatever had happened, had happened in here.

'Maybe they're really on holidays,' said Ziggi.

'Maybe they're on the run,' I added.

'Maybe they're okay.'

'Maybe they got out before this happened.' I pointed to the ceiling, which was brown as well, flakes of mud peeling off just as the gold paint had from Verhoeven's fresco in the Bishop's Palace. The whole room had been filled to the brim.

'Maybe,' Ziggi said, doubtfully.

'Maybe.'

We had no proof of anything. I put the teddy bear and the coral bracelet into a plastic bag and carried them out to the boot; Ziggi didn't want the smell in the cab and I couldn't blame him.

On the highway home, we were passed by an Australia Post delivery truck, then another, and then a non-specific courier van – and finally something clicked.

'Shit!' I dialled Bela while Ziggi kept demanding to know what was wrong.

'Where have you been?' demanded my boss coolly on the other end of the phone. I had a suspicion he already knew I'd been upsetting Wanda Callander.

'Bela, there's a van—'

'A specific one?' Still chilly.

'Len's vehicle – the murdered delivery driver? He was a sub-contractor; he owned his own wheels. Where's that van? I haven't seen it in my street – mind you, I haven't been looking for it because I'm an idiot. But what do you reckon the chances are that the fox-girl's got it? And if she's genuinely not been seen in any of the usual transient Weyrd dosshouses and boarding houses, then what are the chances she's living in it?'

I told him to call McIntyre, because she could get Len's licence details and plates, and put out a BOLF on the van. I filled him in on what we'd discovered about Susan Beckett and her craft-related activities, and I could tell he'd warmed considerably by the time he rang off. I suggested someone spell Mike outside her house for a few hours at least; I was exhausted and I couldn't face talking to her again until I'd had some sleep. Besides, I wanted to give my henna rune a touch-up before I tried anything. The past couple of days' wear and tear, not to mention an unscheduled dunking, had made it fade faster than I would have liked.

Chapter Twenty-Seven

David and Maisie were asleep when I finally got home, but Olivia was up, sitting in the lounge room, sipping peppermint tea and watching Jimmy Fallon not being funny. Her long hair was wet, as if she'd only just showered, and she was wearing my spare pair of flannelette pyjamas, thick socks and my favourite daggy dressing gown, which had belonged to Grandma. As Olivia's clothing selection consisted of a couple of pairs of jeans, three skivvies, one pair of boots and the long black leather coat, I shouldn't have been surprised that David had offered her some stuff from my wardrobe. I still found myself vaguely annoyed to see my things so freely borrowed – as an only child, I'd never had to share. Or maybe it was just because my mother had come back after all these years and helped herself to my jammies. No matter what the outcome of all the crazy shit going on around us, I was going to have to take Olivia clothes shopping in the near future.

I was exhausted, but I knew I wasn't going to sleep any time soon. Despite my intense desire to curl up next to David or to snuggle in the rocking chair with Maisie, I didn't want to wake either of them; David didn't need to be deprived of any sleep. Living in a state of siege was exhausting and having nothing to do while other people watched over you was wearying in a curious fashion, fear and inertia wore at you; all you could do was sit around and wait, and hope someone else could sort out the mess.

'Hey, Olivia,' I said. I made myself a cup of tea, sat beside her and gave a rundown of the day. We talked about Wilbur Wilson and his extraordinary birth, and I warned her about Len's van, especially if should turn up outside the house.

'What do you think Susan Beckett did?' I asked. 'To her family?'

She waited before answering hesitantly, 'I think she did something terrible. I suspect she got the little man to do something really, really awful.'

I sighed. 'I think you're right, and for whatever reason, he's turned against her now.' We sat in silence for a while until at last I bit the bullet and said firmly, 'We need to talk, Olivia, and no weaselling.'

My mother looked at me sadly.

'You can refuse to answer, but telling me the truth may well be the only way to keep us all safe, and I'm especially keen on staying safe.' I looked at the tips of my boots and thought how I was sick of wearing them; that I should have put on my Uggs before I began this conversation – and then I decided that maybe my subconscious was suggesting I shouldn't feel too comfy right now.

I kicked off with, 'I spoke to Sandor Verhoeven today.'

'You have been busy.'

'Don't get sarky with me. He wasn't too impressed that I wouldn't let Bela take you to the Bishop's Palace for questioning. We both know that it probably wouldn't have ended well for whatever guard of dishonour they sent for you, but you could be at least a bit grateful I didn't turn you over to them.'

One side of her mouth quirked upwards and she said, 'Thank you, dear.'

'So, you died. You drowned, didn't you?' She remained silent. 'Olivia, I've read the autopsy report. You were all kinds of dead . . .'

I was too tired to be really angry. 'So what the hell happened? Did Grigor kill you?'

She laughed then. 'Oh gods no! Your father didn't have the balls to kill anything that wasn't a child.' She laughed again, until tears were running down her face, and then she was crying properly.

I grabbed her hand and held on tight – but not too tight – before saying, 'If this is a delaying tactic it's not going to work.'

'Shit, you're as bad as your grandmother.'

'Well, she did raise me.'

She squeezed my fingers. 'Verity, I tried to drown myself – I *did* drown. I jumped off the Story Bridge into the river. I'd found out what your father *really* did for a living and I lost it. I didn't think about anything or anyone else – I didn't think about leaving you behind or what that would do to you. I despaired, and despair is entirely selfish. I'll never forgive myself for it, so how can I expect you to?' She ran her free hand through her hair and took a deep breath. 'Although I drowned, I didn't leave my body – I don't know why. Part of me, my soul, I guess, stuck around, as if it'd been caught on a nail or a hook. So when the cops pulled me from the water around Newstead House I sort of felt it, and when Sandor came waddling down the bank – he nearly fell, too, fat sod – when he leaned over me and touched my face, my hair, I was aware of it . . . it was as if I was in a cage looking out. They put me in the ambulance and took me to the morgue, and when they wheeled me through those corridors, somehow I knew that the place stank. I felt the cold steel table under me, and I knew that when it came time to cut me, I'd feel that too.'

She put her cup to her lips, then resumed her story. 'But it didn't come to that, because a woman came for me – a friend of yours. Eleanor Aviva.'

'*Friend?*' I snarked, and Olivia grinned. Was there a pie Eleanor

Aviva didn't have an exquisitely manicured finger in? 'How did she know?' I wondered.

'Someone's always on the lookout for a miracle, like a soul still stuck in a body. Aviva was a go-between, brokering a good price for herself and ensuring that her client got what they wanted. Somehow she knew I was still *inside* and she turned up before they got to the cutting part. She brought some little creep with her . . . Mercado something?'

Mercado White, rogue Councillor, buyer of illicit wines. Shit.

So I *was* going to have to talk to Aviva – but not quite yet; if she thought the information was of value to me she'd draw the game out like a cat playing with a mouse. I'd have to work out some kind of cunning approach.

'You didn't ride with the Boatman?' I asked, even though I knew the answer. 'You kept your voice because you weren't properly dead.'

'No, I didn't – but he's not the only way to get to the Underworld, my girl. Not the only way at all. When I was *delivered* – not by Aviva and her toady, by someone I didn't recognise – the Guardian touched me and somehow *zapped* life-proper back into me. I guess I wasn't much use to it if I couldn't function fully, and if I couldn't think and talk and walk, then I couldn't agree to its proposal.'

'Which was?'

'The one thing that kept me alive was the idea of your father getting what he deserved,' she admitted. 'I wanted Grigor caught, and then he'd lose you, because you were *everything* to him. By then I regretted leaving you, so much, but I was beginning to think rationally again, and I still hated your father – you have no idea . . .' She closed her eyes. 'And so I accepted what was offered: Grigor's fall, in exchange for my service to the Guardian of the Southern Gate of the Underworld.'

'The who-what-now?'

'That's what it calls itself: it claims to be one of a legion of Guardians who keep the various Gates safe. But . . .' She paused and then said, 'Well, I've had my doubts for a long while about its true nature, but I don't know what it actually is.'

'What do you do for it?' I was really afraid of the answer, but I had to know everything.

'It was easy at first: bullying, stealing, hunting. I was angry and miserable, so it made me happy to pass that pain on to others. I found things the Guardian wanted: escaped souls, items of interest, information, people who would do deals with it. I warned someone off doing one thing, then encouraged them to do another. I did a lot of things I'm ashamed of.'

That sounded a lot like me working for the Weyrd, and it made me uneasy.

'As well as Grigor's downfall I got super-strength and speed, and the ability to fight. I got the sword too – I do like the sword, watch this.' She fished around in her pocket and brought out what looked like a gleaming metal pocketknife, engraved all over. She showed me the barely-there button on one end and when she touched it, a miniscule needle shot up and pierced the tip of her finger (now I could see it was scarred; she must have done this a lot) – and then the weapon transformed: a long blade extended as the hilt, guard and pommel unfolded in her hand.

'Blood-price magic,' I said.

She offered it to me. *Want to hold Mummy's toy?*

'Better not, I'd probably just cut myself.'

She grinned, then sobered. She pressed the little nub again and the sword became a pocket knife once more, then she went back to her tale. 'I still had my soul, though, and I still had my conscience, even if it was mothballed for a while. But I was so angry that I was happy to be powerful, and to use my new strength to punish whoever the Guardian pointed me at.'

She looked down at her hands and intertwined her fingers. 'But after your father . . . After Grigor was dealt with, I guess the fire started to burn low. It was a slow process, but I could feel myself changing . . . I was less willing to hurt; I started trying to negotiate whenever I could. The Guardian claims to be all-knowing, but it's not; that's just a means to control you when you're out of its sight. I was getting away with more and more, and I suppose I'd reached a kind of accommodation with my life, my death. Then—'

She broke off and, shuddering, exhaled deeply. She took a moment to compose herself.

'Then the little girls appeared,' she said softly. 'I don't know why they were in the place I was. They don't speak – they *can't* speak; they'd made their journey with the Boatman – but for some reason, they latched onto me and started following me around. And they didn't deserve to be there. It's always hard for me, with little girls. They make me think of you. And I'd watched your life and I saw you were pregnant . . . and I—'

'How did you watch my life?' I interrupted. 'And I hope you exercised some discretion.'

She snorted, then rose and went into her bedroom. She returned with her fingers clasped tightly around an object. 'It gave me this.' She held out her hand and lying flat on the palm was what looked like a make-up compact, the colour of antique silver, with a spiralling mother-of-pearl inlay. She handed it to me and said, 'Open it.'

Inside was the usual deal, mirrors on either side, but in both there was nothing but the swirling of smoke. 'What is it?'

Olivia reached out and touched the silvery shell, and instantly the smoke cleared. In one mirror I saw myself, in the other, Maisie's sleeping face. 'So I could always see my bloodline.'

I closed the thing and handed it back to her, trying to keep my hands still.

'Did Grandma and Grandy know you were alive?'

'Mum did. After Grigor's death I used to sneak off and hide so I could watch you. One day when I was hanging around, she spied me.' She licked her lips. 'She didn't say anything; she just gave me this slow nod and turned away. I knew you were safe with them, so I went away. I . . . I wanted to talk to her, but what could I say? "You were right?" "I'm sorry?" Nothing seemed enough.'

'Did you watch when I was still with Grigor?'

She shook her head. 'It was all too new, the hatred too fresh then; I didn't want . . . connection. Quite apart from that, the Guardian doesn't like divided loyalties: it said it would know if I kept any kind of contact with my family, and it would punish me through them and for a long time I believed it . . . but eventually I realised it wasn't omniscient or omnipotent, and I could do what I wanted, as long as I was careful. I got away with it too, for a good while.'

'Why didn't you come back for me then?' I hated my plaintive tone. 'Especially when Grigor was gone.'

'Because of my agreement with the Guardian. Where would I have gone with you? Where could we have hidden? What life could I have given you on the run? It *would* have found me at some point . . . And I got into bad enough trouble for skirting the terms of our agreement and just watching you from a distance – the fox-girls spied on me and they snitched. In the end the Guardian gave me the magic mirror, so I wouldn't be tempted to stray again.' She sighed. 'Just breadcrumbs to keep me happy.'

'Who are the fox-girls, Olivia? You know them, don't you?'

'They were young when they came to the Underworld. They arrived a few years after I did. Their lives had been truncated like mine, but they weren't properly dead either. The Guardian made deals with them, just as he did with me. They were my . . . well, colleagues, but they chose the Guardian's way.'

'Why did you come back now?'

'I was trying to make up for my sins where I could, showing kindness, striking bargains that weren't so sinister or punitive, because . . . because I couldn't do the things it wanted me to do any more. I'm exhausted by its demands, worn thin, and I am *so* tired of being alone, tired of being angry, just *so tired*. I wanted to be *out*, just for a little while, even if it took my life, as long as I could see you and the baby. I needed to know that my life had produced something good in the end.' She began to sob again. 'And when I left, I took the two little ghost girls with me, because they shouldn't have been there, alone in the darkness—'

'The corpselights,' I said, focusing on the thing I could deal with most easily, the thing that didn't affect me so much. 'They're here for you.'

Olivia reached out and grabbed my hand. 'I took them with me because I was lucky – someone looked after my little girl for me when I was at my worst, my most selfish, when I did the thing I've most regretted. So I thought it was time for me to do that for someone else.' She wiped away tears, but more flowed. 'They've been out there again tonight. I don't know if I've done the wrong thing, but this has got to be better, right? Better than being *down there*?'

'And we might be able to help them, Olivia, when everything else is done and dusted. There are witches who might assist,' I said, thinking what Aviva might do for a few more privileges, or Wanda

Callander, to make amends. 'But the *kitsune*? They've been sent after you?'

She said wearily, 'The Guardian doesn't like broken bargains. But something I have learned over the years is that it's not all-powerful, *it* can't hurt you from a distance, but it will send its minions, like the fox-girls, like me. It's got a long reach, but it relies on cat's paws. When I kill the last of the *kitsune*, it'll send someone else.'

And there was something in the way she said 'the last' that made me pause; there was something sad and painful in her voice that suggested loss, and I knew that a simple working relationship was not the only thing between my mother and her hunters. I thought about the expression on the Librarian's face when Olivia killed Gothic Alice in that stinking alleyway in the Valley, and I didn't think all the grief was for her dead sister. She still wasn't telling me everything, but by that time I couldn't listen to any more.

'You sent the dresses, didn't you? The Princess Awesome frocks?'

Olivia nodded.

'I think we both need some sleep,' I said. I wasn't prepared to hug her, not quite yet, but I did anyway. And my mother clung to me as if I were a piece of driftwood in a stormy ocean, as if I might be the only thing to save her. I was the one to break away.

The next morning, when I took a large mug of coffee out to Ziggi, he was looking a little the worse for wear. Understandable, I suppose.

'You should go home,' I said. 'Take a shower.'

'I'll shower when we're done.'

'You might have stunk me to death by then, my friend.' I opened the back door of the cab, got in and sipped my peppermint tea. Ziggi sniffed and caught the aroma, which was not what he expected. The eye in the back of his head narrowed as it scoped my mug.

'*Really?*'

'No taste left for coffee, Ziggi,' I said sadly. 'It was all I wanted during pregnancy and now it just tastes like ashes. Peppermint tea? Couldn't stand it before – and now I find it refreshing.'

'That might be the saddest thing I've ever heard.' He took a deep, grateful swig of his own brew. 'The Universe has some sense of humour.'

'The Universe is an arse.' As I looked through the window, the little brown cat wandered up the driveway as if it owned the place; it gave me a look – it wasn't bothering to pretend I couldn't see it any more – and headed off down the street. 'That's Galina, right? I mean, I haven't actually seen her transform, but it's starting to be a bit like Clark Kent and Superman. Interesting disguise.'

'Is it?' He grunted in surprise and sat up straighter so he could get a better look at the departing feline. 'Huh.'

'I'm sure that when the time comes she'll rub herself on the bad guy and set off his allergies and we'll all be saved.'

'So cynical.'

'I've had a hard life.'

I relayed everything my mother had told me last night, and by the time I'd finished, Ziggi's head was hanging low, almost to his chest, and he was shaking. I'd never seen him cry properly before, not even last year when a really big archangel gave him a major walloping. He was mumbling something.

'What's that?'

'I should have been there for her! I should have been around—!'

'You didn't know her . . .' then two bits of memory clicked together like Lego pieces finally angled the right way and something that had been bothering me without me realising it suddenly made sense.

When we'd returned from Ocean's Reach the first time, when

Olivia had arrived at my place, Ziggi had *used her name*. Bela had seen photos of her in the Archives; he'd said that, but Ziggi hadn't any such excuse.

'You *knew* her – you recognised her at once, but I didn't twig. I didn't realise you shouldn't have, not if you didn't arrive in Australia until after she and Grigor were well and truly gone. And don't tell me you'd seen a photo.'

'I . . . V—'

'You know, I asked Jost Marolf for information about *Jäger* because I thought you weren't telling me everything. He had a book for me, and you know what? I refused it because I thought it would be invading your privacy. But that was the least of what you were keeping from me, wasn't it?'

'Verity—'

'So, how about you repay that trust? *Now*.'

Chapter Twenty-Eight

'You can't help what you're born as,' Ziggi said, 'but you can help what you become. You're proof of that.'

I was born the daughter of a murderer. I was born half-blooded, strange and powerful, and I could have gone either way, but I was lucky. My grandparents loved me and cared for me. They made sure I didn't fall between the cracks like so many other kids, Weyrd and Normal, because no one was looking out for them. The truth of his words didn't make me any less pissed off with him.

'There really isn't much more to tell, V, but it's the most important part. I told you my family were *Jägers*, that I refused to do my duty. I told you my brother saved us, but I didn't tell you he wasn't a *Jäger* but a *Kinderfresser*, a butcher of children. I didn't tell you that the princeling he bound himself to was a Nadasy.'

It took a few moments for that to sink in.

'Vadim Nadasy?' I asked at last. 'Vadim Nadasy, the mage I killed last year?'

The mage who'd turned his own grandson into a garbage golem to wreak revenge on the Council of Five. The mage whose wife I'd pushed into an oven to stop her making wine from the tears of children. The mage whose daughter Dusana had been encased in a bronze statue for the better part of fifteen years, who even now was still recovering in a specialised sanatorium somewhere in Europe.

I should have known all of his spiteful acts – his *hatred* – were *personal*.

'Don't get me wrong, V, your father might have saved us—'

'My father—?'

'Grigor. Your father. My brother. *Kinderfresser* to the Weyrd.' He puffed out a breath, and I remembered Wanda Callander calling him my uncle at Ocean's Reach; I'd thought it a mistake, but Ziggi was continuing, 'Your father might have been forced to his decision, but he loved his work; he was regarded as an artist. Verity, I can't make excuses for him. He was proud of what he did, and proud to be in service to the House of Nadasy.' He wiped away tears from all three eyes. 'He took a new name, Fassbinder, to disassociate himself with the shame I'd brought on "Hassman".

'When he met your mother, he fell in love – genuinely and deeply in love and he defied his master to marry her. Grigor and I kept in contact a little, although we were no longer so close, and I met them in Paris when they were on their honeymoon. Olivia was lovely and so very happy and I knew she had no idea what marrying Grigor would mean, how her life would change now she was joined with him. She was ignorant of what he really did – so how could love remain, with all those secrets just waiting to bubble to the surface?'

'And that doesn't strike you as a little ironic, *Uncle Ziggi*?' I was struggling to keep my voice level. 'After my grandparents died, I thought I was all alone. How could you not tell me you were my *family*? When we met, when we started working together, *how could you not?*'

'I'd . . .' His voice stumbled, and he tried again, 'V, I'd left it too long. You were an adult when I met you: you were fully formed, and you were so bitter about being abandoned by the Weyrd – you had walls up, and I figured if I told you I was your uncle, you'd be even more pissed off. I grew to love you, V, and I kept worrying that it would destroy our friendship, that you'd feel betrayed—'

'Like I do now?'

He didn't answer. What was there to say?

'And Bela knew too, didn't he – that you were my only living blood relative here?'

'At least until recent events,' he admitted. 'He wanted me to tell you, V – he nagged regularly – but I was the one too scared to come clean.' He hung his head and muttered, 'I thought I'd lose you.'

I sat quietly for a few moments, then collected his empty cup, not looking at him, and went back inside.

'Your breakfast's cold,' said David as I put the cups in the sink. I touched his shoulder but didn't say anything, just went into the bedroom where Maisie was lying, wide awake. She was watching me intently as I leaned over her and inspected her closely, especially her red-gold locks, then gathered her up. I cupped my hand under her head and gently felt for any sign of a third eye developing, but I – *we* – were in luck. If there's anything a girl needs less than hair on her chest it's an eye in the back of the head.

I sat in the rocking chair in the corner of the bedroom and fed my daughter, rocking to and fro as much for my comfort as hers. I heard my mobile buzz and ignored it. David knew me well enough not to come running in with it; he'd make sure Olivia didn't either. They left me in peace.

But it didn't last.

I heard Ziggi yelling from out on the footpath, then hammering on the front door. Idly I wondered if that was a prized characteristic of the *Jäger* too: yelling so loud that you scared the shit out of your prey.

'V! *Verity!* Bela says there's an orange Datsun Stanza outside Susan Beckett's house!'

It took me a few moments to wonder why I was supposed to give a flying fuck. Then I remembered, all those days ago, almost being run over at Toowong Cemetery.

'It's registered to Acton Beckett—'

Susan Beckett's missing father. Of course, it might be a coincidence. I hadn't taken down the licence plate on that vehicle; it had been covered with mud and we hadn't thought much of it. It might be an entirely different orange Datsun Stanza. Then again, realistically, how many of those things could still be running? And the gods only know, whenever they collided with anything else they crumpled like an aluminium can.

My daughter gave a squeak, her little hands stretching up and up as if reaching for my nose, and tears I didn't know I'd been holding in splashed onto her face. She didn't appear to notice, just gave this little milky burp and sent something white and a bit stinky dribbling down her singlet. I wiped the tears and the muck, and as I kissed her, David came into the bedroom.

He wiped away *my* tears and took Maisie. 'Duty calls.'

'Why can't you be like other husbands – tell me I'm not allowed to go to work, that I have to stay at home and mind the baby?' I hiccoughed and cried a little more.

'Because (a) I'm not your husband and (b) even if I were, I like my testicles where they are.'

'Why aren't you my husband?' I sobbed irrationally; we'd talked about this – but I couldn't stop myself, even though it didn't matter to me. Or at least, it hadn't. 'You got me pregnant and all – shouldn't you make an honest woman of me?'

'There's so much wrong with those sentences.' He held me close and whispered, 'But will you marry me?'

At last the tears dried up and I grinned. 'Yes. As soon as we're all safe.'

'That could take a while. I'll wait.'

'I love you.'

'I love you, too . . . but our daughter has just done something unspeakable, and if you don't go outside, I fear Ziggi will self-combust.' He grinned.

'Right now, I would rather deal with the poopocalypse.' I sighed. 'Okay, okay, I'm going . . .'

I pulled on my jacket and kissed them goodbye, but I didn't say anything to Olivia. She was still keeping secrets.

I didn't know how I was meant to feel about all these people I was supposed to be able to trust.

It was a very quiet, very fast ride to the Paddington workers' cottages on Enoggera Terrace. The orange Datsun in question was empty and parked at a drunken angle right behind the silvery-grey BMW in the carport. The gate in the high stucco fence was ajar. We pulled in behind Mike's red Jeep and I was out of the car before Ziggi could tell me to be careful.

As Mike opened his car door I asked, 'What did you see?'

He stretched his legs, cracked his joints as he did so, and from the corner of my eye I thought I saw dark, leathery wings peeking over his shoulders.

'Little guy, got his right hand bandaged.' He looked at me and wheeled his arms around as if warming up for a fight. 'Are we going in?'

'*I'm* going in.' I heard Ziggi behind me; I'd be arguing with both of them if I didn't shut down the rebellion quick-smart. I pointed a finger at both of them. 'Neither of you are noted for your subtlety.'

'With all respect, nor are you,' said Mike, and I knew Ziggi was thinking the same thing.

'Look, if the three of us go in mob-handed, someone's going to be saying, "Well, that escalated quickly!" in no time. So here's what's going to happen: *I* will go in and chat to Mr Wilson. I don't know what part Beckett's going to play – hostage or mob boss – but my best chance of finding a solution is by going in softly. I know he won't talk to me if I've got a posse.' I grabbed a quick breath before anyone could get a word in edgeways, added, 'Give me ten minutes. Let Bela know what's happening. Listen out for cries for help – and if it comes to that, Mike goes in first because he's the only one who's been smart enough to listen to me and actually get a *Vatnahlífir* tattoo!'

'But what about—?'

I held up my wrist and we all eyed the faint rune there. I'd forgotten to re-ink it.

'V, ' said Ziggi in a low voice. 'V, it's pretty faded.'

'It'll be just fine,' I said with a lot more confidence than I felt. 'And it's better than nothing, which is precisely what you've got. And I've got the Dagger of Wilusa.'

Neither Ziggi nor Mike looked convinced.

Ziggi said, 'Can't see how that's going to help against water . . .'

'Probably won't, but Wilson is flesh and blood. Look, just give me ten minutes—'

'Why is it always ten minutes?' asked Mike.

'Because it's long enough for me to sort it out or fuck it up! Now, will you both stop arguing? I've got my knife, I've got my phone—' And that was when I realised I'd left the house without my mobile; it was still charging in the kitchen

However, they didn't need to know that or I'd never get away.

I lit out across the road and headed for the open gate, hoping my faded rune would be enough to keep me safe – or if it wasn't, that I could get to Wilbur Wilson with the dagger before he could get to me with an eidolon.

Chapter Twenty-Nine

I took off my shoes at the front door and laid them beside a pair of men's oxblood loafers, thinking bare feet might give me an element of surprise. And I suppose it did for the few moments it took me to pad down the sunny hallway – but when I stepped into the lounge I realised it probably wouldn't have mattered if I'd shimmied in wearing a glittery top hat and tails and silver tap shoes.

The little man looked even more ordinary in the flesh than on camera. It was easy to see how he'd have slipped beneath notice. He didn't even look up as I slid in through the door. He was sitting cross-legged in the middle of the room. The furniture had been pushed back so he had more space, and that was enough to tell me that Susan Beckett either wasn't at home or wasn't in a position to protest. Wilbur Wilson was wearing the same chinos and blue dress shirt he'd been sporting the night he'd come to Ocean's Reach; it looked as though they hadn't been washed or ironed since then. There were grass and mud stains on the trousers and sweat had darkened the armpits of the shirt; I could smell him from where I stood. He'd taken his shoes off and I wondered if it was an ingrained habit; I was pretty sure Beckett hadn't had him living here, but he must have been in this house enough times to learn.

He'd surrounded himself with a circle of labradorite, glinting in the sun pouring in through the windows. In front of him was a silver bowl containing a huge labradorite crystal the size of an emu egg: no doubt the stone Kadie Cross was so keen to have restored to her. As I watched, I saw Wilbur Wilson reach out a shaking, badly bandaged hand and sprinkle something from a small leather sack onto the egg; the powder slid down its smooth surface and pooled at the base. I thought how meticulously he must have scouted his locations before he sent the water eidolons out to do his bidding, finding some hidden broom closet or a storage room or stairwell – or maybe a dark spot in the garden at Ocean's Reach – where he could set up his working in secret and still be close enough to control it. Beside him was a silver flask that probably contained water from the well in Wanda's front garden, the place he was 'born', over which he'd have the greatest influence. He reached for it and I noticed the bandage around his hand was seeping. Drops of red hit the polished wooden floorboards, but he didn't notice.

'Hey, Wilbur,' I said softly, trying not to startle him.

He looked up and for all the expression on his face, he might not have known me. Might not have tried to run me over in a cemetery, or drown my child in her cradle.

'Where is she?' he asked in a plaintive tone.

'I don't know. I'm looking for her too.'

'Yes, but you want to hurt her,' he said.

'No, I've been trying to help her.' I moved slowly to sit in the recliner-rocker so I didn't look so tall or so threatening.

'One man's help is another man's hurt,' he sing-songed, and smiled nastily, pleased with his cleverness.

'Her hand was burned,' I said. 'Did you do that?'

'No! She – she just wasn't expecting me and she got a surprise.' He pouted. 'I didn't *mean* it.'

I let it go. 'What're you doing here, Wilbur?'

He gave me a smile, and it was a sly, chilling thing. 'Wouldn't you like to know?'

'I think I already do. Should I guess, Wilbur? Is it a Grand Drowning?' He made a face, put out that I knew. 'See, I'm wondering why you're doing that here when you're looking for Susan, because *here* is where you do the mud thing.'

He looked away, mumbling something.

'What was that?'

'I said, I don't want to hurt her. Just scare her. The mud hasn't worked.' He looked shocked at that. 'She's so stubborn! But she'll see reason. She'll make good on her promise.'

'What promise is that, Wilbur?'

'You came to her door that day – you *upset* her! So I followed you – I tried to scare you off at the cemetery,' he said, then hissed, 'You haven't helped, you know, talking to her, offering aid.'

'She didn't accept any.'

'You haven't helped *me*.' And he spat in my general direction, although it didn't get very far, just dribbled onto his own trouser leg. 'All this time, all this effort, all this *mess*! I thought if I drowned your child you'd be distracted,' he added, very matter-of-fact.

I fought down the urge to beat him to death and instead concentrated on keeping him talking. 'Did Susan send you to Ocean's Reach?'

He shook his head vehemently. 'Not *send*, no. She was angry at me! She told me who you were, that Aunty Wanda had you to stay . . .' He grinned wickedly.

'So you showed some initiative?' I pushed out a calming breath, and found it didn't help much. 'You've hurt some people, Wilbur.'

'That's not my fault! She wouldn't be reasonable. So, I thought . . .' He paused and took a deep breath. 'So, I thought if I did some terrible things she'd realise it was *her* fault, and she would want it to stop.' He began to blink, quite a lot, a rapid butterfly movement, and as he did so, his outline began to shiver and shake, flickering like a TV on the fritz. Beneath the glamours Wanda Callander had so carefully woven I could see something small and pale, with a thick thatch of hair, or fur, more likely, and large red eyes set wide apart on a squashed oval of a face. Wilbur was a *smågubbar*, one of the little folk, as near as spit to a troll, just more articulate, although not necessarily more logical or rational. He was having trouble holding himself together and I wondered if Alex Parrish might see through him properly now.

'You've hurt yourself, Wilbur. Can I clean that up for you?'

'You just want to get close to me,' he laughed. 'Meanie! This is your fault: *you* stopped the price being paid. I wanted that man to stop giving her money every time. It made it easier for her to ignore me, when everything got cleaned and replaced so easily.' So he hadn't known Susan was about to cancel her policy.

'You've been cutting your hand for the starter blood?'

He ignored me and whined, 'But you *didn't* die, you *didn't* drown, no one died! So the debt bounced back on me and infected me. How did you stop it? *How?*' he shouted.

I kept my voice low, soothing. 'Well, if you do bad things, Wilbur, someone's going to stop you eventually.' I really felt like I was dealing with a child. 'Had any of the other people done anything to hurt you? Toby Malone or Faraday Hannigan?'

'No – that was the point, don't you see? I just chose them when I saw them: *random* was the point.' He smiled cruelly at his own cleverness. 'If she didn't know who was next then she couldn't warn anyone, could she? *She should have felt guilty.*' He looked at me plaintively. 'Why didn't she?'

'You did a lot for her, didn't you?'

'Yes.' All sincerity now, and I remembered thinking my first visit to Mindy's Mehndi, when Kadie Cross told me that his request for improvements in his appearance, that it smacked of someone trying to attract another someone who wasn't interested.

'You love her, don't you, Wilbur?'

He smiled then, and it was almost beautiful. 'How could I not? Hers was the first face I saw. She brought me out of the dark places and let me serve her.'

Oh, you poor bastard. 'How did you serve her, Wilbur? I'm sure it was difficult, like going on a quest to prove your love.'

'Oh yes! All sorts of tasks: making sure she had enough wealth, making sure no one threatened her, making sure she did best in all her studies. She trusted me! *Only* me! And I did everything right.' He smiled at the memories. 'And when she moved here, I followed and she let me work with her, really! In her office! I delivered the mail twice a day, and I got to see her every time.'

I wondered how many of Susan Beckett's rivals had met with unfortunate accidents over the years – and then I wondered if any of the 'goods in kind' payments David had found in her firm's accounts covered the *smågubbar*'s salary – although what need would he have of money?

'Wilbur, what was the biggest, the best thing you ever did for her? The greatest proof of your love?'

'The mud,' he said without hesitation, 'definitely the mud.'

'The mud that's been appearing here?' I asked, as if confused.

'Oh, no: the first time. At her father's house.' He leaned towards me confidentially. 'The little bits I've done here? Nothing compared to that! But I was clever there, I kept it contained, I only used one room – and that's a lot of mud per square foot!'

'Why yes, it is. You must have been exhausted afterwards.'

'Nothing is too much to prove my love. When she asked me, when she made her promise, it was like – like plighting a troth. She trusted me to remove her greatest problem, her greatest unhappiness, and I trusted her, so I sent the mud.'

'Was it on a Wednesday? The last Wednesday of the month when you did that?'

He smiled. It did make a warped kind of sense, I could see that: the day he sent the mud was the most significant day in his life, when he committed his greatest act of love. I suspected Susan either didn't realise, or more likely, she didn't care.

'Who was in that room, Wilbur? It must have been someone who treated your Susan very badly.'

He scowled. 'Her father, who'd done bad things. Her mother, who'd let those things happen.'

I swallowed hard. 'What about the little girls? Unity and Hildy?'

'They were . . . unwanted.' He looked away as if not comfortable with that confession. He was so easy to read, this creature; Susan Beckett would have had no trouble manipulating him.

I didn't pursue that; I knew enough. 'And what did she promise you, Wilbur? What have you been fighting so hard to get? What thing did you hope to earn for such a price?'

'Love!' he almost sang, but the word was underpinned with pain and sadness. It was a word painted red with the blood of others, with his childlike screaming need and with Susan Beckett's ruthless determination to get whatever she wanted.

'Why now, Wilbur? I mean, why did she ask you to hurt her parents now?'

'Her father came to visit – he said something mean. I wasn't here. I don't live here.' He shrugged, resentful. 'Not yet.'

So he only knew what Beckett had told him. 'Wilbur, what terrible things did he do to Susan?'

His face – his *faces*, both human and *smågubbar* – darkened, his eyes lit up and I knew I'd put a foot wrong. He raised the injured hand over the egg and made a fist until his blood dripped onto the stone, and at the same moment he splashed water from the open flask and shouted, 'What she wouldn't let *me* do!'

The process was incredibly fast; if I hadn't been so terrified, I'd have been fascinated. From the moment the first drops of blood and water touched the egg, a form began to build, increasing in speed as the liquid ran down the smooth sides and hit the powdered ingredients at its base. There was a swirling, roiling mass of fluid, like watching a waterspout form over the sea, spiralling up and up and up. And like an idiot, I just sat in the chair, watching it like some slack-jawed gawker.

But when it reached person-height, it wasn't quite right, not like the eidolons I'd seen at Ocean's Reach or Soteria. It kept losing its shape, as if the surface tension holding it in place kept forgetting what it was supposed to do. Wilbur grunted, grimacing in concentration, and the eidolon drew itself back together. His hand was bleeding profusely through the bandage now, as if the magic knew the proper price hadn't been paid; that a greater debt was owing than drowning me would cover.

And finally I figured out it really was time to go. How much power was left in my henna rune was anyone's guess, and suddenly I felt a lot less confidant than when I'd told Ziggi and Mike I'd be fine. I stood, which caught the eidolon's attention and it rushed at me – and for the second time in far too brief a period I was certain I was going to die.

But instead of being hit by a wave of water, I was thrust aside, hit by a high-speed object, and I slid across the floor until I crashed into the wall, so winded I couldn't even swear. Panting, trying to get back my breath, all I could do was watch as the eidolon re-sighted on the short, sturdy brown blur, which had started circling the chair I'd so recently occupied.

It dived low, in front of Wilbur Wilson, still sitting cross-legged on the floor, knocking some of the labradorite crystals out of the circle, and the eidolon leaped, just missed the tips of the blur's feet, then hit the *smågubbar* full on in the face—

—and proceeded to drown him.

There was nothing I could do. It was awful to see, but no worse than watching Jerry die; no worse than it would have been to watch my daughter die, or Alex Parrish, or his daughter Alicia, or anyone I cared about . . . or anyone whose only crime had been to wander past Wilbur Wilson's hiding place at the wrong moment.

When he'd stopped struggling, I slowly rose and went to stand over him. In death, Wilbur Wilson's glamours were unknitting fast, revealing him to be nothing more than a small, pale creature, only vaguely human, wearing a shirt and trousers far too big for him. I crouched beside him and put a finger to his torso. I pushed, and watched as the liquid rippled beneath his skin.

'Unpaid debts have a way of coming home to roost,' I said quietly; he was way beyond hearing me. I wondered where Susan Beckett was and how she'd snuck away. I wondered where Wilbur Wilson had lived while he toiled at her law firm; I was willing to bet that if we searched we'd find a storeroom or mailroom or broom cupboard at Walsh-Penhalligon with a little nest where he slept and dreamed that his summoner would one day take him to her heart. I couldn't help but feel a little sorry for him.

I looked up at Galina, who was leaning against a wall, barely puffing. 'Not to sound ungrateful, but shouldn't you be watching my family?'

'Zvezdomir told me to follow you,' she said. Bela's real name rolled off her tongue like a caress and I wondered how they knew each other – and had to remind myself it was none of my business. 'He called me because you weren't answering your phone. He said that meant you were probably doing something stupid.'

I opened my mouth, closed it again. I couldn't argue with that. 'I forgot my mobile.' I glanced at the faded *Vatnahlífir* on my wrist and became even more convinced that I'd have drowned, just a lot more slowly than Wilbur Wilson had, while the weakened marking struggled against overwhelming odds. 'I'm glad you came. I couldn't have moved like that.'

'Zvezdomir also said to tell you that the dead man's van has been located in the Chinatown Mall. He is going there now. You are to meet him if you are still alive.'

'Bela, always with the conditions.' I rose. I'd call McIntyre to send a clean-up squad and leave Mike standing guard over the house that Susan Beckett had somehow managed to vacate without his noticing. Finding her would have to wait, but I was pretty sure the main threat to Brisbane's general public, both Weyrd and Normal, was gone. 'Come on then.'

She straightened, shoulders pushing back. 'No. I am done.'

'What do you mean, done? Like, off-shift?'

'No, I am done. My debt to you is paid.' And with that her outline shimmered and stretched. Gone was the stocky little ninja and in her place stood a tall, elegant blonde woman with blue, blue eyes and a haughty expression.

'You're . . . you're—' For a long moment my brain wouldn't make the connection.

'Dusana Nadasy.'

'Well, fuck.'

To say that Dusana Nadasy's marriage had ended badly was like saying that a few books were burned in the Great Library of Alexandria's Christmas barbecue. Her husband had paid Eleanor Aviva to cast a spell encasing her in bronze and Dusana had spent the next fifteen years as a foyer decoration. It was through my efforts that she'd been released, but I had also killed her parents – who were psychos – and her son, who was trying to eat me. Actually, strictly speaking, I really only killed her mother, because her son killed her father, but looking at her face, I didn't think that sort of subtlety would get me very far. I found myself expecting to hear the words, *You killed my family, prepare to die.* Given Dusana's incredible speed, the odds of my deploying the dagger in time were very bad.

But she just looked at me as if I were nothing more than a servant who'd proved to be disappointing. 'Zvezdomir made it clear that you were responsible for saving me and I owed you for that. Now that debt is paid. But for what you took from me?' She made a motion with her hand like clearing a table. 'When next we meet, there will be no quarter given.'

'My family—' I was overwhelmed with panic – *I'd left her with David and Maisie and Olivia . . .* But she hadn't done anything to them. Had she?

She gave me a look of pitying contempt. 'I will not hurt them to get to you. I will not hurt a baby. Your man is a good man; there are too few of those. Your mother is . . . steadfast.' She knew of what she spoke. 'But I will hurt *you*, and you will be the cause of a lifelong ache for those you leave behind. Carry that knowledge with you.'

And with that, Dusana Nadasy did the disappearing act very few Weyrd could manage, there one moment and gone the next, leaving only warm air and a trace of heady perfume.

Chapter Thirty

I had the presence of mind to collect Kadie Cross' stone before finding the telephone in the kitchen. I rang David and he picked up on the first ring. In the briefest possible way I told him about Galina – that I didn't think she was a threat, but she should under no circumstances be let back in the house; that Mike was on his way. 'I love you,' I said inadequately, just as Mike and Ziggi rushed in; my ten minutes was up, apparently.

I hung up and went back to the *smågubbar*'s sad little body. When I went through his pockets there was just one thing there: a very soggy piece of parchment, carelessly folded. I couldn't read the smudged lettering, but I was willing to bet it was the formula for the mud-curse. I headed back to the kitchen, gesturing for Mike and Ziggi to follow. 'Mike, did you see Susan Beckett leave? At all?'

'No! I swear it, V: she hasn't left—!'

'Well, she's not fucking here.'

I rifled through the drawers and failed to find a box of matches or a lighter, but when I started to search the kitchen I noticed that the high-end hob was gas; when I hit the starter for one of the rings, a bright blue spark sprang up almost immediately and lit the circular plate. I held the damp parchment to the flame, praying it would take. There was some ineffectual smouldering for a moment, but eventually, whatever it was made of, whatever ink had been used, somehow it burned. I held onto it until there was just one corner left, then I dropped that on the stovetop so it could be entirely consumed. Once I was certain there was nothing left but ash and smoke, I turned on the range hood so the fumes would be drawn away and dissipated into the open air. I wanted the spell *completely* gone, for no one to use this one ever again. At least *this* instance of it had been erased from the world.

When I'd finished, I noticed Mike's stricken face and softened. Patting his shoulder, I said, 'Look, she probably went over the back fence – you couldn't possibly have known that. Mike, do me a favour, will you, and get over to my place. Do *not* trust Galina if she turns up, and don't let anyone else you don't know in the house until you hear otherwise from me.'

When we departed I left both the front door and the gate open. I didn't really care if anyone walked in and stole stuff from Susan Beckett.

'Did you know who she really was?' I asked Ziggi once we were heading towards the Valley.

'Who?'

'Galina. She's Dusana Nadasy.'

'*What the fuck—?*' Ignoring all the other traffic, he slammed on the brakes in the middle of Musgrave Road, and somehow avoided a pile-up. He turned in his seat to stare at me. You couldn't fake that level of *what-the-fuck*-ness. 'And she didn't kill you?'

'Not this time. But next time? Apparently I'm in big trouble.' I rubbed the back of my neck, wondering if Ziggi'd given me whiplash. 'You know what? Bela might have just rocketed past you to the top of my shit-list.'

The beeping of horns from the cars that had narrowly avoided rear-ending us finally broke through his shock and he turned around and hit the accelerator. Luckily for us both, Ziggi was an excellent driver, otherwise we'd have been dead long ago. 'How'd she even get here? We didn't see her.'

'Guess she parachuted in.' Which meant she'd transited in the same way she'd gone out, which took a tremendous amount of energy. Even Bela needed an aspirin and a lie-down after he'd done a one-way trip. 'Ziggi, Bela knew,' I said casually. 'Zvezdomir Tepes, still making decisions that affect me without telling me. She was *near my family*, Ziggi. She was watching over my baby.'

'But she didn't do anything, V, that's the thing to remember. Bela wouldn't have let her near you if he thought she was a threat,' he said reasonably, but I thought I detected a note of uncertainty.

'She said she'd paid her debt to me for getting her out of the bronze and back into the world. There's a refreshing sense of honour neither of her parents had.' I made fists, then let them go. 'But, shit, shit, *shit*, Ziggi. Shit!'

'Shit indeed.'

We didn't talk until we reached Fortitude Valley and turned off, driving under the red gates into the Chinatown Mall. Ziggi parked outside a shop selling all manner of Chinese medicine and I wondered briefly if they had anything for a headache, then figured they'd probably have something for everything, but it would have to boil for hours and would smell dreadful and taste worse. Perhaps I'd wait till I could get an aspirin myself.

I walked up the slight incline much more easily this time, now I was unencumbered, and turned into the mouth of the alley where I'd last seen the fox-girls. Two Weyrd were lounging at the entrance to the alleyway, eyeing me as I passed.

Parked right at the back, wedged in so tight that the side doors had no hope of opening, was Len's delivery van, looking much the worse for wear. I wondered where the *kitsune* had taken it to get it so covered in mud, but decided it probably didn't matter. What was more interesting was how she'd got it in here in the first place. It couldn't have been here long or there'd have been complaints to the cops.

Bela, McIntyre and Constable Oldman were standing in front of the open back doors, their backs to us as they leaned in, being careful not to touch anything. As they heard us approach they turned, and to his credit, Bela looked relieved to see me. Nice to know. But I was still furious.

McIntyre and Oldman were both uncomfortably shifting their weight on their feet.

'You look like shit, Fassbinder,' said Rhonda.

'I'm starting to think it's my default state of being.' I didn't talk to Oldman; I wasn't too fond of her after that little performance on my front porch and she was still giving me the side-eye like a defeated four-year-old. 'You should send someone over to Susan Beckett's house, Rhonda. It's empty and messy and there's a body to pick up. I'm sure it's the sort of job Lacy here would love to do.'

'Hers?'

'Nope, Wilbur Wilson's.'

Bela said, 'Galina found you, then?'

'No, *Dusana* found me.'

' . . . '

'Bela, between the fact that you knew Ziggi was my uncle and didn't tell me and the fact that you let Dusana Nadasy get close to my family and didn't tell me, you are in so much fucking trouble that your head should be spinning.' I held up a finger to stop him interrupting. '*But* . . . we have enough to worry about at this point without infighting, so I am going to keep my temper until this is over.' He was starting to look a little relieved, so I continued, 'But just so we're clear: you're an arsehole. A fucking, *fucking* arsehole. And I'm probably going to hurt you. Just not yet.'

'Understood.' He glanced at Ziggi, who might have looked sympathetic if I hadn't been watching them both like a hawk.

'Now, before we go any further, is there anything else either of you'd like to share? Because if anything, even the tiniest secret should come to light that you have kept from me about me or my family or anything even vaguely tangentially connected with me or my family, there will be hell to pay.'

They intoned together, 'No, V.'

'You'd better be telling the truth.' I rubbed my temples. I pulled the emu-egg chunk of labradorite from my jacket pocket out and offered it to Bela. 'This needs to be returned to Ms Cross, but perhaps you'd like to talk to her about keeping such a powerful object in a safer place?' He took it. 'So: Wilbur Wilson is dead, drowned by his own eidolon, and we have Dusana to thank for that – which, by the way, she says is the end of her debt to me, and now I'm in big trouble.'

'She won't hurt—' Bela began.

'—my family. That's what she told me. Mind you, that's what she *would* say if she was trying to disarm me. But I've spoken to David and told him not to let her in and to make sure Olivia is on high alert.'

'No , V, Dusana was a princess, but she always had a sense of fair play, and the time she's . . . been away . . .' – *sealed inside a giant bronze mermaid statue, watching her son grow up motherless, watching her husband gloat over her incarceration* – 'has changed her. That's why I agreed to let her watch over you. But I should have told you.'

'Yes, you should.' I looked around. 'Wilson's gone, the drownings were . . . well, long story short: Beckett summoned him when she was a teenager and has been using him to feather her nest ever since.

She asked him for something really huge and promised him something commensurate in return – but she didn't come through on her part of the bargain. Bela, he was like a child, no sense of morality – it made perfect sense to him to try to manipulate Susan Beckett by killing strangers.'

'*Smågubbar* are basically malicious children,' Bela agreed. 'They lead sailors astray and laugh if they drown – they think it's a great joke.'

'But Beckett didn't give a shit about anyone else. She's spent *years* manipulating him, getting him to do her bidding, making her life better, and all he wanted was to be loved – by which I don't mean cuddle-loved, I mean full-on creepy-loved. He started using the Grand Drownings once he realised the mud inundations weren't enough to make her keep her promise.' I began to pace, thinking. 'He sent the mud as a reminder of what he'd done to her family at her bidding, but it wasn't enough.'

'Why was he making an eidolon at her place?' asked Ziggi.

'He said just to scare her, but he didn't know where she was – he clearly assumed she'd be returning, as her beamer's still in the carport. And he was in a bad way; the last Grand Drowning cost him badly. He's been cutting his hand for the first blood, but it'd got infected and it was breaking him, his glamours. And Beckett's refusal to play ball was clearly doing his head in. He was heartbroken, Bela, but still hopeful.'

I stopped and looked at them. 'So, where the hell is Susan Beckett? Somehow she's snuck out past Mike. She had her entire family killed. Wilson implied there'd been abuse, so I can kind of understand her parents as targets, but the little girls? Her sisters?'

'Maybe . . .' Bela began, then stopped and took a breath. 'Maybe they weren't her sisters.'

'Her . . . *daughters*?' said Ziggi in horror, clasping his hands behind his neck and spinning away on one heel.

'Jesus,' said McIntyre. '*Jesus.*'

I felt sick to the pit of my stomach, but at least I didn't throw up on the crime scene like Constable Oldman did. 'Daughters. *Her own daughters.*'

We were silent, struggling with the implications – then I had a sudden thought. 'The corpselights! Two corpselights have been in my back yard – what are the odds they're Hildy and Unity? Olivia brought them with her; she said they were what finished her in the Guardian's employ, seeing them there.'

'What Guardian?' demanded Bela, and I realised neither Ziggi nor I had had a chance to tell him what my mother had confessed. When I filled him in, he frowned.

'Verity, in all my years I've never heard of a Guardian of the Southern Gate of the Underworld.'

'Does that mean there isn't one?'

'Well, no one knows precisely what happens after death – everyone's got different stories, those who come back: either bright lights and tunnels or blackness, nothingness.

'And those are all stories from Normals; the Weyrd have no such tales. So we don't know. We just don't know.'

'Bela, there are so many religions, so many mythologies, different belief systems, so many pieces of a very fractured whole . . . isn't it conceivable there is something like that, a Guardian? And my mother did come back from *somewhere*, even if it was a kind of purgatory, a waiting room. Isn't it possible?'

He shrugged. 'Anything's possible.'

'Okay . . . So, back to Susan Beckett: is it possible she'll try to bring something else across? Of course, she doesn't know Wilbur's gone – but where is she now?'

'Do you think she's a danger to the population at large?'

'Not as such, no: she's a stone-cold self-interested bitch – but the kind of random wholesale murder Wilbur was indulging in? No, her murders were precisely targeted. She didn't want anyone's help when Wilbur turned on her because she was afraid we'd find out what she'd done to her family. Wilbur said her father had come to visit, before all this started, so I'm willing to bet that was the trigger.'

'But she's not a general threat?'

'No.'

'Right, then the next pressing thing is the *kitsune*.' He pointed to the van. 'Look.'

He used the light from his mobile to illuminate the interior. A pile of undelivered parcels had been pushed up against the back wall. They were crushed and battered; the fox-girl must have been using them as a bed.

More importantly, a black circle had been burned into the floor of Len's van. I could smell sulphur and fat, recently ignited, so we couldn't have been too far behind her. And sulphur and fat . . . I had a vague memory; was it something witches used . . . ?

I looked askance at Bela. '*Flying?*'

'No, transit: from one defined point to another. It's dangerous to do without a receiving place because you might find yourself in a rock or halfway through a piece of furniture or in front of an oncoming vehicle.'

'Is that like what you do?' Bela generally only did it when he *really* wanted to get away. Often from me.

'It's a version of it: an artificial analogue of my natural ability.'

I looked back at the circle. 'Olivia said the *kitsune* were also the

Guardian's minions. She was the Hound – the hunter – then when she fled, she became the Apostate.' I pondered a bit, then gave up. 'So where's the fox-girl gone?'

'Back to the Guardian? This isn't an easy or lightly conducted spell, so she must have a very good reason that makes it worth doing.'

'We found this because she wanted us to – she left the van here because she knew it would be found the moment someone from one of the restaurants tried to get into the alleyway. Turn the torch back on, will you?' I stared into the van, squinting, then scrambled in and walked to the back, avoiding the circle, to where I'd seen something gleam in Bela's light.

Beneath a yellow express post plastic satchel were three things – I couldn't decide if they'd been carelessly discarded, or left there to be found as hints or breadcrumbs or torment.

I recognised my phone by the large scratch on its face where it had scraped across the concrete of this very alley when the *kitsune* had attacked me. A small antique silver compact lay beside it: Olivia's magic mirror. I grabbed them both, kneeled, a little unsteadily, and opened the compact. One reflective surface was shattered but the other was still intact. I touched the glass, but got nothing more than billowing grey smoke. The third item was Olivia's sword, fully extended, its blade rusty with someone's blood.

Olivia: my mother.

My mother who'd been looking after David and Maisie.

Just then, Bela's phone began to ring.

Chapter Thirty-One

'I'm sorry,' said David, bewildered. 'I went to have a shower – I just needed a shower—'

Maisie, draped over his shoulder, was howling for Australia. I'd be howling too, if my mum and great-uncle and some over-sized Weyrd in black jeans and a T-shirt had just burst in on my dinner. I clocked Mike wandering in just after we arrived and made a mental note to demand where the fuck he'd been right after I worked out why David had been so uncommunicative.

'Why didn't you answer when I called after the shower? I just kept getting through to your voicemail, over and over . . .'

. . . and the knot in my stomach was getting tighter and tighter as I became more and more certain that Dusana Nadasy lied to me and my stupidity meant your deaths: that I'd lost you both.

'I was stuck in the chair, V! Maisie was sleeping and my phone was in the lounge and I didn't want to get up and wake her. She's restless enough.' He jiggled our daughter up and down, desperately trying to get her to stop crying. 'Jesus, V, I'm sorry—'

'But why didn't Olivia answer the phone, then?'

'Well, when I got out of the shower, Olivia was gone – and your phone was gone.'

'And you didn't call—?'

'Yes, of course I did! I called your phone, but no one answered, then Maisie started crying and I went to take care of our child.' He pursed his lips and I realised my tone had finally done what months of Weyrd life hadn't. I said quickly, 'I'm sorry, it's not your fault,' and bursting into tears, I wrapped myself around him and Maisie.

My sobbing shocked the baby out of her own fit of the miseries and a tiny hand entangled itself in my hair, holding on tight, and I breathed in the smell of them, pathetically grateful that they were solid and real and alive in my arms.

'It's not your fault,' I repeated, and this time I meant it.

'I thought Olivia had gone to bring you your phone. I'd only just talked to you before I went in the shower. But I'm guessing she . . .'

He finally registered my face and asked urgently, 'V, where is she?'

'She's gone. I think . . .' I swallowed. 'The text from Bela telling me where the van had been found is showing as read, so I think Olivia must have heard the message come through, realised I'd forgotten the mobile and checked to see if it was important. She obviously assumed she could handle the last fox-girl because she'd dealt with the others . . .'

I swallowed and whispered, 'We think the *kitsune* got her. But . . . I don't think she's dead, at least not for real, not yet. There's no body . . .' I started to cry again, sobbing, 'I don't know where she is, David, and I don't know how to get her back.'

He laid his hand against my cheek, but didn't say anything; empty promises would do no one any good. The *Vatnahlífir* on David's wrist had been refreshed, and Maisie's kicking little heel was the same. He saw I'd clocked them and said, 'Olivia did them last night. Before you came home.'

My mother had been looking after my family while I'd been out. I was saved from thinking too deeply about that by the vibration of my mobile, but it was Bela's number flashing up, dashing any foolish hope that it might have been Olivia calling to say she was okay, she was victorious, she'd just popped out for a bottle of milk and a loaf of bread.

'We've got a problem,' he started.

'I think we're currently at critical mass on problems.' I sighed. 'No capacity for any more.'

'Eleanor Aviva is dead.'

'*Shit*—' Aviva had been my next stop. I didn't *want* to talk to her, but she was a powerful witch and if anyone could trace the casting remains in Len's van, it would have been her; apart from that, anything she knew about the Guardian was lost. 'What happened to her?'

He hesitated a little too long. 'Ah. Dusana happened.' It was probably the first thing she'd sorted after she'd saved me – maybe that was why she'd revealed herself then: to distract me by making me worry about my family. That was occurring a lot . . .

'Dusana arrived to speak with Sandor, then asked to use the bathroom. By the time he realised she'd been gone too long, Eleanor was dead.'

'How many pieces was she in?'

'Just the one: her throat cut and she'd bled out.' He sighed. 'Honestly, I'd have thought Dusana would have wanted to make it last longer.'

'Dusana appears to have become something of a pragmatist, Bela: it had to be quick, or she'd get caught. She'll be on her way out of the country right now.' Despite the inconvenience and fear she'd caused me, despite the cold-blooded murder, I couldn't help but feel a little pleased for her. I couldn't help but think that after fifteen years as a metal mermaid courtesy of Aviva's spiteful magic, Dusana Nadasy was entitled to her revenge.

Then I remembered I was also on Dusana's shit-list and felt a little less sisterly towards her.

'No one saw her leave . . . but one of the guards said he'd seen—'

'—a small brown cat running from the house,' I finished for him.

'I should have told you who she was, V. I'm sorry. I'd like you to come to the Palace and look around.'

'Bela—'

'I need your eyes on this. The *smågubbar's* no longer a threat and the fox-girl's gone.' He didn't say, *The fact that she has your mother is irrelevant to my interests.* 'David and Maisie are safe, and Mike will watch over them.'

'Susan Beckett's still in the wind.'

'Do you really think she's going to go after your family? Or Alex Parrish? Or anyone?'

'No. I think she set things in motion for personal gain and revenge isn't her thing because it won't bring her what she wants. I think she's fled the mess she made, or she's hiding out until it blows over. But I've been wrong before.'

'Just get here, V.'

In life, Eleanor Aviva had been an elegant woman; in death, not so much. The powerful glamour that had given her high cheekbones and perfectly coiffed auburn hair was gone. Though her face was still recognisable, she now had eight legs instead of two, all of them considerably hairier than before, a swollen abdomen, less shoulder and more cephalothorax. A pink jersey Schiaparelli dress was pulled tight around her distended – true – shape. The expensive rug beneath her was stained sticky and black, and her eyes were blank and staring, the white veil of death thick on them.

I crouched beside her and noted that there was a wound at each leg joint; closer examination showed the heads of the iron nails that had been hammered in to prevent her from shifting her shape or transporting herself to a much nicer location. They were old wounds, not new. The last time I'd seen her she'd been sporting the stopgap measure of an iron collar around her neck; obviously something a little more permanent had been deemed necessary. It must have hurt like hell, but I still had trouble mustering any real sympathy for her.

Her cell wasn't luxurious but it wasn't uncomfortable: big bed, bookshelves, three dressing tables and a walk-in wardrobe, several plush sofas. The walls were hung with tapestries so she could pretend she had a view beyond them other than the rock of the basement level. The Turkish rugs on the floor were clearly old and valuable, so it was unfortunate that she'd been obliged to bleed out onto one. Her *bag du jour* was open on the floor next to her, its contents scattered far and wide. At first I thought it a random mess, until I realised one of her forelegs was draped over a fluorescent yellow Post-it notepad and an uncapped tube of lipstick – Chanel, worth the cost of a passable meal for two – had rolled away until it butted up against the leg of a coffee table. I could make out smears of the same shade on the tips of what passed for her 'fingers'.

Gently, I shuffled the leg away, praying Eleanor Aviva wasn't suddenly going to shudder back to life, or give one of those death-throe jerks designed to make you wish you'd worn brown trousers. The feel of her limb against my fingers was sticky-soft and velvety, strangely nice, considering how un-nice she looked. But it didn't really matter how soft it was, or how used to the Weyrd I was: it didn't diminish the fact that this woman had been a giant spider underneath all her clever enchantments. I suppressed a shudder and let the leg drop away, then picked up the Post-it pad.

With the lipstick and an unsteady hand she'd inscribed *3 in 1*, which, quite frankly could not have been less fucking help if it had tried. I held up the piece of paper so Ziggi and Bela and Sandor Verhoeven, all crammed in the doorway, could see it.

'Just once,' I said through gritted teeth, 'just once, why can't someone write some *useful* last words?'

'What does it mean?' asked Verhoeven. There was a catch in his voice and I looked at him in surprise.

He glared. 'Eleanor was a friend for a very long time, Ms Fassbinder. Betrayal . . . doesn't always destroy that. She didn't deserve this.'

I thought differently, but didn't say it. 'Right. And you also knew Dusana was masquerading as Galina?'

'Zvezdomir sought the permission of the Council.'

'The *whole* Council?' I asked. If Theodosia had known about this my head might just explode.

Verhoeven amended his statement, a hand raised in apology. 'My permission – he sought *my* permission and I gave it. Dusana . . . She said all the right things.'

'I bet she did. She's not stupid.'

'You must go after her,' announced the head of the Council of Five in the same casual tone rich women use to tell their maids to clean up the puppy's poop on the carpet.

'*Excuse me?*' As I rose and faced him, my arms crossed over my chest, I saw Bela's expression change to the one suitable for noticing a runaway car or a train speeding towards a level crossing where the signals are out.

'You will find her and retrieve her.'

'Well, *that's* not going to happen.'

'What—?' Verhoeven looked apoplectic.

'To recap, the answer is *no*, and here's why: my mother is missing and I'm pretty fucking keen to get her back, and Susan Beckett, a woman who murdered her family and allowed three innocent people to die rather than let her secrets be revealed, is still out there. Not to mention that Dusana Nadasy is crazy-powerful and I am *not* going after her unprepared, *plus*, I killed her family, so whatever she's got in store for me is going to be considerably worse than what she did to Aviva. The cumulative result of all these things is that Dusana Nadasy is *firmly* on my back burner.'

Verhoeven's lips opened and closed a few times. When he turned around for support, Bela was shaking his head. Zvezdomir Tepes knew better than to beat a dead horse. 'I'm sorry, Sandor, but I must agree with Verity on this. Dusana is not to be trifled with, and I would not send anyone against her until we've agreed how we will deal with her. Besides, I received a call a few minutes ago to say she'd boarded a private plane at the International Airport. She has access to her not-inconsiderable inheritance, so we will not find her easily.'

He placed a hand on Verhoeven's shoulder and I watched the Councillor deflate. 'We will find her, Sandor, but it must wait. I will not risk my best resource.'

I supposed I should have been flattered, but I still kind of want to kick Bela in the nuts. My forgiveness stocks were running especially low.

My phone vibrated; I didn't know the number, but I did recognise Wanda Callander's voice even though she was speaking quietly, 'Verity? Verity, she's here. Susan's here.'

'In your house?'

'Outside, in the garden. She's standing there, staring at the turf maze.'

'Is she doing anything?'

'Just standing and staring.'

'Okay, stay inside. Don't let her in. I'll be there . . . soonish.' I looked at Sandor Verhoeven and Bela. 'Susan Beckett's at Ocean's Reach. Don't suppose the helicopter's available?'

Verhoeven said, 'It is in use elsewhere.'

I looked at Bela: he could transit if he needed to, though it took a phenomenal amount of effort and energy. 'I can't take anyone with me, V.'

'What about the sort of transit the fox-girl must have done with Olivia? We know where we need to go – we can get map references for Ocean's Reach, surely? One of you can home in on the turf maze, can't you? It's got to be giving off some kind of signal . . . can we use the power as a focal point?'

Verhoeven said slowly, 'I can do it.'

'She can't go on her own,' said Bela with a pained expression that said quite clearly, *I just stopped you from being killed by one madwoman and now you invite yourself into another situation?*

'She won't be,' said Ziggi.

I said mildly, '*She's* the cat's mother.'

'You will feel ill,' warned Verhoeven.

'Better than feeling nothing at all.'

Chapter Thirty-Two

Verhoeven wasn't joking: when we landed in the centre of the turf maze I fell to my knees and vomited. Ziggi deftly danced out of the way, then graciously helped me up once I'd finished heaving. I wasn't looking forward to the return journey, but at least I'd have an empty stomach for that.

I looked around for Susan Beckett and found her sitting on the stone bench at the edge of the cliff. Beside her, having clearly chosen not to take my advice, was Wanda Callander, one hand on Beckett's jacket-clad shoulder, her face tense. The wind plucked at their hair, tossing red and blonde locks this way and that.

'Cosy,' muttered Ziggi.

'She's just keeping her calm.' I touched his arm. 'Do me a favour and wait here? I promise I'll stay alert, but honestly, I don't think matters are going to go well if she thinks we're ganging up.'

'How did that solo approach work out at her house?' he asked sweetly.

'Sarcasm is such an unattractive trait. Trust me on this, okay? I don't want her panicking. Wanda said Beckett's got no real power; her magic depends on ritual and ritual requires implements. I see no implements.'

'She might have a knife or a gun.' He complained a lot more, but he did at least stay where he was when I left him. I figured there

303

was a good chance he'd creep closer as soon as he saw I had our target's attention. I walked slowly and quietly, but tried not to *sneak*. I didn't want to startle Beckett, not when Wanda was so close to her.

When I was about a metre away, I called, 'Afternoon, ladies.'

Neither of them looked surprised to see me. Wanda rose and came towards me as I made my way around the bench and stood in front of Susan Beckett. I was struck by her pallor, the intense red of the rims of her eyes. She looked at me as if I was of no more interest than a rock. I probably wasn't. I wondered if Wanda hadn't applied a dose of her charm to calm the woman down, make her more trusting than she might otherwise have been. If that was the case, I was grateful.

Wanda touched my hand and said, 'Susan's ready to talk. She hopes you'll take her confession.'

Did I look like a priest now? I said, 'Of course.'

'Be kind to her, Verity,' she said, her tone severe, as if I was likely to misbehave; I gave her hand a little squeeze to register my displeasure.

'Did you know?' I asked. 'Did you know the little girls were hers? Not sisters but daughters?' Her horrified expression told me not. 'Stay or go, Wanda, just don't interfere.'

I sat gingerly on the edge of the bench where Wanda had been and looked at Susan Beckett until she said, 'You.'

'Me,' I said. 'What are you doing?'

'Making an end.'

'Wilbur's gone. You don't have to worry about him any more.'

There was the briefest spark of hope in her eyes, but it died pretty quickly. She must have seen something in my face and said, 'But I've still got to worry about you, haven't I?'

'You made a bargain with Wilbur to kill your own family. Then you stood by and let him drown three people whilst trying to convince you to come good on your part of the deal. He attempted to kill Alex Parrish, who'd never done you a bad turn – indeed, he did his best to help you. Your little pet tried to drown my new-born daughter because he thought it would distract me from investigating you. And you knew he was doing it. You knew, and you didn't say anything.'

True to form, she remained silent. Did she have any nerves to touch?

'I know it wasn't easy growing up here—'

'*Easy?*' Her voice cracked, her skin flushed a deep angry red and she bared her teeth. Okay, nerves there. 'How dare you? *You have no fucking idea!*'

And she was right, but no matter what had happened to her, it didn't justify what she'd done to others.

'Wilbur said your father came to visit,' I said. 'Was that what did it?'

Her expression became positively feral; she must have felt so *trapped* when Acton turned up on her doorstep. 'He came to my *house*.' she spat. 'He came to my house and tried to touch me. *Me!* And then he said if I didn't come home he would start on Hildy and Unity.' She began to sob.

'But you chose not to protect them,' I said. 'They were *yours.*'

'How could I *love* them? I didn't ask for them – they were *forced* on me!' she screamed, and there it was, that most painful of truths: no mother's love was guaranteed; no mother's love should be taken for granted. No mother could automatically be relied upon for protection.

'You could have taken them to live with you,' I said, keeping my voice calm, for all I wanted to scream back at her. 'You could have sent them to boarding school. You've got enough money; you could have given them comfortable lives well away from you and your parents. You could have fostered them out to people who would have loved them, you would never have needed to see them again.' My mouth felt suddenly dry. 'Hell, you could have killed your parents and saved your daughters and *no one* would have questioned that. But you didn't. *You didn't.*'

'My mother didn't protect me,' she said childishly, as if that was some kind of defence.

'Yet you did worse.' I had no pity for her. 'They're wandering, you know, your little girls. They're corpselights. They keep showing up in my back yard.'

Then she began to cry, but I couldn't tell if it was for herself or her children, or part of a big act – or maybe everything she'd ever pushed down inside, every ounce of pain and fear and anger, resentment and bitterness and, finally, guilt, were coming to the surface, threatening to crack her open.

'Where did the mud spell come from?'

'Wilbur . . . sourced it,' she said through her tears. 'I just told him the *result* I wanted and left the details up to him.'

The *result*: four deaths. 'Did you have him steal Wanda's grimoire?'

'No. I didn't know he had it. I didn't know where she'd hidden it after the last time I used it.'

'But you made him promises you had no intention of keeping. You *used* him.'

She hunched over, shuddering as she sobbed.

'Where are their bodies?' I asked, but she didn't answer. 'You don't even know where they're buried?' Still nothing.

'Verity, please,' begged Wanda. Her soft heart must have hated seeing the girl she'd cared for hurt so.

'Wanda, she *commissioned* four murders, and she let three others die because she didn't want to pay her debt. She didn't care about any of them. She didn't confess, and not only did she not ask for help, she *refused* it, in case someone found out what she'd done. Susan cares only about Susan.'

While my attention was fixed on Wanda, Susan Beckett made her move – but not to threaten or hurt me, her tormentor, her confessor. She shot from the stone bench and covered the space to the edge of the cliff at astonishing speed. She was at the precipice in no time and outlined dark against the sky a split-second later, and in the space of a breath she was gone, trying to escape the consequences of her actions . . .

Wanda Callander's scream was still echoing in my ears, although it'd been an hour since Susan Beckett took the easy way out. Clinging to a tree, I'd leaned out as far as my sense of self-preservation would let me and watched her body be dashed against the rocks by an angry ocean. I guessed she'd wash ashore eventually.

I should have been making calls: arranging for Rhonda McIntyre to get her New South Wales Weyrd Liaison counterpart out here to clean up and to search the Morwood Road property for four bodies. I should have filled Bela in on what had happened. Instead, I left Ziggi to do the ring-around and set plans in motion while I took Wanda aside. She resisted when I told her what I wanted her to do, until I pointed out none too gently that she'd had a hand in this tragedy. Once she'd agreed, I sat for a bit, thinking.

Would it have made a difference if I hadn't pushed Beckett so hard, if I'd gone softly, softly? Probably not. Who knew? And I'd pushed . . . because she was a bad mother. She'd had a bad mother, and she'd been a bad mother.

Maybe there was no hope for me either. It didn't matter that everything I was doing was to keep Maisie and David safe; I wasn't caring for my daughter the way her father was. I couldn't recall the last time I'd changed her nappy, and in that very moment it felt like that worst thing in the world.

And I felt like the worst mother in the world, not just because I wasn't there now, but because there was a really good chance that this wasn't going to be just a blip on the radar of my daughter's life. David would always be there for her, *he* could be counted on, but I would always be trying to deal with the latest crisis, or cleaning up a mess not of my making, or trailing along in the wake of something terrible and trying to work out why it'd happened, who'd done it, who needed to be punished and how it could possibly be kept secret.

That was going to be our life for ever . . . or until I fucked up, until I died – or I wasn't there for David or Maisie and *they* died.

The Weyrd world had cast me out when my father got caught doing what he did, and it hadn't helped my mother when she needed it. Even now, when I worked so hard to help the community, still the Weyrd acted as though I wasn't quite right, not good enough, not *one of them*, just some cat's paw they could send out to do their dirty work. Bela and Ziggi, two of the people I loved most, had kept things from me. I understood why, but I didn't feel like being especially forgiving, not just yet.

And my mother was gone again, but not by her choice this time. She'd been trying to make amends and she deserved the chance to do right. The broken mirror sat heavy in my pocket. I didn't know her, not yet, but I could see in my mind's eye the re-inked henna runes she'd put on David and Maisie because she cared.

At the end of all this, there would be hard decisions to be made.

I would need to work out what to do about Ziggi and Bela and Olivia. But first I had to get my mother back. I would not desert her. I wouldn't be a bad daughter.

But that was all easier said than done.

Chapter Thirty-Three

Contrary to my expectations (and hopes), I threw up again when we arrived back at the Bishop's Palace, mostly on myself, a little on Ziggi, who remained annoyingly unaffected by such means of travel. Guess that was due to his full Weyrd blood.

Once I could stand straight again and my ears had stopped ringing, Verhoeven had Guillaume lead me to a bathroom, which turned out to be a steampunk delight, with copper piping and showerhead, and an enormous claw-footed tub. When I finished showering, I found someone had left me clean clothes and stolen my filthy ones. I wished I hadn't recognised the royal blue dress, one of the jersey wraps of which Eleanor Aviva had been so very fond; unlike mine, it wasn't from the maternity section. The long-line grey cardigan coat with deep pockets and the thick black tights were probably hers too, but at least they'd left me my own underwear and rose-embroidered Docs, the dagger and the handbag with its precious cargo of milk. Short of wandering out in a beautifully fluffy towel, I was stuck wearing a dead woman's very expensive designer clothes.

As I left the bathroom, Guillaume silently reappeared and led me to my companions. Any illusions I might have had about pulling off a fashion coup were dashed when Ziggi did a double-take – or maybe it was more the sight of the hilt of the Dagger of Wilusa sticking out the top of my right boot.

Afternoon tea was being served – because what is a council of war without the beverage of the Empire? – in a parlour marginally less decayed and neglected, but there were no comfy sofas, just some very hard dining chairs with gothic arch backs circling a round oak table. An antique Wedgewood Black Basalt tea set sat on an intricate Venetian lace tablecloth.

I really wanted to make a smartarse crack about how civilised it all was, but I was hungry and at least there were biscuits, even though they were very small, looking more like decorations than actual food.

Verhoeven was mother and poured the tea. 'You've done well, Ms Fassbinder,' conceded the head of the Council of Five as he pushed a delicate teacup in my direction, then served Bela and Ziggi.

'Are you referring to the trail of bodies in my wake, the careless loss of my mother – *again* – and the appearance of yet another mortal enemy who's probably going to come after me at some point in the near future?'

Bela interrupted, 'You saved lives, V. Don't be so hard on yourself. You couldn't prevent the other deaths; all you could do was clean up.'

'I exposed the people I love most to danger. Olivia's been taken and Eleanor Aviva has been murdered – on your watch.' I looked meaningfully at Verhoeven, then turned my gaze on Bela. 'Not to mention I've been actively lied to by you and Ziggi for a *really* long time. I am *tremendously* unhappy about all of these things.'

'The *smågubbar* is dead, the drownings have ceased and the woman who was the cause of all this is also dead,' said Verhoeven calmly, sipping at his milky tea. 'You've done what you're employed to do.'

In my mind's eye I saw Susan Beckett silhouetted against the sky for a brief moment, then gone. 'You're forgetting the small matter of an assassin fox-girl who attacked me, murdered an innocent man, then kidnapped my mother.'

'The *kitsune* is beyond your reach – as is your mother. The assassin presents no more threat to this Council or community.'

'Pardon?' I glanced at my colleagues for support, but both Bela and Ziggi were studiously looking elsewhere.

So what I'd taken for a council of war was in fact the wrap party, a chance to crow over the corpses of our enemies, while shrugging off my mother's inconvenient resurrection and very convenient second disappearance. Clearly Olivia Fassbinder alive represented too many problems and was too much a reminder of guilt.

'I *am* going to get my mother, and I *am* going to deal with that fox-girl,' I stated.

'You don't know where either of them have gone,' said the fat man soothingly.

'The Underworld – where else would they go? The fox-girls were sent to bring Olivia back to the Guardian of the Southern Gate of the Underworld – that's what it's calling itself, at least. She broke her bargain with it and it is seriously pissed off. Surely Jost Marolf can find me a map, or an incantation to get me there, or give me a list of back doors or secret avenues in and under – Olivia said there were other ways. And surely you lot owe me enough after all these years to help me out.' I thumped a fist on the table, making the delicate china jump. 'And the Boatman – what about the Boatman??'

Ziggi spoke very quietly. 'V, you won't find any Weyrd willing to go with you. Or even to help.'

I stared. 'Not even you?'

He blinked, looking ashamed. 'We – the Weyrd – get only one trip with the Boatman. Dead or alive, we don't come out again if we set foot in his vessel. Normals talk about bright lights, voices saying it's not their time, returning to their earthly lives . . . we Weyrd? We've got no such stories. None of us come back, not ever, and no one's prepared to risk being drawn down. I'm so sorry, but I *can't* go with you.'

That stopped me cold. 'But what about the *kitsune*? They're Weyrd and they come and go as they please.'

Bela said, 'My belief is that they're like your mother: I think they didn't travel with the Boatman on their way in. As you observed, there are other roads – but I don't want to travel on any of them. The fox-girls are operating under the aegis of this Guardian, whatever it is, and that appears to give them some sort of immunity or dispensation – I don't know why, but it's clearly protecting them, allowing them to operate outside the laws that bind the rest of us.'

'Then I'll go in alone.'

'You don't know where to go, Verity—' Bela started.

Ziggi begged, 'V, think about David and Maisie. You can't go on your own, V – you don't know what it's like down there—'

I ignored the first part of his sentence and said, 'And you've just told me that *no* Weyrd knows what it's like down there, that no one's returned to tell tales, so don't try to bullshit me.'

'V—'

'You let her down. *You*,' I said, pointing at Verhoeven, 'let her down when she was young and married to Grigor. She should have been cared for, whether she was Normal or not, but you let her despair. And as for you two . . .' I looked at Bela and Ziggi, then said quietly, '*You owe me*. Aren't you better than this sack of shit who was happy to leave my mother to suffer just because she wasn't Weyrd?'

'I'm your *family*, V—' Ziggi began.

'Oh, you do not get to play that card! Not now!'

'V,' said Bela reasonably, 'I would help if I could, and so would Ziggi – but we will die if we go with you.'

Verhoeven weighed in, 'Whether your friends would help you or not is irrelevant, Ms Fassbinder, because I forbid it.'

All right, so maybe I shouldn't have called him a sack of shit.

'You are given great leeway in your efforts, because of the work you do for us, because of your bloodline, but I will not allow you to defy this Council. I will not allow you to defy *me*.'

I kept my mouth shut for a long time. My lips trembled, but if they thought I was going to burst into girly tears, then so much the better. Finally, I spoke, my voice tremulous. 'Well, I guess that's it, then. If you'll excuse me, I need to go to the bathroom.'

Ziggi stepped into my path, put one hand on my shoulder and said, 'Verity—,' too loudly. I pushed past him.

You'd have thought they'd be suspicious about women wanting to go to the loo after Dusana's effort earlier that day, but no. You'd've thought Bela and Ziggi would have been suspicious of me giving in so easily. Then again, maybe they were: maybe their pretended ignorance was the only aid they could give me under the circumstances.

Back in the magnificent steampunk bathroom it took a long while for the red rage to stop clouding my vision. Invariably, any decision made when I wanted to strangle someone was probably not going to turn out well. I was just about breathing normally when I felt a vibration in the deep pocket of my borrowed cardy, and a rattling sound to boot. I thought about ignoring it, but then noticed the number was the landline for Little Venice.

'Fassbinder?' It was Aspasia. 'I don't know if it's relevant any more, but Thaïs is awake.'

Then I dug the other thing out of my pocket, the thing that had been rattling: the keys to Ziggi's taxi, dropped in there as he spoke my name loud enough to cover the jingling. I'd left the handbag on the floor beside my chair in the conference room; it didn't matter, I had the dagger and Ziggi could get the milk back to Maisie. I felt a stirring of something that might have been hope or might have been fear and decided they weren't that different anyway.

'Hello, little strangeling.'

'I hate it when you call me that,' I said. 'New kaftan, Thaïs?'

It had a *lot* of fabric in it, which made me wonder if I should pass my maternity clothes onto the third Sister. Then again, my stuff probably wasn't loud enough for her: this dress was the most astonishing combination of fluorescent shades; she looked like a dance party waiting to happen. In the light given off by the candles and lanterns in Thaïs' third-floor abode, the scar at the base of her throat seemed redder, more intense than her sisters'. None of the Norns made any effort to cover them, and they had all refused healing; I think they saw the scars as badges of honour, as well as a reminder not to be complacent. No matter that they studied futures and fortunes, they still had not seen the now-deceased Brisbane angel coming for them last year.

'What can I do for you?' asked Thaïs, gesturing for me to sit.

Most of her furniture had been destroyed by the angel's attack, so the replacement sofas clustered around the new coffee table where she stored all her fortune-telling paraphernalia hadn't yet had a chance to become worn in. I liked that when I sat, my knees didn't end up around my ears.

Maybe Alex Parrish and Soteria had insured them; angel attack would surely come under *Unusual Happenstance*.

'What have you been told by your sisters?'

'That while I slept Grand Drownings were visited upon the unwary, that your mother returned and disappeared once more – and that you have a daughter. Congratulations.'

'Succinct, and thank you.' I leaned back in the chair. 'My mother was taken to the Underworld – supposedly to a thing calling itself the Guardian of the Southern Gate of the Underworld. Is that a name you're familiar with?'

She tilted her head, thinking hard, then said, 'No, I do not believe so.'

That wasn't the answer I'd been looking for. I'd hoped she might have been able to equip me with helpful knowledge. As there was no such luck, I continued, 'There was a van, and in the back of it a transit circle, but no one knows precisely where the receiving circle is. So I can't find her that way – I can't just follow along her path.' I hesitated, afraid she might refuse to help if she knew the Council's stance. 'I'm told . . . I'm told the Weyrd can't come back from such a journey – but I should be able to, right? My Normal blood should mean I'm okay?'

'With your mixed blood, you're a different thing altogether, little strangeling. You won't be drawn in and down. However' – she raised a finger and gave a mocking grin – 'I'm given to understand Master Verhoeven has strictly forbidden you from this undertaking.'

Of course someone would have notified Councillor Theodosia as soon as the decision was made – as soon someone realised I'd snuck out, nicked Ziggi's cab and driven from the Bishop's Palace as bold as brass, and *of course* Theo would have told her sisters immediately, because there are few things the Norns enjoy quite so much as gossip.

'So you won't help me?'

'I didn't say that.' She bit her lip. 'Your mother left you when you were very small.'

'She had her reasons, and that's between me and my mother. I want to find her – I want her back.'

'What's it worth to you?'

'I saved your life, Thaïs.'

'So you are fond of reminding us. But your mother left you. You have a lover and a child now. You have *everything*. Is she worth risking all that you have?'

'Yes, because . . . because she's my mother, and if I don't try then I won't be able to live with myself. If I don't try, then how will I tell my daughter that I didn't make any effort to help my own mother? How could I look her in the face?'

She must have found my answers compelling enough because she said, 'This has a great cost, Verity Fassbinder: this splits another veil entirely. What will you give up for this mother who left you alone?'

I bit my tongue, keeping back an answer or a profanity, and clenched my hands to keep myself from hitting her until she gave me what I wanted. Maybe she saw that, or maybe she just got bored with tormenting me.

'I regret to say that I cannot help.'

'Thaïs—'

'*I* cannot help you, but there is someone who can.'

Somehow, I knew what she was going to say.

'The Boatman is keen for the restoration of his dagger. He has paid a heavy price for lending it to you, and a greater price still for its non-return.'

'And he can take me where I need to go?' I felt the blush heating up my face and imagined the weapon in my boot vibrating at the mention of its master's name.

'He's a deliverer of souls, so he can take you to the Underworld – but you will need to seek what is lost on your own.' She leaned forward. 'But you must pay the toll.'

'This isn't just some dodgy means of getting me to give the dagger back?'

She grinned. 'That would be petty indeed.'

'Right. Anything else I need to know?'

'Now this is where I *can* help you, Verity Fassbinder. You will need an anchor, and talismans to exchange.'

'And . . . ?'

She sighed as if she couldn't believe I needed an explanation. 'A person must act as your anchor in the world, and they must be a Normal – even if a Weyrd weren't too afraid of being pulled after you, defying the Council so openly would put lives at risk. Normals are . . . weightier, more solid for this kind of thing. And you must ensure that you exchange some personal objects, you and the anchor: these things will make the connection between you both. The object you hand over is the item you will need to think of when you want to leave. And as always, there must be blood. There is always a scarlet price.'

'Simple.' I headed for the door.

She asked again, 'Is she worth it, your mother?'

I thought of Olivia saving me in that stinking alley, holding my hand and reassuring me. I thought again of the reapplied henna on my lover's wrist and my daughter's heel and said, 'Yes. Yes, I believe she is.'

As I made my way down the stairs, McIntyre rang. 'Fassbinder, what have you done?'

'Nothing. Yet. I'm going to find my mother.'

'Well, I have just had a very irate Mr Verhoeven on the line – and you know Mr Verhoeven *never* talks to me, so that is how we can tell he's very upset.'

'I might have called him a sack of shit.'

'Of course you did. Well, he's demanded I put a BOLF out for your friend Ziggi's very distinctive taxi, which I'm given to understand you stole—'

'—borrowed—'

'—good, *borrowed*. I will do so in about forty or so minutes, when I finish scratching my arse, but my professional advice, even though we're not having this conversation which would otherwise affect my career quite badly, is that you ditch the wheels. Are we clear?'

'Crystal. Thanks, Rhonda.'

'Don't get killed.'

Outside, the fifty I'd borrowed from Aspasia burning a hole in my pocket, I flagged down a cab and told the driver where I wanted to go. I looked at my dress and cardy and figured that if I was going visiting in the Underworld, a dead woman's clothes were probably *de rigueur*.

Then, praying hard that I wasn't about to do something I'd regret, I made a call.

Chapter Thirty-Four

There's inevitably a point in most, if not all, of my plans when I think, *This was a bad idea.*

That moment came as soon as the cab dropped me off and I saw Sister Bridget waiting for me by the river. It looked like she and Galina had swapped clothes: she'd discarded her habit and veil in favour of black combat pants, a black puffer jacket and a pair of black Doc Martens; no frivolous designs for her. It could been worse: she might have been wearing a beret and toting an Uzi. Fortunately for me, machine-guns didn't seem to be standard issue for nuns nowadays. As it was, she was difficult to see in the gathering dusk.

When I'd called Dr Aarden and fended off all of her questions about my health and Maisie's health and asked for Sister Bridget's mobile number, I'd thought I was in luck when she gave it to me without argument. I thought I was in even better luck when the nun picked up on the first ring, and agreed to help. Now all I could see was an aged woman dressed like Rambo. *What the fuck did I think I was doing?*

My hopes plummeted. *Really: what the fuck was I doing?* Going to the Underworld to find the mother who'd deserted me, leaving my baby and my beloved behind – and the only person on my side in this whole stupid venture was a cranky person of the nunly persuasion. I might as well have taken out a Classified ad. *Wanted: one nun, prepared to stand on riverbank in middle of winter at short notice. Essential skill: ability to battle evil. Desirable but not essential: willingness to commit exorcism.*

Well, Verity Fassbinder, it's too late now. I squared my shoulders and reached deep down inside to where my courage was hiding under the sofa cushions of the soul and hauled it back up by the scruff of its neck.

'Sister Bridget, thank you for coming. I really appreciate this.'

'You're a fool, Verity Fassbinder, but your daughter deserves a mother who comes back, so I'll help any way I can.'

So much for an inspirational speech . . . but maybe it was the best I deserved. 'Glad we got that sorted out.'

'Does your lovely husband know what you're doing?'

I pointed her towards the river and gave her a gentle push to get her moving along the path. 'Not my husband, and not yet, but he's about to.'

I found David's number and hit the call button. It rang and rang and just when I thought it was about to go to voicemail, he answered. I held the phone away from my ear as he shouted at someone in the house, 'Calm down, it's just work. Bela, be so kind as to change Maisie. Not *into* anything, just change the nappy.'

'Hello?'

'Hang on, Bruce, let me get away from these bozos! Got some mates here, getting a bit rowdy.'

'You're cracking out the *b* word?' I heard a door close quietly and figured he'd gone into the bedroom for privacy.

'And you're in all sorts of trouble. Where are you?'

'Going to find my mother. Are you really making Bela change nappies? Are they really shitty?' I asked hopefully.

'The shittiest. He and Ziggi descended half an hour ago looking for you, said you'd disappeared and were not answering your phone. Ziggi seems less concerned than perhaps he ought.'

'As well he might. Disappeared is a bit of an exaggeration. I just did a French Exit from a tea party.'

'Is that a fancy way of saying you farted in company?'

'It means to leave early without saying goodbye. It ensures you don't end up spending more time bidding farewell than you actually did socialising. Also, it helps when you don't want to hear people say you can't do something.'

'You learn new stuff every day. And this *something* would be going after Olivia?'

'It would.'

'Do I want to know the details?'

'Probably not. But rest assured I am not alone, I have a fairly righteous nun on my side. She's keeping an eye on our interests.' Sister Bridget looked offended at being described as only 'fairly righteous'. I thought about patting her shoulder, then reckoned there was a good chance I'd lose a hand if I did.

'I'm not sure how I feel about that. How did you talk Sister Bridget into . . . you know what? No, better if I don't know.' He paused. 'In the interests of not going mad, I'm going to choose to regard it in a positive light. I love you.'

'I love you too. I love you more than anything. I'll come back, I promise.'

'I'll hold you to that. If you don't I'm going to be pissed off, not least because Maisie needs a feed and she hates decanted.'

'You're such a romantic.' I grinned in spite of everything.

'Stay safe.'

'I will.' I managed not to get all teary until after I hung up. Sister

Bridget was powering along like a woman half her age. 'Hang on,' I called, 'this is it.'

We were at the spot on the river below St Mary's Church where last year angels and sirens had battled it out over the fate of a mixed-blood child. It was also the place where I'd managed to summon the Boatman. I bit my bottom lip hard enough to distract me from thoughts of David and Maisie. I needed to focus. I pulled Olivia's broken compact from my pocket and held it up for Sister Bridget to see.

'See this? It's my mother's. You need to hang onto this, come hell or high water. Did you bring something personal?' She pulled a rosary from her own pocket and we exchanged items. 'This forms a link: it'll get a living person back from the Underworld, or so I'm told – I *really* hope someone wasn't just messing with me out of a misplaced sense of humour.'

'That's your mother's ticket. What about you?'

I reached up and undid the chain around my neck. The ring from David felt warm from its contact with my skin. I handed it over, really not wanting to surrender it. 'Be *very* careful with that.'

She rolled her eyes and, with much difficulty, removed the worn gold wedding band from her finger and placed it firmly in my palm. 'The same goes for you with this!'

I slipped it on my own wedding finger; the fit was snug but I didn't want to risk losing it. I looked sternly at the nun. 'Now remember, this doesn't give you a right to take liberties. I'm a good girl, I am.'

'There's a lot of evidence to the contrary.'

'Touché.'

'When will you be back?' she said as casually as asking if I was going to be home in time for dinner.

'I am . . . not sure. Honestly, I don't know precisely where I'm going. I don't know what or who I'm going to encounter when I get there, or how I'm going to find my mother. I'm pretty sure I won't get much of a mobile signal while I'm there.' I cracked my knuckles nervously and she winced at the sound. 'Give me a day – then come back every day after that, if you can. For ever.' I threw my hands in the air. 'I don't know. Use your better judgement.'

She didn't say whatever was on her mind, but pulled a silver hip flask from a pocket and held it out.

I eyed it dubiously. 'Holy water or whisky?'

'Ordinary water, you idiot. But right about now I wish it was whisky. Don't eat or drink *anything* down there. Remember Persephone and the pomegranate seeds.'

'That's not a very Biblical reference.'

She ignored the comment and handed over a bunch of muesli bars. I stuffed everything into my pockets. 'Why are you doing this, Sister Bridget? Why did you say yes?'

There was a long hesitation before she said, 'Because you were right when you said I was you once. I travelled the same paths and supped with the same demons. It never ends well, Verity Fassbinder, and you've got more to lose than I did. I want to try to make sure you don't suffer too much grief, or at least, not more than your allotted portion.'

'Right.' We stared at each other and I thought that at some point, if I survived, I'd like to dig the secrets out of Sister Bridget. 'Thank you.'

I bent down, loosened the sheath that held the Dagger of Wilusa against my ankle and wrapped the leather straps around the knife so it made a neat parcel. I felt suddenly light, but also bereft. The weapon had made me feel safe and I was about to give that away. I reminded myself I didn't have a choice. 'I don't know how long this part of the process is going to take, so don't nag, okay?'

She didn't answer, just watched as I walked down to the water and carefully picked my way out onto a rocky outcropping. I crouched and unsheathed the dagger, feeling it begin to hum and vibrate as I held it over the waves. Things like this are connected to their owners, their custodians; they vibrate on frequencies few ears or hearts can hear or sense . . . This was a sure-fire way of letting the Boatman know I was there, and so was his fancy knife. *Do your thing, God-slayer.*

It didn't take long before I heard Sister Bridget gasp. The mist rose up from the river and the Boatman piloted his low dark boat, propelled by some unseen force, through the fog, directing its course with the single oar set in a rowlock in the stern. He was tall and skeletally thin, clad in a hooded cloak that flapped in the breeze, showing cheekbones and a chin, skin as brown as dried wood, a sparse mouth and a near-ruined nose. He carried no passengers today. He had a neat trick of stopping the skiff from moving on the current whenever he wanted.

I waved. 'Hi.'

He held out his hand. He always was a creature of few words.

'Okay, I'm going to return it – and I love it, by the way, it's been very helpful, saving me on at least two occasions, and that's much appreciated. But I need a favour – and frankly, that's the only reason you're going to get this back.'

He snorted, bull-like, and smoke came from his nostrils. 'You have had it too long,' he said and pulled aside his cloak. The stringy flesh of his torso was partially eaten and worms peeped through holes between his ribs.

'Look, I understand you've been punished for letting me have the dagger and I really am sorry about *that*. But there's no point in trying to scare me,' I said with a sigh. 'I need a ride. I need to get to the Underworld.'

He dropped the cloak.

'I need to find my mother. She doesn't belong there.'

It felt like a very long time before he at last nodded and held out his hand once again. I looked back at Sister Bridget, who gave me a hearty thumbs-up. Initially I'd been worried that someone would hassle her while she waited; now I felt kind of sorry for anyone who was dumb enough to try. I slid the weapon back into its sheath.

I said, 'Thank you,' and turned back to the river to find the Boatman had manoeuvred close enough to my perch that all I had to do was take a careful step into his surprisingly sturdy boat. As soon as I sat down, I reached up and handed him the knife. I faced forward, trying not to brood on its loss or wonder at its hold over me: had its other custodians felt so attached, so certain that life would be less safe without it? It was responsible for many sacrifices over the centuries, not to mention the death of at least one angel. I wondered if anyone had ever given it up easily.

We pushed out into the river and through the evening shadows that lay heavily on it. Everything around me became blurry, as if someone had wiped the glass of life with a dirty cloth. Then I began to see spots. Then it felt as if hundreds of cold dead hands were touching my hair, my skin, my face, trying to force their way between my lips, my teeth, down my throat. Just when I thought I would have to scream, when my mouth would have to open and the prying fingers would get their way, I mercifully passed out, more because it was imposed upon me than because of any internal choice of my own, and knowing only that this had all been a very bad idea indeed.

Chapter Thirty-Five

I woke up lying on something hard and warm, and I had a terrifying moment of certainty that all the rumours were true: that the Underworld was the equivalent of Hell, and it was as toasty as Dante would have us believe. I sat up fast, feeling horribly dizzy, and was steadied by thin strong fingers on my shoulder.

I stared into the eyes of the Boatman, who was crouched beside me, his cloak carefully wrapped to preserve his modesty. This close, I could see the wrinkles in his skin, and that his eyes weren't missing – sunken, yes, but they were there, dark and light at the same time, the gaze measured, maybe a little pitying.

'That wasn't fun,' I coughed, 'but at least I wasn't sick.'

'The living are not meant to travel thus,' he said. 'Rest a few moments.' This was the chattiest he'd ever been: full sentences and everything.

When my head stopped spinning I looked around. I was sitting on a stone jetty jutting out into an enormous lake, thankfully not of fire, to which the Boatman's vessel was moored without any obvious tetherings. A path gently sloped upwards, lit every ten metres by flaming torches. We were in a cave so huge that their light reached only a little way into the air above us. A stream trickled along beside the path, but it took me a few moments to realise what was wrong: it was running uphill, away from the lake, deeper into whatever lay beyond us.

The Boatman must have noticed me looking because he said, 'Don't drink the waters, no matter how thirsty you get.'

I thought of Sister Bridget's warning, and said '*No*', but he seemed to think I hadn't really understood, and went on, 'The Waters of Forgetting are not meant for the living.'

'But this is what the dead must drink?'

'It is . . . voluntary. Those who wish to go forward must drink; they must not be weighted down by memories of earthly existence. Those memories are not lost forever, but they must be set aside for a time. Others cling to recollections of being warm and do not drink. They wander. They do not move on.'

'And some of them escape? From here?' I asked.

He shrugged; maybe I'd impugned his professional delivering-of-souls ability. Obviously some did though: they refused to forget, found cracks in the skin of the Underworld and returned above. Some, like Susan Beckett's poor daughters, were rescued, although I doubted that happened much.

'Yes,' he admitted.

'So this is a kind of waiting room? A place to make decisions?'

'Just the first of many – and the forgetting does not mean being freed of responsibility, of the consequences of your actions in life, although there are those who think that.' He gave a toothy grin. 'They must face what they have done in another place. When they pass over, their remembrances are returned to them. Only then can the heart be properly weighed, their place determined.'

He rose out of his crouch with a dry cracking of joints and adjusted his cloak; I noticed that the mess of his chest had begun to repair, the flesh re-knitting itself. Our time together was drawing to a close. 'I have other questions.'

'And yet I am permitted to give no more answers,' he said, sounding pleased with himself.

'Right. Then any handy hints before I venture off?'

'Follow the stream, do not drink, be wary of the living who dwell here. They do not belong.'

'You don't want them here, do you?' He didn't say anything. 'But *you* can't do anything about them. You're hoping *I* can.' Again, no reply. 'Then thank you, kind sir.' I watched as he loped back to his boat. 'And I'm sorry about the dagger. I'm sorry I kept it so long, I'm sorry for the pain it caused you.'

He looked over his shoulder at me, and said sadly, 'I cannot return for you.'

'I figured that.'

'I trust you have arranged a way out?'

'I sure as hell hope so.'

He hesitated. 'Even this act . . . even my setting foot on this soil . . .' He held up his left hand. A canker had developed on the palm that I could have sworn wasn't there before – but whatever universal balancing act was responsible for inflicting punishment on him knew enough not to hurt both hands; if the Boatman couldn't ferry souls, who knew what might happen? The Boatman was unafraid to pay some costs, it appeared. 'My brothers have warned me time and again not to interfere—'

'Then why do you?'

He just gave me that toothy grin and stepped off the jetty into his vessel. I wondered about his 'brothers', then figured that one Boatman alone couldn't serve the entire world. He wasn't merely a Brisbane phenomenon; there had to be more, analogues, replicas, franchises, elsewhere . . . everywhere.

I watched as he pushed off and began his return journey to light and air, to all the things I'd left behind. Soon enough he was gone and I could see nothing more than the place he'd been. I patted the pockets of my borrowed cardigan coat to make sure everything was still there that needed to be, and set off up the path to find my mother.

How long it took for me to encounter the first of the ghosts is anyone's guess; the display on my mobile had gone dark at some point during the journey to the Underworld and it had been years since I'd worn a watch. Sometimes the path went up and sometimes down, but the stream flowing beside it remained steady and the ground beneath me didn't get any warmer, which reassured me greatly. The rock walls on either side were smooth and the width of the passageway constant, with very few corners – there was nowhere to hide if anyone came at me from the opposite direction.

So when I saw someone coming towards me, I had no choice but to meet them. I trudged on, thinking uncomfortably of Odysseus digging a trench and filling it with blood to make his spectres talk and also to keep them at bay. As I got closer I recognised Jerry Stormare, Hairy Jerry, my drowned security detail. His black hair was a mess, which he'd never have allowed in life, and he still looked kind of damp; even though he was not quite solid, his outline kept shivering. He peered at me as if he couldn't quite believe I was there. We both came to a standstill about three feet apart.

'Are you real?' he asked.

'Real enough. Why are you still here, Jerry?' I almost reached to touch him, then thought better of it.

'I was . . . I heard something at Ocean's Reach, outside and went to check on it. Mike was asleep, Galina was roaming . . . I should have waited. I should have waited for them. I went back inside and then . . . then I was gone. I was gone and I couldn't talk . . . there was a man and a boat . . . and I woke up here.' He whispered, 'Am I dead?'

'I'm sorry, Jerry, but you were drowned.'

'I wasn't swimming,' he said, bewildered. 'I'm sure I wasn't. We were guarding you—'

'You were murdered, Jerry. Someone killed you.'

'What did I do?' His memories were clearly muddled – I wondered if that was what refusing to drink, refusing to forget, did. Perhaps hanging on to your recollections too hard and too long just meant they decayed anyway?

'You did nothing wrong, you got in the way. I'm sorry. It was meant for my daughter, but you saved her,' I said. 'You saved Maisie, and I thank you for that.'

He stared at me for a long while. 'I don't know what happened. Where's Mike? I miss Mike. He's not here.'

'Mike's still . . . above. He's very upset, Jerry. He misses you. He blames himself.'

'I miss him,' he said again, and I thought my heart might rip in two. 'Why can't he come for me? You're here – you're not dead, are you.'

'The Weyrd can't make this journey more than once, Jerry. The trip with the Boatman is the last for your kind. I've come for—' Then it occurred to me that Jerry didn't know about Olivia, and I said instead, 'I'm looking for a tall woman with dark hair, maybe accompanied by a fox-girl?'

'There are others here but I don't know them . . . they wander . . .' Then his eyes lit up and I realised he couldn't hang onto his thoughts for too long; his short-term memory must have been shot in the drowning. 'Can you take me home? Up there? To Mike?'

I thought about Olivia taking the two little girls with her because she couldn't bear to leave them behind, and I thought about taking Jerry back for a full three seconds before deciding against trying; Bela had said the Weyrd couldn't go back. 'I can't, Jerry, I'm sorry. You're dead. You died, you took the trip with the Boatman, whether you remember or not . . .'

'Did I?' He scratched his head, frowned. '*Did I?*'

'Yeah, you did. I can't take you back. I'm sorry, but the Weyrd – *proper* Weyrd – can't go back.'

He looked at me, and I wondered if ghosts could cry.

'Jerry, you need to drink the water before you can move on.' I pointed at the stream beside us.

'It's flowing in the wrong direction,' he said confidentially, as if the watercourse might overhear us and take it as a criticism.

'It's the only way, Jerry.' I didn't tell him that it would make him forget everything, that Mike would be gone from his memory, even if it was only temporary – who knew how long 'temporary' was in the mind of the Boatman and the things that decree Fate? For a moment his face convulsed with rage and pain, then he struck me. I braced for the impact, but there was just a cold shiver as his hand passed through my torso. So ghosts were less powerful here; I wondered if they could only exercise influence if they managed to escape to the mortal plane? Both were interesting questions to ask Jost Marolf if – no, *when* – I got myself home.

The fury was gone from Jerry's expression almost as soon as it had come and he hung his head. 'I'm sorry. It's just frustrating. Everything's a jumble, you know?'

'I know, Jerry,' I said softly, and if I could, I'd have hugged him. 'I know it's hard for you, but you really need to drink. You saved us. You did your job, my friend. Please, drink. Everything will be better after that.' I didn't know if that was true. What if Jerry was carrying around nasty, heavy things on his conscience? What if his heart weighed too much – or too little?

'Will you tell Mike that I . . . that I . . . Will you just tell Mike?'

'Of course I will. I'll tell him you love him.'

And that must have satisfied him, because he knelt beside the stream and dipped a cupped hand into the flow. It pooled silver, then black, then silver again in the eldritch matter of his spectral flesh. As he lifted his palm to his lips and drank, Jerry's expression went from sorrow to joy like a cloud passing from the face of the moon, and then he was gone, as simply and as quickly as that.

I thought of Mike above, alone with his grief and guilt, and hoped that if I told him what I'd seen he'd take some comfort.

I gave a final look at the spot where Jerry had last been and whispered him a good road, then resumed my trek, happy in the knowledge that the ghosts here couldn't do me any harm. Of course, that didn't cover whatever other inhabitants might be lurking around the Underworld.

Chapter Thirty-Six

The woman sitting in an alcove on a large rock looked familiar, although I couldn't place her. Her thin hair was ash-blonde, her face pale and finely boned; she was perhaps in her late fifties, though she looked even older, exhausted, as if the very act of living had worn her out and death had been no relief. Her blue and yellow housedress was faded with age, but that might have been down to her spectral nature, her loss of solidity.

Out on the path, I shifted and my boots scraped on the stone beneath them. The woman's head swivelled and she said with a mixture of hope and dread, 'Acton?'

I knew then who she was.

As I moved closer I could see the mud all over her, as if she'd been poorly cleaned when she came here. *Acton*. The name was unusual, Anne Brontë's nom de plume. It was also the name of Susan Beckett's father, so this could only be her mother, Marian. I'd not seen her in life, but it was clear where her daughter's delicate beauty had come from – except Marian's had been eroded by pain and unkindness, by a life too hard.

The unhappy wife and mother caught sight of me at last and it was as if she'd been blind before; her eyes focused, the pupils contracting as if my skin produced some kind of bright light. Maybe it did down here – who knew how the living appeared to the dead?

'Who are you?' she asked, shock washing over her face as she realised I wasn't another ghost.

'I know your daughter.'

'Which one?'

'The only one. Susan. I'm sort of acquainted with your grand-daughters too.'

Her mouth hung open. 'How can you know?'

'Lady, I know all sorts of things I wish I didn't.' I sat beside her. 'Where's your shitty husband?'

'He drank. He drank from the stream as soon as we arrived.' She looked pathetic. 'He drank and left me behind.'

Why was I not surprised that a shit like Acton Beckett had gone for forgetfulness as soon as he possibly could?

'Well, he's in for a nasty surprise if he thinks it's that easy to run.'

Her expression changed and became something new. She said, 'Good.'

'Why didn't you drink, Marian?'

She began to wring her hands. 'The girls – Unity and Hildy. They were afraid. They wouldn't go with him. They didn't understand. I didn't understand.'

'But you know what your husband did to Susan, right?'

She looked past me. 'I couldn't . . . I couldn't stop him. I left once when Susan was little, but he found us. He said I couldn't go far enough or fast enough, then he beat me until I couldn't walk, until I peed blood and coughed it too. It took me months to heal and by then . . . by then . . .'

'By then you were too scared to try again.' It wasn't a new story, it wasn't unique. Self-preservation won over fear of anything else. 'When did you last talk to your daughter?'

'Not for a long time. She stopped speaking to me when she left

335

home. I tried to call sometimes, but she always hung up.' Marian Beckett blinked and blinked, as if there might be tears coming, but nothing glistened. 'Susan blamed me – and she was right to.'

'What happened to you? To all of you?' I asked, even though I knew, because I wondered what she'd retained of that experience.

'I don't know, not really. Acton went to Brisbane to visit Susan and when he came home, he was angry, said she wouldn't see reason.' She shook her head. 'As if what he wanted was reasonable!'

'So, Acton came home,' I prompted, 'and you were all in Hildy and Unity's room . . .'

'I was putting them to bed when Acton came in. I remember thinking that something stank and when I looked, I found a bowl under Hildy's bed – not one I'd ever seen before. It was ordinary enough, but it was filled with mud and piss and shit . . . and then . . .' She frowned, dredging memories that had already fled without the need for the Waters of Forgetting; still, she was a lot more lucid than poor Jerry had been. 'The door . . . the door slammed shut and Acton couldn't open it, and he couldn't break the window either, and that was just ridiculous because they broke every time we had a hailstorm, because he was too cheap to spring for better glass.'

'And?'

'And . . . and the bowl, that bowl . . . it began to overflow and spread across the floor – I've never seen anything happen so fast. I stood on the bed with the girls, praying it would stop, that it wouldn't get any higher, but it did. I held Hildy and I yelled at Acton to help Unity because I couldn't hold them both, but he just kept kicking at the door, trying to save himself. And the mud just kept rising . . .'

My heart ached for her.

'And I don't remember any more,' she said, but I suspected she didn't want to and I couldn't blame her. 'What happened to us?'

'I don't know,' I lied.

'Bullshit,' she hissed, and tried to grab me but she had as much success as Jerry had.

My arm where her hand passed through felt icy and I rubbed it to get some warmth back. 'I'm here to find my mother.'

'Don't lie to me!'

'Do you really want to know what happened?' Moments ago I couldn't bear to say her own daughter had her murdered, but now . . .

'Yes, damn you!' She was angry, as if it was somehow my fault.

'Susan did it to you. She bargained away all your lives for goods and services. I guess she doesn't have too many fond memories of growing up.' I wondered why Marian's shocked expression should hurt me so much. 'Your husband went to Brisbane to threaten her, to try to make her come home to *him*. You can thank Acton for pushing her over the edge.'

'But the girls, the little girls . . .'

'I think it's safe to say Susan had a lot of issues.'

'*Had?*' she said swiftly.

'Has. Slip of the tongue.' She didn't need to know anything else, except maybe one thing. 'Do you know where the little ones are?'

She looked at her careworn hands. 'They've been gone for days . . . weeks? I don't know how long, time moves strangely here. I have to wait for them, though, I have to wait.'

'Marian, I know where they are. They're above, drifting around as corpselights, looking for something. I don't really know what. *My mother*, I thought, *the one who led them out of this place. The one who made them feel safe, who's trying to make amends*. 'I'll make you a deal: I'll look after them if you drink from the stream. Pass on and I'll make sure your granddaughters are looked after.' *Pass on and have your heart weighed.*

I didn't quite know how I was going to take care of them, but she didn't ask for details; I suspected Marian Beckett just wanted to set aside her burdens at last. She'd have to answer for what she'd let happen, but that would occur somewhere I couldn't go. She'd be judged, but I hoped it would be weighed against what had been done to her.

'Do you promise?' she asked.

'I promise.'

She rose and moved towards the stream.

'Oh, by the way, have you seen a tall woman with dark hair come through here recently? Looks a bit like me, but in her fifties.' I realised I didn't know what my mother had been wearing this morning – yesterday? how much time had passed? – because I'd neglected to say goodbye to her before I left for Susan Beckett's Paddington home. 'Probably a long dark coat?' I finished lamely.

'The only living being I've seen apart from you is the short one.'

'Asian girl, dresses like a librarian? Brown satchel, Mary Janes with sensible heels, glasses?'

'Yes. Keep following the path, when it branches, take the left-hand side. There's a cavern; it's where they sleep. There's a big fire in the middle. She's most likely there. That's where they go, those who still have breath.'

'Right, first cavern on the left. Thank you.'

'Look after my granddaughters.' She smiled and added, maybe in jest, 'Or I'll come back to haunt you.' And she bent and scooped a handful of that changeable water from the steam at the mouth of the alcove and drank. Then she was gone.

I stared down at the glistening fluid for long moments. I stayed on the stone seat, ate a muesli bar, then drank the contents of the flask until it was empty. Then, very carefully, I knelt and attentively refilled it from the stream, mindful to dry my hands thoroughly when I was done.

Although her directions couldn't be faulted, what Marian Beckett had failed to mention was the giant three-headed dog at the entrance to the cavern to which she'd guided me. You've never got a pack of doggy treats when you really need them. On the upside, said canine was sleeping, all three heads drowsing, all four legs twitching as it chased dream-rabbits. On the downside, it was in my way. I took a deep breath and began the slow task of tiptoeing around Fido and Friends. It was only as I got closer that I noticed something that hadn't been there before: bones.

The long bones of thighs, scattered radiuses and ulnas, a few pelvic bowls, tarsals and metatarsals looked as if someone had been playing jacks with them. There were cages of ribs, and skulls that had seen better days. The bottom of my stomach dropped. As I took another step, another bone, maybe a humerus, appeared in the path of my descending boot and I couldn't correct without losing balance and falling onto the slumbering mutt. My foot went through the bone – not as in, broke it in half, but as in, passed right through it.

Ghost bones.

I looked at the dog and squinted.

One of its heads was raised and it was squinting sleepily right back at me. The beast's outline was fuzzy, just like Jerry and Marian, and when I reached out tentatively to give it a pat, my hand didn't connect but plunged into a misty, foggy substance. The eyes closed, the head sank down again beside the other two and it started snoring, a windstorm sort of a noise that lifted only dust motes.

Ghost Cerberus. Huh.

And completely uninterested in me, because I was breathing. Presumably he was here to keep any errant souls in line.

Beyond the dog was a narrow entrance hall. I paused where it fed into a larger space. In the centre was the fire-pit Marian had mentioned, blazing orange and blue, although it gave off no smoke. This was no torture chamber, for all the weapon racks holding swords and battleaxes, knives and crossbows, morning stars and maces. The floor was tidily swept, and the walls were lined with cubicles partitioned off by expensive screens of silk and wood. It looked like a dorm room, each chamber housing a single bed, a wardrobe and a set of drawers. It wasn't the Ritz, but it was entirely serviceable. Only the living needed sleeping quarters down here. I wondered which bed had been my mother's.

Not far from the fire-pit was an antique wooden table with long benches on either side that wouldn't have looked out of place in a French palace. I wondered if they cooked down here or if food just appeared. So many questions to ask Olivia when I found her.

And there, not so far from me, was the means to do just that.

Chapter Thirty-Seven

The fox-girl was grubby from living rough in the back of Len's van. Her dress was stained, her tights laddered, her Mary Janes were scuffed and in need of a good polish, and her hair hadn't been brushed in a while. She wasn't paying any attention to me or to the space around her, only to the perfectly gleaming tantō. She was assiduously polishing the blade as if her life depended on it. Maybe it did.

I wanted to feel sorry for her, alone and without her sisters. I wanted to regret what I was about to do, but I didn't. I *really* didn't, because of Len's utterly unnecessary death.

I didn't have my mother's skill with a weapon, but now, unencumbered by baby weight, I was back to being able to move quickly and quietly. The girl didn't hear me; she was concentrating, the dog was snoring, and she probably wasn't expecting anyone else to be around. I pulled Olivia's sword from my pocket, found the button she'd showed me, pressed hard and felt the miniscule pin pierce my skin – just a tiny prick and the blood price was paid. The sword grew to full size in the blink of an eye, making no sound – no completely inaccurate movie-magic sword-being-drawn *zing* – but it was a lot heavier than I'd expected . . . and I wasn't so lacking in joy that I didn't notice that it looked *awesome*.

Closing in on the fox-girl, I stared at her neat, deadly hands and thought how she'd be a lot less dangerous without one of them. I decided I couldn't do that, not so cold-bloodedly, not without a damned good reason – for all I was also aware that this lack of ruthlessness might just get me killed. I just couldn't bring myself to maim anyone for my own convenience.

I switched the blade to my left hand, made a fist with my right and punched her hard in the side of the head – not with enough force to stave in her skull, but hard enough to have her go down like a sack of potatoes. It was both rewarding and relieving.

By the time she came to I had her trussed up with torn bed sheets and propped against the table. I'd thrown the tantō into the fire and its handle was merrily burning and giving off a terrible smell. I should have felt worse about destroying an artefact like that, but I didn't. *Should have but didn't* was getting to be a theme with me. I sat in front of her on a stool I'd found in one of the cubicles, sword in hand, legs crossed, one foot swinging as if I had all the time in the world.

'I don't believe we've been properly introduced,' I began, and she glared. Maybe I should have gagged her, but it was unlikely there was anyone to come to her rescue now. 'I'm Verity Fassbinder and I'm looking for my mother.'

She didn't say anything.

'I'm given to believe you worked alongside her for some years. So when she fled it must have been a bit of a blow . . . then again, surely you'd have figured out she wasn't entirely content in her employment?'

'She betrayed us,' she said, and spat blood, fortunately for her not *at* me. 'She ran.'

'And you went after her. You got *sent* after her. Bet your boss wasn't happy when she slipped away.' Her eyes shifted and I saw I'd hit a nerve. 'Bet he thought you and your sisters should have noticed.'

'We were punished for our lack of observance.'

Which made it sound a little too religious for my liking.

'Was that why your sister went off on her own, tried to get to me in the supermarket?'

Expressions that slid across her face – love, resentment, grief; the sister in the supermarket was the selfish one, trying to better her own lot, get the attention, the kudos. *Love me best, Daddy!* And this one both loved and hated her, and felt her loss no less.

'All Mother had done for years was talk about *you*, watch *you* in that mirror, moon over what was happening in *your* life.' She grunted.

'*Mother?*'

'She was! She was like a mother to us. She brought us here when we were just kids, raised us, taught us.'

Olivia hadn't mentioned that, and I knew why: *Left one daughter behind, adopted three* wouldn't play well in the Theatre of Abandoned Daughter #1. 'That must have hurt.'

'You tell me: how did it feel to be deserted by her? She left you to your father. She left us to the Guardian. One look at those little girl ghosts and she was out of here. The Guardian said we must have known. It said we must have helped.' She wept then, through blood and snot. 'And then . . . And then it told us what she'd truly done to us.'

'What?' I asked faintly.

'*Orphaned* us! She murdered our parents and brought us here!'

I swallowed hard, thinking fast. I couldn't in all conscience claim to know what Olivia would or would not do; I couldn't even lay claim to having a gut instinct about it, because my mother was still a stranger to me, alien and unknown. So I did the only thing I could do: I sowed doubt with logic.

'So, the Guardian who's just lost one of his finest employees needs his other employees to hunt her down. It needs them to hunt down their *surrogate mother* – needs them to be *angry and hurt and vengeful*, even more than they already are.'

She stared at me.

'The Guardian who sends you out to find things, steal things, trade for things, kill people, corrupt people – the Guardian who punishes you for Olivia's flight. This is the Guardian whose word you've taken, that my mother murdered your parents?' I kept my voice steady, reasonable. 'The same Guardian who didn't mention this piece of information until it absolutely needed to? And who would have given the order for your parents' deaths, do you think?'

The fox-girl didn't answer. If I was right, then she and her sisters had been played; her sisters had died for nothing and she'd killed for nothing. Or of course I could be utterly wrong about my mother.

'Why do you think she broke then, with the little girls? Surely she'd seen kids here before?'

'They bothered her a lot. Dunno why.'

'Right. And where would my mother be now?'

She grinned, showing red teeth. '*Below.*'

'And by "below" you mean the basement?'

'Down where the Guardian keeps all the things that displease him.' She smiled again.

'Right.' I slid the sword between her ankles and it parted the bonds there as if they were water. Grabbing her arm, I heaved her upwards. I underestimated my strength and her lack of weight, so she travelled rather further up than I'd planned, which gave her the opportunity to kick me in the ribs.

I should have seen it coming; I really should. I'd forgotten for a moment that she wasn't some little girl but a supernatural creature and it hurt. I was knocked onto the table behind me, and by the time I was upright, she'd sprinted halfway across the room, towards one of the cubicles where I figured she had at least one other weapon. I suppose it was closer than the display racks on the walls.

I picked up the stool I'd been sitting on and threw it at her just as she reached the curtains. It struck her squarely in the back and sent her flying. My ribs ached as I jogged over to fetch her.

'No more of that shit or I will take off a limb, do you understand?' I wrapped her hair around my hand and hauled her to her feet, using more control this time. She nodded, with difficulty. 'You might still get out of this alive. Lead me to my mother, and do it as quickly as possible and without any more of this crap, yes?'

'Yeah,' she said shortly.

I pushed her back towards the entrance; the dog didn't even bother to open an eye. 'Just out of curiosity: what's the deal here?' I thumbed in the direction of the mutt.

'Your mother killed it. It attacked her – it was a lot more active when it was alive – and your mother didn't like that. The Guardian wasn't too happy.'

'He should have controlled his pet better.'

'That's what your mother said.' The fox-girl snorted. 'Anyway, that's how she got the name the Guardian's Hound. It said she could replace what she'd destroyed.'

So the hound was a dead thing that couldn't move on. Maybe it didn't matter if it drank from the stream or not. Did animal memories work like human ones? Perhaps they had nothing to give up or leave behind, except maybe the mystery of who was a good boy?

I kept thinking about my missed chance to talk to Eleanor Aviva about her 'brokering' for the Guardian; still, spilt milk and all that. But what might she have told me? Or would it just have been another chance to mess with me? She'd certainly have tried to negotiate new privileges for whatever information she possessed, so maybe it was for the best, because I'd only have resented rewarding her. Was the lipstick message just another torment?

But I couldn't do anything about Aviva now; I had to focus on the task at hand.

We stepped out into the stone corridor and paused. 'Which way?'

'Left. Keep going left.'

There were no tricks. She led me straight to Olivia, and I think she enjoyed doing it because she knew what we'd find.

The torture chamber had clearly been set up by someone with fond memories of the Middle Ages. There was the obligatory rack, of course; a chain hanging from the ceiling for *strappado*; a trough big enough for a person to be immersed in, should either drowning or waterboarding be required; not to mention that perennial favourite, the Judas chair. Metal cages shaped like bodies were suspended from great beams; I also spotted a breaking wheel, a Spanish donkey and a brazen bull, but no iron maiden – oh, correction, there it was, lurking in the corner. On a freestanding table were all the tools of the trade: pears of anguish in varying sizes, breast rippers, pliers, saws, hammers, head-crushers, knee-splitters, thumbscrews, a scold's bridle, a tongue-tearer, a heretic's fork and an iron boot. And that good old standby: iron shackles bolted to the floor.

And there was a cross at the back of the room, to which my mother was attached.

'Hello, *Mother*,' sneered the fox-girl.

I couldn't pay attention to both her and Olivia. Pragmatism won out over any concerns about giving her permanent brain damage and

I whacked her in the head again, then shackled her, out of reach of anything she could use as a weapon.

I moved to my mother's side.

Her eyes were still closed, and her breathing laboured; she probably hadn't even heard the fox-girl's greeting. The front of her white T-shirt (one of *mine* in fact) was stained red and there was blood on her jeans, but she was alive. And she was attached to the crucifix by ropes, not nails, so that was a mercy.

'Mother? *Mum!*' The word felt strange tripping from my lips. 'Olivia?'

She groaned, rolled her head, opened her eyes and said, 'Shit.'

I laughed, relieved. 'Can you walk?'

'Won't know until you cut me down, Verity,' she said, her voice limned with pain.

'Right.' I took the sword and released her legs first, then quickly followed up on the wrists. She was only about a foot off the ground and I did my best to catch her so she didn't jar as she landed, which meant I got a knee in the ribs, precisely where the fox-girl had kicked me. It was a small price to pay. She leaned forward, hands on her knees, breathing shallowly for a while, then she straightened and I helped support her over to the single non-torture-inflicting chair in the chamber. Had the Guardian sat there to watch while the fox-girl tortured my mother? I knelt in front of her.

'Stupid question, but are you okay?'

She laughed, then gasped. 'Mostly.'

'Great, we'll get you to a healer. We're out of here,' I fumbled in my pocket and brought out Sister Bridget's rosary, which I pressed into her hand. 'You need to hold onto this and think really, really hard about your magic mirror. There's a nun waiting on a riverbank and she's probably cold and annoyed by now. You'll recognise her because most likely she'll yell at you.'

'What about you? Will this bring you back too?'

'I'm good, I've got my own talisman.' I blithely waved my wedding finger where Sister Bridget's ring was starting to feel a wee bit tight. 'I'll be right beside you,' I lied. I was about to cut her finger on the sword to pay the blood price when she touched my hand.

I thought for a moment I'd been rumbled, my ill-thought-out plan scuppered.

'We can't go. Not yet.'

I groaned. 'Why not?'

'Because I'm missing something. I'm not entirely . . . whole.' And she lifted her red-soaked T-shirt and showed me: the left side of her chest had been sliced open. The flesh was still raw. 'It's got my heart.'

'Then how the hell are you still alive?' I squeezed her fingers, making sure she was solid, real, not mist like the souls that drifted along the byways of this place.

'It's beating somewhere else,' she said, 'and I'm going to need it if I want to live *above*.'

'Fuckety-fuck! Why can't *anything* ever be easy? Just a tiny bit fucking easy?'

'You know, of all of them I liked Joyce the most,' Olivia mused, looking at the prone fox-girl on the floor. I huffed out a frustrated breath and flicked a glance at her. *Joyce?* My mother asked, 'What do we do with her?'

I still didn't like *Joyce* but the urge to kill her – for Len, whose death had been so pointless, for the fear I'd suffered in that alley when I thought I was going to die and my unborn daughter with me, for my mother, who'd been hunted so mercilessly – was almost gone and now I felt sorry for her: she was alone and she'd lost. I thought of Dusana Nadasy giving me a second chance and I hoped I wouldn't regret paying it forward.

'Leave her here. Those shackles look mighty sturdy.' Then I turned to my mother and said, 'Well, do you know where your heart is?'

Chapter Thirty-Eight

We'd left the torture chamber far behind, and rejoined the main corridor with its companion stream, padding along the steadily rising path, passing niches, alcoves and caverns, some decked out with antique furniture as if someone spent time there, others filled with books, either on shelves or stacked on the ground. Olivia had stopped me from going in; she'd seen the book greed in my face and said, 'You can't take them with you.'

'But—'

'No.'

'Just one—'

'No.'

'Just a little look—'

'Every one has a price paid in blood. Every one bears a curse, Verity Fassbinder. You don't want them, not in your home or your life.'

I wanted to argue, but I felt the pull from the tomes and recognised it as unhealthy. Most books will give you something back, but there are those volumes that will only ever subtract. I stopped looking into the chambers after that.

'So, is this place far? I mean, it's probably not a wonderful idea for you to be exercising in your current . . . condition.'

She was walking almost normally, with just a bit of a limp; not at all like a woman whose heart was beating elsewhere. She laughed and patted her chest cautiously. 'Not to worry. As long as I'm here and as long as it's being kept safe, I'll be okay. It's happened before. I just can't leave without it.'

'*It's happened before?*'

'When I was sneaking away to watch you, and then again when—'

'—you killed the three-headed dog?'

'I'm not proud of that one, but it was a shit of a beast. I've always been more of a cat person myself.'

I chose not to mention the Galina-Dusana feline and the whole vendetta gig – not yet, at any rate; we'd have plenty to talk about when we got home. *If* we ever got out of here. I didn't ask her about Joyce and her sisters, about what the Guardian had said to fuel their hatred; I'd tell her soon enough, when we were *Above*. 'How do we know it's being kept safe? Your heart?'

'I'm still moving.'

'Good to know.'

We continued in silence for a while longer. Olivia hadn't asked for the return of her sword and I hadn't offered, even though I reckoned she'd still do better with it injured than I would able-bodied. In a pinch, I'd let her have it and pop someone's head off if I had to, but for the moment I liked the idea of hanging onto it. Its weight in my palm was comforting.

'You . . . you called me "Mum",' she said quietly. 'Back there.'

'Well, I did think you were dead,' I said, then relented. 'You are my mother, even if you haven't acted like it for a very long time.'

'Get the digs in while I'm still feeling guilty enough to take it, Missy.' She grinned. 'You're not too big to put over my knee.'

'Actually I am. I really am. I've taken down bigger than you,' I said, and felt like an idiot.

'I know,' she said. 'I saw some of it – not all, not your whole life. I couldn't just sit looking into a mirror 24/7. I'd have liked to but I had to earn my keep.'

'About that—'

'What? Ask me, I'll answer.'

'Truthfully?'

'I swear.'

'The little girls. You didn't just see them drifting by, did you?' I didn't look directly at her, but side-eyed

She blinked a few times, then eventually answered, 'I was the one . . . I was the one who carried the mud-curse to the *smågubbar*. We met near the house on Morwood Road; while I waited for him to show I saw the little girls playing in the yard. I didn't know about Susan Beckett, that she'd already made a deal with it and that it was making its own deal with the Guardian.' She rubbed at her chest again. 'Not long after I handed over the curse parchment, the little girls appeared.'

'Did they speak to you?'

'No – maybe the trauma took their voices. Maybe they didn't get them back after the Boatman brought them here.'

'How did Wilbur Wilson even know about the Guardian?' I scratched my head. 'Maybe all the things from Below and In-Between just know of each other?'

'I doubt it. But the Guardian does deals: it finds people who have a need, people who can give it something in return. It finds things, collects them – sends me or the fox-girls or other agents to get them – then swaps things for other things – favours, artefacts, items, other stuff it stocks away for later. Wilson had something it wanted.'

'What was that?'

'A book: red cover, gold lettering, in a language I couldn't read but it looked a bit like Hebrew. And the little bastard had wrapped a ribbon-lock around it so it couldn't be opened by the likes of me, which was rude and suspicious.'

I'd not thought to ask Wanda Callander what her grimoire looked like — was that what Wilbur Wilson had swapped in return for the curse parchment? Perhaps he had intended to use the Grand Drowning spell for the Becketts, but wouldn't it have taken the whole family down at once? Then when Susan remained unmoved by his entreaties the Grand Drowning was just what he needed . . .

'You'd have opened it, though, if you could, right?'

'In a heartbeat. These last few years I've been trying to gather as much information as I could whenever I was above. The first two decades I was still too angry.'

'That's pretty angry, Mum.'

'I had a lot to be angry about. Or I thought I did. Maybe age is mellowing me.'

'So, you collected this book . . .'

'The important thing is that I *delivered* a means of murder — the mud inundation is the worst sort of curse: it's cruel and filthy and it's filled with contempt. And if you use it to kill, it's inescapable.'

'But you didn't know it was Susan Beckett at the end of it all?'

'As far as I knew, it was the *smågubbar* doing the deal, and he never gave his name. I don't know if the Guardian knew much more either.'

'Beckett's dead now. She jumped off a cliff.'

'Did you see her here? Her mother's around . . .'

'I haven't seen Susan,' I said, but didn't say why, 'and her mother's not here any more. I spoke with Marian, let her unburden herself.' I rubbed my face. 'Didn't you feel the urge to talk to her?'

'And say what? "Sorry I helped kill you"?'

'Maybe not.'

'This life . . .' began Olivia. 'This life is a series of doorways, just as death is a series of doorways. Always remember that.'

'That sounds like a fortune cookie.' I asked what I'd avoided asking for so long. 'How . . . how did you find out about Grigor?'

'He kept disappearing, said he was working late, and I thought . . . I thought he was having an affair, so I followed him one night. He went to this big house in Ascot – huge glamour, amazing job – and I went in after him. There were . . . There were—'

'I know what was there,' I said, so she didn't have to go on. I was all too familiar with that house at Ascot where Dusana Nadasy's mother had made wine from the tears of children. It hadn't occurred to me that Grigor must have set up his butcher shop there too. 'And you knew about Ziggi – you knew he was my uncle, but you didn't rat him out.'

'I didn't know if he'd told you who he was. In his position I might have kept quiet about it too: the fact that my brother was an enthusiastic butcher of children. It's not really something you want to get tarred with, is it? You were a teenager when he arrived, yes? I bet you were revolting.'

'That's a bit strong. Maybe.' I paused. 'Yeah, okay, I was revolting.'

'Why are you asking me and not him?'

'Because I've already talked to him,' I said with an edge, 'and now I'm trying to work out who I can trust, because quite frankly a lot of porkies from my nearest and dearest have been exposed in recent days.'

'Well, if it's any comfort, Grigor *detested* his brother – he loved him, but he hated him too. Not because Ziggi was the reason Grigor had pledged to the Nadasys – I realised a long time ago that Grigor *was* delighted by that – but because what Ziggi did brought shame to the Hassman name.' She rubbed her eyes like a tired child. 'I knew who he worked for and I knew bits of the story, of how it had come about, but I didn't know what your father actually *did*. I thought he was a chef!' She laughed, the hardest sound I'd ever heard. 'We met Ziggi in Paris on our honeymoon and had a nice lunch, which all went pear-shaped when Grigor lost his temper and called his brother a coward, and a few other things besides. When they started arguing, they switched between English and the Old Tongue, which I didn't understand, and when I asked your father about it later, he lost his temper again, so I stopped asking.' She looked at me, speaking slowly, as if to make sure I took in the importance of what she was saying. 'Your uncle was *always* the good guy. Ziggi's kind and considerate. He doesn't take joy in the hunt or the hurt, which in his family meant he was the white sheep, an embarrassment. Don't be too tough on him.'

Olivia grabbed my arm just before we hit the end of the corridor – I couldn't figure out how she knew where we were, because I couldn't see any actual markings to distinguish one long passageway from another: no road signs, no handy arrows, no breadcrumbs. Yet she'd navigated flawlessly through the halls of the Underworld and here we were at last: the lair of the Guardian of the Southern Gate of the Underworld.

'It's sleeping a lot nowadays,' she whispered.

'Wait – what? That's its *bedroom*?' I pointed towards the doorway before us, then whined as quietly as I could, 'Muuuuum!'

Her expression was conflicted: one part annoyance, one part embarrassment and one part joy that her daughter finally got to say that word in that tone.

'Last I saw it, the Guardian put my heart in a box beside the bed. It's got *Hello Kitty* on the top.'

'*Your heart is in a Hello Kitty box?*'

'You know, the cat.'

'Yes, I know the fucking cat! That's not the point . . . it's a fucking Country and Western song! "My Mother's Heart is in a Hello Kitty Box"!'

'You swear too much.'

'It's a bit late for that, Olivia. Honestly, this Guardian is getting less frightening by the minute. I mean, look at this place: it's virtually empty. The thing sleeps a lot. It's only got four people working for it — or did.'

'Don't underestimate it, love. There are other barracks, other places across the world and under it; not all those who work for it live Beneath, there are many on the surface too. And as for the lack of other folk down here? Most drink as soon as they arrive because they want to forget, to move on. Those who hang around because they're too scared to take responsibility for what they've done in life, or because they want to cling to their old days . . . that's a very small proportion. Trust me, I've watched for a long time. This is a way-station, a passing place — that's why the Guardian can hide out here.' She rubbed at her chest again. 'No matter what religion they followed in life, as far as I can tell, people make their own heaven and their own hell. They all take a ride with the Boatman and they all end up somewhere like this to start the next part of their journey.'

'You know, it's that kind of talk that will get you burned at the stake, Mother. C'mon, let's get your heart and get the hell out of here.'

The entrance to the chamber was blocked by vintage room dividers, the carved frames painted gold, the silk screens printed with pictures of phoenixes and fires and ashes. It looked pretty damned fancy . . . Then again, maybe this was completely normal. I confess, I hadn't really given much thought to the furnishings of the Underworld.

Olivia and I peeked around one of the dividers.

It wasn't an enormous cavern, but it was still crammed full of *stuff*; someone was operating on Fassbinder's Law of Handbag Physics, only they'd applied it to rooms. There was a lot of furniture, expensive things decorated with gold leaf and gems, shaped from rare woods or cast from precious metals: chairs and lounges, roll-top desks, wardrobes, tables and bookcases. And there were chests and paintings and caskets of gold and silver, Russian icons, all manner of rich plate – more than one church had clearly been robbed – and in one corner, propped on a chaise longue upholstered in worn gold velvet, sat three heavily bejewelled skeletons: saints, maybe, from who-knew-where, made into reliquaries for and from themselves. And there was a sizable baptismal font at the mouth of the path that led towards the centre of the room. It all reminded me of the second floor of Little Venice, where I always imagined Theodora and Aspasia playing amateur *Antiques Roadshow* in their downtime.

Whatever else it might have been, this Guardian had a serious hoarding problem. Or issues concerning religion. Maybe both. Probably both. Definitely both.

Such richness, such treasure and it had put my mother's heart in a *Hello Kitty* box? I wasn't sure if I was more bewildered or offended.

In the middle of all this was a bed: an enormous four-poster with a blue velvet canopy and hangings, bigger than even the notorious Great Bed of Ware, which was three metres wide and could reputedly fit four couples – possibly more, if they were stacked horizontally. This one was three times as big . . . and it needed to be, in order to accommodate its sole occupant.

It was a broken thing, mostly burned black, although some patches of pristine marble-white skin shone through. There were strands of hair left on the large head, entire locks even, of a red so deep it looked almost ebony in the candlelight. The wings were in no state to bear it anywhere: a blackened set of feathers, with sinews and bones that hadn't just been scorched but actually appeared hacked at. The hands that clenched on its pillows did not have all their fingers, but I spotted a thick silver band on one of the remaining ones. Crimson still showed in spots where the flesh hadn't healed.

Even in this state it made my heart clench with fear.

By the size of it, this was an archangel. I'd dealt with one before, but I hadn't been the one to kill it, not to mention that I was no longer in possession of the weapon that had made possible the death of a *lesser* angel. That explained how the *kitsune*, Weyrd though they were, could move back and forth between the Above and Below: the angel had created some kind of dispensation. Given the ill-feeling between the Weyrd and the heavenly host, that wasn't something many of them were likely to get.

Shit.

Shit, bugger and soddy fucks.

I ducked back around the screen, pulled Olivia to me and whispered, 'How long's it been like this? Wounded?'

'Always – well, all the time I've known it.'

'And you said it's been sleeping a lot? As if it's getting worse?'

She nodded, and I wondered if I had a chance. Olivia hadn't tried to attack it all the time she'd been here – but was that fear, reasonable or otherwise? Or did the Guardian have some kind of hold over its minions to keep coups and rebellions to a minimum?

'Right. The box?'

'On the bedside table on the left.'

'Of course it is. You stay here.'

She didn't argue, and I realised she didn't want to go near the ruined creature any more than I did. I rounded the screens and felt a tug on my coat: a nail had worked its way through the frame, pointy end out: a real safety hazard. I pointed to it so Olivia could avoid it, then felt a bit despairing at my priorities when the scale of things was so out of proportion. *Don't wake up the angel, and don't break a nail.*

I was careful: there were many rugs piled up, overlapping each other, a lot of tripping hazards – this place really was an occupational health and safety nightmare – but I managed it. I couldn't work out if it was an intentional obstacle course or simply the product of a mind that didn't care about clutter, as long as it had its possessions all in one place, in sight. The box was right there and as I reached for it, the angel gasped in its sleep, its breath laboured and pained, and I wondered again how long it had been like this. I froze, gripped the sword hilt hard, waited until it settled, then carefully, oh so carefully, snatched up the pulsing box and made my way back to where Olivia hid behind the screens.

The box gave a rhythmic tremor every second or so, which was quite distracting. The lid made a tiny clanking protest as it opened and we both froze, expecting a waking roar from the bed, but there was only the rasping huff of breath in and out. Inside the box was my mother's heart: a meaty thing that was indeed still beating. I wondered if the angel would miss the low sound of its *lub-dub, lub-dub*. I stared at it, then at Olivia. She'd lifted her bloody T-shirt up and now she dug the fingers of one hand into the cut in her chest and pulled it wide. I could see that where there should be ribs that would prevent me from simply replacing what she'd lost, there was nothing. Had the angel removed them too?

She looked at me and said, 'Go on,' then turned her head to the side so she didn't have to watch.

I'd have liked to close my eyes too, but I didn't.

I reached into the box, grabbed the thing that quivered in my hand

and thrust it into the hole in Olivia's chest, and almost as soon as I did so, I felt the flesh closing around my wrist and the poke of rib bones reinstating themselves. I pulled free before I got stuck there and had yet another bizarre thing in my life to explain. Olivia shuddered, bit back a cough and took deep breaths, her eyes wide and watering. I didn't ask her about the mark I'd seen on the skin over her heart – a mark that didn't disappear after the mending was done. The scar in the shape of a quadrate cross was just like those on the Sisters Norn, and I remembered the silver band on the ruined angel's finger.

I asked, 'If this has happened more than once, who put it back in?'

'Joyce, once. Agnes another time. Sybil another.' The fox-girls, performing the service for their *mother*.

'Got that rosary?' I whispered, and she pulled it from her jeans pocket. I nicked her index finger with the blade of the sword: the scarlet price. 'Okay, think of your compact.'

'What, no ruby slippers?'

'And people say I'm a smartarse and wonder where I got it from. Just remember the cold angry nun who has your prized possession. I'll be right behind you.'

And she closed her eyes, which was good, because it meant she didn't did see I'd not taken out my own talisman to link me back to Sister Bridget. For a long moment she was still there and I was terrified something had gone wrong, that Thaïs had played some shitty joke on me, or Sister Bridget had wandered away, lost the compact or, worse still, been found by Bela and Ziggi, who were even now interrogating her instead of letting her do her job.

But then it was okay: Olivia dissolved into a stream of silvery particles that sped away, presumably back along the winding paths we'd taken, back and back and back to a chill, lonely bank of the Brisbane River.

I breathed a sigh of relief. With my mother out of danger I could concentrate on the next crazy idea.

If I left this archangel here, my mother would never be free, and nor would I. As long as it still drew breath it would just keep sending the next minion and the next and the next, until it wore us down and we made a mistake. If I wanted my family to be safe, then it had to end here.

I tightened my grip on the sword and felt a rush of adrenalin warm me. Though I made no sound, a beautiful, broken voice rumbled from the room behind me and shook my very bones as it said, 'Verity Fassbinder. At last.'

Chapter Thirty-Nine

The Guardian was sitting up in bed and staring at me as I stepped around the screen and back into the chamber. It was near impossible to make out any expression on that blackened face, but its open lids showed the greenest of eyes, and they told a tale of avid interest, of greed, of *anticipation*.

'I have been waiting for you.'

'I did not get that memo.' I tightened my grip on the sword, concealing it close by my leg.

'Impudent, just like your mother.'

I wasn't sure how to take that. 'You know my name. It's only polite to tell me yours.'

'I am the Guardian. Did you mother not tell you? The Guardian of the Southern Gate of the Underworld,' it said rather grandly, lifting a hand that had only three fingers and no thumb to gesture to itself: *Here's one we prepared earlier.*

'Really? Because you look a lot like a broken-arsed archangel to me.'

The eyes flashed and it shouted, '*I am the Guardian!* This territory is mine! This trust is sacred and mine alone, *to guard the gateway to Elsewhere!*'

The Guardian's condition hadn't affected its volume, and I wondered if all angels were prone to bouts of crazy. I'd only ever met one – in my admittedly limited experience – who appeared to have his shit together and no delusions of grandeur; mind you, Tobit was also something of a slacker.

'Guardian it is, then,' I said. It might be sticking to its story in the hope that I'd believe it, or perhaps it really had bought into its own fiction. I wondered what had happened to it to turn its mind? The one thing I was sure of was the wisdom in *not* pissing it off. Or at least, not pissing it off too much; I had to get some enjoyment out of this. 'So, waiting for me, hey?'

'I have watched,' it said grandly, and gestured towards the font, which I approached cautiously. I peeked into the basin, but there was nothing there but water with the same dull sheen as the surface of Olivia's magic mirror. The Guardian was apparently not interested in giving a demonstration; he went on, 'Your mother served well for as long as she did. For as long as she *believed*.'

I wasn't going to get into an argument that exposed how much or how little I knew. I just tilted my head to show I was listening.

'But she lost her faith.'

I bit my tongue and didn't say *Her rage burned out so you had nothing to work with any more.*

'She is gone. You, however, stayed.' Its tone was gleeful.

'Why do you think that is?'

'You were *drawn* here. I have waited so long for the right moment, for you to be in this place, for you to feel the rage you must feel.' It grinned, showing white, white teeth and splitting the skin, displaying cracks of red meat. I forced myself not to look away as it went on, 'When you have been so betrayed by your nearest and dearest – when there is so much anger inside you: just as your mother was. Now *you* shall serve me.'

Oh, you idiot, I wanted to say. Cross as I was with Bela and Ziggi and Olivia, that did not render me a moron, and I was a bit peeved that this archangel would think me so easy to manipulate. Then again, my previous experience with angels probably should have prepared me for some pretty huge entitlement and assumption.

'I knew you would come to me. Now you can be put to the great work.'

It was full of shit; it knew no such thing. It was just used to selling dreams and promises to those as broken as it was: people who'd grasp at any opportunity for revenge, any chance to pass on even a little of the hurt they'd suffered. 'Which would be?'

'Two items. They are connected, but you must find one before the other.'

'That's cryptic.'

'There is a being of power, greater than an angel. And there is a vessel. Both are hidden from me.'

'And what will you do when I find these . . . things?'

'Punish one and use the other to heal myself.'

'And what are they?' I had an idea I knew what was coming, but I was only half right.

'One is a tyrant, a torturer. The other is a hope – my *only* hope. You must find this one first so I may become whole once again. Only then can I cast down the tyrant.'

'Are we talking a holy grail type situation here?' I asked, barely able to keep the disbelief out of my voice, which was kind of unfair on my part, because if anyone knew there were miracles in the everyday, then it was me. Angels traditionally dislike the Weyrd even more than they dislike humanity (it's a sibling rivalry thing), but here was this angel – an arch no less – with an identity crisis, willing to ally itself with a Weyrd, and a half-blood one at that. Maybe 'ally' was too strong a word. It was more about *using* me. Most angelics wouldn't stoop so low even if their lives depended on it.

The Guardian nodded with too much enthusiasm and the skin at the base of its throat ruptured. Again, it didn't appear to notice; perhaps it had been in pain for too long for little hurts to bother it. 'It has been called many things—'

'The Holy Grail, holy chalice, *Sanct Grael*, the Cauldron of Plenty, Bran's big bucket.' I looked at it and said, 'So you're what? The Fisher King?'

And again that flare of madness, again with the yelling, 'I am the Guardian and *you will help ME!*'

Ignoring the ache in my ears, I held up the shining length of the sword so the angel could see it.

It laughed. 'I will kill your mother, your lover, your child. I will murder those so-called friends who told you lies for so very long. You will serve me, or all of them will die.'

'And what's to stop me from killing you now?' I asked, hefting the blade. 'Whatever you might say, you're an angel, or at least, what's left of one. I've dealt with your kind before – if you've been watching me, you'll know what I'm capable of. You're broken, you're not invincible.' Which was a pretty stupid thing to say when the angel I'd killed hadn't been an arch and had given me an impressive beating before I managed to stab it with the dagger I no longer had.

'Yes. I know how you dealt with those brethren.'

'So, I repeat: what's to stop me killing you now?'

'See for yourself.' It pointed to the font and I gave a quick glance.

The surface reflected the inside of my home like a small round TV screen. David was holding Maisie, feeding her from a bottle. Bela and Ziggi were close by, talking to Mike, whose face flickered as if two transmissions were coming in to the same receiver. Somehow I knew that I was the only one who could see his expression held rage and guilt and blame and the desire for revenge.

'Joyce can be very persuasive, given the right means to motivate someone.'

The *kitsune* had talked to him – I was willing to bet it was while he sat in the Jeep, maybe when he'd fallen asleep or was in that *between* state. He'd hesitated when I'd asked him about dreams, as if unsure – Susan Beckett had probably slipped out of the house then, found a hire car and headed towards Ocean's Reach with Mike none the wiser. It would have been easy enough for Joyce to cast an erasure afterwards so he'd only subconsciously recall the deal he'd made. A Weyrd Manchurian Candidate. My sympathy for the fox-girl vanished again.

'What did you offer him?' I asked, my throat suddenly constricted.

'His dearest wish, of course: a chance to win back his beloved.' It gave a low laugh.

'Jerry isn't here any more, and the Weyrd can't return.'

'Ah, but the grieving believe what they want to. I need only whisper a command and it will fly from my lips to his ears. Your family will be dead before you can draw another breath because Mike Jones *owes* me a debt of my choosing.'

I fidgeted uncertainly with the sword, and the angel stretched its black-burned digits towards me. The blade in my hand turned red with rust, then crumbled in my fingers. The creature grinned. 'Do you think I have no control over the gifts I lend to my *menials*? Do you think I cannot destroy what was forged by my own will? You have your strength, of course, and I am weak – you might well kill me, little scrap, but you cannot be faster than the breath of God.'

Ziggi and Bela wouldn't expect an attack from Mike. They would go down first, and David and Maisie would be gone soon afterwards, and *then* I would be filled with the right kind of rage for the Guardian to manipulate – but by then, of course, it would be dead. 'He'll find your mother, too, eventually.'

I couldn't be sure the angel wasn't lying but one thing was certain: I wasn't going to risk a death sentence for those I loved.

'Are you willing to chance it?' the thing fair hissed, and I thought of snakes hanging from trees, offering naked folks slices of apple. *Eat the fruit.*

'What do you want of me?'

'Serve me: find the cup, then the tyrant. Be my sword.' It tried another smile, and I wondered how desperate anyone had to be to trust this thing. 'Serve me, and your loved ones will be safe, even beyond death.'

I had experience of archangels and their bargains. I was also naturally suspicious. 'I have some conditions.'

Its green eyes flared again, but it must have realised a little give and take was in order. 'Go on.'

'You release my mother from her bargain with you, no comeback on her.'

It nodded.

'You leave David and Maisie, Bela and Ziggi, well the fuck alone.'

Again, the gracious incline of the head.

'And I am *not* living down here.'

'I find your terms acceptable,' it said, which was all a little too easy. Of course, it was. 'I also have conditions.'

I lifted my chin: *go on.*

'You will have no contact with your family. Divided loyalties make for terrible employees. You will send them away.'

That felt like a kick in the guts; I wanted to argue, but the sensible part of me said it was okay, it was a good idea. If I could get them out of harm's way, I could get this whole thing over and done with much faster, much more cleanly, and with far less risk to those I loved. 'I'll need a few months to arrange that.'

'You have one month.'

'Anything else?'

'You will cease your work with the Weyrd Council. Again: divided loyalties. I have no doubt you will understand.'

Its plan was clear: strip me of my supports, isolate me. Well, it didn't know me very well, no matter what it thought. 'And keep your fox-girl the fuck away from me and mine, understand? She's got impulse-control issues. I'm sure she'll chew through the restraints eventually.'

'Agreed.'

'And tell me this: did my mother kill the fox-girls' parents?' I needed to know. I needed to hear it from someone other than Olivia or Joyce. I held my breath.

'Joyce and Agnes and Sybil were easy to convince,' it said lightly.

'So, *no*.' I breathed out and the breath somehow tasted rotten from all the fear and suspicion that rode on it. 'You lied to get them to hunt her.'

'Information is power, Verity Fassbinder, or at least I have found it so.'

'You've got that right. I will find your vessel and your tyrant, as long as you leave my loved ones alone.'

'I will take the powers I gave your mother and gift them to you,' it said, the very soul of magnanimity. 'Great speed, reflexes, strength—'

'Y'know, I'm good for strength. Leave Olivia alone; leave her as she is. She'll need to protect herself and David and Maisie, no matter where they go – and if *anything* happens to them because you made her less . . .'

'I . . . I cannot give you both—'

I saved its dignity; I'd already figured it wasn't strong enough. 'That's okay. I like the way I am. I don't need any enhancements, thank you.'

'You will require one thing.' It pointed to the bedside table from which I'd earlier snatched the *Hello Kitty* tin. 'There, the top drawer.'

I moved away from the font and picked my way back through the furnishings, getting far too close to the ruined creature watching me greedily. The drawer wasn't locked. Inside was a box covered in midnight blue velvet.

'Open it.'

I moved out of reach and lifted the tiny silver latch. Lying against the plush cushioning inside was an ancient locket on a dirty gold chain, and a pendant that looked like glass but on closer inspection was a clear crystal. Inside the crystal was something *incredibly* white.

'A piece of bone,' the Guardian said. 'It will glow when you are close to what you seek, both tyrant and grail. They are made of sympathetic substances. Keep it on you at all times.'

'A reliquary,' I corrected. I closed the box and slipped it into my pocket. It clunked against the dead mobile. 'Any ideas where to start my search?'

'In that backwater you call home.'

I bridled at that: it's okay for *me* to criticise my city, but not some stray psychotic angel.

It didn't appear to notice. 'Somewhere there, both of those prizes hide, yet no one has ever been able to find them. What magic conceals them?' It looked at me as if I might have an answer.

So, it seemed like I'd be spending a lot more time in the Archives – although how I was going to do that when I wasn't working for the Council was going to take some finagling.

'Well, I guess I'll be going then,' I said. 'A family to displace, a job to quit, arrangements to make.'

'I will return you to your home.'

'No, no, I'm good.' I had no desire to rely on this creature any more than I had to. Getting Sister Bridget's gold ring off was a tad challenging, but I managed it without too much undignified tugging. I backed away from the archangel and found the privacy screen with the nail hazard, then jabbed my finger onto it to pay the price (hoping that I didn't have to worry about tetanus). I wrapped my fingers around the band and felt the blood slip across the surface, and thought hard of my own emerald ring in the old nun's possession. Then my body felt as if it was falling apart, spinning and speeding and floating.

There was less sickness than when I'd travelled to Byron, though I still threw up when I landed on the riverbank, but by that point I was happy with small mercies.

Chapter Forty

It was ridiculously early when they began to arrive and we were still in our pyjamas, but Maisie loved the sight. It was good to hear her laugh; she'd become prone to fits of crying over the last few weeks, as if she sensed something was wrong, that the time of our separation was drawing near. But for now, she was chortling, warm and smelling of talc as she snuffled into my neck. David stood beside us on the deck, his arms around me. I wanted it to last for ever.

An odd assortment of vehicles chugged down the steep driveway into the back yard: ancient kombi-vans, family sedans that had seen better days, some in a spectacularly abhorrent shade of orange, others with rust patches that threatened to entirely undo them as they rattled along the concrete. There were eight in all, and as they circled the base of the giant jacaranda tree, a change came over the battered chassis as chrome and steel and glass turned to glossy brown, the wood grain obvious even from where we stood. The vehicles became larger, reshaping themselves into gypsy wagons with shuttered windows, exquisite copper and glass lanterns hanging on either sides of carven doors, then brightly painted patterns crept across the planks: blood reds, daffodil yellows, emerald greens, extraordinary purples with gold trim. Where engines had been proud horses stamped great iron-clad feet, tossing magnificent manes – although there were no drivers on the box seats.

'Well,' I said. 'That's new.'

David whistled. 'I did not expect *that*. Cool!'

Maisie gave a particularly delighted *coo* and I thought my heart might explode, then she drooled down my neck.

'You think she likes the horses?' David asked, examining our daughter.

'Lots of little girls like horses, but I suspect . . . it's the magic.'

David mock-sighed. 'No point in telling her fairy tales then, she'll just point out the inconsistencies.'

I leaned against him. He kissed my forehead, and his lips burned where they touched the cool skin – or maybe that was just my imagination working overtime as D-Day drew closer. Below us, the doors at the back of each wagon creaked open and stairs unrolled themselves from where they'd been stored. No human hand was touching anything. All in all, it was an impressive display.

'Is this good or bad?' David asked uncertainly. 'I know Ziggi's desperate to be back in your good books, but—'

'Honestly, I just don't know,' I said helplessly. 'But we let him organise this, so we'll probably get what we deserve.'

As if the Fates heard me, someone appeared from what had once been a kombi-van: a short woman with a shock of silver hair wearing a bright blood-red peasant top and hippy skirt, her fingers glittering with rings and the silver hoops in her ears almost reaching her shoulders. She looked up and saw us, waving enthusiastically.

I waved back. Ziggi was inside with Olivia; they'd been whispering and plotting for what felt like months. I handed Maisie to David; neither of them complained. 'I'll handle this.'

Five hours after Belle McTavish had fair sung at me, 'We're the band! We're here for the party!' there was indeed a party in full swing in my back yard.

The Norns had kindly done the catering, and even brought along their emo-Weyrd waitresses to pout and slouch through the crowd offering food and doing a bad job of pretending not to enjoy themselves. There were sweets, dips, chips, finger sandwiches, fruit platters, pies and sausage rolls, and a bewildering variety of cheeses and preserved meats. A table, manned — or rather womanned — by Theo and Aspasia had been set up by the jacaranda tree; it groaned with all manner of beverages. Naturally, there was no sign of Thaïs, but she'd sent her best.

The crowd mingled happily, any arguments forgotten, at least for today. Some Weyrd had approached Olivia and offered apologies for past sins; she accepted graciously. Maybe I could learn something from my mother. Rhonda and Ellen, proudly displaying her new tattoo — thanks to Kadie Cross, who was currently in an animated discussion with Sandor Verhoeven about the safekeeping of her labradorite rock — arrived bearing more gifts and were directed to another table on the other side of the tree where the wedding presents were already piled high. It wasn't like we actually *needed* anything, but it was nice that so many people gave us stuff. The cake (marshmallow and caramel) was upstairs, where it would remain until it could be safely brought down for cutting. McIntyre whispered to me that a very sheepish Constable Oldman had finally found Wilbur Wilson on both the Mt Coot-tha security footage and the video of the shopping centre where Faraday Hannigan met her end. Not that it mattered any more.

Ziggi had been a little grumpy with me when I'd put my foot down about the pig on a spit he so dearly wanted, but as the band got into full swing, belting out a fine, fiery mix of folk music from places unknown — after they'd assured me a dampening glamour would keep the noise from blasting my neighbours near and far — he was more forgiving. After a few drinks, tails, pointed ears and wings started to poke through faded or exhausted glamours. David, who was firmly planted between two flirtatious sirens, watched our daughter being passed around by people who were genuinely delighted to make her acquaintance. Bless him, he didn't bat an eyelid when Maisie tried to swing on the horns of a guest whose true shape leaned towards minotaurish, but he did calmly rise, apologise and retrieve her.

Sister Bridget had settled down next to the old siren Ligeia and the slacker angel Tobit and was gazing at them with undisguised wonder as the three talked avidly about I didn't know what; it didn't matter, because she looked *happy*. Mel and Lizzie had returned, tanned and relaxed, and Lizzie had been pressed into service passing out the platters of food, while Mel and Jost Marolf were staring at each other and talking and ignoring most everyone else around them. Mel occasionally threw me a glance that said, *Thank you, thank you, thank you*. What are friends for?

More guests arrived and the gift table looked like buckling, so Bela offered to help me ferry them upstairs, which should have – and did – make me suspicious. Bela wasn't a man given to volunteering for heavy lifting.

'I don't like this, V,' he said, stacking boxes against the tiny sliver of free wall in the library; I'd have trouble getting to my desk later. 'You don't need to do this.'

'There's no other way, Bela; we've got to put them somewhere,' I said, deliberately obtuse.

'I mean the quitting,' he began.

'I know what you mean, but it's not up for debate. I have to fulfil my obligations to the Guardian. There're no ifs or buts about this thing.'

'V—'

'Bela, if my previous dealings with angels has taught me *anything*, it's that they're determined and monomaniacal. If I don't hold up my end of the bargain, it'll send someone – or some*thing* – after me and mine.' I thought about Joyce the fox-girl and how much she'd like some payback. I wondered if the Guardian had punished her again for her failures. 'And frankly, I don't want to talk about this. Not again. It's not safe to do so.' I leaned close and whispered in his ear, 'I *will* find a way to communicate, so just calm the fuck down.'

He opened his mouth again and I hastily said, 'How's Mike?'

'Getting there, slowly. He's still at Ocean's Reach with Wanda. She's trying to clear the last traces the Guardian's girl left in his brain. It helped when you told him about Jerry. It hurt, but it helped. We're keeping an eye on him.'

I'd wondered if it wouldn't be too painful, being where Jerry had died, but Mike himself had told me that it made him feel closer to his partner, more at peace. Whatever worked for him was fine by me. He still had no memory of Joyce talking to him, but he had admitted there had been times he'd drifted off from exhaustion, so he couldn't swear that the fox-girl hadn't been there.

And a little while later, Olivia held Maisie tightly while David and I stood in front of Sandor Verhoeven. He looked a little unsure what he was doing there, but he married us nevertheless. That's not to say there hadn't been a heated discussion about his participation, but in the end, I think he gave in because he realised I'd never give up. But, damn it all, every other Weyrd got to stand before him when they chose to do this stupid knot-tying thing and I sure as hell wasn't going to miss out on that. I belonged to them as much as I did to the Normals and I would *not* be treated as an outcast any more – which was kind of ironic, given that I was about to cast myself out.

David had tried to buy me a new ring, but I said no, all I wanted was my silver and emerald birthday ring, retrieved from Sister Bridget's possession. It was the first gift he'd ever given me, and the thing that had brought me back from the Underworld. What more did I need?

Later still, when the sun was down and everyone had gone and all the dishes had been done by the emo-Weyrd waitresses (I'd think twice about bitching about them in the future), when Olivia and Maisie were asleep and Bela and Ziggi had gone on their not-so-merry ways, then David and I sat out on the deck, even though it was cold, holding hands and staring at the silhouette of the fat kookaburra in the upper branches of the jacaranda tree.

'Promise me you'll read Maisie fairy tales, ones where the missing mother comes good. Ones where she gets a second chance.' I bit my lip. 'They're not just stories, you know.'

'It's already happened once. If it can happen for Olivia, then why not for you?' He laughed, then grew serious because he knew I'd spend the next however long fretting over every conversation, every last word, just everything. 'V, this is *not* your fault.'

'It is, you know. It really is.' I closed my eyes against the tears I felt welling, blinked them away. 'It really, really is. But I promise, David, I promise when this is over, no more of this life.'

'That might be one of the most stupid thing you've ever said, Verity Fassbinder, and I wish you would stop saying it. You are who you are, V: this is the life you have and this is the life I've chosen because I've chosen *you*.' He pressed his forehead to mine and whispered, 'Just do what you have to do, my love, then we'll come home . . . Wife. You're my *wife*.'

'Well, more fool you: no backsies.'

'For better or worse.'

'I'll try to make sure the better outweighs the worse.'

'That would be good. Shall we go to bed, Mrs Harris?' His

expression changed, looked stricken. 'Oh, shit, that sounds *so* wrong. Mrs Harris is my mother!'

'Yeah, I think I'm going to stick with Fassbinder.'

'I think that's for the best.' We grinned at each other like idiots, then he said again, 'Bed?'

'You go on ahead. I've got one last thing to do.'

And because he knew what that thing was, and because he was David, he didn't whinge, just kissed me on the forehead and went inside. I waited a few minutes, enjoying the quiet and the knowledge that, for a little while yet, my family was here and they were safe. Finally, I got up and went to collect a shallow silver bowl, Sister Bridget's flask, a box of matches and the plastic bag from the house on Morwood Road, then headed down to the back yard.

Jost Marolf had told me what he thought would work, and I was willing to give anything a go. I needed all the loose ends neatly tied before I could move forward.

I sat at the foot of the jacaranda, put the bowl in front of me and opened the carrier bag. I laid out in a row three little tea candles, a stinky mud-encrusted teddy bear and a grubby little coral bracelet. From the left pocket of my jacket I pulled the necklace Wanda Callander had given me a few days ago: a leather thong with a miniature apothecary's bottle strung on it – Wanda hadn't wanted to when I told her to trap Beckett's soul, but she'd done it anyway, reeling in the silver thread before it made its way to one of the Brotherhood of Boatmen – and set it between the other two items. I was careful as I unscrewed the flask and even more careful when I poured about three-quarters of the contents into the bowl. The Waters of Forgetting looked just as strange in that mundane receptacle as they had in the Underworld stream that ran the wrong way.

I lit the candles and very softly, I sang the summoning chant Jost had found in a book located deep in the Archives. It wasn't long before one, two, three corpselights were dancing before me and soon enough they resolved themselves into Unity and Hildy, with their mother Susan Beckett in the middle. Her expression was strange, or maybe not strange in the circumstances: I saw guilt there, and anger and resentment, fear and love . . . but most of all I think I saw love, and that was what surprised me most of all. She looked uncertain, but she also looked determined.

'You've got one last chance,' I told her. 'Take them on their way, take them to their rest. Answer for what you've done, have your heart weighed.' I pointed to the bowl with its silvery-dark liquid and said, 'You have to drink, all of you.'

For a long moment Susan Beckett hesitated; she didn't speak. I didn't know if she knew what was to come, but at last she nodded. She let go of her daughters' hands, reached down to take the vessel I lifted up, then held it to each child's rosebud lips, one after the other. Finally, she herself drank, a long, deep swallow, as if she was embracing whatever would happen next.

And then they were gone, all three; the bowl fell to the grass with a dull thud. I hoped it was somewhere good, even for Susan Beckett, as much for myself as her. If she got a second chance with her children, then maybe I'd get one with mine.

As I sat in the darkness I contemplated Eleanor Aviva's note about the 3 in 1 and pondered what that meant. I wondered where to start my search for what the Guardian was looking for, how long I'd take to find both tyrant and grail – and what I'd do when I found them. I wondered what Dusana Nadasy was doing and where, and when I'd see her again. I wondered what life would be like without Bela and Ziggi. I wondered how long it would be before I had David and Maisie and my mother back with me again.

That was the worst uncertainty of all, and it ached, but it was the sort of pain that spurred me on, giving me strength and stubborn determination. I'd move heaven and earth to get my family back.

I also took comfort, dark though it might have been, from the knowledge that there was no bargain that couldn't be renegotiated and no deal that couldn't be broken some way down the track.

Verity Fassbinder will return in

RESTORATION

Author's Note

Thanks to all the mums who read *Corpselight* for me and gave me guidance on the finer points of the Care and Feeding of Offspring. Special thanks to Kate Eltham for her willingness to share her experience of having a premmie baby. Does Verity express milk enough for a new mother? No, she does not; at least not 'on screen'. I'm sorry, you'll just have to imagine it happening in the between spaces. Any mistakes are all my own.

Acknowledgements

Thanks to:

My family for their patience as I tell wild stories.

My BFF and Brain, Lisa L. Hannett, for cheerleading.

My beta readers, Peter M. Ball and Alan Baxter, for looking over very ugly early drafts.

Ron Serdiuk, Alexandra Pierce, Tehani Croft and Maria Haskins for being first amongst readers' readers.

Kathleen Jennings for emergency art fixes, and Kate Eltham for all things premmie.

Pulp Fiction Booksellers for All of the Things.

Jo Fletcher for her exquisite editing skills, her openness to discussion and her infinite patience.

Stephen Jones, for professional advice and steadfast friendship.

Ron and Stef, Lulu and Johnny for the sanctuary.

Sam Bradbury and Olivia Mead of JFB/Quercus for their unfailing professionalism, excellent author support and willing participation in GIF wars.

Ian Drury for his expertise on brand auguries.

The lovely folk at Hachette Australia, especially Ilse, Jessica, Sean and Kathie and Adele, for helping me with the home turf.

David Pollitt for his support. Nicola Howell and Marianne Ehrhardt for proofreading.

To the Katharine Susannah Prichard Writers Centre for the time and place to complete the edits, and to the Copyright Agency for assistance with funding.

Angela Slatter is the award-winning author of eight short story collections, including *A Feast of Sorrows: Stories*, *Sourdough and Other Stories*, *The Bitterwood Bible and Other Recountings*, and *Winter Children and Other Chilling Tales*. She has won the World Fantasy Award, the British Fantasy Award and five Aurealis Awards. Her short stories have appeared widely, including in annual British, Australian and North American Best Of anthologies, and her work has been translated into Spanish, Russian, Polish, Romanian, and Japanese. *Vigil* was her first solo novel, and the sequel *Corpselight* is out now. Angela lives in Brisbane, Australia.

Stay in touch with Angela!
Follow her on Twitter at
@AngelaSlatter

Find out more about Angela at
www.angelaslatter.com

Visit her on Facebook at
www.facebook.com/angelaslatterauthor

Read on for an exclusive story,
written especially for this edition.

Swan Girls

Sister Bridget Hazelton is twelve when she sees her first angel.

Of course she's not a Sister then, just a sister – to Eleanor, who's half her age, with twice her capacity to get into trouble – but she sees the angel nonetheless. Eleanor, of course, does not.

Bridget is walking home from school, her sister dancing along in front, singing the national anthem – in 1964, it's still 'God Save the Queen' and they have to sing it every morning at assembly, standing to attention on the burnt red parade ground. But at this very moment Eleanor is chanting it to the same tune as the *Gilligan's Island* theme song. It sounds wrong, but Eleanor doesn't care.

There are a lot of things Ellie doesn't care about; Bridget is the one with a thing for rules. She's the eldest, so all their parents' expectations and hopes, terrors and fears have been vested in her. Ellie reaps the benefits of Megan and Will's exhaustion with making and enforcing their own decrees; it's a known fact that as long as the first-born isn't obviously broken by the time the second comes along, parental units tend to relax/collapse on the whole 'boundaries' front. They inevitably try to make up for this by handing a degree of responsibility to Child Number One.

Bridget is aware of the weight of these expectations and it has affected her posture: she doesn't slouch, but stands straight, feet always braced a little bit apart, so that anything trying to knock her down will have to work extra-hard. Her shoulders are held back with the discipline of a soldier, which makes her look taller. It's a stance that will stay with her for ever, that and the way she juts her chin forward, daring the world to have a go and see what happens.

Bridget knows, courtesy of her parents, that she is Responsible. She is Responsible for her own good grades. She is Responsible for collecting the mail when she comes home from school. She is Responsible for laying the table and for drying the dishes her mother has washed up. She is Responsible, most of all, for her little sister.

Ellie makes that particular task so much harder by being a thorough-going little brat. If there is a means to get into trouble, she will find it. It is invariably Eleanor who locates the hidden wasps' nest and stirs it up; expensive electrical equipment will either short out when she touches it or curiosity will overwhelm her and she will take it apart, and even if she does put it back together (which is not guaranteed), it will never work again, for some critical component will have gone mysteriously missing. If she so much as looks sideways at a piece of their mother's jewellery, it (or part of it at least) will disappear. Megan Hazleton has long ago accepted that she's destined to have more unmatched earrings than anyone else on the planet. She continues to hope that one day it might become fashionable.

'Ellie, slow down,' Bridget calls, for the sprite – her still-blonde hair catching the sun hasn't yet darkened like Bridget's – has got too far ahead for comfort, even though the street they're on is straight as can be, and long, with no surprises: post office, church with matching hall and graveyard, children's hostel, pub with accommodation upstairs, all those little houses with their tin roofs and wooden verandahs. Yet Bridget, already perspiring in the heat of a Queensland summer's day, feels more sweat breaking out on her brow. Bridget doesn't like it here. *It wasn't so bad in Brisbane*, she grumbles to herself, *although Cairns was much, much worse with its humidity that made me feel like I was breathing soup.* They've moved around quite a bit, seen more of the state than most kids ever will, because of their father's job, although it will take Bridget a long time to realise this. Only when she does will she understand her own itchy feet, the wanderlust that keeps her moving every few years.

Here is Sullivan's Drift, Somewhere in South West Queensland, almost eight hundred miles from Brisbane (but it might as well be a light-year or twelve). When they arrived a month ago so her father could take up the position of the town's sole copper, Ellie, curious as a dog, was hanging half out the window, despite her mother's demand that she *Bloody well sit down before I smack your bum.* Bridget had her nose in a book – Andre Norton's *Key Out of Time*; she'd found that if she hunkered into the seat so she couldn't see the movement of passing countryside in her peripheral vision she didn't get quite so carsick.

Their father, driving the new white station wagon, had kept up a steady patter of information: Sullivan's Drift was one of the first towns in Australia to have hydro-electric power pumped from the Great Artesian Basin beneath the earth's surface. They were near the Barcoo River and could go swimming. There was some memorial they'd have to visit, to some early explorers who'd failed to plan adequately and as a result had died of starvation and thirst; Bridget had noticed in her Australian history classes a tendency to make heroes of halfwits, especially those too stupid not to die, but she kept that thought to herself. They'd visit some of the big cattle properties where the girls could go horse riding, although, having been chased too often by dogs and scratched too often by cats, Bridget now regarded all animals with suspicion and was quite certain she would not be trusting her safety to anything as big as a horse. The school was small, he said (just forty-five kids), so it would be easy to make friends. Bridget wonders if her father has a clue at all.

Sullivan's Drift, thinks Bridget, *is red dust, flies and, when the wind blows in a particular direction, the smell of rotten eggs, which comes off the water from the artesian bore*. There's so much red dust it coats her skin on the walk to and from school – even now Ellie is kicking it up with her dancing.

'Ellie, slow down!' she yells again, knowing that Ellie will simply do more of whatever is causing annoyance to her sister. To Bridget's complete lack of surprise, she speeds up, almost sprinting past the small church and cemetery, heading towards the police house that lies just at the end of the main street (it's on a block of land next to the police station, which means Bridget's mum walks her husband's lunch over at 12.30 p.m. every day). Watching her sister raising more crimson clouds, Bridget grits her teeth and shakes her head; that's when she sees the angel.

She knows it's an angel because he looks like the ones in the books they used to have at her old Sunday School: a proper warrior-angel, not fluffy, but ready to battle evil at the drop of a hat, to put the head of the snake beneath his heel.

He's sitting in a tree, a big, old, gnarled coolibah. The trunk had been split by lightning at some point in its history, but it had stubbornly continued to grow, just in two different directions. The angel perches on the left branch, casual as you like, his weight making the wood creak and sway just a little. He's big, enormous really, even taller than Bridget's father, who's well over six feet. He wears a short white dress – there has to be a better term for it than 'dress', but she just doesn't know what it is – and armour on his forearms and shins, shining like jet, sable boots with pale pearl lacings, plus a gleaming breastplate carved with all the hollows and rises one might expect of a well-formed chest. His hair, black as ebony, flows past his shoulders. She can't tell what colour his eyes are. He's too far away, and Bridget has a thing about distance: she knows that going over to get close enough to see would constitute 'talking to strangers'. Bridget has a sense for these things: if you get within two feet of someone, that somehow triggers the conversational force field and you're obliged to talk.

The angel, well, he sees her looking. She can tell from the way his wings twitch – oh, those wings! Gleaming like the mother-of-pearl earrings her mother once had two of – and the dip of his head. He nods and she knows, just *knows*, she's right not to get any closer. This distance, she can ignore him; no one expects you to be polite from this distance. Bridget hitches her school bag up a little higher, sticks her chin out a little further and walks on, staring straight ahead.

But her brain's already trying to work out who she can tell about what she's seen; the answer she comes up with is *no one*.

Her parents would say she has an overactive imagination. She has no friends – despite her father's optimism, it's never a sure thing, making friends when you move around a lot, and it's extra-hard when you're the local cop's kid. There's always some smart-arse who thinks it's funny to say, 'Hey, do you smell bacon?' and make snorting noises whenever you walk by. She sure couldn't tell Ellie, because Ellie couldn't keep a secret if her life depended on it. Ellie's loose lips could sink a whole *armada* of ships.

As Bridget trudges towards home, the weight of the secret settles on her, although she barely notices because it doesn't add too much to all the Responsibility that's already there. She comes to the fence, one of those wire things woven into a diamond pattern with hollow pipes at intervals set as posts to hold up the ones running across the top as railings. Ellie is standing outside the gate that creaks whenever they go in and out – their father says it'll stay that way, 'cause it warns them that someone's coming up the garden path, and most coppers prefer a creaky gate to a surprise guest. Ellie is frozen there, one hand wrapped around the strap of her satchel, the other on the gate – she's got it pushed open just to the point before it squeaks, where the girls can slip in without making a sound. Coppers might well outsmart potential crims, but seldom their own slender, clever daughters.

Ellie is staring across the road at the big old house that's been empty for a long time, according to Kylie Howard, the neighbour on the other side of the police station. The place is nothing special, just bigger than most, with a wide verandah that runs around three sides; the white paint is peeling, the red roof looks like a canvas of rust and the windows are dark and dirty. Nothing special – except the garden has run wild and lush in strange defiance of the climate, and a rose bush has grown rampant over the front of the place. It screens the verandah so you can't see much from the road except the four steps that lead up to it, the door with its old brass knocker, and a little of the windows either side. The red roses are beautiful, impossible really, and Bridget's mother has been surreptitiously nicking them since they arrived, one a week: they get put in a slender ceramic vase on the sill of the kitchen window until the petals give up the ghost.

Today, though, the front door is open, and so's the back one, apparently, because the girls can see all the way through, down the hallway to the blast of light at the end of it, with a Hills Hoist leaning to the left.

As they watch, there's movement; a dark shape obscuring the tunnel of light makes them blink. Bridget's heart clenches and Ellie makes a little noise, a sharp intake of breath, then the form resolves itself into an older woman with curly steel-grey hair, white shirt and wide-legged trousers, a pair of blue rubber thongs on her feet.

Cat's-eye-shaped glasses rest on her good-natured face. She notices the girls, gives a smile and a wave.

Surprised and relieved, Bridget waves back, even though it's one of those things that signals a willingness to converse. Ellie does too, and begins to take a step towards the new neighbour, but Bridget puts a swift hand on her sister's shoulder and turns her towards their own yard. As Ellie, surprisingly compliant, skips up the path, Bridget makes a point – although she's not sure why – of pushing the gate back far enough to squeak. She doesn't look behind as she follows her sister to the police house, which has its own verandah enclosed by mesh to keep the flies out.

'Won't you have some more pudding, Mrs Bell?'

'Ida! Now, I told you to call me Ida,' Mrs Bell pretend-scolds Bridget's mother, and Megan Hazleton laughs.

'*Ida*, won't you have some more pudding?'

'I will, thank you, I simply cannot resist a lemon delicious. You've found my weakness!'

'I can't believe you whipped this up so quickly, Megan,' Kylie Howard says admiringly, a little enviously, of the meal that's been thrown together in the two hours since Mrs Bell first knocked on the front door. Hastily convened guests arrived, all showered and primped at speed, but the heat hasn't tailed off yet and the men are all sweating through their shirts; the women, with their strange magic, look cool and unruffled. A small group, for certain, but not unreasonable given the short notice, since no one knew there'd be a new neighbour. It's only fitting that the police family be first to welcome them, along with Kylie Howard, the head of the local chapter of the Christian Women's Association. (Her husband, a stock agent for Elders, is taciturn with the ladies, but Bridget's seen him grow expansive around other men.)

Mrs Bell wears a long sleeveless black silk dress with a column skirt that smells a little like mothballs whenever she shifts or the languid breeze motivates itself to move around her. Her hair's still grey and curly, but it's now got the rigid set of something that's been tamed by hairspray and will. Megan and Kylie, younger, more daring, are in shorter, full-skirted cocktail frocks with capped sleeves, one in green, the other in orange.

As soon as the newcomer knocked on the door there was no doubt there'd be a gathering for dinner – country hospitality and all that, plus Megan knows her job as a copper's wife. She's there to make an impression, do his reputation no disservice, to welcome and feed anyone he chooses to bring home at whatever hour of the day or night. She takes freshly baked bread and cakes to families in need, offers a shoulder to cry on, an ear to pour secrets into. She's his helpmeet, his companion, she's the soft side seen by townspeople wherever the Hazletons happen to be living. She makes him look good, human, especially if he's had to arrest a drunk or three, or a battered wife who's had enough and been found holding a .303 rifle over a dead or bleeding husband. Megan lets Will know when she's seen bruises on faces or arms of women and children; he'll make a mental note to have a chat with husbands and fathers with big hands and short tempers, letting them know he *knows*. Folk see her in the grocery store, at church, at the school, and they remember she's kind no matter what, so they sort of forgive him for keeping the peace and stopping them from hurting each other and themselves.

Even though it's a grown-up occasion, which means she and Ellie aren't invited (they ate earlier, before being packed off to bed), Bridget made a special effort with the setting tonight, ensuring the cutlery all lined up with the edge of the table, and she folded the starched serviettes into fans that sat up on their own, just like Grandmother Hazleton had taught her last year; they stayed with her for a whole month for a holiday when Mum and Dad weren't talking to each other very nicely. The best dinner plates have been brought out from the silky oak sideboard that belonged to Mum's Great-Aunt Oriel, and the crystal wine glasses that Great-Aunt Lois bought on her honeymoon in Venice a *long* time ago. In the slender vase in the centre of the table is the last pilfered red rose.

Bridget sits in the doorway of her room: she can only see the end of the table that accommodates Mrs Bell, Archie Baldwin the grocer/butcher, brought in because you cannot have an uneven number of bodies sitting down to a meal, and the back of Kylie Howard's bottle-blonde head. Mr Baldwin's roadmap of a face wrinkles as he smiles at the newcomer in a manner he seems to think is charming. Mrs Howard uses her hands a lot when she talks, and Bridget watches with dread anticipation as the glass in Kylie's loose grip, which still contains wine, is pushed and pulled hither and yon. The liquid flies and flows and sloshes, but it never quite spills out. Bridget likes Mrs Howard, who always speaks to her as if she's a grown up; she doesn't have any kids of her own, so maybe she's got no preconceived notions about them.

The adults are taking their time over dessert and port, which her father discovered about a year ago and has since become the final course to all their dinner parties. Mrs Bell's a good conversationalist: she's travelled a lot and used to be a teacher so she tells loads of stories about faraway places and the habits of the locals there. She talks about wine with Bridget's father, who knows less than he pretends, but she's kind enough not to notice. She talks cattle with Bruce Howard, who opens up like a rose in a good garden, and she talks cuts of meat with

Mr Baldwin, even though she resolutely refuses to acknowledge his attempts at flirtation.

Bridget doesn't like Mr Baldwin; he stands out front of his shop every day, watching all the kids as they go to and from school. It makes her uncomfortable. She's a copper's daughter; she senses more than she should for an entirely cosy childhood, but perhaps it'll help keep her safe later in life. She doesn't quite understand why he's looking in that uncharacteristic way at Mrs Bell, but maybe she does understand about camouflage.

Conversation has moved on to the healthy gossip industry that keeps the bored housewives of Sullivan's Drift enthused about their lives in a dust-bowl.

'Oh, you'll hear some things!' Kylie's voice goes high with alcohol. 'Small towns thrive on gossip, you know.'

'My dear, I never listen – just like eavesdroppers, one never hears any good of one's self.' Mrs Bell makes only the slightest adjustment of her head, gives the merest flick of her eyes, but Bridget knows her presence has been noted. Too clever to jump to her feet and let *everyone* know she's there, she slowly slides backwards on her bum into her room.

In the bed closest to the French doors that lead onto the verandah, Ellie is sleeping. That's one thing about her the family is grateful for: how good a sleeper she is. Exhausted at the end of each day, she goes straight off as soon as her head hits the pillow. Bridget's never had that ability, and sometimes she has to resist the urge to wake her sister with a pinch or a shake, just so she won't be quite so rested in the morning.

But this night, for a blessed change, mere moments after she gives the empty bookshelves a yearning look (the boxes with the last of their belongings have yet to arrive) Bridget drops straight into slumber. She doesn't know how long it lasts, but the sounds of the dinner party have disappeared and there's no light coming from the dining room when she wakes. But there is a tapping noise on the glass panels of the verandah doors. She doesn't know why they're closed – weren't they open when she came to bed? Normally they're left ajar so the breeze flows through, trusting the mesh that encloses the verandah to keep the mozzies and flies from carrying them off in their sleep.

The glass panel looks strange: something is moving against it, something that covers the whole pane. At first she thinks it's a single thing but after a moment of squinting she makes out lots of bodies, hundreds, maybe: black flies, obscuring the glass, occasionally shifting aside to let shafts of light through.

Bridget's never seen anything like it. Her throat closes over. She's so busy staring that she doesn't notice Ellie's bed is empty. She doesn't notice until it's too late that Ellie's tiny white hand is reaching for the handle of the door. It's only when she hears the *kerklunk* of that handle being turned that she shrieks—

—but when the door is pushed open, there's nothing.

No influx of insects, not even a single one.

'I heard singing, Briddy,' says Ellie in a sleepy voice, soft and warm as the goosedown quilts that go on the beds in winter. 'It was so pretty.'

Bridget rolls herself up off the bed, flinging the sheet aside in the movement, and takes the ten steps, jerky with fright, to where her sister is standing, staring out at the sky illuminated by the full moon. The street, too, is bathed in silver. Bridget puts her hands on Ellie's shoulders and turns her to her bed with its pink sheets and the old teddy that used to be Bridget's once upon a time.

'You were dreaming,' she says in voice that's harsh with leftover terror. Her fear, if she's honest, had felt as silvery and cold as the moonlight; now it's like something has faded from her system, leaving her angry and drained. 'Go to sleep.'

Bridget turns back to the door, unsure why, as behind her Ellie sighs, 'So pretty, Briddy,' as she drifts off.

When Bridget reaches for the handle – should she close it? It's awfully hot in the room – she notices a shifting outside.

The stocky, bald shape with light bouncing off his skull is familiar: Mr Baldwin. She can't see his face, but she recognises him, the hang of his dress shorts, the socks pulled up too high on ankles and calves too thin for his barrel-body, the pale blue of his dinner-party shirt washed out by the white of the moon. He's not looking at her, or at the police house. He's across the road and he's staring at Mrs Bell's home. He stands there for a long time and Bridget realises at some point that she's forgotten to breathe. She gasps a little, fearful that the sound might carry.

The man shakes himself as if waking, but he still doesn't look her way. He gives one last glance at Ida Bell's new abode, then begins his walk up the main street, towards his shop with the house attached to the back. His gait is a little more shuffley than normal, and Bridget thinks he might have had too much to drink.

Bridget pulls the door closed, latches it and goes back to bed.

When Bridget and Ellie walk home the next afternoon, Mr Baldwin is standing in the doorway of his shop, polishing his glasses with a frayed hanky that doesn't look too clean. Bridget is wondering why her parents invited him to dinner, but she knows the answer: Mr Baldwin is very cunning. He doesn't look at children the same way when adults are around; he keeps his face very carefully controlled, barely gives the kiddies a glance. He does nothing to alert another adult to any interest that might be deemed unhealthy. He's an upstanding citizen, a pillar of the community: he gives to charities, he chats with all the widows and wives at the CWA dances on Saturday nights, just as he tried chatting with Mrs Bell. *Camouflage. Never married*, Kylie Howard had said in passing on her first gossip run with Megan Hazleton, *but no one holds that against him.*

Bridget thinks they probably should, and she boldly meets the man's gaze as she strides past, keeping Ellie close; her sister shows an unwonted willingness to comply, staying to Bridget's left, only occasionally peeking around as they pass the store at speed.

When they reach home, Bridget glances over at Mrs Bell's house. The old lady is on the verandah, trimming the lush red roses. She gives the girls a casual wave, then returns to her task. Bridget pushes Ellie inside the gate, makes sure it creaks so Mum knows they're home, then pulls it shut. 'Won't be long,' she says, and runs across the road.

'Hello, Bridget,' says Mrs Bell without turning around. 'What can I do for you?'

'Mr Baldwin,' says Bridget before she can think better of it, 'isn't very nice.'

Mrs Bell stops what she's doing and looks at the girl in surprise. 'Really?'

'He was outside your house last night, late.' There's more she might say, but she doesn't quite know how to phrase it without sounding like a child who doesn't have the proper vocabulary to put her suspicions into words.

'Was he indeed?' Mrs Bell sits down on one of the old rocking chairs, brushing away some of the peeling green paint, and stares at Bridget as if it's the first time she's truly seen her. Through the window behind the old lady Bridget spots a room lined with shelves, those shelves lined with books. Her fingers itch.

'Why do you think that is? Am I so irresistible?' Ida Bell smiles, primps her hair like a pin-up and is briefly transformed by the power of her own amusement into someone far lovelier and younger than she has a right to be. Then the woman laughs and the illusion is gone: she's grey-haired, wrinkled and grandmotherly.

There's a sound at the mailbox – Mrs Bell's house has no fence around it – and Bridget knows without needing to look that Ellie has come over to collect her, no doubt after dobbing her in to their mother for revenge.

'Mum says you're to stop bothering Mrs Bell.'

Bridget pulls a face and Mrs Bell laughs. 'Oh, no bother, little one. Well, thank you for letting me know, Bridget dear. And you're *both* welcome here any time.'

But it's a week before Bridget gets across the road again; after school she's always got homework to do or chores for her mother, or there's some sort of sporting event which she loathes but her parents insist she participate in: tennis, vigoro, basketball. Sport, she is rapidly coming to believe, is a form of punishment for those who'd rather read books in a nation that would rather throw things at each other. She'd have given anything to curl up with a book of mythology or science fiction or Bible stories instead, or anything that bore no relation to physical activity.

But at last the afternoon comes when Mum and Dad are going to a Chamber of Commerce dinner with Kylie and her husband, and Megan asks Mrs Bell if she'd mind babysitting. Mrs Bell agrees happily, offering to feed the girls at her place, then when it's time for bed she'll walk them back home and sit with them until their parents return.

Dinner is Vegemite on toast with melted cheese (no cause for complaint), and a chocolate sponge cake for dessert. After they've eaten, Mrs Bell lets Bridget look through the bookshelves in the lounge room and choose some to borrow. There are two Nancy Drews she hasn't seen in the local library, so it feels like finding buried treasure. While Mrs Bell is in the kitchen making herself a cup of tea, Bridget looks at the other shelves, at the bigger volumes with their covers all bound in leather of different colours, with gold titles in languages she doesn't recognise embossed on the spines. She thinks Mrs Bell might be the smartest woman she's ever met, which makes her feel disloyal to her own mother, but not so disloyal that she dismisses the thought.

When Mrs Bell comes back in, Bridget is buried deep in an armchair, the first Nancy Drew open in her lap; Ellie is sitting on the floor, facing her sister, playing with her ancient teddy bear. The old lady comes up behind Ellie, a surprised expression on her face. 'Oh my!'

She puts her teacup and saucer down on a little side table and reaches towards Ellie's back with quick, thin fingers. The little girl gives a squeal of outrage and jumps; her expression, Bridget recognises, is the one that says she's giving serious consideration to kicking someone.

'Look, Ellie!' she says rather too loudly, trying to derail her sister's intent, although she'd no idea what she should point to as a distraction.

'Why I do believe,' says the old lady, 'that I've found myself a swan girl!' She holds up a feather, white with a tinge of grey, shortish, still a little downy, but undoubtedly a feather. The tip of the quill is dark red.

Bridget's mouth falls open, but no words come out. Letting the book drop, she struggles out of the chair and spins Ellie around to examine her back, left exposed by her yellow sundress. Between the right shoulder blade and the line of her spine is a small hole dripping blood, as if the feather had been pulled from the girl's flesh. Bridget carefully scans the canvas of her sister's skin, but she can find no trace of any other feathering.

'It happens slowly, Bridget,' says Mrs Bell gently, kindly. 'The transformation is a gradual thing. Have you noticed any signs about yourself?'

And Bridget says 'No,' even though she doesn't know. Then, hesitating, she asks, 'Are you sure it's a swan and not something else?'

Mrs Bell tilts her head. 'What *else* might it be, dear?'

When Bridget doesn't answer straight away, Mrs Bell says, 'Eleanor, love, go and get yourself a tissue from the bathroom, and there's a little tube of antiseptic cream on the sink – bring that too.'

When Ellie is gone Bridget spills her tale about the angel, quickly, lest Ellie come back and hear it.

Mrs Bell purses her lips. 'Well, Bridget, I can say with some authority that girls don't become angels. But they do become swans. It's a known fact in parts of Europe.'

'But we're not in Europe.'

There's a crash from the direction of the bathroom and Ellie's voice floats back. 'It's okay!' is always code for, 'It's less than okay.'

'No, but not everything that starts in Europe stays in Europe,' says the old lady tartly. 'But this angel you saw, that is a puzzle. Go and help your sister, dear. Let me have a bit of a ponder.'

Later still, when Ellie has at last fallen asleep on the embroidered loveseat under the window, Bridget thinks she will get some more answers, but before she can begin the conversation there's a noise from the back of the house, the whisper and protesting thud of the kitchen door opening and closing. Mrs Bell gives her a look and puts a gnarled finger to her lips as she gets up rather more nimbly than she ought to be able to from her own chair. There's a heavy grey marble bookend on one of the shelves at the right side of the hallway and the old lady picks it up as if it weighs nothing more than a thought. She holds her free hand palm out like she's stopping traffic: *Stay there*.

And Bridget does, although her heart's in her mouth and she's terrified that Ellie is going to wake up and ask aloud what everyone's doing and why does Mrs Bell have that bookend and why's she hiding over there? But Ellie stays soundly asleep and Bridget is free to watch the dark shape, a lumpen silhouette, shuffling up the hallway. She tries not to blink lest it somehow get closer in those fragments of a second between when her lids shut, then flicker open again.

Eventually the intruder steps into the light: it's Mr Baldwin. In unconscious mimicry of Mrs Bell, he puts a finger to his lips. Bridget bites down on a cry, and she's very careful not to look beyond Mr Baldwin's shoulder to where Mrs Bell is standing, bookend raised, then she takes two paces up behind him and swings the chunk of marble down onto the top of his head with remarkable force.

Mr Baldwin drops like a sack of very heavy potatoes and begins to bleed into the blue and red woven rug. Ellie still doesn't wake up.

From outside Bridget hears a car, the white station wagon, driven slowly, the way her dad always does when he's had a couple of beers and is trying to be careful. Mrs Bell hears it too, and breathes a sigh of relief.

'Go and get your dad, love.' Mrs Bell is puffing like a steam train. She's got her hands wrapped around the bookend. 'You go as fast as you can, before this bastard wakes up and I have to hit him again.'

From the kitchen, Bridget thinks, comes a buzzing sound like a trapped bee. She looks down the hallway and the noise seems to rise – then Mrs Bell urges, 'Go on now, fetch your father.'

Bridget sets off across the road like her life depends on it. Her parents are laughing, barely out of the car, when she skids to a halt and shouts hysterically that they must come. Because they've never seen their elder daughter so upset, they follow without asking too many questions, without too much delay.

But when they reach the old lady's house, there's no trace of Mrs Ida Bell and no sign of Ellie either. Bridget, who gets through the door seconds ahead of her father, spots, just where Mr Baldwin fell, the angel, rubbing his head, a rivulet of silver-red blood running down his face. She sees him for a second and he sees her, then blinks out of existence.

The investigation is huge, quite the largest ever mounted in Queensland. Eleanor Hazleton is police family, she's a child of one of their own. Her loss is felt very personally. Coppers don't take kindly to an attack on their fellows; they don't like being reminded that they've not been rendered invincible by donning a uniform.

They never do find a trace of Ellie, or Mrs Ida Bell – in fact, they find no record of anyone of that name or vintage, and the realtor in the next town has no record or recall of having rented the house out to *anyone*; the owner didn't want it let. Nothing remains of Mrs Ida Bell: no clothing left in the wardrobe, no toothbrush in the bathroom, no toiletries. There's no food in the refrigerator and the pantry's empty but for the corpses of a few thousand flies. No furniture, no books. No one can remember ever seeing a car outside the place, nor does anyone remember seeing the woman arrive. Or leave.

There are only the roses, which blossom and bloom even more

vigorously in the days and weeks that follow the disappearance, reminding Bridget (and, she has no doubt, her mother) of the ones stolen to sit on the windowsill of the police house.

Mr Baldwin denies ever having been to dinner at the policeman's house, and no matter how often the Hazletons and the Howards swear he was there, he swears with equal vehemence that he was *not*. Ultimately, the stress of the investigation, of having so very many policemen around, day after day, proves too much and Mr Baldwin hangs himself in the cemetery; he is found dangling from the lightning-struck coolibah one morning. Although he *could* have demonstrated his innocence in the matter, it would have required him telling all and sundry that he'd been busy convincing a thirteen-year-old boy to do 'favours' for him in return for as many lollies as he could eat.

Bridget doesn't cry, though her eyes always look red, as if she's constantly on the verge of it. Her mother worries, when she surfaces from the depths of her own grief, that her daughter is locking something away that will surge up and wreck her in the future. Will doesn't say much to Bridget, although he always ruffles her hair when he comes home in the evening and when he goes to work in the morning, pats her shoulder after dinner as he leaves the table. She spends a lot of time thinking about what happened, figuring bits out in her head, but even at that age she knows she won't be believed if she tells what she does know.

Bridget sees the angel one last time before they leave Sullivan's Drift. The day of the memorial service for Ellie, in one of those increasingly rare moments that her parents take their eyes off her, she wanders outside the church hall. There's a memorial service even though there's been no funeral. There's a memorial service because Megan couldn't bear a funeral. There's a memorial service because the Hazletons have given up but can't bring themselves to truly admit it.

The angel is sitting on a wrought-iron bench in the far corner of the graveyard. He looks different: he's wearing shorts and a navy singlet with a pair of battered brown boots on his feet and he'd easily pass for one of the shearers that come and go from the surrounding properties. He doesn't stand out quite as much, except that he's very beautiful.

'You're smaller,' says Bridget. 'Where are your wings?'

For a moment she can see them as he lets them show, for a moment he's so very tall, a prince of Heaven, then the moment's gone and he's just a handsome young man again.

'You'd better go. No one's very trusting of strangers any more,' she says.

'I'm sorry,' he tells her. 'I thought she was looking for you. I didn't pay enough attention.'

'Why didn't you do something?'

'She was . . . hard to determine . . . she was very well hidden . . . *beneath*. I was not certain.'

'But you came sneaking around. You came in his form, just in case you were wrong?'

The angel nods. 'If I was wrong then I did not have to explain anything if she thought I was him.'

'Is my sister alive?' she asks without much hope. Her voice breaks.

'I don't . . . No. I don't believe so.'

'What kind of an angel are you? Can't save one little girl.' Her tone is cold and coiled by rage.

He gives no answer, for he has none. After long seconds, Bridget sits beside him on the bench; the metal contains all the heat of the day and radiates up through the fabric of her black dress. She's wearing shiny black patent shoes with silver buckles and short white socks that have scratchy lace around the top. The red dust is threatening to turn them pink. The outfit is too young for her, but it's the only dark thing she owns, and black's the only appropriate colour for the service.

'Your parents,' he asks, 'do they blame you?'

Bridget pauses before answering, 'They keep telling me it's not my fault, but what they mean is I'm not Responsible.' She doesn't think the angel will understand the subtlety and she doesn't wish to elaborate, so she asks the question that's been troubling her ever since her little sister disappeared, 'What was she? Mrs Bell?'

'A bad thing. They come out the darkness but they're good at looking normal.'

'A demon?' The old lady, she's long ago figured, had that feather in her hand, concealed, before she stuck it into Ellie, broke the skin, drew blood to draw conviction. She doesn't know why the old lady played such a game – why she told a tale of swan maidens – nor how long it was meant to go on. She only knows that the angel's interference, or rather Bridget's disclosure of his existence, sped matters to their close much sooner, she suspects, than intended.

'Perhaps. Something older, perhaps, a Lilith.'

'Adam's first wife.'

'The terror by night.'

'Eater of children.'

'Yes.'

'You couldn't have known,' she says.

The angel looks at her quizzically.

'About Mr Baldwin, what he was doing.'

The look the angel gives her is one of shame. If he'd not disguised himself as Archie Baldwin at the dinner party, she'd not have been afraid of him; she'd not have trusted Mrs Bell so implicitly. Camouflage, yes, but not of the sort she'd thought. Bridget would not have confided in her about the angel and alerted the old woman to the fact that she was being watched. She'd not have left her sister with the beldame, and now she wouldn't be an only child whose parents were going to great lengths to not let her know they blamed her.

'Do you have a name?' she asks. She figures she's only got a minute more, tops, before her parents notice she's missing.

'Yes.'

But he never gives it to her. What he gives her instead is a feather, one of his own, plucked from one of the great pearly wings. He places it in her right hand: it's so long and so broad that it covers her entire palm. She will keep it with the other one, the one tipped with her sister's blood, the one she found on the lounge floor of Mrs Bell's house when her parents started shouting. The one she keeps in a box of treasures beside her bed. As she's staring at the new feather, a shout comes from the door of the church hall; a scream really, in her mother's voice. The angel winks out and Bridget is left alone, tears falling at last onto the stiff white barbs.